SAVING THORNWOOD

JULIA RUST
&
DAVID SURFACE

Haverhill House Publishing LLC

978-1-949140-59-0 Hardcover
978-1-949140-58-3 Trade Paperback

First Edition

YAP Books is an imprint of Haverhill House Publishing LLC

For more information, address:
Haverhill House Publishing LLC
643 E Broadway
Haverhill MA 01830-2420

Visit us on the web at www.haverhillhouse.com

"Fast-paced and compelling, *Angel Falls* is a page-turner with well-drawn characters and a terrific supernatural mystery propelling a story that is, at its core, about love, loss and the inevitability of change. I couldn't put it down."

~**Lynda Rucker**, author of *You'll Know When You Get There*

"What a lovely horror it is to enter Angel Falls where the air drips with fog, and the tender heart of human desire becomes a fetid root of loss. What a balm it is to go there and heal old wounds, without risk, through the gift of this well-told story!"

~**M. Rickert** author of *The Shipbuilder of Bellfairie* and *Lucky Girl, How I Became a Horror Writer: A Krampus Story*

David Surface's THESE THINGS THAT WALK BEHIND ME

"An exciting, fresh voice. A writer whose artful style and subtle depictions of the weird should be relished."

~**Adam Nevill**, author of *Some Will Not Sleep, Hasty for the Dark, Wyrd and Other Derelictions*

"Another extraordinary collection by one of the more accomplished and consistently fascinating authors of literary weird fiction. We all know the feeling of an unknown yet undeniable disturbance just out of sight, watching and waiting. Surface takes this natural fear and builds it into an overwhelming feeling of dread with no antidote and no escape."

~**S.P. Miskowski**, author of *I Wish I Was Like You*

"What makes these stories so powerful is Surface's simultaneous commitment to the realistic and the strange--and his understanding that they're not opposing realms but are adjacent and intertwined. These are nimble and satisfying stories that take the best qualities of literature and genre to create a creature that is its own distinct, dark thing."

~**Brian Evenson**, author of *A Collapse of Horses,* and Shirley Jackson Award Winner.

"The stories in David Surface's These Things That Walk Behind Me are so steeped in horror and ghost story traditions, they almost built a Vermont December around me as I read in the dregs of Georgia's hot, sticky summer. A comforting illusion and a gift of atmosphere bring to mind the great M.R. James and the ghosts of Aickman and Blackwood haunting our modern world. Inventively oblique, ominously clear, and never losing touch with his characters, Surface digs beneath his name to find the raw beating heart of what it means to be human in the darkness."

~**Michael Wehunt**, author of *Greener Pastures* and *The Inconsolables*

"In *These Things That Walk Behind Me,* David Surface gathers dark and haunting tales that explore the thin line between nightmares and daydreams. From unsettling encounters with the past to eerie whispers of otherworldly beings, each story lingers with a sense of dread and anticipation. A chilling exhibition you won't want to miss."

~**Christopher Barzak**, Shirley Jackson Award-winning author of *Before and Afterlives*

"*These Things…*" is a superlative collection by a master of the genre. Not only does he create nightmare images that stay in the mind long after you've put the book aside, but—here's the key—his themes are deeply rooted in universal emotions. Surface digs deep, and his personal honesty pays dividends, putting him at the top of the tree of contemporary short story writers working in the realm of the uncanny. These are truly horror for grown-ups, and I highly recommend you savor them."

~**Stephen Volk**, author of *The Dark Masters Trilogy, Monsters In the Heart,* screenwriter for *The Awakening* and *Ghostwatch.*

Praise for SAVING THORNWOOD

"*SAVING THORNWOOD* takes on two weighty subjects—the awful history of mental health care institutions in the U.S. and the need for accessible and destigmatizing mental health care today—but the voices of its two main characters make the topic feel lived-in and approachable. Its nineteenth-century narrator, Mary, trapped in Thornwood Asylum, is as fierce as they come. Modern-day Annie, who is navigating her dad's new mental health diagnosis, is Mary's match in thoughtfulness and care for those she loves. Watching the two girls interact through their supernatural meetings, as well as through the interplay of history, was fascinating and moving."

~**Erica Waters**, author of *All That Consumes Us*

"*SAVING THORNWOOD* bridges the gap between gothic and wonder, the supernatural and sanity, heart and horror, casting its own mysterious web that tethers the centuries together and fastens the reader to this spellbinding book. You'll never want to leave Thornwood once you're finished reading it."

~**Clay McLeod Chapman**, author of Wake Up and Open Your Eyes

"When I can truly feel and care for characters in a book, I'm drawn in immediately. Saving Thornwood did just that. It is a compelling and brilliantly written novel, exploring the dark history of care for those with mental illness and creates a supernatural bond between two women of two different times, Mary and Annie, who must fight courageously against the walls of resistance to gain their rights and those of their loved ones."

~**Elizabeth Massie**, Bram Stoker Award-winning author of Sineater, Hell Gate, and The Wages of Belief

"Gritty, gothic, and compelling, this tale of mental health stigma and friendship boasts two lead heroines who give *SAVING THORNWOOD* its driving heartbeat. A moody, dual narrative across time that will appeal to modern readers. Highly recommended!"

~**Gaby Triana**, author of *Moon Child, Wake the Hollow,* And *RIVER of Bones*

"A gripping tale of courage and connection, where the haunting past of a crumbling asylum intertwines with the present, revealing the indomitable spirit of those who refuse to be forgotten in a system designed to silence them."

~**Christopher Barzak**, author of *Wonders of the Invisible World*

"This is time travel at its most believable and most entertaining. A fascinating look into the stigma of mental illness then and now, and a real tribute to the power of young women across different eras to overcome helplessness and not only form their own futures but rescue those they care about."

~**Mary Carroll Moore**, best-selling award-winning author of *Last Bets* and *A Woman's Guide to Search & Rescue*

Praise for David Surface and Julia Rust's previous award-winning novel ANGEL FALLS

"Folks, this is an excellent read with real, compassionate teenage characters and how they grow up. The inner turmoil they went through with their feelings was expressed point-on…. You'll nod in agreement as you read some of these passages, just as their self-reflections did in this tale. Their Moxi is second to none in dealing with this supernatural force alive in *Angel Falls* and the decisions they make."

~*Buttonholed Book Reviews*

"Angel Falls is a touching, tension-filled young adult novel that had this old guy engrossed from start to finish. The authors absolutely nail the emotional angst of two teenage characters fraught with familial and supernatural terrors, all while developing deep feelings for one another. When it comes to supernatural young adult fiction, Angel Falls is the best novel in the genre I've ever read. It's that good."

~**Tony Tremblay**, Bram Stoker-nominated author of *The Moore House*, and *Do Not Weep for Me*

ACKNOWLEDGEMENTS

Saving Thornwood began when we first visited the Trans Allegheny Lunatic Asylum in West Virginia, designed by the architect and reformer Thomas Kirkbride. We then knew we wanted to write a story set in a historic mental asylum. We've both worked closely with people with mental illness and were determined not to make the patients or inmates the objects of fear.

In October of 2018, we visited Tewksbury Hospital in Massachusetts. The nearby inmates' cemetery, "The Pines," made the strongest impression on us. When we walked under the shadow of the towering pine trees, we saw no gravestones, just small metal markers half-hidden in the pine needles and weeds, only a few of the 10,000 graves of the men and women who died unclaimed; the mentally ill, the neurodivergent, the poor and homeless. It truly felt as though, at any moment, we might come face-to-face with one of them. What kind of stories might they have to tell?

Many thanks to our beta readers: Lou Lamb, Carolyn Macdonell, Doug Moser, Mary Rickert, and Beth Rust. Their thoughtful reads and insightful comments were so welcome. A special thanks to Thomas Hamm, Emeritus Professor of History and Quaker Scholar in Residence at Earlham College, for his kindness and assistance in keeping the story faithful to 19th-century Quaker speech. Thanks to John McIlveen and Haverhill House for giving this book a life and a home. They say it takes a village, and when that village is Haverhill House Publishing, you know you're in good hands. Thank you, Tony, Chris, the late great Jim Moore, Matt, Errick, and all the good people in this village. We are honored to be a part of you.

People with mental illness have been with us always. They are all around us. They *are* us. Please spend a moment to get to know them. To welcome them. To give them a seat at the table. There's room.

For those living with mental illness and for their helpers and advocates.

SAVING THORNWOOD

Chapter 1 - Annie

The directions the police gave us make no sense. Mom keeps saying, "Where do I turn? Is this it?" I can't tell her. I study the lined paper in my hand, covered in Mom's awkward scrawl. *About 2 miles down from the post office.* I haven't seen the post office and have no idea what two miles feel like.

I look at Mom. She's leaning forward over the steering wheel, hands clenched tight at ten and two, eyes rimmed with red and drooping. She hasn't slept in three days. I barely have.

"Should you even be driving?" I ask her.

"Do I have a choice?"

A squat red building beside a pole holding a limp American flag rises up on the left, *U.S. Post Office* in small letters over the door. "Two miles on the left," I read from the paper then look up. One- and two-story buildings glide by *For Sale, For Rent,* or *No Trespassing* signs in the empty black windows. Houses with untended yards, a few looming old Victorians that need paint. Not a single person anywhere.

I don't say what I'm thinking—*ghost town.*

I hadn't said much since the second day Dad went missing, when Mom went from being angry to being scared and called the police. I don't know what they told her, but it made her brittle. She started snapping at me for anything I said, and the only way to make her stop was to stop talking.

I see a long stretch with trees on one side and an open field on the right. Then, a driveway. I read aloud from the notes. "Take the second driveway on the left."

A series of old brick structures with large wide doors appear, and then behind these, a sharply steepled building rises. The trim is covered in peeling white paint, and dirty windows glint in the late-day sun.

"That can't be right," Mom mumbles, even as I start to read aloud from the ironwork gateway rising over the driveway.

"Thornwood Lunatic Asylum."

It hits me in the gut. *Lunatic.* Is that what Dad is?

The building looks worse as we get closer. The facade needs major repair, and the windows look like pupil-less eyes. Scaffolding comes into view, climbing the far side of the building as we drive up to broad stone steps and the wide double doors of old wood and glass. There are no other cars, so Mom stops, gets out, and climbs the stairs without waiting for me.

She bends to read a small white sign. Her lips move, but she doesn't make a sound.

It reads: *Please enter here. Museum hours 10 to 2, Tues and Thu.*

We look at each other, and Mom goes around to the side door, but it's locked.

"You're blocking the drive."

A man in overalls and a bright orange vest has materialized next to our car. He looks at each of us slowly, first at Mom, then at me.

"If you're looking for the hospital, it's up the hill over that-a-way," he points behind the building. When I turn to look, I can just make out the tops of a few square brick buildings, much newer than this one.

"Oh," Mom finally speaks. "Yes. We are." And as she moves towards the car, motioning me to follow, "Thank you."

I look back at that man and notice something wrong with his face. The bones look as if they were taken apart and reassembled by a child. The right side looks partly caved in. I know I'm staring, so I force myself to look away.

"Stay away. It's no good for you here," are the last words he speaks before lumbering toward the scaffolded side of the building and disappearing. Again, Mom and I look at each other but say nothing. The laughter bubbles up without warning.

"*Stay away…*" I intone with a spooky voice.

Mom smiles before joining in with, "*no good for you…*" And suddenly, she's laughing, and all those new lines between her eyebrows and around her mouth fall away. Something inside me relaxes. Maybe everything will be okay.

The hospital is a big, ugly, yellow brick building, just a box with small windows. This parking lot is full, and it takes us a few minutes to find a space. The sun is high and hot, making shimmers above the asphalt. My sandals stick to patches of tar, and the whole thing stinks. Finally, sweating, we reach a pair of steel-framed glass doors and pull them open.

Inside smells bad, too. I'm not sure what it is, and I don't want to know; I just start breathing through my mouth. We approach a woman behind a desk who stares at us blankly.

"We're here to see Jackson Blake," Mom says, pronouncing each syllable carefully. The woman shoves a clipboard with a stack of papers toward Mom, and my pulse races. *He's here!*

Mom fills out the papers, then we sit in uncomfortable metal chairs for a long time until a door opens, and a man in a white coat with a name tag appears. Mom leaps to her feet.

"Stay here," she says and goes over to talk with the man. I can't hear what they're saying, but the worry on her face is hard to look at.

Then she calls me over and we pass through the door together. It's a long march down an empty hall. When we get to the door labeled *Psychiatric,* Mom stops and puts her hands on my shoulders.

"Wait here. Please."

"No way. I'm gonna see him," I push her hands off and move to the door, but she grabs my arm and holds on as I try to break free.

"Annie, please. I have to see him first. See what he's… if he's… I'll come right back and get you, I promise, I just … need to see him alone. It's too…" and she starts to cry. She doesn't make a sound.

Her face just crumples, and tears run down her cheeks. I can't bear it.

"Okay, okay. You go." And then she's gone.

I try to imagine what she'll find. Is he in a hospital gown, the kind with a gaping back? Maybe he's sitting somewhere rocking himself. Will he know her? But the images won't hold. What I see is just my dad, the way he was the last time I saw him. He was staring at his computer when I walked into the living room from work. He looked up at me with that expression of pure joy he always gives me. Joy and surprise, as if he couldn't believe I'd come home to him. I imagine him looking up now, seeing Mom and smiling. As if the last two days had never happened.

The first night, Mom grumbled and then raged, "How can he be so thoughtless!" The next day, Mom looked groggy and strange. She made me go to work that day at the library, which made it worse somehow. So little to do, so much time to imagine bad things.

When I got home, Dad's car was still missing from the drive.

Then came the call from the Massachusetts police; the look on Mom's face when she'd picked up, the hope there, nearly killed me.

And worst of all, walking down the long line of faded red doors at the motel to room 19, the motel manager opening the door and turning on the light. Sheets of paper covered in black swirly marks were tacked to the walls, words and numbers, drawings and calculations, all in Dad's handwriting. Some of it had bled onto the wallpaper. Every wall was covered from baseboard to ceiling.

The door clicks open and there's Mom, smiling at me. "C'mon, sweetie. It's okay." I can't tell if she's been crying. Her eyes are still red, but the smile doesn't look fake. I go inside, and the air changes as the door sucks closed behind me.

We walk down another long, bleak hallway and finally enter a room without a door. I see Dad sitting at a table, writing. He's wearing jeans and a black t-shirt, and when we come in, he stops writing and looks up. And there it is – that joy.

In two seconds, he's across the room and holding me. It feels so good, but I start to cry. He rocks me a little, saying, "Shhhh, it's okay. You'll be okay," as if I were the one in the hospital.

"Sorry," I say when I can talk, but he pulls me back into a hug then offers me a chair. And this is when I see the shape he's in. There's something off about his eyes, and when he sits down, he can't stop moving, his leg bouncing up and down, his fingers drumming, one eyelid twitching.

"Nothing to be sorry about," he says. "I'll be out of here today, right Caro? And everything will be fine. Sorry you had to come all this way."

"Jack," Mom's voice is tight. "We have to see the doctor first."

"Doctor, schmoctor," Dad says, standing up. "It was the motel people. I had to get out of there, and they wouldn't let me go. That's why I'm here. But now you're here and we can all just go home and forget the whole thing."

Mom puts her hand on his arm. "We will. Soon. After we see the doctor." He shakes her arm off.

"I need paper."

I look down and see the pages full of scribbled words, and the writing has started to cross over onto the tabletop.

"Okay, Mr. Blake, come with me." A burly man in scrubs and jeans puts his hand on Dad's arm. Dad shakes him off.

"In a minute, I have to get this down."

"We'll get you paper. Just come with me now." The man removes the pen from Dad's hand and gets him to his feet. Dad looks around the room and then at Mom. His face crumples.

"I'm sorry, Caro," he says, and then he looks at me. He's not crying, not yet, and I have to force myself not to look away. "C'mere, kitten," he says, and I'm in his arms again. *I'll get you out,* I tell him silently. *I promise.*

Chapter 2 - Mary

I ought to send you to Thornwood.

I must have heard Aunt Bridget say those words a thousand times. But I never thought she'd do it.

This road is rough and rattles my bones, but I'm holding on as best I can. The clatter of wheels is so loud I can't hear Jamie crying, but I feel him shake and shudder in my arms. I call out for him to be still, but the noise of the cart and the howl of the wind carry my words away.

This cart was meant to carry grain or animals, not human beings. Those men in the seat above us, the ones who put us here and whip the horse toward the place they're taking us—I pray that every bone-breaking bounce of the wheels makes them suffer at least half as much as we do.

Jamie pulls my hair. I grab his fist and hold it steady while I stare down into his thin, pale face, at his bright eyes searching mine, until his grip loosens. I don't hit him or yell like Aunt Bridget does. His fits, his strange and halting way of talking, the days when he doesn't talk at all, none of it is his fault. Aunt Bridget thinks it can be beaten out of him. Even on his worst days, Jamie is worth twenty of her.

A whiff of alcohol reaches my nose. I look up and see the men passing a flask between them, drinking to keep away the chill. I hope it rots their livers and turns their faces yellow.

I knew what they'd come for when they showed up at our door. Rough-looking men, unshaven, with faces like slabs of raw meat. Not like the young doctor Aunt Bridget brought in to look at us, that soft-looking fool in gentleman's clothes. He'd peered through his spectacles, first at Jamie, then at me, looking for what Aunt Bridget had told him about us, trying to find it in our faces. I watched him prod at Jamie like a calf being sold at auction, and my blood ran hot, so when he came to me and brought his fingers close, I cursed him and spit in his face. Aunt Bridget shrieked bloody murder, and just before her fists came down on my head, I saw fear in the young doctor's eyes.

Good, I thought you should be afraid of me.

The first time I heard Aunt Bridget say *I ought to send you to Thornwood*, it was to my da. Every time she said it, he'd laugh at her. That made her furious. She'd been angry at him for years because of his odd ways and the strange and heathenish things he'd say. Aunt Bridget would threaten to send him to Thornwood for the hundredth time, and he'd laugh, his strong, white teeth flashing from under his thick, dark beard.

When the men had hold of Jamie and were herding him toward the door, I stood in front of them. "Take me!" I shouted at them. "Take me too!"

The men stared down at me with dumb brute faces, but I heard Aunt Bridget laugh, "Oh, they're taking you, alright. Did you think I was going to let them leave you here?"

One of the men moved to take my arm, but I gave him such a cold look that he withdrew his hand. "If you hurt him," I said, pointing toward Jamie, "I'll fucking kill you." The men laughed harshly, but they turned loose of Jamie and let us walk to the cart on our own.

Take care of your brother, Mary. Those were the last words Da said to me before he vanished into the night. *Promise me.* At first, I wasn't sure how I was supposed to do that. I'd seen Jamie bloody Da's nose more than once when the fits come over him, though my da never lifted a finger against him. Now it was all going to be on me. *You'll have to find your own way with him,* was all Da would say.

I feel the cart start to climb higher. The men call out to the horse and crack the lash to urge it onward. I turn my head and see a massive dark shape rising against the night sky, blotting out the stars. As we draw closer, I can see high stone walls and a single dark tower pointing an accusing finger toward heaven. Jamie sees it too; he turns his face away and buries it in my chest.

Every child around here knows about Thornwood. We all know the stories—lunatics in cages who eat blood and bone marrow from the slaughterhouse that the guards keep in buckets and throw at them. Lost creatures who howl at the moon like wild beasts, who escape from their cages and scratch on children's windows at night. I know those stories; I'd even told a few of them myself when I want to frighten the other kids who'd try to frighten me. The truth is you don't have to be crazy to go to Thornwood—all you have to be is helpless. Or poor.

I hear a low rumble of thunder. The first drops of cold rain sting my face and arms, then the skies open up. This cart isn't covered, so Jamie and I are drenched in less than a minute.

A single light flickers on in a window, and a door in the great wall swings open. Through the door comes a figure wrapped in a dark blanket. The figure walks up to one of the men who brought us here, drops something into his outstretched hand, and I hear the clink of coins. The other man opens the back of the cart. "Get out," he snarls.

I look down at Jamie who still has his face buried in my lap. "Jamie," I whisper into his ear. "Jamie boy, come on. It's alright." I want him to come on his own—I won't let those men put their hands on him again.

Jamie and I climb down from the cart. One of the men tries to take Jamie by the arm.

"Keep your fucking hands off of him!" I say.

"Yes, Your Majesty," he says. They both laugh, climb back into the cart and ride away.

The figure in the blanket stands at the edge of the road, waiting for us. We approach, and it lifts the lantern to get a better look at us. "You two," it says in a woman's voice, flat and joyless, "Come with me."

I think about taking Jamie by the hand and running off into the woods. But if we're caught and brought back, I know it will go hard on Jamie, and that's why I choose to follow the woman and her lantern through the door in the stone wall.

We cross an open brick courtyard while the rain keeps beating down on our heads. The woman with the lantern leads us to a dark wooden building. The door is already open, dim light spilling out onto the wet brick walkway, and we follow her inside.

The woman removes the wet blanket, gives it a shake, and hangs it from a peg on the wall. When she walks back into the candlelight, I can see she's not young, but not yet old, her graying hair pulled back tight from a lean, hard face. She walks behind a raised wooden desk, opens a heavy-looking ledger, and turns through its pages.

"Your name," she says in the same flat, joyless voice.

"Mary," I tell her. "Mary Donovan."

"How old."

"Fifteen."

The woman writes in the ledger. Without looking up, she says again, "Your name." I know she's talking to Jamie. He's clinging close to me, looking anxiously at the darkness all around us. He doesn't like the cold, wet clothes clinging to his skin or the harsh and unfriendly sound of this woman's voice prodding at him like a sharp stick.

"Jamie," I tell her. "Jamie Donovan."

The woman looks up from the ledger, her eyes hard. "Can he speak?"

"He can," I say.

"Then let him," she says. "Boy. What is your name?" Jamie looks at her for the first time, his eyes frightened, and I feel my anger rise. She knows his name—what she's really asking for is obedience, respect, all the stupid, invisible things men and women like her crave.

"What is your name, boy?" she asks again, her voice loud and harsh.

"Don't yell at him!" I tell her. The woman glares at me, then calls out a name.

A man steps out of the shadows, grabs Jamie by the arm, and begins to drag him away. Jamie starts shrieking and flailing, and the man steps behind him and wraps one strong arm around Jamie's neck. I'm on him in a second and sink my teeth into the man's arm. He roars and shoves me away. Other men and women appear out of nowhere, pulling me and Jamie apart and dragging him down a dark hallway. I'm screaming Jamie's name over and over so he can hear me wherever they're taking him, screaming till my throat is raw. The man whose arm I bit pulls something from his pocket and swings it at my head. Pain explodes down the left side of my skull, and I fall to my knees.

Then I see nothing.

Chapter 3 - Annie

The sounds are wrong. A deep humming and cold air across my face. Rhythmic beeping; a truck backing up? Rumbling of loose wheels on a sidewalk right outside. My nose fills with something astringent, antiseptic, strange. I open my eyes and see nothing. No night light in the hallway, no dim light through my curtains, just black. Close by I can hear soft snoring. I sit up.

And it all comes back: motel, New England, Dad.

I can still see that other motel, the walls covered in Dad's writing. A wave of fear and sorrow hits my gut. I slip out of bed and stumble in the direction of the bathroom, a thin line of light showing the way. Inside, I click the door closed as the first sob escapes. I turn on the water full blast to mask the noise. I put the toilet lid down and sit there curled up as wave after wave of sobs wrack my body. It feels like something being pulled from me, a half-scream, half-moan. When it's done, I sit still for a while, breathing through my mouth. My face and nose are a mess, so I run hot water and splash my face over and over again. When I leave the bathroom, I feel lighter.

I can see a little now. Mom is turned to her side, but her breathing is slow and even. I remember what she said last night. *"Tomorrow we'll make some decisions."* And as I slide back under the covers, I see the clock. It's already tomorrow.

After we get up, Mom doesn't say anything about my red puffy eyes. Maybe she doesn't notice. Last night I heard her talking to someone on the phone, saying, "There are too many decisions to make, and all of them are wrong." It scared me. Mom's supposed to know what to do. If she doesn't, where does that leave me?

We go out for breakfast. The diner is in a real train car; the ceiling is low and curved, and the place is cozy. I don't know if I can eat, but Mom makes me order the Farmer's Breakfast, and as soon as I see it, I'm starving. Mom gets a muffin and yogurt, and I'm happy to see her finish them both.

As we drive past the old buildings, I see a figure standing there, bright orange vest nearly blinding in the sun.

"Hey, look," I tell Mom, but we don' t laugh this time. He just stands there, face in shadow, but I can feel his eyes on us.

The hospital lot is emptier today, and we park close to the doors. It's warm already, and it's going to be a hot day, so the cold lobby is bracing.

"I'm going to talk with the doctor," Mom says. "Wait here."

"Can I see Dad?"

"After." She takes one of my hands and gives it a quick squeeze. "I'll be back soon." And then she's following someone down the hall and through swinging doors, and I can't see her anymore.

The morning after the night Dad went missing, I wanted to call Bess so bad. I was sure that her voice was the medicine I needed, that she could somehow explain the unexplainable—if she was still speaking to me.

The next few days had felt like I had a wire inside being pulled tighter and tighter, ready to snap. No one had heard from Dad. Hospitals and state police hadn't found him, nothing. Mom was freaked, and I was pretending to be better than I was for Mom's sake. It took everything I had.

When we finally got the call from the police, I started to text Bess.

My dad went missing, but he's okay. We're going to pick him up in some place called Pineville.

I thought about sending it. I imagined Bess hearing the buzz and seeing my name on the screen. What would she do? I imagined waiting for a response that might never come. So I deleted it.

I stare at the door where Mom's gone, the one with the sign that says 'Psychiatric.' I stare, but it doesn't open. I move back to the waiting area, pick up a magazine and sit down. *Vanity Fair.* I drop it and pick up another one. *Psychology Today.* The cover image is a leaping dancer and the words 'The Moments That Make Us Who We Are.' I turn to the article and try to read it, but the words don't stick in my brain.

I have to get out of here.

I go to the reception desk and wait for one of the attendants to notice me. A big woman with dark skin and long braids looks up and smiles. "What can I do for you, sugar?"

I smile back. "My mom is seeing a doctor back there…" I look around, wondering if I should be asking them this. "Can you tell her I'm out walking? She can text me. I won't go far."

"The tall woman? Short hair? Red top?"

Is she wearing red? I can't remember, but I nod. "No problem," she says. The kindness in her voice makes me want to cry. "You just go along now."

The damp heat is good after the chill in the lobby, and I walk down the hill right towards the old buildings. There's no sign of the lopsided-face guy, so I walk around to the front and look at the small sign. *Museum hours 10 to 2, Tues and Thu.*

I check my phone and see it's a little after ten. I move to the side door, a heavy wooden thing with glass panes, one of which has a diagonal crack across it. I grab the handle and pull. The door opens easily, and I step inside.

It's cool in here but not frigid. The place smells old, like wood, ceramic, and iron. The hallway looks abandoned. Large posters depict hospital equipment from a long time ago, nurses in old uniforms. Lists of diseases from different times in large block print: *Influenza, Polio, Tuberculosis.*

In a glass case against the wall are objects with small hand-printed cards in front of them.

Above a card that reads 'Asylum Fork' is a long wooden handle holding a metal rod that splits in two. The ends are connected by another piece of metal with short teeth.

My phone buzzes. I look at the screen.

I'm out. C'mon back and we'll see Dad.

Mom's waiting for me by the white door. She warns me, "Your dad is sleepy because of the medication they gave him."

When we enter the room, the change in him is a shock. He slurs his words, and his eyelids look like they'll drop at any moment. When he blinks, it's slow and tenuous.

"Hey," I say and sit across from him. His eyes focus firmly on mine, and he grabs my wrist. He leans forward and gestures for me to come closer. When our heads are nearly touching, he whispers, "I need you to get me out of here. Can you do that?"

I smile and nod. Mom told me the doctor said we should go along with anything he says, at least for now. "Sure, Dad. We will."

"No." He seems upset. "You. You have to do it."

"Do what?"

He looks around the room, then leans in closer. "Distract them."

He wants to make a break for it with me as a decoy? I almost laugh, but there's nothing funny in this room. Instead, I look him in the eye and say, "What are you writing?"

His grip on my wrist lightens, and he sits back. "Oh, wouldn't they like to know," he says, nodding and glancing around the room. I see there are a couple of other patients sitting at tables with their visitors. I wonder who he means.

I look at the paper. I can make out some of the sentences, although the writing is especially bad.

Keeping patients uninformed. Doctor refuses to see me for days. A social worker takes his place but doesn't have the right file…

Is this true? "Dad?" I lean forward, but Mom's hand is on my shoulder.

"Annie, your dad needs his rest now."

I look up at her, frowning. "Is that true?" pointing to Dad's paper.

"Jack, we'll be back this afternoon."

"I'll be packed," he says, his eyes and head starting to droop.

I can see Mom wants to say something. *Wait and see.* The mantra of the medical profession. But she doesn't say it. Dad struggles to his feet, and after a limp hug for each of us, he shuffles out of the room.

He left his papers, so I grab them up and run after him. "Dad, wait!"

He turns slowly and looks at me with surprise. "Annie?" Almost like he didn't remember just sitting here talking with me.

"You forgot your writing." I thrust the papers towards him. He grabs them from me, and one of the pages rips.

"Whatever you do, don't let them see this!" he whispers harshly, then turns away and shuffles through the doorway and down the hall.

Mom gestures for me to sit. She takes Dad's chair and reaches for my hands.

"I know it's scary..." she starts.

"When's he getting out?"

She blinks and looks away. "Soon. I don't know. The doctor wants to..." She stops.

"What? Tell me." Now I wish I'd gone with her and heard what the doctor had to say. Maybe I could have asked my own questions. *How did this happen? When will my dad come back?*

"Just... I think he said...till he stabilizes."

"What does that mean?"

She alternates between staring somewhere behind my head and at the table between us. Anywhere but me. "They use the drugs... the medication to calm him. Right now he's... volatile. Manic."

"Manic? He's manic-depressive?!"

She grabs my hands and finally looks at me. "They don't know what it is yet. Maybe bipolar, maybe not."

No, no, no, NO! I stare at the tabletop underneath our hands. There's some ink there, from Dad's pen where he went off the paper. I can just make out the letters *p-l-o-t*. Mom is still talking.

"They need to get him back to normal in order to figure out the next step. Annie, we have to be strong, okay? I know it's hard, but we'll get through it. I promise."

I look at her, biting the inside of my lip so hard I can taste blood. *Not gonna cry.* I blink hard and nod once, then pull my hands away and stand up. "What do we do now?"

She stands up and says, "I'm taking you home."

The relief and joy that floods through me is a shock. *Home.*

We leave the hospital and head toward the car.

"You don't mind being on your own, do you?" Mom says. "We'll stock up on food before I leave again."

"Leave?" I stop walking. "Where are you gonna be?"

"I'll come back here. You can video chat with your dad. I'll let you know…"

"I want to be with you."

"Honey…"

"You shouldn't be alone."

She sighs, closes her eyes, and pulls me into her arms. I feel her chin rest on the top of my head. "You shouldn't have to deal with this," she says.

And you should? I can just make out the rooftops of the buildings down the hill, the flaking white paint of the steeple. I remember the writing on the walls of the motel room. The word scrolled in iron on the gate. *Lunatic.*

No, I tell myself. That's not him. That's not my dad.

Chapter 4 - Mary

Something stings my head, cold and sharp. I open my eyes and see a girl's face hovering over mine. Pale and thin, maybe a couple of years older than me, she's washing out the wound on my head with a dirty-looking rag.

"Hold still," she says. I grit my teeth against the stinging until she's done. There's a ringing in my head and bruises all over me, but I drag myself up till I'm sitting and have a look around.

The room we're in is long and dark and lined with dozens of beds and single iron cots with dingy-looking sheets. On a few of the cots, women are sitting, some rocking gently back and forth and talking to themselves. Some just staring into space.

"Where am I?" I ask.

"You're in Thornwood," the girl answers in a flat voice. "The women's ward." She stands up, getting ready to leave, and I see for the first time how tall she is.

"Where's Jamie? Where's my brother?"

"If you have a brother here, he's in the men's ward."

"Where is that? How do I get to the men's ward?"

"Women aren't allowed there." She wrings out the rag into a bowl, and the water comes out tinged with red.

I struggle to stand up, and the room seems to move around me.

"Wait," she says. "You took a beating. You need to lay here a while."

"I can take a beating," I say.

"Yes," she says in a cool voice, "I believe you can."

I look at her more closely. Her mousey-colored hair is tied back tightly; her grey eyes are sleepy-looking and don't meet mine.

"So where is it?" I ask. "The men's ward?"

"I told you. You can't go there." She's finished gathering up her things, the dingy-looking rag and bowl of water. "You lay here and rest," she says, then walks away. I start to call out after her, then stop. She's probably crazy anyway—I'm in Thornwood, aren't I?

I glare at the walls all around me and try to figure out which one is hiding Jamie from me. All his life, Jamie has never been without me. I think of how scared he must be now.

A door opens and a tall and thin woman in a long black dress appears, her hair pinned back tight. I recognize her. It's the woman who let us in out of the rain the night we arrived. She blows on a whistle that's hanging around her neck, three loud and shrill blasts. Ten or twelve women in their shapeless cotton smocks shuffle toward the door and get in line.

Someone touches my arm. I turn and see the young woman who washed my head, fixing me with a hard stare. "Come on," she whispers and nods toward the line of women waiting at the door. "Just follow me."

We enter a large room with long wooden tables holding deep trays of water and washboards. Steam drifts from a large metal boiler, and the burnt smell of lye is everywhere. The women line up at the deep metal trays while two more women walk about, dumping soiled clothes and bed linens into the water. The young woman who led me here stands at the tray next to mine. When a load of clothes is dumped into my, and then into her tray, she picks up a bar of soap and starts scrubbing, soaping down the wet clothes and then rubbing them vigorously against the washboard.

"Go on," she whispers, cutting her eyes toward the tall woman in the long black dress who's walking back and forth between the tables. "Don't let her catch you standing around like that." I notice how red this girl's hands are, how her fingers and knuckles are covered with little red scars. I pick up my bar of soap and start scrubbing, wondering how long it'll take before my hands look like hers.

"What's your name?" she asks, not looking at me.

Who wants to know, I almost say, then stop myself. If I'm going to find Jamie, I'll need someone who knows their way around this place.

"Mary," I say. "What's yours?"

"Kathleen."

I take another look at her. She looks to be maybe a couple of years older than me. I thought she was thin, but watching her work, I can tell how strong she is. Not thin as a wisp of air like Jamie. I picture those men's rough hands on him, his sweet face crying out for me, and my heart hurts in my chest.

"Where's the men's ward?" I ask.

She looks down into her washing tray and scrubs even harder as the woman in black walks past us. When she's gone, the girl looks back at me again, a scowl on her pale, dirty face. "I told you. You can't go there."

"Why not?"

"Because," she looks up at me, annoyed and astonished, "You're not a man."

"That's a stupid reason," I say. She stops scrubbing and glares at me, then goes back to her scrubbing. "My brother's there," I tell her. "They took him."

"Then there's nothing to be done," she says, still scrubbing away. "The sooner you settle your mind on that, the better."

My temper starts to seethe like the water in the big metal boiler. Then my eye settles on the woman in black walking slowly back and forth between the rows of girls, and on the ring of keys hanging around her neck.

"What about her?" I ask, nodding toward the woman. "The one with the keys. She knows where the men's ward is, doesn't she?"

The girl looks up at me, a flash of alarm in her eyes. That's all I need to see. Right away, I drop the wet clothes back into the tub, wipe my soapy hands on my dress, and walk toward the woman. I hear the girl behind me whisper, *"No!"* but I keep walking, right past all the other girls who are looking up from their washing with looks of surprise on their faces, all the way up to the woman in the black dress who turns to glare down at me.

"I need to see my brother," I announce. "He's in the men's ward."

The woman's face grows red. "Get back to your work," she says, her voice hard as iron.

"No!" I shout. "Take me to my brother! Now!"

The woman turns and calls for someone. The keys on her chest rattle at me like she's taunting me with them, so I grab the key ring in my hands and start pulling on it as hard as I can. The woman clutches at the chain around her neck, trying to stop it from choking her, but I keep pulling. Three men surround us and pull me away from her, then I feel the chain break and the keys clatter to the floor. The other girls are all shouting and calling out now, and the last thing I see as they drag me away is the woman in black down on her knees, her angry face blood-red, gathering up all the keys from the wet floor.

I don't know how many of them are holding me, but they pull me along so fast that my feet barely touch the floor, down a dark hallway into a small room. Then they're pulling some kind of rough garment over my head, forcing my arms into its sleeves and binding them to my sides. I hear someone bolt the door, and now I'm alone. I can't move my arms, so I run into the door, banging against it with my whole body. It makes a loud noise, so I do it again and again, screaming and cursing till my throat is raw.

Finally, the bolt slides back, the door swings open, and two big men come in with two women—one is the woman with the keys. Her eyes blaze at me, and I can see the red marks on her neck where the chain dug into her. Then the men's hands are on me, and they're dragging me down the hall. I scream and try to struggle, but my arms are bound tight.

They bring me into a room with dirty tile walls. I see a large bathtub filled with water and chunks of ice. They lift me up on my back, then drop me in.

The shock of ice-cold water seizes my lungs so hard I can't breathe. A memory comes to me from when I was five or six, the day we were playing by the river and I fell through the ice. I never knew cold water could burn like that. I can feel it now, creeping in through my skin, through muscle and bone, until the cold is all there is. I tell myself the same thing I told myself back then—this will not kill me because I won't let it.

All I have to do is hold on.

Chapter 5 - Annie

There's a rank smell when we open the front door to our house. A black streak hurtles around the corner and bangs up against my legs.

"Gremlin," I murmur, picking up the cat and hugging him. "Poor baby. Did you miss us?"

I look around. The place is a mess. Even before we got the call about Dad from the police, we let the dishes pile up and forgot to take out the trash. The house is hot, and stuff is rotting on the counters. The butter dish was left out. A pool of yellow goo has oozed onto the counter and over the edge, dripping onto the floor.

It didn't take much to convince me to leave that awful place and come home. I'm ashamed how glad it made me, the longing for my town, my home, my room, my bed, leaving Dad alone in that hospital.

I look around at these familiar rooms and realize I was wrong. There's nothing comforting here. Not anymore.

I put Gremlin down and fill his food bowl. He gives me a look. "What? It's food. Eat."

He stares at the dry kibble for a moment before diving in.

"I'll take out the trash. You get started on these," Mom points to the dishes.

I drop my backpack and turn on the faucet. It sputters once before gushing out, cold at first. When it's hot, I put a stopper in, squirt in soap, and let the sink fill, putting dirt-encrusted cups and bowls into the water to soak.

Bipolar. That's what the doctor said. Dad is bipolar. He had a 'psychotic break.' An attack of mania. *A man who is never depressed suddenly goes off the rails and writes on walls?* I remember the shock of seeing those words scrawled where they should not have been. It was clearly his handwriting. Bolder and more wild. Dad, but not Dad.

"Why don't you call Bess?" I jump at Mom's voice, hand to my heart.

"Okay," I say, feeling a little breathless. I imagine telling Bess about Dad, about everything. I can see her raised eyebrows and widened eyes. The way one hand will slowly lift to cover her mouth, the shape of a perfect 'o'. And then her expression transforms into the last one I saw—disgust.

My phone buzzes. I see it's Dad and freeze. My limbs too stiff to move, I almost miss the call, but I manage to break out of it.

"Hey, Dad."

"Sweetheart. I need you to do something for me." He almost sounds normal.

"Sure. What's up?"

"There are papers in my office. I want you to find them and bring them to me. Can you do that?"

The doctor said to *Go along.* "No problem. Where are they?"

"On top of the desk and in the top drawer. Just bring everything you find, okay?" His voice is even and calm despite the urgency of his words.

"You got it. What are they? Something you're working on?"

"Yes… but Annie," his voice drops down low. "Don't let anybody see them. Especially here. They'll take them from you. You can't let that happen, understand?" And there it is, the mania creeping back into his voice.

"Okay," I say. "See ya soon."

"Good night, kitten," he says.

By the time everything's cleaned, it's late. Mom pulls me into her arms and rests her head on top of mine. "Time for bed."

I'm ready for it. Ready to dive under the covers and sleep as long as possible.

"I'll get you up in time for work…"

Work?! I'd forgotten about the library. Was it only two days ago I was there?

"…and then I'll go back. To get Dad."

I pull back a little so I can see her face. "Are you sure you don't want me to come?"

She looks me in the eye, making her gaze steady. "Yes, I'm sure." Turning me around, she gives me a gentle shove toward the stairs, "Now, bed!"

I'm not sure I'll be able to sleep, but my bed is heaven; the sheets smell like everything good. I sink down deep, and the next thing I know, Mom's shaking my shoulder gently and saying, "Time to get up."

Gremlin is lying behind my knees, pinning me between the wall and the edge of the bed. "Over, you," I say as I pull my legs up to my chin and swivel around him.

I'm brushing my teeth when Mom knocks on the door.

"Leaving now. I'll call you when I can. Love you!" I feel the tug inside me, hearing her footsteps go down the stairs, the kitchen door opening and closing. The car tires spit gravel as she pulls out.

Why didn't I go with her?

Gremlin weaves between my legs and puts his paws up on my legs, begging to be picked up.

"I can't, buddy. Gotta go to work." But I pick him up anyway, burying my face in his fur and breathing in his warm skin. There's still a trace of his kitten smell, even now that he's—what?—four? Five? Dad's face floats in front of me, a tiny black fluff ball with grey-green eyes pressed against his cheek. Gremlin is his cat. I wonder what he thinks about Dad's absence.

"Don't worry, bud. He'll be home soon."

Mr. Kaplan is opening the heavy inner door just as I walk up the steps to the library. He eyes me with suspicion.

"Good morning, Anne," he says with no warmth at all. For a moment, I wonder if he knows about Dad.

"Morning, Mr. Kaplan," I force my face into a smile.

"How are you feeling?"

I almost say, *Fine,* until I remember calling them from the motel room yesterday. Telling them I was sick.

"Uh, better, thanks." I start to pass him.

"I'm glad to hear it," although there's nothing glad in his voice. "Ms. Greene has some tasks for you."

"Okay," I say, moving fast now to the back room where the reference desk is.

"Annie!" Ms. Greene cries on seeing me. "How are you?"

I swallow hard, forcing a wave of sorrow back down into my chest. "Better, thanks. Sorry I couldn't be here."

She studies me for a few moments, her head cocked sideways. Then she says, "No worries. None at all. Here…" She points me to a full book cart. "Yesterday, I started moving these to make room for new editions. Come." She stands and walks through the stacks behind her.

"Here's what I thought we'd do. Move the volumes at the end to these empty shelves, leaving a gap like this one." She points to a low shelf full of bound periodicals. I see *Zoetrope* and *Yankee Magazine* on the dark brown spines.

She leaves me, and I start shelving from the cart. Finishing up the 'Y's, I take the cart and load up on *Vanity Fair*. I flash on the hospital lobby, then that room with Dad writing at the table.

Why was Dad in Pineville? Why didn't he call us? I'm suddenly furious.

I slam the books into shelves, my hands become covered in dust, and I start to sneeze. I go to the bathroom to wash up. While I wait for the water to get hot, I study my face. Round, circled with curly brown hair. People say I look like Dad, but I can't see it. I wish I looked more like Mom. Regal, beautiful.

By the time I leave work it's 3pm, and still no word from Mom. My heart lifts at the sight of Dad's car in the driveway till I remember Mom saying she was taking her car back to Massachusetts. Still, Dad's coming home with her, I'm sure of it. Maybe late tonight, but they'll be back. Won't they?

I send a text:

Hey. How was the drive? How's Dad?

After typing that last part, I hesitate, but my thumb hits the screen, and it's sent.

I go inside and call for Gremlin. He doesn't come, so I pull out his food and shake it. Still nothing. I go to my room and open the closet, expecting him to jump out, furious at being locked inside, but he's not there. I look under the bed and pat down my comforter in case he's making himself flat underneath, but he's nowhere.

My phone buzzes. It's Mom.

"Hello?" My stomach clenches even as I tell myself nothing's wrong. She's going to tell me she has Dad, and they're coming home.

"Hi there." Her voice sounds tired. Tired and careful. "Sorry I didn't call before. How are you?"

How am I?! I force my jaw to release and say, "Fine. How are you?" I almost laugh. The formality of it.

"I'm okay. But I have some…not great news." She pauses. "The doctors… they say he should stay a little longer."

She continues talking but the roaring in my ears stops me from hearing it. *No!* My legs are wobbly, so I sit on the stairs as Mom's voice starts to fade back in, "…between different regimens and a little therapy."

"What?" my voice doesn't sound like me. "What did you say?"

"Oh honey," the sympathy in her voice nearly kills me. "It's all so… the doctor thinks he's at risk of another psychotic episode. That he needs supervision round the clock until the drugs have stabilized him. Then they can move forward with a treatment that will bring him back to normal."

I have a million questions, but they all boil down to one. "So, when can he leave?"

"I don't know. A few days? A week? We'll know more tomorrow."

A week... Not one or two days. It's real, not a nightmare I can pretend never happened.

"Honey? Are you still there?"

I stare at the phone for a moment before lifting it back to my face. "Yes. Sorry. What are you going to do?"

It's Mom's turn to be silent.

Finally, she emits a weak laugh. "I don't actually know. I haven't thought…"

"Are you going to that motel? The Sleep Inn?"

There's a long pause and then a sigh. "Would you be alright? Alone?"

I want her home with me. I want them both home. "Sure. No problem."

"It's just that I'm so tired…"

"Yeah, I know. It's fine. Really. Hey, did you let Gremlin out?"

"No. Why? Can't you find him?"

"He didn't come for his food," I say, then remember holding him after Mom had gone. "He's here, I'm sure." I look in the hall. From this vantage, I can see the edge of the door that leads into Dad's office. It's slightly ajar.

"I love you, sweetheart. I think there's some lasagna in the freezer."

When I end the call, I look up again at the door to Dad's office.

I push the door open. The late afternoon sun is streaming through the windows, glinting off the wood floor and making everything look shiny. It smells like Dad, his sandalwood aftershave, the paper and glue he uses to make his models and the old book smell from his overloaded bookcases.

My chest hurts. I've always loved being here. When I was small, Dad would set up toys on a small blanket and sit me there so he could work. I remember gazing up at him, so high on his stool at his drafting table. Big and handsome and sane.

His desk chair is swiveled out like he's just gotten up. The seat is dark and lumpy, and as I walk closer, the lump moves. Gremlin raises his head and makes a little sound, "*mwert?*"

"There you are, you bad boy." I kneel down and scritch his head. "Why didn't you come?" He leans into my hand for a moment, then lays his head back down, a perfect donut. I want to hold him, squeeze a warm living thing, but let him be. He misses Dad, too.

The desktop is obscured by papers covered in blue ink. Calculations and measurements. Lists and types of building materials. Nothing crazy here. If he's asked me for this stuff, he's thinking about his job, his work. And that's a good sign, isn't it?

As I straighten the papers into a neat pile, I notice a drawing of a building sketched on graph paper. It looks familiar, so I pull it out. I see an imposing brick building with a tall steeple at its heart.

A chill runs from my heart through my limbs, and my ears fill with white noise. My knees buckle, and I sit down on Gremlin who growls, squirms from beneath me and runs away.

I look away from the paper but can't get free; several drawings pinned to the wall show different angles of the same building. There's an enlarged photograph, which looks like it was taken from the steps where Mom and I stood. I turn my head to find more drawings, photos, and newspaper clippings, all of the same building.

That's when I see his draft table, flat and covered with pieces of foam core, a steepled building rising in the center. A perfectly scaled model, right down to the tiny gate, the small letters imitating the wrought-iron scrollwork: *Thornwood Lunatic Asylum.*

Chapter 6 - Mary

The whistle blows, and they march us through the iron gate to the road outside where the wagons are waiting, each one filled with heavy baskets full of laundry. The woman in black is watching us closely as we unload the wagons. She's no longer wearing the ring of keys around her neck; she must be hiding them inside her apron. I feel a hot rush of satisfaction, knowing some small part of her is afraid of me.

The whistle blows again, and they march us back through the iron gate into this steamy, stinking washroom. I go to my spot at the washtubs next to that girl, Kathleen, pick up my bar of lye soap, but there's only one thing on my mind. I've got to keep my promise—find Jamie and get us out of this goddamned place.

Kathleen glances at me, then looks down at the clothes she's scrubbing. When she speaks, it's so quiet I can barely hear.

"Are you alright?"

I nod once and plunge my hands into the lukewarm, soapy water. I look closer at what's in the tub in front of me–a fancy-looking bedspread with flowers printed all over it.

"What's this?" I ask. "It's not from here, is it?" I ask.

"No," she says. Then I understand.

"You mean people send their washing to this place?" I remember Ma bent over our sink, scrubbing away at sheets and clothes she could never afford to own herself. "And they pay for it?"

"They sure as hell don't pay *me* for it," she says, her mouth twisting at one corner. It's the closest I've seen her come to a smile.

The bedspread is heavy, sopping wet, and Kathleen helps me heave it into the rinsing tub. The way she's helping me makes me want to try one more time.

"How do I get to the men's ward?" I ask.

She glares at me and then looks down at her work, her lips tight.

"I won't tell anyone you told me," I say. "I swear."

She doesn't speak, but I catch her eyes flicker toward a door in the far wall.

Thank you, I want to say—now I know.

I never take my eyes off that door the whole time I'm washing. All I know is that Jamie is somewhere on the other side. I watch the matrons and the male guards pass back and forth through that door. But for me, it might as well be locked and bolted.

We're taking the matrons' gray uniforms down from the drying line when I get the idea. I find one that's about my size. When no one's looking, I roll it up as small as I can, turn my back, and stuff it inside my smock.

That night, I lie on my cot, waiting for the other girls and women to fall asleep. Clutching the uniform under my sheet, planning the whole thing out. When I get to the men's ward, I'll find Jamie and escort him out like I'm doing my job. Then we'll walk through the front door and keep walking. I don't know where we'll go or how we'll survive, but I can't let not knowing stop me the way it did before when we first got here and had a chance to run—I'll never let another chance slip through my fingers again.

When the ward is finally quiet and dark, I slip into the matron's uniform under my sheets. I take a strip of cloth I've torn from my smock and tie my hair back as smooth and tight as possible, the way the older women wear theirs. When I'm sure no one's looking, I slip out of bed and start walking past all the rows of cots.

The door to the washroom is still open. I go in, hoping it will be empty at this hour. It is, and I walk across the damp stone floor to the door I need to pass through to get to Jamie.

A guard is sitting by the door on a wooden stool. He looks half-asleep. I remember the brutes who brought us here, and I wonder if he's drunk. I pause for a moment, but only for a moment. The trick, I know, is to walk calmly and with purpose, like someone who has every right to be here.

Holding my head high, I walk quickly—but not too quickly—past the man on the stool. My heart pounds so hard I'm afraid he might hear it. He stirs but doesn't stop or challenge me. I keep walking steadily, straight ahead. Soon, I see a sign in front of me at the end of the hallway. *MEN'S WARD*. I keep walking, trying to slow the pounding of my heart.

A woman wearing the same grey uniform I'm wearing appears at the far end of the hallway and starts walking toward me. For a second, I almost freeze, but I force myself to keep going and look straight ahead. She comes closer and closer, the sound of her leather boots striking the floor echoing in the silent hallway. As we pass each other, she looks at me curiously. Then I see her glance down at my feet. A frown passes over her face, and my blood freezes when I realize—I'm still wearing the canvas slippers the inmates wear.

She calls out, and I start running for the doorway to the men's ward as fast as I can. I'm too close to turn back now. I start calling Jamie's name over and over as the sound of angry shouting and pounding feet approaches from behind me. I keep shouting his name even after they tackle me and pull me to the floor.

Rough hands drag me down the hallway to a small room where I see a wooden box the size of a crate against one wall. They shove me inside, and the smell of sawdust and piss makes me gag. The door slams shut, and I hear a chain rattle and the click of a lock.

It's black-dark in here. I try to push my way out, but the wooden walls press close on every side, so I can barely move. I remember when they buried Mother in that small pine box. I'm not screaming Jamie's name anymore; I'm just screaming and beating my fists against these wooden walls until my hands are numb and my voice gives out.

It's as dark as death in here, so I close my eyes and try to think of light, bright light, and fresh air to keep from going mad. I keep thinking about it until I can finally see it; a faraway glow as small as your fingernail at first, then bigger and bigger until it pushes the dark away. I see the trees at my da's farm, big, strong apple trees that give sweet, tart fruit to eat and strong limbs to climb. I'm walking under them, feeling the long grass against my legs and the warm summer sun on my face, playing the game Jamie loves to play. I say, *Oh, I wish I had an apple, but they're all so high I can't reach them.* There are apples all over the ground, but I pretend they're not there; that's part of our game. *I'm so hungry*, I sigh, *Oh, how I wish I had an apple.* I sigh again. The leaves rustle above me, I hear a muffled giggle, and an apple falls just before me, bouncing and rolling on the ground. I bend to pick it up and take a bite. It's warm from the sun, and the juice is sweet on my tongue. But I know the game isn't over yet. Jamie is waiting for the best part. *Oh, how I wish...* I start, but before I can finish, another apple falls, then another and another, until it's raining apples and Jamie's laughter pours down around me from above like sunshine. I stretch my arms wide to receive this gift and say what I know I'm supposed to say now: *Thank you. Thank you. Thank you.* I say it again and again. I'm still saying it when they finally open the door and drag me into the light.

Chapter 7 - Annie

I look again at the model on the table, marveling at the detail; hand-drawn tiles on the slanted roof, a cut-out of a bell in the small steeple.

Why did he make this? What do all these drawings and photographs mean?

I can't stand looking at them, so I go downstairs. Gremlin hisses at me. I pull him from under a table, and he twists onto his back in my arms and purrs. "What's wrong, buddy?"

I want Mom to come home. She'll know what it means—why Dad made all that stuff. I set down Gremlin and call Mom, but it goes to voicemail.

I get up, microwave the lasagna, then sit at the table staring until it's cool enough to eat. I expect rich tomato sauce and salty cheese, but it sits like Play-Doh on my tongue, so I throw the rest away.

Why did Dad make that model? Is this part of what happened to him? Was it a job, or was he just obsessed? Again, an image of his writing on the walls appears and I work hard to push it away.

My cell rings. Mom's picture on my phone looks like a professional headshot. She's smiling, head tilted, bright white teeth shining against tanned skin. When I press the green button, her actual face is a shock—fake smile and so very pale.

"Mom, did you know what Dad was working on?!"

She looks confused. "What?"

"Thornwood Lunatic Asylum."

She shakes her head slightly. "How did you…"

"There's a model in his office. And pictures… everywhere. Mom. What's going on?"

"I know he was working on a restoration project. Maybe he said the name, I can't remember…." more silence. "I guess it explains why he was here. I'll ask him tomorrow. Maybe he came up for a meeting…"

"But he said 'don't let them see it' about his papers. Is someone out to hurt him?"

"No, of course not." Her voice is firm. "Your dad's… not in his right mind. You saw that."

She sounds so tired. I remember all the days she didn't sleep, the worry, the terror, the relief at finding him, the fear at what he's become. Suddenly, I'm exhausted, too.

"I'm sorry you had to … be surprised like that," she says. "We'll sort it out. I have to get some dinner. Did you eat yet?"

"Yup," I lie. "See you tomorrow?" *Please come home now.* I want to say this so badly.

"Yes. Tomorrow. I love you."

"Love you too." She needs sleep. I know this. And maybe Dad will surprise us all. Maybe he'll be better tomorrow, and she can bring him home.

I start to put my phone down. Then, before I can stop myself, I open the browser and type *Thornwood Lunatic Asylum*.

The number of results surprises me. I scroll down, skipping the website in favor of Wikipedia:

Thornwood Lunatic Asylum and Alms House, later known as Pineville Mental Health Association. It was the principal facility for the care and treatment of Massachusetts's mentally ill from 1830 to current day. Its surviving buildings represent one of the oldest surviving complexes of mental care facilities in the United States. The Massachusetts Department of Public Health currently operates a Joint Commission accredited, 275-bed facility at Pineville Hospital, providing medical and psychiatric services to challenging adult patients with chronic conditions.

The Asylum and Alms House, in 1863, was the subject of a legal dispute headed by the Massachusetts governor. He accused Thornwood management and staff of a variety of abuses.

The case was dismissed, but the resulting publicity resulted in a management change and widespread reform in the care of the mentally ill, spearheaded by famous activist Mary Donovan.

Currently, the main building operates as a museum in a limited capacity as most of the structure is in disrepair.

There is a block print of the main building with rows of people standing in front; women in long dark dresses and men in hats.

There is a photo of the strange utensil I'd seen in the museum, as well as a leather collar with a padlock and chain.

I scan the search results for something more recent and click 'Local government at impasse.'

'Save Thornwood' non-profit fails to meet its fundraising goal required for the State to continue running Pineville Mental Health Association. Last week, owners presented their proposal for the property, which includes razing all existing buildings and creating new private hospital facilities. However, Pineville's mayor, the board of trustees, and the building department have rejected this proposal as elitist and neglectful of serving the community and its needs.

The photo accompanying the article shows a village green, complete with a gazebo and a ring of shade trees. All I remember are the dingy streets and empty storefronts—the hot bleakness of asphalt outside the building where Dad is now.

Was Dad about to lose his job, this contract? Is that what triggered his—what did Mom call it—psychotic break?

I suddenly miss Bess. I want to tell her about this so she can help me figure it out. But she's not talking to me. She's never talking to me again.

Chapter 8 - Mary

The light floods in and blinds me as rough hands drag me out of this stinking box. Two men carry me down a dark hallway, one holding each of my arms. I don't have the strength to fight them, so I go limp and let them carry me where they will.

We stop before a large set of double doors. One of the men knocks. A voice answers from the other side, and the men bring me into a large room different from others I've seen. There are bookcases full of heavy, important-looking books, a fine loveseat and armchair set of mahogany and red velvet. A large desk with a single oil lamp burning is at the center of the room. Behind the desk is a well-dressed man with a pointed grey beard. The man has a ledger open before him and peers down at its pages through his spectacles.

"You may leave," he says to the men who brought me here. I hear the big doors close behind me. Now I'm alone with this man behind the desk. He continues to gaze down at the ledger in front of him as he speaks.

"Do you know where you are?"

For a moment I don't understand his question. Before I can speak, he answers for me.

"You are at Thornwood Lunatic Asylum and Alms House."

I've never heard the full name of the place before. It sounds strange and formal. The man pulls a white handkerchief from his breast pocket, removes his spectacles, and begins to wipe them.

"Do you know *why* you are here?" he asks. I don't answer—why should I? "You are here because your aunt is concerned about your behavior."

"My aunt is a bitch," I say. "She's only concerned about herself."

He glances up at me, replaces his spectacles, then picks up a pen and writes something in his ledger.

"I want to see my brother."

The man keeps writing and doesn't look up. "Your brother is in the men's quarters."

"I know that," I say, my voice rising. "I want to see my brother now."

"I'm afraid that's not possible," the man says, not even looking at me.

Something inside me explodes, and I rush at him, sweeping the big ledger to the floor and spilling ink across his desk. He looks up at me, his eyes wide and startled.

I scream in his face, "You fucking take me to my brother *right now!*" Before all the words are out of my mouth, the door behind me swings open, and the two men are here again, pinning my arms behind my back. As they march me out, the man behind the desk calls out.

"Stop!"

The men pause and look at the man who is now standing up and wiping at the black ink stains on his waistcoat.

"Leave her here," he says.

The men look at each other like they're unsure what to do. Finally, their grip loosens, and I hear the door close quietly behind me.

He's going to beat me or kill me; I know it. I look around for some kind of weapon to defend myself. Instead, the man sits back down, folds his hands in front of him, and leans across his desk. His eyes behind his spectacles are cold and hard.

"Let's try this again, shall we?" he says. "You want to see your brother, and I tell you that's not possible…"

"What do you mean, *not possible?*" I say. "Why the hell not?"

"That is beside the point," he says. "Let's talk about what happens next. You're going to keep asking me for what you want.

And I'm going to keep saying no. Then you're going to get angry. When you're angry enough, you're going to attack me again. Those men behind that door are going to come in again and remove you, put you in restraints, possibly back in isolation. And none of that, *none of that* is going to get you any closer to what you want."

I clench my fists. Every angry word I know rises inside me, but I bite my tongue and hold them back.

"Or…" he continues, "You can choose differently. The real measure of a person is how they behave when what they want is not possible. That's what you're going to show me now. You're going to show me who you are. Do you understand what I'm saying?"

I glance at the door and picture the men behind it, waiting for what I will do next. I let out one long breath and lower my eyes.

The man peers at me for a moment, then bends back to his ledger, scratching back and forth with his pen. "You will be faced with many choices in this place, so you will have the opportunity to make many decisions. Some of them, no doubt, will be bad. You have just made a good one."

Still writing with one hand, he reaches out with the other and rings a bell on his desk. I hear the sound of the big doors opening behind me. I suddenly remember something my aunt once told me: if I wanted something, I should learn to say *please.* I always refused to say that word—except when it was for Jamie's sake.

"Please," I say. "Can I see my brother? Please."

The man puts his pen down again and gazes at me with a curious, puzzled expression.

"That's a word someone else taught you, isn't it? It doesn't sound natural coming from you. I believe it must have cost you something to say that. Am I right?"

My face flushes with heat, but I say nothing. The man lifts one hand and gives a small, beckoning wave, and the men behind me take hold of my arms again.

"We will continue this conversation later," he says. The last thing I see before the men lead me from this room is the man slowly wiping his spectacles with the same white kerchief, now stained with black ink.

Out in this darkened hallway again, it feels like coming out of a dream, and for a second, I start to doubt that the fancy room and the man behind the desk are even real.

Please, I said. *Please*. For all the good it did me, or ever has.

I swear to God, I will never say that word again.

Chapter 9 - Annie

I'm waiting for Mom to come home, and that's when I think of Bess. I've managed to avoid it; it hurts too much. But being home and alone, the memories come.

Nursery school where we met; Bess's fuzzy red hair haloing her face, cheeks puffed and red, eyes squinched into upside-down 'u's.

Several years later, making up each other's faces for Halloween. The year I was Jack Skellington, and she was Sally. I can still feel the bristles of the brush as she smoothed on the greasy colors, my mouth extending up into my cheeks, the depth of black around my eyes making them sink and disappear.

The day she fell out of the tree. The shape of her arm, the wrongness of it. How Dad whisked her away, leaving me with Mom and tears and not knowing.

Decorating the cast at her direction: More vines here. No! Here! And a fox, I want a fox.

Pouring over the "The Joy of Sex" side-by-side on the floor of Dad's office while he and Mom were out. Laughing hysterically at the drawings of a couple doing unimaginable things to each other, then scrambling to return the book to its hiding place when we heard tires on gravel.

Then, the bad memory arises, and I try to block it out. I loved her. I've always loved her. That has to count for something.

For the next several days, we live in limbo. Dad has to stay another day. Then another. Each day Mom drives four hours to Pineville and waits for a doctor to talk to her. Then, another four-hour drive back home. We talk or watch a show. Most nights she falls asleep on the couch, and I cover her up so she doesn't have to move.

This morning, she wakes up coughing and sniffling. "A cold," she tells me, coming out from the bathroom fully dressed, her makeup barely covering the dark circles under her eyes.

"Just a few emails and I'm out the door," she says, sitting on the couch with her laptop. I lean over to kiss her forehead. My lips burn.

"Ow! You're really hot. You are not going anywhere."

"But your Dad…"

"You don't want to make *him* sick, do you?" I'm standing in front of her, prepared to block her way. "They wouldn't let you in, anyway. Not with a fever, right?"

She lies back against the couch cushions, blinking bleary eyes. "I don't know what to do…"

My chest seizes. Mom always knows what to do.

She insists I go to work and promises to rest up and stay put, so I head toward the library. The morning air smells fresh and familiar.

As the front of the library comes into view, I wonder—what would I do if Bess dropped in? My stomach twists as I remember the look of disgust on her face, and all I feel is the great gnawing loss.

Halfway through my shift, Dad calls.

"Hey, pumpkin, is your Mom okay? Is she on her way? I called, but she didn't…" *Mom didn't call him?*

"She's staying home today. She has a fever."

"Has she seen a doctor?"

"Not yet. I made her stay home and rest."

"Kitten," his voice is serious. "Promise me you'll make her see a doctor if she's not better by tonight."

"I promise." Then there's a long pause. "Did you talk to your doctor today?"

"Yeah," he sighs. "He says I'm better." Another pause. "God, I miss you." He sounds so normal I want to cry.

It's hard to speak with the lump in my throat, but I manage. "Miss you too."

"Call me in the morning and let me know how your mother's doing."

"Of course. Yes. I love you."

"I love you too."

When I get home, Mom's sitting at the dining room table, still in pajamas. Her laptop is open, and she's typing furiously. Next to her there's a cold cup of tea and a plate with crumbs. She ate something. That's a good sign. She looks up when I come in, her smile coming slowly, painfully across the dry skin of her face. Her eyes look glassy.

"Hey," she says. "How was the library?" Her phone rings before I can answer. She stares at the number, then holds up a finger to me and picks up her phone.

"This is Caroline."

It's not Dad, then. I grab her cup and take it to the sink.

"Thanks for returning my call. Did you get a chance to look over the records?"

I fill the electric teakettle and turn it on, rinse out her mug, and put in a 'Breathe Easy' teabag. There's a glass of water here, so I empty it, rinse it out, fill it with cold water, and take it to her, along with the bottle of ibuprofen.

Her face looks pinched and the frown lines between her brows are deep. "I understand about involuntary commitment...but he's already in the hospital. All I want is to transfer him..."

She's trying to get Dad moved. The tea kettle is bubbling, so I move back to the counter and fill her mug. I fill one for myself, too, putting in a teabag called 'Stress Relief.'

"But he's already..." She's interrupted. I can hear the measured rise and fall of a male voice on the other end of the line.

"There has to be a way," she says.

I want to cheer her on and bolster that confidence. But the voice on the phone is murmuring something that's making the lines in her face deepen.

"So you're saying we're stuck? Without his agreement, my hands are tied?" That's when she starts coughing. I hand her the tea, thinking about tied hands, and my stomach aches.

She's writing, scribbling furiously. "Consent. Hearing. Mmm-hmm." She finishes and takes a sip of tea. "Thank you. I'll let you know."

I watch her staring at her notes for a long time, then she looks up. "Can you bring me some ibuprofen?" I pick up the bottle I brought and shake it.

"What's going on?" I ask.

"Because he went to the hospital voluntarily, if he doesn't agree to move..." she pauses and winces like it hurts, "we have to file a petition for involuntary admission under an independent psychiatrist. If we get it, the independent doctor can sign papers to have him moved." It sounds all legal and messy. She sighs. "What it means is, I'll need to stay in Pineville for several days."

"*We'll* need to," I correct her.

"I thought you could stay with Bess."

No! I know I have to tell Mom about why Bess won't see me. I know it. Just not now, please.

"I want to come with you," I say. "I want to be with you. With Dad. Please?"

She studies me for a few minutes, then leans back against the couch, exhausted. "If you're sure. Okay."

We get up early the next morning. I pack while Mom is making arrangements for someone to care for Gremlin, then I force myself to go back into Dad's office to get the papers he asked for. I avoid looking at the drawings and photos, but that damn model draws my eye, and I stare at it, knowing Mom and I will be seeing the real thing soon.

On the road, Mom has me call Dad from her phone so it connects through the car speakers.

"Hi, dear. How are you?" she says when he picks up.

"Caro! Hi. I'm good. I'm … okay. How are you? How's that cough? When are you coming back?"

"We're in the car now."

"Hi Dad," I add.

"Annie! How's your mom? You're in the car? Does that mean you're both coming?" He sounds happy.

"Yes," Mom says, "On our way. Have you seen your doctor today?"

"I'm so glad," he says, and then we hear someone in the background. "Not now," Dad says, his voice muffled as if he's pulled the phone away from his mouth.

"Jack, listen to me. I need you to tell your doctor I want to speak with him. I'm calling him in a moment, but I doubt I'll get him."

"You want to speak with him."

"Yes."

"Why?"

Mom is silent for several seconds. "I want to talk about moving you."

"Moving me? Where?"

"Jack. You need to be home or closer. It's not working out…."

"NO!" his voice is too loud. "I told you, they need me…."

"We'll talk about it when I get there."

"No, we won't talk about it. There's nothing to talk about. I'm not leaving." Suddenly, there's another voice, someone standing close to Dad.

"Easy, Jack. I think you should go back to your room," the anonymous voice says.

"I'll go there when I'm fucking well ready," Dad says, making me wince.

"Jack," Mom says, and when there's no answer, "Jack! I've gotta go. We'll see you in a few hours, okay?"

"Caro." Thankfully, the anger is gone from his voice.

"Just a little while now. You'll be fine," and then she starts coughing.

"Caroline! Annie, you still there?"

"I'm here."

"Take care of your mom for me, will you?"

"Of course."

"I love you."

"Me too."

When we finally arrive, Dad is waiting for us in the same room as before. His eyes droop, blinking slowly.

"Hi kitten," he says to me.

"Did they change your medication?" Mom asks.

He nods but then frowns and shakes his head. He turns to me and whispers, "Did you bring what I asked for?"

"I… they're…" I stare at Mom, and she answers.

"They're in the car. We can bring them later."

Dad looks disappointed. "It's what they want, don't you see? To keep me in here, forcing me not to work…."

His words slur and his head begins to droop. I take one of his hands. It's cold, although the room is warm.

"Hey, Dad. You in there?"

He raises his head with great effort, and his mouth moves, but no sound comes out. He tries again, smacking his lips and moving his jaw. The words come out slurred, garbled, "I'm glad you're here."

"Us Blakes have to stick together, right?" My voice sounds too loud.

His head keeps coming up, falling backward until it slumps against the back of his chair and settles there, eyes closing.

"Dad? Are you okay?" He doesn't look asleep; he looks dead. I'm terrified. "Mom! Look at his face!" We both stare as the muscles of his face work with effort, his skin turning red.

"He can't breathe..." Mom says. I see the raised welts on his arms and neck.

Mom yells, "Get a doctor! Quick!" Several people enter the room and move fast toward Dad. A gurney's wheeled in, and Dad is hefted onto it and rolled into the hall, his body writhing. Mom grabs his hand, running alongside. "Jack, I love you. You'll be okay." Then they push through a set of double doors, and a nurse stops us.

"I'm sorry. This area is for staff only." Mom tries to pass her, but the nurse steps in her way.

"What's happening to him?"

"We're taking care of it..."

"TELL ME...what's happening to him?"

"It looks like an allergic reaction," the nurse says. "The doctor will know more soon. Please wait in the room at the end of the hall." She waits, still blocking the way, and Mom turns back to me, her face unrecognizable.

"Mom?"

And then she starts coughing. The nurse studies her face, then says, "Ma'am, if you have a fever, you shouldn't..."

"I'm fine," Mom says when her coughing fit ends.

The nurse looks at me, then back at Mom. "Let me get a thermometer..."

Mom stops her. "Please. Let me stay."

The nurse looks at her, then says, "I shouldn't do this..." She looks down the empty hall and says, "Follow me."

We walk down a different hall. She stops at a door with a window, peers inside, then opens it. "Wait in here. I'll tell the doctors where you are."

It looks like an examination room with two chairs. Mom sinks down into one.

"Mom?" I don't know how to ask, can't say the words. All I see is Dad's face going from red to purple. *Is he dying?*

"It's my fault," she says. "I should never have let him stay."

"Mom?"

"This fucking place…"

She never swears. Not in front of me.

"I wanna go home." It just comes out, and then I'm crying. Mom stands and pulls me to her, her arms strong and sure, but her body is shaking, and I realize she's crying, too.

"I shouldn't have brought you here," she says. "I should have made you stay home. I'm sure Bess would be glad to…"

"No!" I pull out of her arms and can't stop the memory.

I can still feel every bit of it, the laughter, the dare, the kiss. I don't know why I thought I could do it. That she would like it, but we were drunk. It was a dare. And for a few sweet moments, she kissed me back. I know she did. I can still feel it, her mouth, soft as snow. If I could stop the memory here… But it's the next bit that's burned in my eyes and arms and face like a brand. How she grabbed my arms and pushed me away, her face twisting, ugly. *What are you doing?*

Mom's trying to pull me back into her arms, but I twist away and open the door.

"Annie!" she says, but I'm halfway down the hallway.

I don't remember an elevator or more doors, only bursting through glass doors to the outside, free of the building, of whatever's happening to Dad, and running across a field in hot sunlight. A line of pine trees rises up and swallows me. I trip over rocks, but they're not rocks; they're some kind of metal markers. I keep running deeper into the woods, trying to escape the pain until my knees give out. I'm on the ground, a scream forcing its way from the pit of my stomach through my throat and out:

"NO!"

Something changes. The air, the trees, something's different. The sweat drying on my arms and face makes me cold. It's too quiet. No birds, no traffic, nothing at all… until a girl's desperate voice, a voice

that seems both far away and very close:
    "PLEASE!"

Chapter 10 - Mary

When the whistle blows this morning, I line up with the others. Instead of marching us into the washroom, they lead us down a hallway toward a wide-open door with daylight pouring through.

When I step outside, the sunlight almost hurts. The woman in black is here with four other matrons in gray. Another blast from her whistle, and they lead us down a dirt path away from the old brick buildings and into the trees. It's cool here, cool and green. I close my eyes and breathe in the fresh scent of pine needles.

Another whistle blast, and the women around me bend down and start pulling weeds and fallen leaves from the ground, tossing them into piles. I wonder what they're doing until I see what's under the weeds—little markers made of metal, shaped like crosses. There are no names on them, only numbers.

Someone touches my arm. I turn and see Kathleen glaring at me. "Here…" she says, pointing to a spot on the ground below me.

I bend down and start to pull up weeds by the handful, laying bare one of those cross-shaped markers. There's no name on it, only a number. *757.* I look down at the little metal cross at my feet. I know what this place is. We are walking on the dead.

"Are these..?" I say.

"Yes," Kathleen says, not looking up from her work.

"Who are they?"

"From there," she says, nodding toward the brick walls of Thornwood.

I stand up and look to see how far these markers reach. There are so many of them. So many. "Does…" I'm finding it hard to put the words together, "Does no one ever…"

"No," she says, then nods toward the scattered markers around us, "This is the only way you get to leave Thornwood."

I look again at all the unnamed metal markers sprouting up from the ground, and a great wave of sorrow rises inside me. Then I think of Jamie.

"Kathleen." It's the first time I'd ever said her name. "You've got to help me."

She looks over at me and frowns. "How?"

"I need to see my brother."

She turns away and goes back to weeding. "You really want to get killed, don't you?"

"He's not well," I say. "He needs me. I promised our Da I'd take care of him, that I'd never let anything happen to him." Kathleen keeps pulling weeds and tries to ignore me, although I can see her biting her lip. "If I can't see him, I just want to know if he's alright." Then I say it, the word I swore I'd never say again. "Please."

Finally, she lets out a long, weary sigh.

"I'll talk to someone," she says.

My heart leaps in my chest. "When?" I ask. "Tell me when."

She scowls at me. "Jesus, you're a pushy one. Just…try not to be so impatient. I'll tell you when I find out something."

Take care of your brother.

That's what I promised our Da. And that's what I've always tried to do, though it's not always been easy.

The tantrums, the long quiet spells that make other people shun him and call him a *little devil* or *freak*. It was the summer when he turned seven that I finally learned to see him differently.

One morning, Jamie came over and handed me a sheet of paper. It was a drawing of me. He'd drawn my long, tangled hair so you felt like you could reach in and run your fingers through it. He'd even caught the little scar on my lip where I'd fallen when I was five. He'd also drawn a pair of wings rising up behind my back, the white feathers sketched in soft shadows.

"Is this me?" I asked him, meaning *Is this how you see me?* I looked into his face, into his eyes looking back into mine, and I knew I'd never see him the same way again.

Take care of your brother. Those were my Da's last words to me before he left us. And I promised I would.

I've kept that promise ever since. And I'm not about to stop now.

Every day, I wait for Kathleen to bring me news about Jamie. When I see her in the dining room at breakfast or in the washroom at midday, she turns her eyes away. It's been a week since she made her promise, and still no word.

Today, I approach her when we're clearing our plates after breakfast.

"What's taking so long?" I whisper. "If you're not going to help me, tell me now."

Her face turns dark red. She doesn't look me in the eye, but I hear her whisper, "Alright."

Later, I see Kathleen in the corner, talking with one of the guards, a stout man with an unkempt beard and ruddy face. The man scowls and shakes his head. I see her lean in close and say something into his ear. The man's dull face slowly forms a wide grin, and I don't like the looks of it.

At dinner, I see Kathleen's place at the table is empty. I look around the room for her, but she's not there. Neither is the man.

At bedtime, Kathleen's cot is empty. I expect one of the matrons to notice and report it, but no one does.

Later, I wake in the dark. Someone's hand is on my shoulder, shaking me gently.

"Mary…" It's Kathleen's voice, but there's something wrong with it. It sounds thin and worn, like the voice of an old woman.

"What?" I whisper, "What is it?"

"I'm sorry…" she whispers, and a dagger of ice stabs my heart.

"It's Jamie, isn't it? What's wrong? What's wrong with him?"

"He's sick. With a fever."

"Did you see him?"

She shakes her head. "Someone else did. They told me."

My eyes are starting to make out Kathleen's face in the dark. Her long hair is disheveled, her lips look raw and swollen, and an ugly bruise shades her right eye.

"Kathleen…what happened? What did you do?"

She looks away, her tangled hair hiding her expression from me. "Never mind," she says. "It's done now."

"How sick is he?"

I wait for her answer. When she finally speaks, her voice sounds even more faint and brittle.

"He's very sick, Mary…I'm sorry."

Take care of your brother.

I've failed. I've broken my promise. If Jamie dies…*when* he dies…it will be me who killed him.

Then I'm up and running away from Kathleen through the dark ward and down the deserted hallway. I run until I'm outside under the night sky, deep into the trees with the cold air and these little graves all around me.

I fall to my knees in the dry pine needles. It's been years since I've been to confession. I try to say the words, *Mea culpa… Mea culpa…* I close my eyes and try as hard as I can, and it all comes out of me, a long, soul-wrenching scream that's tearing me wide open. Then that word, the one that's so hard to say, I'm saying it over and over like it's the only word I know.

"Please…please…"

There's a change in the air. Something is different.

Someone is here. Here with me now. I open my eyes, afraid of what I'll see.

There's a presence. A space in the darkness in front of me that's filling with something bright and living. A living form. The form of a girl, down on her knees as if in prayer. She sees me—I know that. She sees me as surely as I can see her.

More words come to me, words I remember from church.

Fear not.

But I *am* afraid. More afraid than I've ever been. Still, I have to know. I open my mouth, and like a miracle, the words come.

"Who are you?"

Chapter 11 - Annie

"Who are you?"

A girl stands in front of me, just six feet away.

My heart lurches. Where did she come from? It's not possible. I blink, and she's still there, looking as real as anyone. She's wearing a dark, old-fashioned dress. There's dirt and tears on her face, and she's looking at me in absolute terror.

I blink again, and she's gone.

"Wait!" I say, then I hear my name.

"Annie!" It's Mom. "ANNIE!" I stagger to my feet and hurry toward the sound, breaking out of the pines and into the blinding sunlight. I see her turning away from the woods, looking around for me.

"Mom."

She turns back, her face ghastly pale, and then she's running to me, pulling me tight into her arms.

"Don't ever do that again." It comes out as a whisper, and I wonder how long she's been calling me. She's breathing hard, maybe crying, but I'm afraid to look. I scared her. Really scared her. What's wrong with me?

"I'm sorry, I'm sorry," the words pour from me, over and over, but she hugs me harder, saying, "Shhhhh."

"Is Dad…"

"He's in ICU, but he's going to be okay."

Time stops. Dad's okay.

We hold each other for I don't know how long. Eventually, Mom's arms relax, and I pull away, wiping my face. "Let's go see him," I say.

"They won't let me in," she says, her jaw tight. "Fever."

"Can I see him?"

She looks toward the hospital, frowning. "They might not let you."

I glare at the ugly building.

"But...you don't have to tell them where you're going," she says.

I stare at her. "What?"

"I'm not telling you to break any rules, understand?" She looks at me, eyes sharp. I nod. "Go straight to the ICU. Even if they ask you to leave, you'll get to see him. Now go."

I enter the building and go straight to the elevators. No one says anything to me. The elevator is empty. I get in and press 3 for ICU. The doors open to a large area with a circular desk and monitors, and men and women in scrubs moving quickly past. I look around; there are no rooms, just beds with curtained dividers, most open.

Avoiding the eyes of the nurses, I scan each occupied bed until I find him. Just then, he sees me. The smile on his face nearly kills me. I force myself to walk, not run, until I'm beside him and take his hand.

"Hey, Dad."

"Hey. How are you?" His voice is scratchy, but there's color in his face.

I laugh and then cover my mouth, looking around quickly to see if anyone's noticed. "I'm fine. How are you?" I don't know why, but that starts me laughing again.

He joins in, and it's good to hear.

One of the nurses comes to the other side of Dad's bed and looks at me. "Well, what do we have here?"

Dad says, "This is Annie. My daughter. Come to cheer me up."

She smiles, big and wide. "Looks like she's doing a good job. Keep it up."

When she's moved to the next bed, I ask, "Can I hug you?" He takes my arm and pulls me between the tubing and wires so I can rest against his chest. He feels so strong.

We stay like this for quite a while. Then I remember Mom waiting. I pull away but keep hold of his hand. "Mom sends her love. She's still got a fever, so they won't let her in."

"Tell her I love her," he says. His eyes droop suddenly. "This is nothing. Just a setback, okay?" He yawns and closes his eyes.

I press his hand to my cheek, feeling its warmth, and wish I could take him with me. "See you tomorrow," I whisper, then pull away and return to where Mom is waiting.

The next day, we see Dad's doctor. He looks too young. Acne threatens eruption on one of his cheeks, which are partly covered by a new beard. *Is that why he's growing it? Or is it to make him look older?*

"I believe we can discharge your husband in another week."

"That's great," Mom says. "We'll take him home, and—"

The doctor holds up his hand, its palm facing us. "He doesn't want to leave."

Mom and I look at each other. "He wants to stay here?" I ask.

"Not here," the doctor shakes his head. "He told me he wants to stay in town and complete the project he started. It's very important to him."

"I know what's important to my husband," Mom says, her voice sharp.

The doctor looks at her for a moment before responding. "Do you know what he was working on?"

It feels like a trick question.

"He told me a little," Mom says. "About the restoration…"

When the doctor speaks again, his words are clipped, his face tense. "All the buildings you see here, the hospital, clinics, labs, everything, including the old Thornwood building, are up for demolition."

The word sticks in my brain: *demolition.* A wrecking ball

crashing into the wall, the steeple collapsing…

"The development company has no interest in providing services for the mental health patients in the area," the doctor continues, a note of anger creeping into his voice, "And the closest hospital after ours is over an hour away."

"I'm sorry," Mom says. "But what does that have to do with Jack?"

"Jackson was working with SOPHATA, a local organization trying to save the hospital. His research on restoration and the historical relevance of Thornwood is invaluable."

I frown and look at Mom. She's frowning, too. "I'm sorry, but Jack can't possibly stay. He needs to come home."

The doctor fidgets in his chair and turns his head away. When he turns back to us, his expression is bland. "While we're still here," he clears his throat. "We can continue to treat Jack, stabilize him here in the hospital, oversee his care as an outpatient, and get his medications to where he can take up his life again. If you move him now, he'll be starting from square one with new doctors—strangers. They won't understand his project and his need for access to…"

"You're putting your project before Jack's care?!" She stands up and says to me, "Let's go."

"Wait! Please," the doctor says. Mom stops but doesn't turn towards him, her back ramrod straight—I wonder if this doctor knows what he's up against.

"I apologize," he says. "I misspoke. Of course, Jackson's well-being comes first. It's at the forefront of my recommendation to keep him here. He *wants* to stay. No one is asking him to."

Mom turns sharply, and the angry look on her face makes me cringe. "*This* is the reason he's here in the first place." She gestures around the room. "*You* are the reason. The stress of that project, coming here all the time. He needs to get away from…"

The doctor interrupts, "Do you think he'll stop working on the project just because he's not here? The stress of travel may have been part of what exacerbated the psychosis. Forcing him to stay away is not conducive to his recovery."

"You want him to *move* here?"

"I want him to stay here a few weeks. No longer than a month. Long enough to balance his medication and make sure he's on the way to recovery. An active mind will only help him. On my end, I will keep the responsibility for the success of the project off his shoulders. That is my promise to you."

Mom stares at him for several moments but doesn't speak. Is she giving in?

"If I can convince him to leave," she says, "Will you sign the necessary papers?"

Everything about the doctor falls, his face, his shoulders, but he nods. "Of course. Yes."

Mom nods once, then says to me, "Let's go."

On our way to the visiting room, I hear Mom muttering to herself. I can only make out a few words: "selfish" and "gall". When she starts coughing, she muffles her face in her sleeve.

Dad appears in the doorway. "Caro!" he calls, moving into Mom's arms. "Pumpkin!" He opens a space for me, and I move in, a huddle of three. His color looks good, although the skin around his eyes is puffy. But the eyes themselves are clear.

"I have something to show you." He sits catty-corner to Mom and takes her hand.

"Jack. We need to talk about your treatment."

"I know, I know. Just check this out." He slides an envelope across the table and removes some papers from inside. On top is an old black and white photo of a woman. The woman's hairstyle and serious face remind me of suffragettes like Elizabeth Cady Stanton from the 1800s.

"This is the key," Dad says. "Mary Donovan."

"Okay..." Mom says. "The key to what? Who was she?"

"Mary Donovan! You don't know her? She practically invented

humane treatment for the mentally ill, not only in the US but across Europe. Her book on reform was the Bible for mental health professionals by the end of the 19th century."

"That's nice," Mom says. "But Jack, we want you to–"

"Mary Donovan was at Thornwood." Dad pauses, looking at us as if he's just done a magic trick, waiting for applause and wonder. "She was here! At the old building. If we can prove it, I mean, prove that she started her reform work here, we can save Thornwood!"

"Jack..." Mom says.

"Historic Landmark Status," he continues as if she hadn't spoken. He speaks slowly, giving each word equal weight. "If we get the state, then the feds to list Thornwood as a Preservation project, no one can tear it down."

"That's… nice…but–"

"Nice?" Dad's voice is louder. "It's not *nice*, it's crucial! Ask these guys," he sweeps his hand around the empty room. "Ask the men and women who meet here two, three nights a week for AA or NA or Al-anon or any of the hundreds of programs provided by this hospital. Ask them if it's *nice*."

Mom touches his hand. "Jack…"

He pulls away, standing and beginning to pace. "What do you think is going to happen to all the people who take services here? Not to mention the rest of the locals who need hospital care. What will *they* do?" His voice is getting louder and he's talking faster. "They'll die! That's what will happen. By their own hand, by overdose, or they'll go to jail. Get fired. Become homeless. Is that what you want?!" He's shouting now. Mom stands up.

"I'm sorry. I didn't know. Sit down. Please."

I hear quick steps, and then a man in scrubs appears in the doorway.

"Jack!" He smiles and opens his arms as if he expects Dad to hug him.

"Hey," Dad's voice is at an almost normal level. "Martin, you know my family." Dad gestures to me. "This is Annie."

The guy in the doorway nods and smiles, "Nice to meet you."

"And this," Dad puts his arm around Mom. "Is Caroline. Martin, maybe you can talk some sense into her. Tell her how important it is to save the hospital."

Martin doesn't move. "Nice to meet you," he repeats. "Jack, the doctor wants to talk with you. Do you have a moment?"

Martin is tall and muscular, and I realize he's here to make sure Dad doesn't get out of control. The thought makes me both relieved and sad.

"I'd like to see the doctor with you," Mom says, standing.

Dad stares at her, then looks at Martin, who says nothing. Then Dad looks at me.

"You okay, sweetie?" he asks me. I nod. Then Martin steps aside, and I watch Mom and Dad move through the door and disappear.

Chapter 12 - Mary

I look across the empty field at the walls of Thornwood and see the lights going dark, one by one. I curse and start to run. What if they've locked the door?

When I reach the building, I touch the door and it swings open. The breath I've been holding leaves my body in one long sigh.

It's only then that I allow myself to think about what just happened back there under the trees—and the thing I saw.

It was like looking at a reflection in the water that's been stirred up, the outlines all broken apart and swirling like they were trying to come together again.

I can still see it. The way it shimmered.

The way it looked at me.

It wasn't a ghost. I know that much. It felt too *real* to be a ghost. It was more than that.

The kitchen is dark as a pit, so I walk toward the door that leaks light from the hallway. When I reach the girl's dormitory, the lights are out, and they're all asleep in bed or pretending to be.

I climb into my bed, close my eyes, and try to sleep. But the image of that thing I saw in the woods keeps rising in the darkness behind my eyelids. I might never sleep again.

Am I going crazy?

I've been called crazy plenty of times by Aunt Bridget and the other children at school. I've had that word thrown at me for so long I stopped trying to deny it.

But whatever kind of crazy I am, it's not the kind where you see things that aren't there.

Who are you? I said, and I saw it shimmer, that thing in front of me. I know she could hear me—just like I know it was a "she."

Maybe she was trying to answer. I couldn't hear anything, but I feel her trying to get through. If I'd waited, maybe she would have.

But I didn't wait—I ran. I ran because I was afraid.

I remember the first time I heard the Christmas story about the angel appearing to the shepherds. I thought the shepherds were ignorant cowards because they were afraid of an angel. I was sure that I would never do that.

Who could I tell about what I saw? The only person I could tell is Kathleen, but she must hate me now after what happened. I swear I never meant for her to get hurt like that.

The next day, they put us to work in the garden. The sun beats down on the back of my neck while I dig into the earth with my hoe. I spot Kathleen a few rows beyond mine, and my heart twists. I turn away before she can see me looking.

We carve long furrows into the hard ground while the matrons stand under the shade of the pine trees and watch us work in the hot sun. I know what they're trying to do. Work the Devil out of us. That's what Aunt Bridget used to call it. I scrubbed clothes and pots and pans for her till my fingers bled. The hard look she gave me when she watched me, that's the same look I see in the eyes of these women watching us now.

I stop for a moment to wipe the sweat from my eyes. The walls of Thornwood rise up above us, that single tower like a church steeple pointing an angry finger up at the sky. I think of Jamie lying sick in bed on the other side of those gray walls. Does he wonder where I am—why I haven't come for him? Late at night, when these thoughts come and fill my head, I shut my eyes and try to send my words through the wall to him. *I'm here, Jamie. I'm here.*

But today, it's like the wall is becoming thinner and thinner as if, at any moment, I can step right through it if I want.

I wonder if it's because of what I saw in the graveyard or if somehow something passed between us, some kind of secret message or blessing.

Maybe that's it. Maybe I've been blessed.

I never believed in blessings before; I'm not sure I do now. But I want to find out.

Standing here in the hot sun I know what I have to do. Go back to the graveyard and find that girl again. This time I won't run. I will stand and humble myself before her and open my heart to whatever she says or gives me.

I remember hearing that if you want to talk with the saints or the angels, you have to make yourself clean. Clean on the outside and clean on the inside, too.

I walk right over to where Kathleen is digging away at the ground. By the time she looks up and sees me, it's too late for her to get away. One of her eyes grows wide with surprise, and the other is still bruised, swollen, and halfway shut. It pains me to see it, but I swallow hard and say what I've come to say.

"I'm sorry. I never should have asked you to help me. If I knew that was going to happen…" Kathleen's face hardens as I speak, but I go on. "I'm not asking you to forgive me. You don't have to ever talk with me again. I just…I just want you to know that I never meant to hurt you."

I've run out of words. Kathleen is looking down at the ground. A little of the hardness seems to have left her. Or maybe that's just what I want to see. I walk away and leave her to herself. My heart is beating fast. There's a light feeling inside my chest, like a weight has been lifted from me.

It's not quite dark yet when I go outside to dump the scraps from dinner. I set the empty pail down on the ground and keep walking. I figure I have just enough time to make it to the tree line ahead of me before they realize I'm gone. I don't run—running will only make the fear grow, and I don't want to be afraid now. I need to be brave for what I'm about to do.

I find my way into the trees. The thick carpet of old fallen needles under my feet feels strange like I'm walking on water or on air. Then I stop and wait until I start to see the long straight shapes of the pines rising up around me in the dark, then those small metal markers sprouting from the ground. I find the spot where it happened before and stand there.

What should I do now? Go down on my knees? Should I pray? Who or what do I pray to?

Suddenly, the thought that I might be wrong sweeps through me like a cold wind. What if there's nothing? What if it's all a dream and a lie? I'm ashamed, ashamed of my belief, and ashamed of my doubt. I'm alone. I was always alone, and I always will be.

A sob I can't stop rises up in my throat, and I'm crying now in this lonely place where no one can hear me. I say the word I said before. *"Please…"* This time it hurts even worse, like a wound opening up, but I can't stop saying it. *"Please…please."*

Then something changes. The emptiness inside me fills with something like light, though there's no light around me.

Now I see it like those spots that float behind your eyelids when you've been staring at the sun, drifting in the darkness in front of me. I shut my eyes, and when I open them, it's still there, closer now. I can see something starting to take shape. Two eyes framed by long curly hair. A mouth. A face. A young girl's face.

Before I know it, I fall to my knees in the deep bed of pine needles and ask the same question I asked before.

"Who are you?"

Chapter 13 - Annie

I'm sitting in the hospital waiting room when a young man walks in, stares at me for a moment, then crosses to a corner table and sits. He pulls out a phone and starts swiping. A woman comes in, cries, "Carson!" and runs over to him.

He looks up briefly before turning his attention back to his phone.

"I told you not to come," he says.

She stands there looking stunned. I can't figure her age. She's older than he is. Could she be his mom? Older sister? Finally, she speaks.

"You're upset."

"*You're* upset," he says without looking up.

She finally notices me. I look away quickly, but it's obvious I was listening.

I hear a chair scrape, her voice low now. "I'm glad to see you." He looks up briefly before turning his attention back to his phone. There's a long stretch of silence before she speaks again. "Carson? Talk to me."

Wrong move, and sure enough, I hear a chair scrape, then footsteps, and feel the air moving as he walks past me to the door.

"Wait!" Now she's up and following him, but he doesn't stop, and they' re both gone in a moment.

Mom marches in and says, "C'mon. We're leaving."

"What about Dad?"

"He's sleeping. They gave him something. C'mon," and she leaves without waiting to see what I do.

In the car, her face is grim, jaws clenched, so I decide to wait. She'll tell me when she's ready.

At the motel she asks me to sit by the pool while she makes some calls. Although I want to know what happened at the hospital, I'm grateful not to hear whatever angry conversations are about to take place.

I change into my swimsuit, grab a towel, sunscreen, my phone, and head for the pool. It's blissfully empty, and I dive in the deep end and swim underwater to the shallow end. I do laps, feeling the stretch of arms and legs — when was the last time I exercised?

There's a penny on the bottom of the pool near the deep end. I dive to fetch it, and I'm instantly taken back to another pool, another motel, with my dad. He races past me, and I grab his leg. My hands slip, but I manage to get a grip and pull him back as I zoom ahead, deeper, closer, my fingers so close to the penny… and then his large hands are on my waist, pulling me back. I can see his grin, bubbles escaping his mouth as he pushes past me.

My lungs are bursting and I turn around, kicking hard for the surface. As my head breaks the water, I'm sure I'll see Dad beside me, penny in hand, I can't make sense of the emptiness.

I climb out of the pool and dry off. I pick up my phone and search for *Mary Donovan*.

The same grim photo Dad showed us pops up. Her hair is parted in the middle and looped behind her ears, and her eyes look into mine as if to challenge me somehow. I scan the article, looking for something that might help Dad. It says she taught school at a young age but became a governess because of poor health. Later she was a suffragette, started a school in Boston, taught in prison, started petitioning local, state, and federal governments for reform in mental health treatment...

I look for some mention of Thornwood but can't find any. Then I read, *It has been suggested that Mary suffered from major depressive episodes, which contributed to her poor health.* Does that mean she could have been institutionalized? Maybe at Thornwood?

The wind picks up, and there's a sudden flash of light. Thunder bellows, and great drops of rain begin to fall. I cover my phone with the towel and run back to our room.

Mom's staring out the window, phone in hand, and gives me a grim smile.

"Thank God. I was about to come get you." Thunder crashes, startling us both. She starts to cough.

"How are you feeling?" I ask. She starts coughing again. I take the bottle of codeine from her, pour out a dose, and hand her the tiny cup.

"Puts me to sleep," she wheezes as she shakes her head.

"You need sleep." I put the cup in her hand. She has another coughing fit, but when it stops, she drinks the medicine. I fill her glass with water and put it next to her. "Lie down." I turn out the light, and even with the curtains open, the room falls into dusk. The rain begins to fall hard, making me sleepy too.

Mom drinks the water, doubles up the pillows and lies back against them. "Your dad asked me to go to a meeting tonight. Town Hall."

"You're helping him with his project?"

"I'm handing over his notes. That's all. Then he can focus on getting better."

"Can I come?"

She studies my face, then nods. "Okay. May be boring. We'll see. I'm going to talk to the committee head after. Dan-something. I promise not to be long."

"Okay. Rest now."

"Just for a little while," she says softly, and in no time, she's quietly snoring.

My eyes droop, so I lie down, too, but I hear that voice from the woods, and behind my eyelids, the shape of the girl comes into focus. Long dark hair, dirty face...

My heart starts to race. I try to picture Bess's expression if I were to tell her about the girl, but all I can see is her disgust. I picture Dad, his head lolling back on his neck, his facial muscles clenching as he struggled to breathe…

I can't lie here anymore. I stand up and look out the window. The thunderstorm has passed, but the rain is still coming down. I've got to get out of here.

I rifle through my backpack, pull out an old blue rain poncho, and throw it on. I tear a page from my notebook, scratch out a message for Mom, then plunge out into the rain.

The rain feels cold, but it's good to be outside and moving. I don't plan on it, but as soon as I realize the direction I'm going, I head straight towards Thornwood and those pine woods.

I plunge into the trees, stumbling a little on the path, till I find a bench in front of a marble stone with writing too faded to make out. I wipe some of the water from the bench and sit.

The rain slows. My poncho clings to my skin. I look around, but there's no one else here.

I was hallucinating. Of course, I was—after all the stress of the past few weeks, it's not surprising. I saw graves, so I conjured a ghost.

But she seemed so real.

The sound of drops on leaves is all around. Otherwise, the place is silent.

Then I hear a voice.

"Who are you?"

My head snaps up, and I see the girl standing with one hand on a tree, looking like she's about to bolt.

"Anne," I answer quickly.

She falls to her knees, hands clasped in front of her chest. "Please, ma'am, you have to help us. Help Jamie. Please, he's going to die if you don't!" Something is odd about her voice, some kind of accent. She's wearing the same dress. It reaches to her ankles, and the material looks scratchy and worn.

"Do you need a doctor?" I ask.

Her eyes narrow, and her jaw clenches.

"Doctor! That place is full of them. Useless bastards. We need a miracle." Her fine, proud head droops, eyes cast down.

I stand up, but she's gone before I can take a step toward her. Just like the first time. I feel faint; now it's my turn to fall to my knees.

The ground is mossy and wet, cold against my bare skin. After a few moments, I force myself off the ground and walk to where she first appeared. I look all around, hoping to catch a glance of a fleeing girl, but there's nothing.

Ghost. The word is instant and terrifying, and my mind rejects it.

"Hey, where'd you go?" I call out, but my voice is shaky and weak. I wait for a few moments, but there's no response. Only the sound of rain on leaves.

My whole body starts shivering, my teeth chattering, the cold filling me through and through. I turn and find my way out of the woods, forcing one frozen leg in front of the other. Somehow, I make it back to the motel, shivering all the way.

Mom is still asleep, so I slip into the bathroom, close the door, and fill the tub with hot water. I slide into the water, and I slowly stop shaking. Breathing the steam in, I close my eyes.

I instantly see the girl. Every detail. I can hear her voice, her accent. Was it Irish? And her dress, something old-fashioned, like from another century.

A ghost, I say to myself, believing it this time. I'll tell Dad. He'll sit me down and ask me to give him the details, step by step, never doubting me, just trying to logic it out. I want him here so badly.

I think about telling Mom. Before coming here, she might have listened to me. Now, all she'll do is try to talk me out of it or take me to a shrink.

I think about telling Bess. But that's never going to happen.

I try to think of someone else. But there's no one.

I can't tell anyone.

Chapter 14 - Mary

Hot steam and the smell of lye rise to my face as I plunge these dirty sheets again and again into the tub in front of me. I can still hear a voice saying one word. A name.

Anne.

That's what she said. I asked, *Who are you,* and she said, *Anne.*

Whatever she is, she's not a ghost. I know that now.

What is she, then?

The words are right there in the front of my mind. *Angel. Saint.* I don't want to let them in.

But I saw her. Right there in front of me.

I'm running through the names of all the saints I can remember from church and school, and there she is. Anne. Saint Anne. Mother of Mary, grandmother of Jesus. Patron saint of pregnant women, embroiderers, and miners. Something else, too...

Then I remember. Washerwomen.

I laugh out loud, my voice echoing loudly from the damp walls of the laundry room. The matrons scowl at me, then lose interest and look away. They're used to voices crying out here. I hold back the laugh and keep scrubbing, my thoughts running wild.

Is *that* why she came to me?

I remember stories that Da told me about a holy well near Dublin dedicated to her and how the pilgrims flock there once a year. Then it comes back to me, a prayer the nuns taught us in school.

Good Saint Anne, mother of her who is our life, our sweetness, and our hope: pray for us.

I used to sneer at those words behind the nuns' backs. Now, they prick at my heart like a thorn from a rosebush. I want to sneer at that feeling, too, but I can't. Something has happened to me.

She has happened to me.

I don't know what she is. But she came to me. Whoever she is, whatever she is, she came to me. There has to be a reason for that. The more I think about it, the more certain I am.

A loud bell rings, breaking my thoughts into pieces. I see the matron in her black dress, the bell in her hand, calling out orders. She orders another girl and me to take the wash water outside and dump it. Together, we lift the heavy wooden tub and carry it through the door and into the sunlight.

Something catches my eye. At the far end of the building, two matrons and a guard are pushing something through the door and onto the path. It's a wheelchair. A child, a boy, is tied fast to the chair with leather straps to keep him from falling or running away.

I see him turn his head and look right at me. Even at this distance, I know those big, dark eyes.

Jamie!

I run toward him as fast as I can, shouting his name. I'm close enough to see the freckles on his pale, sweet face, the dark circles beneath his eyes. When he sees who I am, he starts to laugh and clap his hands. I'm laughing, too—then I feel rough hands on my shoulders, pulling me back and dragging me to my knees.

Ugly, angry faces crowd in above me, blocking out the light. I twist and turn to get away, but there are too many of them. I sink my teeth into the hairy arm wrapped around my neck and hear a loud bellow of pain. Fists grab my hair and pull my head back, strong hands pin my arms behind me, and now they're dragging me back inside. I keep screaming Jamie's name as loud as I can so he'll hear me, but the big door slams shut behind me.

I know where they're taking me before I even see it. I struggle and twist in their arms, but it's too late—they're already shoving me into the same stinking box where they left me before. I hear them slam and lock the door, footsteps moving away, and then nothing but my ragged breathing. Tears come, and I can't stop them. I don't even try. I can't remember the last time I cried, but I cry my heart out now until it's good and empty.

I stare into the darkness, my thirsty eyes trying to drink up what dregs of light are here. Soon, I see that the walls around me are not really blank. Words are carved into them, names of girls and boys who've been here before me. Ugly words, desperate words, pleas and curses carved into the wood. All the anger and fear of every person who's been here before me. It's too much. I shut my eyes, and other words come to me again, like before. *Good Saint Anne, mother of her who is our life, our sweetness, and our hope, pray for us.*

My fingers find a small rock on the floor beneath me. I pick it up and look for a place to carve my prayer. I see a small space, big enough for only two or three words. I press the rock into the wood and dig deep, saying the whole prayer as I carve my message. Hoping she'll hear.

HELP ME ANNE

Chapter 15 - Annie

"Get dressed," Mom says. "The meeting starts at 7:30."

"What meeting?" I ask.

"At the Town Hall. For your dad, remember? You don't have to go."

"No...I forgot. I want to come."

I throw my suitcase on my bed and rummage around for something to wear. The idea of being alone here with my crazy thoughts is too much.

We need a miracle. The girl's words come back to me now and I shiver.

So do we.

We arrive at a school that looks the same age as Thornwood; old dark brick and big windows with many panes. The school smell of chalk and cleaning fluid greets us as we enter. On our way toward the auditorium, we pass a table spread with flyers. One of them catches my eye. *EVENT PLANNER WANTED* in red letters with the silhouette of Thornwood at the bottom. Something makes me grab it, and I stuff it in my pocket as Mom hustles us into the auditorium.

There's a low rumble of voices as we enter. People are seated in rows of wooden chairs, mostly gathered toward the front. On stage are a mic stand and four chairs, three occupied by two women older than Mom and one man about Dad's age, talking among themselves.

As we move down the aisle, Mom scans the crowd for the man Dad told her to find.

"That's him," she says, pointing at a red-headed man in a white shirt and dark pants climbing onto the stage. "Let's sit here." She pulls me into an empty row of seats.

The man Mom pointed out is shaking hands with the other people on stage and laughing. He's younger than Dad. I think, *too young to be heading an organization trying to take down a big development company.*

One of the women stands and walks to the mic. She taps it and then says, "Good evening, everyone. Could I have your attention? We're going to start now."

The murmurs settle down to a whisper as those standing move into their seats. A baby's cry pierces the air and is abruptly silenced. I realize that, next to that baby, I am the youngest person here.

"Good evening," the woman says again. She's got *businesswoman* written all over her, from the blunt chin-length haircut and thick professional makeup to the dark grey fitted suit and bright red blouse.

"In case you don't know me, I'm Jennifer McManus, Mayor of Pineville." She goes through the night's agenda and then sits.

The next woman to talk is less well put together. Her hair, pulled back into a scrunchy, comes loose in places and flies around her face as she speaks. She's doing a recap of another meeting, and I tune out.

It seems like forever till I hear the word 'Thornwood,' and the man Mom pointed out is suddenly speaking at the mic.

"Hello, everyone. I'm Dan Michaels. The Committee is still looking at ways to prevent the demolition of Thornwood and surrounding buildings. While we've had offers from the building company to keep or rebuild a small portion of the facilities, what they offer is completely insufficient. This project continues to threaten our ability to provide mental health services to the community. At this point, demolition is still scheduled for August 26th."

There's a collective gasp in the audience, and the man raises both hands. "But we haven't given up. We are continuing to press the governor to put a stay on their operations. We expect to have an answer by the end of the week. I will have more to share next meeting."

He sits down among a rising buzz of people making unhappy noises.

"Where am I supposed to get my prescription?" a woman in front of us says.

"I've been going to meetings there since 2002. This is bullshit," says a man behind us.

Another person steps up to the mic, and it quiets down eventually as other business is discussed.

When the meeting breaks up, Mom moves through the crowd to the stage.

"Mr. Michaels? I'm Caroline Hansen, Jack Blake's wife. He asked me to give you some information."

The man looks at her, then smiles. "Jack? Yes, that's great," and he steers her away from other people.

"This is my daughter, Annie," she tells him.

"Oh. Yes. I see." He puts out his hand. "Nice to meet you. I'm sorry for the circumstances."

I'm momentarily confused, then I realize he means what happened to Dad.

"How's he doing? I wanted to come see him, but..."

Mom interrupts. "He found something, and he wants you to follow up on it. Jack thinks you might get Historic Preservation status and save the old building. Someone important who was incarcerated there. A woman, Mary Donovan..." She hands him the manila envelope.

He looks at the envelope and scowls. "Won't Jack be following up once he's released?"

"When Jack is released," she speaks quietly, "He will be coming home." She turns around and walks toward the door. I follow her as quickly as I can.

"Mrs. Blake," the man calls, "I'm sorry if that was insensitive..."

She turns to him, waiting.

"Your husband called me. Last night. He's really invested in this. And he's been crucial to our work so far." He stands looking at Mom for several moments. When she doesn't say anything, he continues. "Do you have any idea what's at stake here? How many lives will be negatively impacted by the loss of these facilities?"

"My husband's broken, Mr. Michaels," she says louder than before. "Something in your project helped trigger this. And it is my job to get him fixed. You're on your own."

She turns away again, and we're halfway out the door when the man calls out, "My son is broken, too, Mrs. Blake. He takes services in the same building as your husband. Without them, he'd be dead. My wife's cousin is broken, too. Our best friend's dad. We have close to three hundred broken people in our community who'll have nowhere to go. Jack's work is crucial to saving these facilities. Saving these people. Please reconsider."

Mom's eyes look glassy. She seems shaken. I watch as she swallows hard, blinks, and then gives him a curt nod. "We'll think about it," she says, turning and vanishing out the door so quickly I barely have time to move.

At the motel, Mom calls Dad to report on the meeting. I can hear Dad's voice arguing, and Mom's face grows grim. I grab a book and go out to the pool. The streetlight isn't strong enough, and the pool lights are off, so I just sit there enjoying the cool night air while Mom and Dad hash it out.

My husband's broken…my son is broken, too…three hundred broken people… We need a miracle…

A miracle. Dad needs to get better. Mom needs to stop fighting with him.

I feel for the flyer in my pocket and pull it out.

'Save Our Pineville Hospital and Thornwood Asylum (SOPHATA) is hosting a fundraiser this August. We need a creative and organized event planner to help us with the main event.'

My heart speeds up. This is what Mom does. Event planning. It's perfect!

I picture Mom kicking her damn cold, settling in, and planning the event–working side by side with Dad for the same end. I picture Dad's face relaxing.

Then I think of the girl in the woods. My ghost. If we stay, maybe I can see her again.

The next day, we visit the doctor, all three of us. Dad is so much better I can almost believe he's healed, cured. The doctor is cautiously optimistic.

"I believe we've found the right balance of medications. It's too early to know for sure, and, as Jackson and I have discussed, the best way to know is to keep him here for a little longer."

Mom nods once. I jump in.

"How much longer?"

"A few days," he shrugs. "Maybe a week. Even when he's out, he'll need to check in daily to ensure he's stable." He looks pointedly at Mom.

She looks back steadily. "Jack's explained this to me. Is there anything we can do to help in the meantime?"

"Pretty much what you have been doing. Come around a lot. Call frequently. Jackson, do you have anything to add?"

Dad looks from the doctor to Mom, then me. He smiles, then his eyes suddenly fill with tears.

"Forgive me?"

I'm sitting by the pool with Mom, where I've dragged her after our morning with Dad. She hasn't got a suit, but she's wearing shorts, a T-shirt, a big floppy hat and sunglasses.

"Hey, Mom...can I show you something?"

"Sure," she says. I can't see her eyes behind her dark glasses.

"I found this at that meeting," I pull out the flyer. "They're looking for someone to create an event at Thornwood for a fundraiser in August."

She doesn't take the flyer. "I don't need a job."

"Just read it. It's kinda cool."

"Moving here is not an option," her words are clipped.

"Just for a couple of months—"

"Not gonna happen."

"What's Dad supposed to do?"

"What?"

"When he gets out. What's he gonna do? You heard him. You heard the doctor. He needs a project—"

"He needs to come home."

"He won't drop it. You know he won't. You take him home, he'll just fret."

"What about you? Do you really want to spend your summer with a bunch of strangers?"

"I want to be with you and Dad."

"What about your job? Your friends? You'll be bored to death…Maybe you could stay with Bess…"

Here it is again. Bess. I'm going to have to tell her sometime. Just not yet. Please, not yet.

"What happened between you two?" I see she's staring at me, trying to read my face. I keep it as blank as I can.

"I don't want to talk about it."

"You can tell me."

"Mom, please?"

She sits up and leans forward, taking off her sunglasses to study me. "Okay. But what would you *do* here?

"Help you. Help Dad. Do research, whatever. It could be fun. Here..." I read to her from the brochure. "*Events being discussed: Zombie paintball...*that's a winner. *Asylum Ball?!*" I look at Mom, and she's rolling her eyes. "*Paranormal Tours.*" I think of the girl in the woods, and I shiver.

Mom takes the flyer from me, scanning the rest of the text before dropping it on her chair. She squints off into the distance.

"These people," she says softly. "They deserve better."

Chapter 16 - Annie

In the car, driving to the museum, I look at Mom and try to read her face. She hasn't said much since reading the flyer, and I'm not sure what she's thinking.

"So," I say. "Are you going to take the job?"

She purses her lips. "I don't know yet."

She wants to see the museum before she makes up her mind. I want to see it too.

When we arrive, a few people are standing on the steps leading to the side door. After a minute, the door opens, and a nurse leans out.

"Come on in. Just line up in the lobby, and I'll be right with you." She's dressed in a white, tight-fitting buttoned blouse with long sleeves—isn't she hot?—a skirt ending just below the knees, white stockings, and white shoes. Not like the nurses in the hospital in their colorful scrubs. And that's when I realize she's in costume.

Inside is the same as when I came before. Lots of wood: floors, walls, old desk, and chair. Posters on the wall.

"Here's the intake form, if you would all please sign."

Someone laughs nervously, but we all line up. Mom signs her name. Then I step up and sign mine.

The "nurse" turns to us and puts on the broadest, fakest grin I've ever seen.

"Welcome to the Lunatic Asylum! Don't be scared. There's nothing here that can hurt you....I hope."

A few people laugh, but I'm disgusted, and when I look at Mom, I see she is too. I'm tempted to leave.

The nurse begins her spiel in a monotonic drone. "Thornwood

Lunatic Asylum and Almshouse were established in …" It's hard to hold onto her words. I remember the theater director at my school, Ms. Tachen. *Open your mouth,* she'd tell this woman, *Enunciate!*

I look at the portrait on the wall of a man with a pointed beard and unsmiling eyes. Just then, she turns and points at it.

"This is a portrait of Dr. Jonathan Blackwell. Dr. Blackwell was the director here in the early to mid-19th century. He was credited with improving patients' treatment." The man in the portrait stares at me with a hard look. He doesn't strike me as kind.

The "nurse" leads us down a long hallway. At the end, we turn and enter an open room with large circles engraved into the floor. Twisted pipes extend from the walls, and the floor slopes slightly toward a drain.

"Watch your step," she says. "This was the laundry room from the 1850s when they had to carry the water in. There were free-standing tubs here," she points to the circles on the floor, "which emptied into troughs here..."

On the wall is a photo of several women standing by large tanks. They are not working but posing for the photographer, their eyes grim. They are all dressed in rough-looking clothes, tight bodices, and long skirts. There's something familiar about them. I study the figures, trying not to let the sad, hostile faces get to me.

I've read about how soap was made from lye and how corrosive it was to skin. Maids were evident from mistresses by whether or not their hands were ruined. The photo isn't sharp enough to see their hands, but you can see the discomfort in their faces. They don't look crazy, just deeply unhappy.

When I look up, I see the group has moved on. I walk into a wide spot in the hallway where everyone has stopped. Against the wall is a wooden box. A large iron padlock hangs from a latch.

"This," our guide says, "was the isolation box. Patients exhibiting violent behavior would be locked in here for several hours up to several days."

A chill runs through me. The box barely reaches my waist.

She pulls back the latch and opens the front of the box. The hinges shriek as it swings open. We all lean forward to peer inside.

The light from the hall spills over a dirty wood floor, making me think of rats and spiders. I imagine a body cowering against the back, hands raised to block the sudden light.

"Along the sides, you can see scratches made by the patients," our guide says. "Names, dates, messages." She holds up a flashlight and shines it on each wall inside. There is a collective gasp. Every surface is covered in writing, scratched with what? — fingernails? I can make out a few names and some numbers. I remember the motel room, Dad's handwritten notes, and drawings on every wall. I imagine him locked up here in the dark, and I start to shake.

"Want to go?" Mom is right there, her hand on my arm. I look into her face, wondering if she's picturing what I am, but her face shows only concern for me. I shake my head.

The guide herds us to the end of the hall, which faces the hill where the hospital and other buildings are—where Dad is. She talks about the grounds and how the patients tended gardens that provided most of their food.

"Across the fields," she says, "you'll see a stand of pines. In those trees is the cemetery for Thornwood. Between 1834 and 1930, over 15,000 patients were buried here. If you follow me, we will continue the tour there."

The number hits me. *15,000.* It makes my heart hurt. So many unwanted, unloved. I think again of the girl I saw there. Is she one of them?

The group is moving back toward the lobby, but I hang back. The thought of tromping around in the cemetery with a group of strangers makes my skin crawl.

"Can we skip this part?"

Mom studies me for a moment, then says, "Sure. Are you okay?"

I nod, but I'm looking past her at the isolation box at the end of the hall.

"I just want to check out something," I tell Mom. "Meet you in the lobby, okay?"

She studies my face again before nodding. "See you out front."

I wait for them all to leave and then walk back to the isolation box, which is still open. I momentarily pause then climb inside and pull the door almost shut. I sit and close my eyes, waiting for something to happen.

It smells vaguely of urine — how recently was it used? —also of smoke. The thought of fire almost makes me bolt, but something makes me stay. I take a few deep breaths and open my eyes. It's not pitch black, but it's near to it. The dark begins to have texture and weight. I can hear my own heartbeat, a soft-sounding *thud-thud*. Part of me finds it soothing; heartbeat means life. But part of me starts to panic. I reach out quickly and open the door to let in more light.

There are scratches on the back of the door, more and deeper than on the walls. It's easy to imagine fingernails – people trying to scratch their way out. I stare at all the words carved into the wood, and one catches my eye. I look closer and feel a cold hand on my heart when I see my name.

HELP ME ANNE

Chapter 17 - Mary

I've seen this door before. They've dragged me here again to face whatever punishment waits for me on the other side.

My brain is still dizzy from the heat of that awful box, and when they push me inside, the colors nearly blind me. Rich gold curtains, red and gold rugs, massive shelves full of books bound in every color.

At the center of it all, behind a large oak desk, sits the man I've seen before with his dark suit, neatly trimmed beard, and round spectacles.

"Please," he says in a low, calm voice. "Sit down."

I don't want to sit, but I'm weaker than I realized, and I find myself sinking down into one of the fancy chairs. It's the softest thing I've felt for a long time.

I watch the man remove his spectacles, take a handkerchief from his pocket, and start cleaning them slowly and methodically. Then he leans back in his chair and looks at me.

"Do you remember what I told you," he says, "the last time we met? I said that in this place, you would have the opportunity to make many choices. And that some of those choices would be bad ones. Would you say that has turned out to be true?"

"Where's my brother?" I ask. "Take me to him."

"I'm afraid that's not possible. Your brother is very ill. He's been taken to quarantine."

"You've got no right to keep me from seeing my brother," I say. "And you've got no right to keep me here either. You want me to think I'm crazy. I'm not crazy."

"It's not your sanity that's in question," the man says. "It's your behavior. Sanity. Insanity. Those are labels. Words for things one can't actually see. Behavior, though, one *can* see. And correct."

"My behavior's none of your fucking business."

"That's where you're wrong," he says. "Did you or did you not threaten to stab your aunt with a pair of sewing scissors?"

"My aunt's a bitch," I say.

"That may be so," he says calmly. "But did you, in fact, threaten to stab her?"

"She was beating Jamie."

"Why was she beating him?"

"She threw some of his drawings away. He got upset and started yelling, so she hit him."

"And you threatened her."

"Yes."

"You wanted to make her stop. And threatening her with a pair of scissors was the only way you knew how to do that. What does that say about you?"

He's trying to trap me into something, so I say nothing.

"I'll tell you what it says about you," he continues. "It says that you're the type of person who's not intelligent enough to get what you want without resorting to violence." He pauses and leans closer. "…except I don't believe that's true. I don't think that's who you really are. The question is, why would you want people to believe that about you?

My breath catches in my throat. What's he trying to do?

"Mary…" he says. It's the first time he's said my name. "Aren't you tired of fighting? Fighting everyone and everything? How long have you been doing that? It must be very difficult for you."

I feel sharp pain, like something inside my chest is being pulled out of me. I hate him for making me feel this.

"What do you want?" I ask.

"I'd like to make you an offer," he says.

I stare at him. Did he really say *offer?*

"I'd like you to come here for one hour every day. You'll have a certain number of tasks to perform. And when those tasks are complete, we'll talk."

"What kind of tasks?"

"Simple ones. Some filing."

He's trying to make it sound easy, but I don't like the sound of it.

"What about the laundry room? What if I just want to stay there?"

Blackwell stares at me over his desk, then says, "Show me your hands." My face turns warm, and I hide my hands behind my back. "Very well," he says. "You don't need to show me. I know what they look like. Do you know what your hands are going to look like if you keep working in that place?"

He's got me exactly where he wants me. But I'm not going to admit it.

"You don't belong in there," he says. "With the others. You're better than that."

Something is happening here. I don't know what it is, but I know I have to be careful.

"What do you want?" I ask again.

"It's not about what I want," he says. "It's what *you* want. If you accept this chance I'm offering you, and if you apply yourself, then you may see your brother."

I see he's still talking, but my heart is beating so loud that I can't understand. *You may see your brother.* Did I really hear him say it?

"Yes," I say.

He looks at me carefully, like he's unsure what he just heard. "Yes?"

"Yes," I say again.

"Very well. Be here tomorrow at twelve o'clock. You may go now."

When I walk out of that room, I feel like I'm floating. *You may see your brother.*

It can't be this easy. I know he's got some other kind of plan going on, and when I'm thinking straight, I can figure it out.

For now, though, I'll make him keep his promise no matter what happens.

Chapter 18 - Annie

Back at the motel all I can think of is that box. I close my eyes and see my name scratched into the wood. *Help me Anne.*

What if it was that girl?

I'm going mad. Or someone's playing a terrible trick on me.

I grab my phone and Google *bipolar, schizophrenia, mental illness, and heredity,* but I end up with too many questions and not enough answers. I google *hallucinations* and end up feeling just as twisted as when I started.

I remember that photo in the museum's laundry room, the clothes the women wore, the reason they looked so familiar.

I go back to the phone and type in *ghost.* The page fills with exaggerated stories about ghostly encounters, fuzzy photos of white blobs, and double-exposures of ethereal figures. I keep scrolling and find a website called 'Science or Ghosts.'

Scientists using reliable research methods have found zero evidence that ghosts exist. What their data show is you can't always trust your eyes, ears, or brain. Supernatural beliefs are common in patients with schizophrenia.

I nearly drop my phone. *Schizophrenia.* Is that what's wrong with me?

I start shaking again and hug myself to make it stop. My stomach feels like someone's wringing it with both hands.

What is happening to me?

I picture Dad writing on the walls of his motel room. Did he think that was normal? How am I different, going to the cemetery again and again to see a girl in an old-fashioned dress, a girl who isn't really there?

Mom comes in and I hide my phone. "Everything okay?" she asks.

"Just fine," I say, hoping she can't see the confusion in my face.

After dinner we watch a movie, which keeps my mind off the girl until it's time for bed.

I lie down and press my face against the pillow. *I don't want to be crazy.* That girl is a ghost. She's real. I know she is.

And the first thing I think when I wake up is, *how can I see her again?*

At breakfast Mom surprises me.

"I'm taking that job." She exhales loudly. "which means your dad can keep his doctors here...maybe keep working on the Thornwood project. I don't know. We'll have to wait and see."

The way she looks out the window after saying this, one hand tapping the table, makes me worry.

"Is Dad going to get better?" I didn't plan on asking, but there it is.

She stands and wraps her arms around me, squeezing hard. "Of course he will. Very soon. I promise."

At the hospital, Dad's all smiles. "My girls are here!"

"Hey Dad." I walk into his arms and get a good, long hug.

I trade places with Mom. They kiss, and then he holds her, and something inside me relaxes, just a little.

"Jack..." Mom starts after we've all sat down. Dad looks at her patiently, but she doesn't continue.

"Mom's taking a job here," I blurt. "So you can stay in Pineville a little longer."

I hold my breath. Dad looks puzzled.

"A job?"

"You wanted to stay here longer, and I...we..." Mom says, looking at me, "We want to stay with you. I'm going to plan the fundraising event for the hospital. I called this morning, and they hired me on the spot."

Dad's eyes grow red, and he takes Mom's hands. "You'll do that? You'll stay?"

Mom nods, and Dad leans across the table and hugs her. He calls out, "Martin! Hey Martin!"

The orderly comes into the room and looks at us calmly. "Champagne all around!!" Dad says. "We're staying in Pineville!"

Martin looks at each of us, then smiles broadly. "Will ginger ale do?"

We leave soon after our mini-celebration, and Mom drops me off at the motel. She's got a full schedule: meetings, looking at rental homes. As soon as I'm alone, I start thinking about the girl again, about that old photograph in the museum.

What if she's in it? What if she's one of the girls in the picture? I imagine looking at it and finding her face looking back at me.

My heart starts beating hard. Something in me doesn't want to see her there. But I have to know.

When I reach the museum, it looks like no one's there. What if it's locked? I hold my breath and pull on the door, and it opens. I exhale in relief and go inside.

There's no one in the main room, but I can hear voices at the far end of the building. Maybe there's a tour going on. I walk right down the hall toward the first big room. By the time I get to where the photograph is hanging, my heart is beating so hard I'm having trouble catching my breath.

I lean closer and look. It's just as I remembered, about twenty women, from age ten or eleven through adult. I look closely from face to face.

She's not here.

The voices come closer, so I move quickly to the front of the building and out the door, walking fast and trying to think.

It doesn't prove anything. It doesn't matter that she's not in the picture. She's real. I know she is. I saw her.

Unless...

No! I'm not crazy. I can't be. But I have to find out once and for all.

I head toward the cemetery. It's a bright sunny day, with cars and trucks rolling nearby and somebody with a power tool grinding in the distance.

I enter through that straight line of trees. Silence falls. Even the birdsong has ceased—nothing but a faint whispering of leaves high in the trees. I expected a temperature drop from sun to shade, but this cold is extreme. The light sweat on my arms and face turns to ice.

The markers here are thick underfoot and hard to see. I stub my toe on one, then step on another. They're so close together that I wonder if they share graves, bodies lying one on top of one another.

I step around the markers, looking for a path. In a small clearing are a few stones. Some have names and dates: 1872, 1894, 1908.

I find a bench and sit. I close my eyes and wonder how to conjure her. I picture what she looked like, wearing the same dark dress as the women in the photo, the cloth looking scratchy and uncomfortable, a little large on her narrow frame. I remember how she threw herself at my feet, begging for help.

"Hey..." My voice sounds young and small, the trees swallowing the sound. "Anybody there?"

In the silence, I become aware of a distant roar like the ocean. It grows louder, and I open my eyes, looking up in case it's a storm, but the trees aren't swaying. The roaring grows louder, stronger, like static in my ears, the kind I once heard just before I fainted after giving blood.

I gulp air, bending over as my vision begins to swim. A little more air, and then it all stops, my bendy vision, the roaring. Even the chill lifts a little.

And she's there. Standing a few feet away, as solid as the trees around her. Feet in canvas slippers planted firmly on the ground.

What looks like the same drab dress hangs a little loosely from her shoulders. Her hands grip the sides of it in her fists. I can see white knuckles and red patches across the skin. And I think *Lye*.

She stares at me with small eyes, a frown causing her forehead to crease. I can see dirt in the creases. It is not a welcoming look.

"Jamie's still sick. Are you not Saint Anne?"

I realize I'm shaking and hug myself to make it stop.

"Are you…" my mouth is dry and my voice shaky. "Are you a ghost?"

She stares at me a long time, her mouth making strange movements like she's trying to make words. Then her eyes fill, and she angrily swipes at them.

"Who are you? Why are you here?" She turns and begins walking away.

"Wait!"

She stops.

"My name is Anne. Just Anne." I look around; the markers are everywhere, so many dead. I remember ghost stories and movies where the spirits don't know what they are. "I think… maybe you died."

The sound she makes is a cross between a gasp and a cough, but when she turns back to me, I see she's laughing.

"Sure, and soon you'll be asking if I'm from Faerie." She throws back her head and gives a muffled scream. "Not that I wouldn't be better off dead and buried with this lot." She focuses on me, looking me up and down. "That's a nasty trick you played. Appearing and disappearing, making me think you were holy. How do you do it? Did Doctor Blackwell put you up to it?" The bitterness in her voice cuts me. She moves close and leans so our faces are inches apart. I can smell her. Sweat and harsh soap. "Don't you dare tell him I cried!"

She doesn't touch me, but it's like she's twisting some part of me, and I gasp. I'm amazed at how real she is, how solid she is.

"Okay," I say, and the twisting stops. "Are you a patient here?" That could explain it—she's delusional. Escaped from the psych ward. In costume?

Again, she makes that coughing sound, not a pleasure laugh, harsh and deep in her throat. "Patient?" she practically spits the word. Her eyes narrow, "And what would you know about it? Who are you? *Just Anne.*"

Her tone stings, but I say, "My father's a patient here. And he's trying to save Thornwood."

"Save it? Why would anyone want to do that? It ought to be burned to the ground!"

I can see it. Flames licking around broken windows, and the bell tower collapsing and disappearing behind the brick walls.

"If your father's in there," she says, "you should understand. Who are you, really?"

"Who's Jamie?"

Her face turns pale so quickly I'm afraid she'll faint, and then the color comes rushing back, first around her eyes, then great patches on her cheeks. *Blood.* Real blood is flooding the skin of her face. This is no ghost.

"Jamie," she sounds like she's about to cry. "is everything." And she turns and is gone.

One minute, a solid human being is standing in front of me, and the next, she's gone. No walking away, no disappearing behind a tree. Gone.

"Hey!" I call out, expecting her to come back, to rematerialize and erase what just happened. "Hey. Where are you?"

But there's only silence.

Chapter 19 - Annie

The next morning at the hospital, Dad looks better than I've seen him since this whole thing started.

"Guess what?" He grabs Mom's hands. "Dan knows someone with a carriage house they use for guests, and he says they'll rent it to us for almost nothing. Two bedrooms, an office, private grounds. And they'll let us bring Gremlin."

"Really? Sounds great..." I turn to look at Mom and she's frowning.

"We don't need all that. I have a few..." she begins, but Dad interrupts.

"Caro, you'll love it. Just see it, please."

She's tight-lipped and her nostrils flare. All the danger signs. "I don't want to be indebted to these people."

These people? I look around the room. Other families are gathered around their loved ones, as we are. Encouraging them to get well. The boy from last week is at a table with his parents, still sullen, eyes down. I wonder which people Mom is talking about.

Dad says, "Just look at it, please. Let someone be kind to you. It won't kill you."

Judging by her expression, it actually might kill her. But she forces a smile and nods.

"Anything I can do?" I ask.

He gives me a broad smile. "Yes, actually. You can." Dad opens the folder he's been fingering and pulls out a paper.

"Go to the library and see if they have intake and release records for Thornwood covering this period," he points to the paper. It looks like a Wikipedia article with biographical information on Mary

Donovan, including dates.

"Look for anything about Mary Donovan. Ask the reference librarian. They should be able to help you."

"I know how to use a library, Dad," I say. But it's good to have something to do, and when we rise to leave, I give him a big hug.

Across the room, the sullen boy and his family rise also. I watch the boy look up at them once they've turned away and can't see him, and for a moment, his eyes soften.

The parents come over to our table, and the woman leans in toward Mom and Dad. I can tell she's trying to keep her voice low, but I can hear every word. "It's so hard to see them hurting and be unable to help them."

I realize she's talking about me. She thinks I'm the crazy one.

"It takes time," my mother's voice is kind, and she doesn't correct her.

"See you tonight," Mom says to Dad, kissing him. I kiss him, too, and the boy's parents stare as Mom leaves the room, not with Dad, but with me.

We go look at the carriage house. It's perfect. Everything looks new and scary-clean, a country design, plaids and paisley, and bright accent colors on the walls.

I throw myself on the overstuffed couch, making sure my sandals don't touch. "This is heaven."

Mom comes over, lifts my legs and sits next to me.

"Okay then. We'll go home tonight, pack and bring back Gremlin."

Tonight I'll be home. Normally, that should make me happy.

Mom's busy for the rest of the day, so I head toward the library and Dad's mission. I pass the entrance to the cemetery and find myself detouring onto the trail.

I've managed to put the girl out of my head most of the day, but here she is again, a weight on my chest I can't shrug off.

I head toward the bench and sit. I wait for the rushing sound, the faintness, the sudden appearance, but nothing happens.

"Hey," I call. "It's Anne. Are you there?"

No answer. Nothing but the sound of birds and distant traffic. I try again.

"Hey! Are you there? It's me..."

More silence.

Suddenly, there's a sharp crack as if someone stepped on a stick, followed by rustling, and a figure emerges from behind a tree.

"Who are you calling?" It's a boy's voice. I blink away the figure I was expecting and find the boy from the hospital looking at me.

I let my breath out in a whoosh; I didn't realize I was holding it.

"What are you doing here?" I say. "Did you get released?"

"You shouldn't ask that." He's scowling, and I realize I'm alone with a stranger—alone with a mentally unstable boy.

"I'm sorry. You're right." I don't like the pitch of my voice. I sounds terrified.

"Who were you calling?" he asks again, scowl fading making his expression neutral, non-threatening.

"Nobody," I say, and turn around to leave.

He laughs and says, "Sure didn't sound like nobody." I look at him for a moment before taking a step to leave. In a lower voice, he says quickly, "Don't say you saw me."

I turn back. "Why?"

His eyes fill with tears, and I want to crawl inside a hole in the ground. "Just don't, okay?" And then he's moving away fast and silently through the trees until I can't see him anymore.

I head to the library, but the reference librarian is unhelpful. They don't hold the records I'm looking for, and she spends several minutes trying and failing to find who does. When she finally stops saying, "Let me try one more thing…" I thank her and start to leave.

"You're Jackson Blake's daughter, aren't you?"

Feeling caught, I turn back and say, "Yes."

"It's such a good thing he's doing. You should be proud of him."

I wonder if she knows what's happened to him. "Yes, I know. I am."

"He won't find what he's looking for, though. Mary Donovan. She was never there. I'm sorry to say this, but he's barking up the wrong tree."

I look at her, hating her. But part of me is afraid. Dad's banking everything on this.

What if she's right?

Mom and I leave Pineville just before dinner. The plan is to spend the night at home, pack, then move into our carriage house tomorrow. We travel in silence. I can almost hear the cranking of Mom's brain as she plans what we need to do. If I interrupt her she'll snap at me, so I just stare out the window and watch the light leaving the sky. *Home.* Home means Gremlin and fresh clothes…and Bess.

Before I can stop myself, my phone is in my hand, and I'm typing a quick text: *I've been away. Back home tonight. Can I see you?*

I don't know where I found the balls to write that, but it's too late to take back now. I never believed she'd ghost me like this, but ever since that night, I don't know her anymore.

Gremlin is at the door and winds around my feet, practically knocking me over. I pick him up and he's purring so hard he shakes. "It's okay," I tell him. "Are you ready for an adventure?"

I feel sorry for him. Cats don't like moving. But given the choice, I'm sure he'd rather be with us.

None of us wanted this to happen.

I wake up the next day and find a text from Bess.

Call me.

The text came after 1 a.m. I must have been asleep. My palms start to sweat as I press her number. She picks up after two rings.

"Hi."

"Hi."

She doesn't say anything for several moments. Then, "Mom told me about your dad. That sucks. Is he better?"

She knows? She knows, and still, she didn't call me?

"He's… better. Listen, I'm sorry. I miss you." It hurts to say it. The truth of it hurts like an arrow gone wrong, curving away from the target, ricocheting back to pierce me.

"What? What do you miss?" Her tone is another arrow. I don't know how many I can take.

"Us. I miss us." I'm about to cry and hope I can keep it silent so she won't know.

"Annie, listen," another wound, no nickname, no 'Gryphon.' "It's not the kiss, okay? I don't care about it. That's not the problem."

I don't want her to continue.

"It just showed me something," she says.

"Showed you what?"

"You always want too much."

"What?!"

"Like that night. It was fun, it was nice, and then you wanted more. Why do you always want more?"

It's like small explosions going off in my head, bright lights behind my eyes, blinding me. I don't understand. She goes on, "I just can't do it anymore."

"Why…" I start, my throat closing. I have to inhale hard before I can continue. "Why didn't you say something?"

"I did! I did. So many times. And you'd say 'sorry,' and I'd say 'okay.' But it wasn't okay."

"But…what exactly? Tell me what I did." I don't want her to answer. I can't bear it, but the world is upside down; nothing's normal anymore.

She sighs. "I'm always cheering you up. I'm sorry, but I'm not your therapist. I've got problems too. It's exhausting hearing yours all the time."

She thinks I'm depressed?

"If I want to go somewhere without you, you get hurt. You're so clingy. And if you don't come along, you grill me later for all the details."

Clingy?

"You talk about your dad like he's Jesus. He's not a god, Gryph. Just look at him, will you?" At my gasp, she says quickly, "Oh my God, I'm sorry. I shouldn't have…"

"Is that everything?" My voice is cold, my blood, too. Everything is cold.

"I'm sorry. I went too far. It's just…"

"Just what?!"

"I can't do it anymore. Let's just wait and see, can we? Like, give it a break, okay?"

"You don't want to see me."

"Not now. I'm sorry. Maybe…" I wait but she doesn't say anything more.

"I'm sorry I was such a burden." My voice cracks, but I take another deep breath, cutting off a sob. I pull the phone away and look at it—at the bright red button saying 'End'. I can hear her saying something, my name, the word 'sorry', but she's already called it, already ended things, so I press the button.

Chapter 20 - Annie

I lie on my back with Gremlin on my chest, staring at the bedroom ceiling.

There's something wrong with me.

You always want too much...Exhausting... Clingy...I'm not your therapist...

I remember the mother of the boy in the hospital, the pity on her face as she assumed *I* was the one needing treatment. Did she see something in me that everyone else missed? Everyone but Bess?

I want to hate her. It would be so much easier than hating myself.

I remember the collar and manacles on display in the museum, meant to restrain the "insane," and I picture them on me. Would Bess feel differently if I was certified bipolar? Schizophrenic?

Gremlin is purring right over my aching heart, the vibrations deep in my chest, and it soothes me a little. Right now, I am a source of joy for this one creature. I pet him and blink away the tears. I think about Dad. Is he lying awake in the hospital? Hearing other patients crying or moaning or calling out for help? Will he wake up forgetting we're not there with him? I picture him calling out, looking for us, but not finding us.

Gremlin moves down to settle between my legs and starts licking himself. I used to hate this, the little jerks as he bites, his claws keeping me awake, but now it's a welcome distraction. I roll onto my side, sliding one leg up and over him, and he settles in behind my knees.

And, just like that, it's morning.

The drive back to Pineville is as silent as the drive home had been, except for the occasional howl from Gremlin and the wind whistling through the bikes we fastened to the roof rack.

The first thing we do is set up Gremlin in the room I've chosen as mine, with his litter box, food, and water. "He'll need a few days to get used to the house. We can let him out then." Mom says, pulling out her phone and checking the screen. "I'm going to the hospital. Do you mind staying with him? You can visit your dad this afternoon."

Gremlin is curled up on my lap and purring hard—the way he does when he's scared. I want to see Dad now, but how can I leave this poor cat? "Okay. Squeeze him for me."

After Mom goes, I stay on the couch, petting Gremlin and trying not to think.

He's not perfect. Bess's words about Dad sting me again. How cruel! Maybe I'm better off without her.

Not that you have a choice. My inner voice is also cruel.

When Mom comes back, I move Gremlin off my lap and go in to find out how it went.

"How's Dad?"

She doesn't say anything.

"Mom?"

"You know, he looks good. Really good." Why doesn't she look happy about it?

"That's great," I say, but Mom is still frowning. "Did you talk to a doctor?"

She nods slowly. "Yes, briefly. If all goes well..." she frowns again.

"What? Will they release him?"

Her face twists, and she nods as tears run down her cheeks. She wipes them away. "I don't know why I'm crying. He can come home...here...in a few days. Isn't that good news?"

I put my arms around her. "It's good news, Mom. The best."

After a while, she pulls away, "I'm a mess," she says, wipes her face again, and laughs lightly.

"It's okay," I say. "You're allowed." But inside I'm scared. If Mom can't hold it together, what will happen to us? I can't keep myself together, let alone her *and* Dad.

"I need to get a little work done," Mom says. "Then we can have lunch. You want to go out for a while? Explore the town? You've got your bike."

When she'd suggested bringing the bikes, I'd pictured us biking together, all three of us. The thought of it makes my heart ache. I want Dad with us now. But I nod and say, "Sure."

"Take water. It's hot."

The roads are lined with trees, so most of the ride is completely shaded. The road I take is mostly level, too, which helps. Then I come to a hill, downshift, and down again, all the way to the lowest gear, and even zigzagging across the road, I can't keep going. So I get off and walk.

A breeze hits me at the top of the hill, lifting the hair off my face. Below me is Pineville, spread out like a painting. Winding roads cut through swaths of green trees, wide lawns, and a small square with a statue of a man on a horse.

And right there, a short downhill ride away, is Thornwood.

I mount my bike and pedal down the hill, even as my mind says *Turn around*. I ride straight past the old building to the trees and cemetery beyond.

I turn down the path, lock my bike in a rack at the trailhead, and walk in.

Something settles in me then. The air is cool like it was before. My sweat dries, and goosebumps rise. I make it to the same stone bench, and after a quick look around, I sit and close my eyes.

Dad's motel room rises in my head, all that stuff on the walls, his harried face, gray skin in the hospital, the way his head fell back on his neck, the orderlies rushing the gurney down the hall, the doors closing, cutting me off from him.

Then I see Mom weeping, sobbing, torn apart in a way I've never seen before, and something starts to break inside me.

I see Bess's face looking at me with so much revulsion, horror. *Something's wrong with you.*

This time, when I start to cry, it's like I'm retching up tears like my insides are trying to escape through my eyes and mouth. I cry until I feel a sudden change in the air, then there's that rush of sound. And the feeling that I'm no longer alone.

Chapter 21 - Mary

It's noon, and I'm standing outside the door of Blackwell's office, right where I promised to be.

Help me, Anne. Please help me…

It makes me sick just thinking about it. Groveling on my knees to that… that girl. That's all she is. Not a saint. Not an angel. Just a girl. Sent to torment me by that devil Blackwell.

What kind of trick is he playing? How much lower does he want to push me? And him, acting like he wants to help me, lift me up. No man ever lifted me up. Except for my Da.

Maybe it's another one of his experiments. He's supposed to help insane people get better—maybe he wants to see if he can make people go insane, too. If that's what he wants, he's got a fight on his hands.

I knock on his door so hard my knuckles hurt.

"Come in."

I open the door and find him standing near one of the giant bookcases. "I want you to file these for me," he says, pointing to a table with three tall stacks of books.

"File them…" I say. "Where?"

"In this bookcase, obviously. Alphabetically. That shouldn't pose a problem for you, should it?"

"I can read if that's what you want to know."

"I'm assuming you can read. What I want to know is how organized you are." He returns to his desk and sits down behind a stack of papers. "Take all the time you need."

I glance at the titles on the spines of these books. They mean nothing to me. *Psychological Review, Proceedings of the Second*

Annual Meeting of the American Psychological Association, Principles of Physiological Psychology.

I take a quick look at his shelves to see what kind of order his books are in. I go back to the table and start sorting the books into stacks, not wasting time walking back and forth to the shelf with every single book. Then, I carry the stacks to the shelf and put them where they belong. Soon, I'm done.

"What else do you want me to do?"

He looks up from his desk. "Very good," he says. "Now, pick any book you like from that bookcase."

I look at him in confusion. What's he trying to prove now?

"Go on," he says. "Pick one. Any book."

I turn back to the bookcase and look at all the strange titles. I have no idea what to do. So I just reach out and put my hand on the first book in front of me, a heavy book bound with royal blue cloth and gold trim—*Principles of Physiological Psychology.* I pull it down from the shelf, then turn to look at him, waiting for more instructions.

"Good," he says. "Now read it. You may sit over there," he gestures toward a small red couch near the window. I stare at him, not understanding.

"You mean…" I say, "You want me to read this whole book?"

"Read for one hour," he says. "You can start again tomorrow."

I stand there a moment longer, letting his words sink in. Then I turn and walk over to the red couch and sit down. I put the heavy book in my lap, open it, and look down at the page in front of me. A small picture in the center of the page shows two unicorns standing on their hind legs under a tree. I turn to the next page and read the large words at the top. *Contributions Toward a Theory of Sense Perception…*

The rest is a jungle-maze of words I know the meaning of and words I've never seen before in my life. I can't make sense of most of it, but I force myself to push on. An hour later, my head is dizzy and heavy. The clock on the mantle tolls one.

"That's enough for today," Blackwell says. I close my eyes, but all those long words still drift back and forth behind my eyelids.

Blackwell folds his hands on his desk in front of him and leans toward me. "So, that book...what is your opinion of it?"

Why is he doing this? Is he trying to make me feel stupid?

"I...I don't know," I say. "The fellow who wrote it...he'd probably do better to not use so many big words."

Blackwell leans back in his chair and nods. "Yes, yes," he says. "An honest response. Come back tomorrow at twelve o'clock."

Then he starts shuffling through some papers as if I'm not there. Just like that, he's done with me.

I'm halfway down the hallway when I remember—what about that girl in the graveyard? Why didn't he say anything about her? Doesn't he want to know what effect his little experiment is having on me? Or is this part of his game, to act like he knows nothing and wait for me to say something first?

When I turn the corner, I run head-on into the women coming out of the laundry room, their dresses damp, their faces and hands red and raw looking. They stop talking, and their eyes go cold as they watch me pass by. They know where I've been. And who I've been with. I can see it in their eyes—I'm not one of them anymore.

They think I belong to him.

That girl. The one in the graveyard. She's the one who belongs to Blackwell, not me. She's the one doing his bidding, trying to break me down and make me believe I'm crazy.

If Blackwell won't tell me what kind of game he's playing, maybe she will.

I wait till no one's looking, then I slip out the kitchen door and walk across the field toward the line of trees and that place I swore I'd never go back to.

I enter the woods and look around for her, but there's no one here but me— unless she's hiding somewhere, waiting to make her big entrance like before. I remember stories about mediums and sideshow magicians, smoke and mirrors. Is that how she does it?

"Come out," I whisper, "Come out, you little bitch. Come out, come out, wherever you are…"

And then I hear something. The sound of someone weeping.

I step deeper into the trees, and there she is, on her knees in the dead grass. No mist this time, no shimmering lights. Just a girl kneeling on the ground, crying her eyes out.

I stop where I am and try to get a better look at her. She's hardly wearing any clothes at all, just some strange bloomers that look like they're made of canvas and leave her legs bare. Her face is hidden by her hair, and her whole body shakes every time she sobs.

What's wrong? I want to ask, but I don't trust her. Not yet.

As if she can hear me, she lifts her head. Now I can see her face. It's a pretty face, streaming wet with tears. Her reddened eyes find mine and grow wide.

"Oh my God!" she says, raising one hand to her mouth. "Oh my God, it's you!" Her eyes lock on mine.

"What do you want from me?" I ask, trying to make my voice sound hard.

"I…I've been coming here…so many times. I just wanted to know. If you…if you were real…"

If I'm *real?* Now I understand. The poor girl is mad. But that still doesn't explain the way she appeared the first time I saw her, like a wraith made of smoke. This girl is as solid and real as I am.

"What's your name?" I ask.

"Anne."

So, I did hear her right the first time. Not Saint Anne. Just Anne. Mad or not, I still don't trust her. She's staring like she's afraid of me. Why would Blackwell use a poor, mad girl like this to do his bidding and play tricks on me?

"Did Blackwell make you do this?" I ask. "What did he tell you?"

"What…Blackwell? I don't know who that is."

"Don't fucking lie to me!" I say, taking a step closer to her. She starts to shrink away, then holds her ground.

"I told you!" she says, "I don't know who you're talking about!"

There are still tears in her eyes, but they blaze at me. She thrusts her chin out defiantly, and I see it tremble. If she's acting, it's the best acting I've ever seen.

"Do they know you're out here?" I ask.

"Who?"

"The matrons," I say, cocking my head back toward the building. "The guards."

She looks confused. "Matrons?"

Poor girl. She's in worse shape than I thought. I take a good look at her. She's slim but not scrawny. At least she's not starving yet. It's easy to see because so much of her is bare; her long legs, arms, and shoulders, too.

"What happened to your clothes?" I ask.

She glances down at herself.

"These...these *are* my clothes."

"Well, don't let them see you like that," I say, "Or they'll put you in the box for certain."

A strange look comes over her face. "The box?" she says. "You mean...the isolation box? Oh my God! Did they put you in there?"

I'm getting tired of this. I'm the one who came here to ask questions, not her.

"Never mind that. You know the doctor you're seeing? I need to know what he's told you. What he's trying to do. I need ... help." My voice seizes on that final word.

She studies me for a moment, and there's nothing mad about her. There's intelligence in those dark eyes.

"You need my help?" She looks away from me, biting her lip. Then softly, "You must be a ghost..."

This again? "No! I'm not a ghost! Why the hell do you think that?"

"Because...I mean, your clothes...the way I saw you

disappear…the way I found you…in a graveyard…"

"I found *you* in a graveyard," I say, "Maybe *you're* a ghost! You ever think of *that?* "

"I'm not!" she protests.

"How do you know you're not?" I ask.

"Because. I didn't die."

"Well, I didn't die either!" I say. "You think I'd fucking well remember *that,* wouldn't you?"

The two of us just stand there looking at each other. Then I hear the curfew bell start to ring.

"I've got to go back now," I say. "You better go back too. They may throw you in the box for a night, but at least you'll be warm." She just stands there, not moving. "What's the matter with you?" I ask, "Don't you hear the bell?"

"What bell?" she frowns. "I don't hear anything."

Poor girl. Mad *and* deaf. I start to leave, and she takes a step toward me.

"Wait…" she says, "When…when can I see you again?"

Then I realize. Of course. She's hungry.

"Meet me here tomorrow," I say. "After dark. I'll bring you something to eat."

The bell rings again. I can't stay any longer. I turn and start walking back through the trees toward the building. When I turn to see if she might be following me, the place she was standing is empty.

Like she was never there at all.

Chapter 22 - Mary

There's no answer when I knock on Blackwell's door this time. For a moment I wonder if I've come at the wrong time. Then the door opens and there he stands in his waistcoat, his sleeves rolled up like a common workman. I can even see a sheen of sweat on his brow.

"Come with me," he says, and without another word, turns and leads me to a table covered with thick stacks of paper tied with ribbon and twine. I see a number of heavy-looking wooden crates nearby.

"All of these," he says, waving his hand over the papers on half the table. "Put them here, in this crate. Be careful not to bend or tear them."

I look at the piles of paper, all covered with the same small, tight handwriting, and understand that it must be his. I pick up the one nearest to me.

"No," he says and points to a different stack. "Start here. Put that one on the bottom. Then go down the rest of this row."

I put the first stack back and do as he says. As I work, I glance at the words on the page, but they mean nothing to me.

When the row I'm working on is finished, I reach out to start on the next one. I look at the top page and notice that the handwriting is different than all the others; it is not tight and crabby-looking but loose and flowing.

Before I can read it, Blackwell slams his hand down on the stack of paper in front of me.

"*No!*" he says. It's the first time I've heard him raise his voice. I look up and see his face flushed red. "Not these. You work on *those,*" he says, pointing toward other stacks at the far end of the table.

He scoops up the stack in front of me and carries it over to his desk. I keep my eyes on my work, but I can hear a drawer slide open and shut, then what sounds like a key turning in a lock.

We keep sorting and boxing the papers. After a while, he says, "That's enough. Time to return to your reading."

He goes to the bookshelf, pulls out the heavy blue book I was reading yesterday, and hands it to me. Again, I sit in the red velvet chair and start turning through the pages, trying to make sense of what's in front of me. My head is beginning to ache when I hear him say, "Very well... What do you think of that book now?"

"I don't know..." I say. "There's a lot of words I don't know."

"Yes," he smiles, "I'm sure there are. Still, you must understand *some* of it..." I feel like he's trying to trap me into saying something stupid, so I don't say anything. "Was there anything that…stood out for you?" he asks. "Something that you liked, perhaps. Maybe something you didn't."

"There *was* something..."

"Really?" he says. "Read it to me."

My face grows warmer. I don't like reading out loud. But I don't want him to know he's made me nervous, so I open the big book and flip through the pages until I find it. I clear my throat and start to read.

"The mind is a creative, dynamic, and…vo..vo-lish…"

"Volitional," Blackwell says. "That means to use one's own will. To choose. Now do you understand?"

"I'm not finished…" I say, my face growing even warmer. He's got me flustered, so I have to go back and start over.

"The mind is a creative, dynamic, and…volitional force...which must be understood through an…analysis of its activity…its processes." I look up from the page and ask my question. "Understood by who?"

Blackwell looks at me for a moment before answering. "I believe Wundt is referring to his theory of psychology as an experimental, inductive science…"

"I mean…who's doing all this *analyzing?* Doctors and such?"

"Yes."

"How can they *do* that? Study someone's mind?"

"Through scientific observation…"

"But…what are they *observing?* They can't really do that, can they? See inside someone's mind."

"A trained scientist can observe someone's behaviors and make deductions based on those observations."

"You mean they're just guessing."

"No," Blackwell shifts in his chair. "Scientific deduction is not the same as guesswork."

"Sounds like guesswork to me. Talking about something you can't really see." I wave my hand at his shelves. "Is *that* what all these books are about? Just a lot of smart people guessing?"

Blackwell stares at me. There's something different in his expression that I can't make it out. Then he walks to his desk and opens a drawer.

"Here…" he says. I see a few sheets of paper in his hand and a sharpened pencil in the other. He's holding them out toward me, but it takes me a few seconds to realize he wants me to take them.

"What's all this for?" I ask.

"I want you to write down what you just told me. I want you to write it down and read it. Then I want you to write more."

"Why? Why should I?"

"Consider this part of our bargain," he says.

I stare at the pencil and paper in his hand. "You mean…now?" I ask.

"No," he says. "Not now. Take it with you."

"I don't understand. What is it you want me to write?"

"Whatever you wish," he says. "Write about this place. How you would make it different. What you would change."

I can't believe what I'm hearing. Still, he looks like he means it. I reach out and take the paper and pencil from his hands.

"That's all for today," he says. "You may go. Be back tomorrow at twelve."

I walk away from Blackwell's office, my mind racing. What is it he wants from me? How many more papers do I have to sort and put in boxes? How many stupid questions do I have to answer? How many times do I have to keep coming back here before he lets me see Jamie?

After dinner, I'm at the wash bin scrubbing my plate. When I look up, I see Kathleen standing right next to me. She hasn't spoken to me for days, not since I told her I was sorry for what happened, so I'm surprised to hear her voice.

"I hope you're watching out for yourself."

"Why?"

"You know why," she says. I look over and see her mouth set in that grim way she has.

"No, I don't know why," I say. "Suppose you tell me."

Kathleen scrubs hard at her plate, her mouth twists even tighter. Then she says it. "Blackwell."

"I'm not Blackwell's fancy girl if that's what you and the rest of these bitches are thinking. You think I care what they say behind my back?"

"I don't give a fuck what they say, either," Kathleen glares at me. "That's not…" She stops, looks around cautiously, then says, "Come on…"

I follow her through the kitchen door and outside, where the sky is turning dark. She turns and looks me in the eye, and I can see that the bruises on her face are mostly gone.

"You think you're the first one he's done this with?" she says.

"Done what?"

"Plucked out of the lot for himself like he did with you. Two years ago, there was a girl here from Newbury. Pretty looking, smart as a whip. He took a fancy to her, started bringing her into his office every day. Teaching her to read, Lord knows what else. Four months later, she was gone."

"What do you mean, gone?"

"You know what I mean. *Gone*. And just last year. This little slip of a girl hardly talked at all. He took her in too. Kept her in his office every day. Then she was gone, too. No one knows where."

"So you're trying to scare me?"

"I just want you to be careful," she says. "I don't want to see you end up like them."

"I know how to look out for myself," I say. "Why do you think I'm doing this, anyway? Just to get out of doing chores? You think I like that old goat's company that much?"

"For fuck's sake, Mary, I know why you're doing it. You think you're going to get to Jamie through Blackwell, don't you?" She glares at me, then lowers her eyes. "I know you, Mary. It's why you do everything. It's Jamie. It's always Jamie."

She glances around to make sure no one else is looking or listening, and I'm surprised to see tears rising in her eyes.

"Look," I say, a little softer this time. "I know you're just looking out for me. Don't worry. I can look after myself."

"I know," she says. "You already said that."

"Okay then," I say and turn to go. But it doesn't feel like enough, so I pause and say, "You take care."

Kathleen doesn't answer, but I think I see the trace of a smile at the corner of her mouth.

I've made up my mind. Today's the day I'm going to ask to see Jamie. I've been as good as I can, playing along with Blackwell, doing what he says, not rocking the boat.

Not any more

I knock on the big door, Blackwell says, "Come," and I enter. Instead of putting me right to work, he points toward a fancy red chair near his desk.

"Please, sit," he says. I sit and wait. "So," he says, "How are you finding your stay at Thornwood?"

It stuns me. *How are you finding your stay?* Like this is some kind of fancy place people can't wait to get into.

"I must be difficult for you," he says, "Having no friends."

His words stun me. "What…what do you mean?"

"I mean, it must be hard to be so completely alone. No one to talk to. No one to ask for help. No one to trust."

"I've got someone," I say.

"Really," he says, lifting an eyebrow. "Who?"

"My brother."

"Yes, well, but you don't really *have* him now, do you?"

The room goes black for a second. There's a heavy-looking paperweight on his desk. I want to pick it up and smash it into his head.

"I want to see my brother," I say, trying to control myself. "You told me I could see him."

He leans back and slowly folds his hands in front of him. "I told you you could see him if you apply yourself to this opportunity I've given you. And so far, you haven't done that."

"What do you mean? I come here every day when you tell me. I do everything you say…"

"Yes, but you're merely biding your time, going through the motions. Your mind is somewhere else."

"I want to see my brother," I say. "Please."

"Ah, there's that word again. Do you know what you sound like when you say that word? You sound like someone trying to hold something in their mouth, when what they really want is to spit it out."

I'm so close to screaming. I can feel it in the back of my throat. Why is he doing this?

He smiles at me, a thin, cold smile, the way I've seen people smile down at their dogs. I want to go over and smack that smile right off of his face.

Then it comes to me— that's what he's trying to do. Push me to see if I can control my temper. I take a deep breath and hold it. When I let it out, my heart's already beating slower. I speak as calmly as I can.

"When can I see my brother?"

"You will see your brother when he is no longer ill."

"If he's sick, he needs me. Let me see him."

"Like I told you," he says, "you can see him when his condition improves."

"Promise me," I say.

"People who trust each other don't need to ask for promises," he says. "But you don't know what that's like, do you?" He cocks his head like a bird and peers at me while I breathe deeply again, waiting for the anger to die down again.

"Good," he says, almost to himself. "Very good. You may go now."

Tonight, when I'm in the kitchen scrubbing out the pots and pans, I wander over to the larder, reach in, and pull out a loaf of bread. It's hard as a rock, but it'll fill a stomach as well as a fresh one, so I tuck it inside my frock when no one's looking.

I think about that little slip of a girl in the woods, how she's out there now, waiting for me. Hungry and alone.

When can I see you again?

I can't get it out of my head. The way she said that to me. Poor little slip of a girl, hiding half-naked in the woods like an animal. She's hungry. If there's one thing I can recognize, by God, it's hunger.

I step outside and keep walking, away from the building and across the field toward the trees where I know she's waiting.

Maybe she's wondering if I'll keep my promise. Maybe she's already given up.

That's the thought that keeps me going. I won't have anyone doubting my promises.

Not her. Not anyone.

Chapter 23 - Annie

As I ride my bike, the street and houses look different, and for one scary moment, I wonder how I'll find our home again.

I remember staring at the same empty spot in the cemetery. How the girl had stood there, saying something about a bell. Then she simply vanished.

She's real.

The way she spoke, the things she said. *Matrons, guards, the box.* I can see the tiny room with words scratched over every inch of wall and ceiling. *Help me, Anne.*

Was that her?

I crest the hill, my clothes stick to my skin, and sweat trickles into my eyes. Then the carriage house appears through the trees, our car parked beside it.

Mom looks me up and down when I walk through the door. "You're soaked! Jump in the shower, then we'll go see your father."

After my shower, I pull on a fresh pair of shorts and a T-shirt. I remember the girl's question. *What happened to your clothes?* How it made me feel naked.

Mom and I get in the car and drive to the hospital. As we pass Thornwood, I look up at the cupola to see if there's a bell inside. *Don't you hear the bell?*

Dad stands up when we walk in the room. "Annie!" he crosses to me and gives me a strong hug.

"Hey, Dad," I say, my face pressed against his cotton shirt. I breathe in that clean laundry smell, and my mind goes to that large room in Thornwood, the dark circles on the floor where tubs had been. The girl's hands…

"How d'you like the house?"

I pull away and look at him. He looks normal. "It's good. Beautiful. You'll like it. I picked out your office."

He smiles, grabbing Mom's hand and squeezing before pulling out a chair for her at the table. "I'm sure it's great. How's Gremlin?"

"He's okay," I say. "A little scared. I think he misses you."

"I miss him too." Suddenly, Dad leans close to me and whispers, "Did you have any luck at the library?"

I don't know what he's talking about. Fear rises in me that he's still not well. Then I remember the task he gave me.

"Not much. I'll keep looking."

He slumps and some light goes out of his face. Then suddenly he's angry. "I'll be able to help look…as soon as I'm out of this stupid place."

Mom places her hand on his arm and leans toward him. "Yes, Jack. We should talk about that. The doctor said, 'very soon.' Have you talked with him?"

Dad's face relaxes, and he looks at Mom with so much love my heart hurts and I have to turn away.

While they talk, I look around the room—only two other groups visiting. No sign of the boy and his family.

Did he escape? Should I have told someone I saw him?

A chair scrapes, and Mom stands up. "I'll be here bright and early to meet with your doctor." Dad stands and pulls her into his arms. "Love you."

"Love you too."

The next night, we have dinner outside, lingering after sundown.

"Star light, star bright," Mom says, and I look up. Stars start popping out as the sky grows darker until it's filled with pinpricks of light. I think of the time it takes for their light to reach me. How, on Earth, it was a hundred years ago when that light first flickered, but I'm just seeing it now.

"I have a meeting at Town Hall tonight," Mom says. You can

come if you like. It might be boring."

"Do you want me to come?"

She studies me before smiling. "That's kind of you. Maybe not this one. Unless you'll be lonely…" she gestures at the house.

"I'll be okay."

As soon as Mom's gone, the girl's face rises up in front of me. *Meet me here tomorrow,* she said, her accent making that final word exotic, *Tamarra.*

Where is *here* for this girl?

What was the name of the doctor she mentioned? Blackwood? Blackwell? That was it. She'd practically spit the name, her face screwed up in anger. Like she'd just seen him living and breathing.

I open my computer and type *Dr. Blackwell, Thornwood.* Instantly, a portrait appears.

It's identical to the one in the old building.

Ice runs through my veins. Thornwood. Blackwell. 1842. I close my computer. It's too much. My hands are trembling, and I'm cold all over.

1842.

My vision starts to swim, and I hear that rushing sound, like the one in the cemetery. *Am I going to see her here? Now?* My face breaks out in sweat, and I realize I'm close to fainting. I bend over and take deep breaths until the feeling starts to pass.

After a few more breaths, I sit up. I'm still alone, but I can hear the girl's voice. *Meet me here tomorrow after dark.*

If this is real and I'm not crazy, I have to know more.

She asked me for help. Maybe there's something I can do.

There's still enough daylight to find my way to the cemetery. It'll be dark soon, and I'll need my phone's flashlight. I check and find the battery on 20%. It should be enough. It'll have to be.

Even with lingering daylight, the woods are dark. I stumble a few times and almost miss the clearing and the bench. If she's going to appear, does it have to be here?

At first it seems like everything is getting lighter, but I realize it's just my eyes adjusting. Then, like a mist, the color starts to fade, and everything becomes shades of gray. That's when I realize I'm alone in a cemetery at night next to a hospital full of mental patients. That boy. He was so angry. What if he shows up? Anyone could come here. Teenage boys. Older men looking to lure women somewhere no one will ever find them.

It was stupid of me to come here. If anything happened to me, what would happen to my parents? How would Dad hold onto whatever sanity he's got? I stand up to leave, the anger at myself keeping the fear at bay.

Then it happens. The rushing sound, the faintness, like a change in air pressure, and the girl is just *there.*

Because she's moving, it's like she's stepped out from behind dark curtains into the light. Except she *is* the light; she's holding a lantern with a real flame. She and her light were not there, and then they were. My heart begins to race.

I watch the moment she sees me, the surprise, how it pulls her up, and wonder if I materialized to her the way she did to me.

"Well, and so you're here." She sounds breathless, her voice pitched higher than I remember, and her eyes, lit upwards by the lamp, are wide.

Before I can respond, she reaches inside her clothes and pulls out a lump wrapped in a rag. She steps up closer and thrusts it at me.

"Here. 'Tisn't much, I'm afraid." When I make no move to take it she shakes it at me. "Take it!"

I reach out, expecting it or her to vanish. Instead, my fingers close around the rough cloth and something hard inside, and when she lets go, I'm still holding it. I unwrap the cloth to find a lump of bread with a thick piece of foul-smelling cheese.

"Don't turn your nose up. It'll last you till they find you or till you decide to go back." She looks around for a moment before striding to the bench and sitting down. She takes off a shoe and shakes it out.

"Thanks," I manage to say, wrapping up the food and putting it in my pocket. "I...I need to ask you something."

I wait while she pulls on her shoe. Suddenly, she leans forward, putting her head in her hands. Is she crying? Her voice sounds normal as she says, "I'm so feckin' tired." *Feckin.*

"What..." I'm not sure what to ask until I say it. "What do you do back there?"

She looks up sharply and frowns. "What do I *do?* Same as you, I suppose. Laundry, sorting old books. Isn't that what Blackwell has you do?"

I swallow hard. "Jonathan Blackwell? You mean...the one whose portrait's in the office at Thornwood?"

"So, you *do* know the good doctor?" Her eyes are mean and bore into mine.

"What? No! I don't..." How can I make her understand?

"Don't lie to me! I know you've been there. I know he's messed with you too." She stands, grabs my arms, and gives me a good shake. "What's his game? Tell me. I need to know."

"Listen," I say, "I think something really strange is happening here. My year is 2022. I think you're in the 19th century…"

"*Twenty-twenty-two?* What the hell is that? Of course it's the 19th century. How long have you been out here?"

I take a deep breath. *Of course it's the 19th century.* She's just confirmed it.

"Shit," she says, looking over her shoulder. "Someone's calling." Again, I hear nothing. She turns back to me. "Don't worry, they're too scared to come here after dark. I should go." She turns and walks to the edge of the clearing, lantern swinging.

"Wait!" I can't let her disappear again. "I want to show you something." I pull out my phone and type in a search. When the article comes up, I show her the screen with Blackwell's face.

"Jesus, Mary, and Joseph," she says, pulling back a little. "What is this?"

"It's…it's a phone." I want to kick myself. She's never seen an iPhone, a computer, and probably not even electricity.

"It's a wee thing," she says. "How'd you make the light? Is there a candle…" she takes it in her hand and turns it around.

"Never mind…" I take it back and point at the screen. "Is that your doctor?"

Her face changes as she takes in the image. "It says he died in 1870…" Her voice barely has breath. She looks at me with fear in her eyes. "Who are you?!"

"I…I told you. I'm in the year twenty… two thousand twenty-two." I start to cry. "I don't know what's happening." Through my tears, I watch her rub her own eyes hard, her lips trembling.

"If he's dead…I'm dead too," she says. "And Jamie…" She turns away, putting a fist against her mouth. Then she whips around fast and glares at me. "Why?"

"What?"

"Why is this happening? What do you want from me?" She looks at me closer, frowning. "And why are *you* crying?"

"I don't know. I thought I was crazy. I thought you were a hallucination. But you're not. You're real."

"Of course I'm real!" She steps close and pinches my arm hard.

"Ow!" I step back, rubbing my arm.

"That real enough for you? But what are *you*, Anne from *twenty-twenty-two?* You aren't even *born* yet!"

My tears stop instantly as ice pours through my veins. She's right—in her world, I don't exist.

Suddenly the light goes out and I can't see anything. "Hey? Where are you?" There's no answer, and when I finally get my phone's flashlight on, she's gone.

My head is spinning—then I remember the food and put my hand in my pocket. The rag and lump are still there. I pull them out and open the rag. Then I watch the food disappear slowly, leaving only the rag. I clench my fist, trying to keep hold of it, but when I open my fingers, nothing's there.

Chapter 24 - Mary

Did I kill her? With my words?

You aren't even born yet.

That's what I said. Then the light in that thing she was holding went out, and she was gone, too. It's like she *was* the light and when it went out, she went out with it.

Those strange things she told me, the things she showed me; what am I supposed to do with them? It doesn't make any sense. She, a girl who's not even born yet. And me, a dead girl who's still alive.

When I walk up to the building, I reach out and put my hand on the wall just to make sure it's really there. It is, hard and cold under the palm of my hand. I can feel it, just like I felt her when I pinched her arm. Her skin, soft and warm between my fingers. She felt it too.

She's real. I'm real, too. I know that much.

Why did she show me those things? What good does she think it will do?

The kitchen is dark when I step inside. Good. No one to stop me or ask me questions.

"So, been out with your boyfriend, have you?"

I turn and see a girl I recognize from the laundry room standing in the shadows, and two more standing behind her.

"You think we don't know where you've been?" the girl says, taking a step closer. "Or what you've been doing?"

My brain struggles to make sense of the sounds coming from her mouth. Is she talking about the girl in the woods?

"You think you're better than we are?" The girl takes another step closer.

"Leave her alone."

I turn and see Kathleen standing in the doorway. The other girls shift their eyes from me to her, then back again. Kathleen steps out of the doorway and into the kitchen. I'd forgotten how tall she is.

"Did ya not hear me?" Kathleen says.

The girl who spoke to me opens her mouth like she's going to say something. "Go on, then," Kathleen says, nodding toward the door. The girl shuts her mouth, then turns and leaves, the other two girls close behind her.

As soon as they're gone, Kathleen turns to me and gives me a hard look up and down.

"So," she says, "Where have you been?"

"I…" the words catch in my throat, and I try again. "I can't tell you."

"Jesus, Mary," she says, "it's one thing to spend time in his fecking office. That's different. But to sneak out at night…"

"You think…? Christ, no! That's not where I've been! How can you think that?"

Her look softens a little and she casts her eyes down. "Alright, then" she says. "Where *have* you been?"

For a moment, I want to tell her. About the girl in the woods. About the strange things she showed me and the strange thoughts and questions she put in my head. But I can't.

"I know," Kathleen sighs. "You can't tell me. Jesus, Mary, you don't make it easy, do you?"

"Thanks," I say, nodding toward where the girls had been standing. "For that."

"What, them?" she says and lets out a little mirthless laugh. "They weren't going to do anything."

"Alright then," I say. "I'm for bed."

Kathleen nods. "Watch your back, though," she says. "Not all of them are as harmless as that lot."

Walking down the long hallway toward the dorm, everything feels strange now. These walls around me, the floor under my feet.

Da used to tell stories about sailors who'd been too long at sea with no food or water. They thought they saw an island until they tried to set foot on it and found it wasn't really there. What if everything around me is like that?

When I get to the dorm, all the other girls are already in bed. The lights go out, but it's not quiet. It never is. The little red-haired girl is crying into her pillow like she always does. There's the pale, skinny woman who talks in her sleep, sometimes with her eyes open so you can't tell if she's dreaming or wide awake. That's how I feel now.

Is this what being mad is like?

I'm in a madhouse, aren't I?

No!

I don't realize I've said it out loud until I hear some girls mumble and move in their beds. They go back to sleep, the ones who can. They've heard worse.

A girl who's not even born yet. What if it's true?

Think of all the things she must know. Maybe something that can help me. Me and Jamie. I don't know what it is, but I've got to find out.

When was the last time I prayed or even came close to it? I remember. It was in the box. Those three words I carved into the wood. *Help me, Anne.* It's funny now. *Saint Anne. Mother of Mary.*

Patron saint of washerwomen…

A little burst of laughter spills out of my mouth. I try to stifle it, but I can't. Before I know it, I can hear the skinny girl four beds down laughing, too. Then another girl, and another, until we're all laughing together in the dark, none of us knowing why. But it feels good, this laughing. Sort of like being free.

Chapter 25 - Annie

What would you do if you saw a ghost? I imagine asking Dad but then change it…not a ghost. A time-traveler.

Maybe *I'm* the time traveler.

I close my eyes, and the girl is there. Everything about her completely real. I remember her taking my phone from my hand and turning it over. *Where's the flame?* I pull it out, hoping for a fingerprint, a hint of dirt or something, but I can find nothing.

When Mom comes home looking tired, she has a coughing fit. I'd almost forgotten how sick she was just a few days ago. I jump up to fetch water. She takes the glass and swigs it, her eyes watery.

"Are you okay?"

She half shakes, half nods her head. She takes another drink before hoarsely saying, "Fine. Just talked a lot. Tea sounds good about now." She walks toward the kitchen, but I stop her.

"I'll make it."

I bring the steaming mugs to the coffee table and then put my palm on Mom's forehead. It's cool. "No fever. That's something. Do you still have the codeine?"

She makes a face. "Yes. I'll be fine. Don't fuss."

We sip our tea in silence, then she says, "This is going to be harder than I thought."

"The show-thing?"

She nods. "There's no budget. And they've got their hearts set on spooky ghosts of crazy people and sadistic nurses."

"That could be good," I can't hold a straight face and start to laugh. Mom gives me a look, and she's laughing, too, then coughing.

"You should rest your voice," I say, handing her the glass of water. We sit quietly for a few moments.

I want to tell her about the girl so badly. I picture it, the surprise on her face followed by worry. Would she even come with me to the cemetery? Would the girl show up if someone else was there?

Then I ask, "Do you know about the cemetery in the woods by Thornwood?"

"Hmm?" She looks at me over her mug. She looks so tired.

"Forget it," I say. "I'll tell you tomorrow."

The next morning, Mom is coughing when I get up. I reach to feel her forehead, but she pushes me away.

"I'm fine," she croaks.

"Then why can't I check your temperature?"

Something like panic flashes across her face and disappears. "Yes, doctor," she says, leaning back so I can reach her forehead.

She's hot, and I can see her eyes are red-rimmed, bleary. She can't be sick again. She just can't.

I take a deep breath, pushing my own rising panic down. "Supermom needs to take a super break."

"I can't. I have so much work to do."

"It'll wait." I check the clock. "I'll go see Dad. We can video chat with you so you can see him, but you need to stay here and rest."

"Annie," she starts.

"Mother..." I match her tone exactly, and her lips twitch but don't break into a smile.

"I feel okay. It's not that bad–"

"Do you want to make Dad sick?"

That stops her. "Of course not. Or you either."

"Don't worry about me. Let's get you rested up and healed. Okay?"

She agrees reluctantly, and I head out.

The hospital doors open, and cold air smacks me in the face as I enter the lobby. The receptionist barely glances at me before she buzzes me onto the Psych floor.

Dad looks up from something he's writing and beams at me, warming my heart. "Hey, kiddo! Where's your mom?"

"She has a fever again. I made her stay home."

His face crumples just a little, then he smiles. "The good daughter."

"Only daughter," I say, leaning forward to kiss him.

The room is half full. A couple of people Dad's age sit alone, and there's a woman at a table with another woman holding hands.

"So," Dad says, "What do you think about springing me tomorrow?"

"Springing you? Are they letting you go?!" My voice catches in my throat, and my eyes water.

He takes my hands and squeezes them gently. "Yes, they're letting me go. I'll have regular sessions with my doctor, but I can come check out the carriage house. See what you've done to the place."

I laugh, blinking the tears away, and squeeze his hands tight.

"You think it's funny?" Dad says in a goofy voice, making me laugh harder.

"Stop!" I say. The relief, the sudden joy is too much. "Here," I hand him my phone. "Call Mom."

He leans across the table and tilts the phone so she can see us both. She picks up quickly, and we both grin at her.

"What?" she asks, frowning.

"He's getting out!" I almost shout it.

"I can come home tomorrow," he adds.

Mom starts to cry.

"Caro, sweet. Annie laughs, you cry…"

This makes her laugh. And then she starts to cough.

"Sheesh, that doesn't sound good," he says.

"I'm…fine," she says when the coughing stops.

"Yeah, right," he says. "I'll send Annie back to take care of you until tomorrow. From then on, it'll be me."

Chapter 26 - Annie

When I get back home, I convince Mom to take her codeine. Maybe because of Dad's good news, she agrees. Shortly after, she falls asleep.

I'm tired, too, but my mind keeps landing on the girl, the feeling of her fingers pinching and twisting my arm. She's real. I know she is.

Why am I seeing her? Why is she seeing me? I don't know the answer, but the thought of seeing her again makes my heart beat faster.

A moment later, I'm out the door and on my way to the cemetery.

I find my way through the pines to the place where I've seen her before. No one else is here, so I sit on the bench and wait. I'm not here long when I hear a voice behind me. It's a boy's voice, deep with some rasp in it.

"Thanks."

I turn around, and there's that boy from the hospital. Playing hooky again. *Thanks?*

"For what?"

"For not telling anyone you saw me. Here, outside."

I still feel guilty about that. What if he'd hurt himself, run away?

"Why are you in there?" I ask. Immediately, I realize how stupid that is and start to look away, but he's already pulling up his sleeves, thrusting his forearms towards me so I can see, and I just stare. Long red lines crawl up his arms, crisscrossed with black stitches. Healing but painful-looking.

"Sorry."

He rolls down his sleeves and steps back. "It's okay." We're quiet for a while. I get nervous—will the girl come if he's here? Will he see her, too?

"You're Annie, right?"

"What?"

"Jackson's daughter? I've seen you with him."

I frown. How does he know Dad's name? Is he stalking me? I remember how isolated these woods are and wonder how fast I could run without tripping over grave markers.

"He's nice," the boy says. "We talk, you know? He doesn't treat me like an idiot. He told me what he's working on."

I let out a breath. That sounds like Dad. Friend to the world.

"I'm not crazy about the hospital," he starts, then breaks out laughing. His entire face transforms, all the sharp edges relaxing. "Crazy… yeah. Not crazy." His laughter dies down. "I'd be dead, though."

Before I can ask what he means, he's talking again, his face wiped clear of joy, anger, or any emotion. Completely blank.

"County Hospital is way too far. I'd be dead if this place was gone. Like those assholes want." Now his face grows dark, and his cheeks flush.

Didn't he want to die? Isn't that why he cut himself so horribly? He continues.

"I'd like to help him. Your dad. When we get out, you know?"

I want him to leave. Why did he pick this place anyway? There are other woods by the hospital. Why here?

"It's quiet here," he says, and I stare at him. Did he read my mind? "I just have to get out sometimes. I'm not running away or anything."

"I didn't say that."

"It's what you were thinking."

I shake my head. "I don't care."

"They'll let me out soon. Soon as they think I'm not *at risk*." He looks up into the trees and lifts his arms slightly as if contemplating flight. "I don't want to die as much."

"Sometimes I do." My heart stops in my chest. Why would I tell him that?

"Everybody does," he responds calmly. "At one time or another. I read that. Just...most people don't do this," he lifts his arms and drops them.

"Why?"

"Why don't they? Or why did I?"

I feel ashamed and angry. I shouldn't ask this. Why am I?

"My parents think it's because I failed this past year. I have to do 11th grade over. With younger kids. It sucks, but it's not why." His face starts to close up in anger, though his voice remains calm. "My doctor thinks it's because I have *low self-esteem.*"

"Cop out," I mutter, and he nods.

"Totally. Jackson thinks it's the world, the town. We're all fucked up. The environment, government, crazy people with guns... He says it's a miracle any of us stay living."

Was Dad depressed? And why would he confide in a boy, a stranger, in a psych ward instead of me or Mom? The thought makes me crazy.

"He's getting out tomorrow," I say quickly. *He's mine.* "After some treatment, we'll leave Pineville and go home."

He flinches. "Tomorrow?" His eyes get red and hopeless, and I'm sorry I said anything. "He said he's here for the long haul. That he's fighting to the end. He told me you're staying at Amy Lee's house? The Carriage House they've got on Airbnb?"

"Who's Amy?" I don't like this. He knows where we're staying. And Dad isn't planning on coming home until Thornwood is saved?

"What time is it?" he asks sharply.

I fumble for my phone. "Two-fifteen."

"Shit," he says and turns and walks fast in the direction of the hospital.

As soon as his footsteps fade away and the woods fill with

silence, I take a deep breath and sit back down on the stone bench.

"Okay, girl," I say softly. "I'm ready." Nothing happens. I can't sit here calmly and wait for the girl to show up. So I ride my bike, not toward home, but the town, looking for distraction.

There's an ice cream stand with a line of overheated parents and whining kids. A 'Help Wanted' sign is posted beside the open 'ORDERS HERE' window. The picture of a root beer float makes my mouth water. I take my place in line.

After I order my drink, I study my server. She's a couple of years older than me, and her arms are covered in ink, not quite sleeves, but a menagerie of animals and circus tents—an entire carnival. Half are black and white, and half are in wonderfully bright colors.

"I like your tattoos."

She looks at me with distrust, then gives a half-grin. "Thanks."

"Do you like working here?"

She now stares at me like I'm out of my mind. She looks over at the 'help wanted' sign and nods once. "Because of that? Need a job? How old are you?"

I bristle. "Fifteen, and I have my work permit."

She laughs, "Okay, okay," and reaches under the counter. She pulls out a piece of paper and a stubby pencil and thrusts them at me. "It's an application. Take it."

"You didn't answer my question," I say, taking the application from her.

"You gonna be much longer?" A short, angry woman behind me is practically shouting. The child attached to her hand is crying. I move away from the window quickly, catching a smirk from the serving girl before she takes the woman's order.

I pick up my float from the other window and find a table in the shade to enjoy it. I take the stubby pencil and start filling out the application. As soon as I'm done with my name and social, I'm stumped. Address. I don't know the Carriage House street, let alone the number. I scan through the rest of it. Previous Employment. Shit.

Would the library confirm I worked there since I ditched them? References. Hell. There's no one here who knows me. And if I ask anyone back home, I have to get into the entire thing of why we're here. Or make something up. And I'm not up for either. Fuck.

"Your ice cream's melting." I look up; it's the girl who served me. She takes the application and looks at it. "Hey, Anne Blake. Didn't get very far, did you? Any relation to Jackson Blake?"

I stare at her. I've heard of small-town stuff, but this is ridiculous. Two people within an hour, name-checking Dad.

"He's my Dad."

She looks at me more closely. "He's terrific. I heard him speak at a rally downtown last month. I hope he wins."

"Wins what?"

"The case. The suit. You do know why he's here, right?"

"Of course I know." I nearly spit the words; I'm so sick of people telling me what my Dad's up to. I stand, grab my cup, and toss it in the trash, stirring up a couple of yellow jackets.

Walking to my bike, I hear, "Aren't you gonna apply? We need the help." But I keep walking. All the way back to the woods.

I want to see that girl.

This time, I'm not leaving until I do.

Chapter 27 - Mary

Walking across the field toward the cemetery, my heart starts beating faster. *A girl who hasn't been born yet.* That's who I'm going to talk to. I still can't get it through my head.

She knows things. Things that can help me help Jamie. That's the thought that keeps me going.

I step into the tall trees, feeling the cool shade cover me. What if she's not here? I wonder what I'll need to do to summon her. Call her name? Close my eyes and pray?

I move deeper into the woods, where the little metal grave markers are scattered all around—and there she is. Just sitting on the root of a tree, like she's been waiting for me.

She looks up and her eyes go wide when she sees me.

"Oh…" she says, "I thought…I thought maybe you weren't coming."

"Why?" I ask.

"I thought…maybe you were like, mad at me or something."

She's got a wary look about her. Then I remember. Pinching her. I guess I did it pretty hard. Before I can speak, she does.

"This…this is weird, right?"

I nod.

"I mean…" she says, "how is this even *possible?* That I'm seeing you? And you're seeing me. Why is this happening?"

"I don't know," I say. But inside, I know the answer. *Because you're going to help me.*

She stands up and takes a few steps toward me. She's still wearing those strange skimpy garments, but she's tied all that wild and curly hair behind her head where it looks like it's about to burst out again.

"Are you…" she says, "Are you, like, hungry?"

"I thought *you* were the hungry one," I say.

"Sorry," she says, "It's just…" I see her run her eyes over me. I'm not exactly skin-and-bones yet, but I know I'm on the way there.

"How many of you are in there?" She nods over my shoulder toward the building.

"I don't know. Two thousand's what I heard. Maybe more."

Her eyes go wide again. "Two thousand…? Oh my God. You mean, *all* of you? In there?" Tears rise in those big eyes, and I want to slap them away.

"Don't feel sorry for *me*," I say. "You're the one living out here in the woods by yourself."

"But…I don't," she says. "I don't live out here. I live in town. In a house with my mother."

"What about your father?" I ask.

"He's in the hospital," she nods toward Thornwood again. "I mean, he's here *now*…where *I* am."

"Why do they have your father in there?"

She looks at the ground and bites her lips. "He was working too hard," she says. "And he had…he's having some trouble. With his mind …" I see her eyes glisten again, and she turns her head to wipe away the tears.

Don't, I want to tell her. Don't you dare be ashamed. Not of any of it.

She turns back to me, her tears mostly gone now. "What about you? Why are you here?"

"My aunt," I say. "She sent me here. Me and my brother."

"Your aunt? She sent you here? Why?"

"Because she didn't want us around anymore. That's why *everyone's* in there."

I see her trying to take in what I've just said. The light shifts, the sunbeams coming down through the branches above start to fade, and now I'm afraid she might disappear any minute. I don't know how much time we have. It's hard to say it, but I push the words out.

"I…I need you to help me."

She stares at me, startled. "How?"

"My brother. I need you to help me find him and get him out of here. Get us both out of here."

"Your brother? I…I don't know. I don't know if I can."

"What do you mean you don't know if you can?"

"I mean…it's not like I have some kind of *power* or something. I can't just, like, walk through walls and *take* him."

"How do you know?" I can't keep the anger out of my voice. "How do you know you can't do that?"

"Because every time we're together, when you walk away and leave this place, you disappear. Right there," she points, "At the edge of those trees. You just…vanish."

That's when I remember. Watching her disappear like a candle flame winking out.

"It's the same with me, isn't it?" she says. "You saw it happen too."

"Can't we just try?" I ask. "Please."

"No. If we try to leave this place, one of us will just disappear like before."

"Then…you can't help me…?" It's too much. The unfairness. The cruelty of it. "What fucking good are you, then?" I shout at her.

"I'm sorry," she says, her voice cracking. "I'm really sorry…"

"Listen," I say, "You *know* things, don't you? You *see* things. Things I can't see."

"Like what?"

"Like those things you showed me on your little light box,"

"You mean…the future?"

"Yes," I nod. "Can you do one thing for me? Find out what happened to Jamie. I want to know…I need to know if he ever gets out of here. If he gets to grow up." My throat grows tight, but I continue, "Can you just find out that one thing for me?"

"Maybe," she says. "But…whatever happened, I can't *change* it. You know that, right?"

"I don't care. I just want to know." Once again, I make myself say that word. "Please."

"Okay," she nods. "Okay, I'll try. Can you tell me your brother's name? His whole name?"

"Jamie. Jamie Donovan."

I see something change in her eyes, like a light coming on. "Wait...what's *your* name?"

"Mary. Mary Donovan."

The light in her eyes blazes bright. She claps one hand over her mouth, stares at me, and starts to gasp over and over, *"Oh my God, oh my God, oh my God…It's you!"*

Chapter 28 - Annie

Mary Donovan.

And then it rushes through me, a torrent of words and images, the old photographs, the names and dates. It's her! It's really her!

"What's wrong?" she says. "Are you going to faint?"

I shake my head. I can't faint, not now. Now that I've found her.

My mouth is open, so I snap it shut and try to get my brain working again. I look at her standing right in front of me, her dark eyes blazing.

"What is it?"

"You…you're famous!"

Her eyes screw up, and she says, "Yeah, sure."

"No, it's true! You wrote books, gave speeches and everything! You went to Europe and Washington DC…I can't remember it all. You started the whole mental health reform movement."

Her face remains screwed up in doubt. "That's not funny."

"I'm not lying. It's true!"

"Me? How do you know all this?"

"My dad's been looking for a way to save the old building, make it a national preservation site, maybe save the whole hospital. We've been reading all about you."

"The old building? What are you talking about? There's only one building."

"Your building, in my time it's the oldest one. It's a museum now. There's a hospital and other buildings, a medical center. An ER, different wards. That's where my Dad is. The Psych ward." It hurts me to say it, and I realize she's the first one, next to Bess, that I've told.

"E.R.? Sike? What's that gibberish?" I watch her face as she processes this. There's a line between her eyebrows, and I try to imagine what she's going through, what it would be like to hear the future.

"Emergency Room. Where they take people who are hurt, usually in an ambulance. And Psych, psychiatric. My dad had a… an episode. They've put him on medication… he's coming home tomorrow. There's a group of developers who want to tear it all down…"

The blood has drained from her face. "I… I don't feel right…" She sways — then she's gone.

"No, no, NO!" I cry out. She can't disappear again. Not now. "MARY!"

The sound is eaten up by the tall dark pines. There is no response.

What have I done? I should have gone more slowly. Figured out how to break things to her, one at a time. Instead, I just piled it all on. Stupid! Why am I so stupid?

I know she won't come back, not today, but I stay anyway, hoping I can see her again, apologize, explain better. Anything but this silence.

My phone vibrates. I pull it out and see a text from Mom: *Where are you?*

I look up from the screen and scan the trees all around me. I'm still alone.

"I'm sorry, Mary," I whisper. "I'll come back tomorrow."

Mom looks up as I walk in. "Where'd you go?"

I have to come up with something quickly—I remember the ice cream stand. "Downtown. They're hiring at the ice cream stand. I thought I'd apply."

"Yes, yes, of course. If you'd like it. You must be so bored…"

I'm about to say no when she pats the couch beside her and says, "I want to talk with you."

Shit. Am I in trouble? I cross the room and sit, tucking my hands under my legs as they jump up and down.

"Since your dad is coming home tomorrow, I thought we should talk about… expectations."

I'm not in trouble. But what does she mean? It's all so formal. "Do you have a PowerPoint?" I joke.

Mom blinks at me, and I look away. "Sorry."

She sighs. "It's okay. I don't want to scare you. It's all so…" she trails off.

"Did something happen?" my throat is so tight I can barely get the words out.

"No! No. Nothing's wrong. Your dad's better, of course. Much better. But we have a ways to go."

What she's saying makes me anxious. He's been so normal the last few times I've seen him.

"We need to look out for…for escalating behavior. Like talking too fast or too much."

"Or not talking?" I add.

"You're right. Not talking, withdrawn, depressed."

"What do we do? If he's like that?" I'm so tired. The thought of catching Dad in a mood swing is depressing.

"Talk to me. Talk to him, to his doctor. Whatever you do, don't ignore it. Promise?"

"I will if you will."

"Deal," she says and pulls me into a tight hug.

I want to tell her about Mary, how she's the answer we've been looking for. But I know what Mom would do if I told her—she'd think I was going crazy too. That would break her even more than everything with Dad has broken her already.

We rush through breakfast and toward the hour scheduled for Dad's release.

"I want to go alone," she tells me, holding up a hand when I start to protest. "There'll be a meeting with his doctor, and paperwork.

You'll be bored to death. Stay here and tidy up. Please?"

I nod.

I've barely cleaned the dishes and put away the breakfast things before I hear the crunch of gravel under tires, and they're here.

Dad bursts in the door, and we hug like it's been weeks or months since we've seen each other. He still smells strange, like the hospital, but I tell myself that'll fade soon enough. He's here. He's home.

When we let go, he looks up at the high ceiling and turns slowly, taking in the central room. He whistles. "Will you look at this place?" He starts to walk around, peering into the other rooms. "Wow. What do you think, Caro?"

Mom moves next to him, and he puts an arm around her. "We like it," Mom says. "Very much."

We tour the house and right when we're done, a car pulls into the driveway. When Dad opens the door, the man standing there looks familiar—then I realize he's the one Mom went to see at the community meeting.

"Dan! Welcome." Dan pulls Dad into a hug, and they slap each other's backs in that man-way. I look at Mom's face and don't like what I see.

"You met my wife, Caroline?"

"Oh, yes. Of course. How do you like the place?" He gestures around the living room.

Mom's face softens. "Yes. Thank you. It's very nice."

"And my daughter, Annie," Dad says.

"Hey," he says, turning his friendly smile on me. "You were at the meeting too, right? I hope this hasn't upset your summer plans, coming here. We're just a few doors down, and we have a pool. You can use it any time." He looks at Mom and Dad. "All of you. Welcome any time."

"Thanks," I mutter, wishing he would leave. Mom's frowning, and I know she wants him gone too.

"Come in my office and I'll show you what I've got," Dad says, moving toward the office door like he's been here for weeks and not an hour.

"Jack," Mom says, clearly warning him. "Don't you think you should settle in before you go back to work?"

"I'm settled, and we have a lot to catch up on." He turns to Dan, who's looking at Mom.

"I can't stay. I just stopped by to see if you need anything. I'll call you tomorrow."

"But… I want to hear about your call with Sullivans," Dad says. "And there's the Preservation application…"

"It can wait a day," Dan says firmly. "Caroline, Annie, let me know if you need anything. Anything at all." He walks to the door and turns back. "And I mean it about the pool. Come anytime." He opens the door and leaves.

Mom sighs and turns to Dad. "You know what Dr. Olleris said."

Dad waves his hand. "Yeah-yeah."

"About taking it slow?"

"I can't take it slow!" Dad snaps. "The bastards at Sullivan Development aren't taking it slow. There's nothing about this project where I can afford to take it slow."

"Jack."

"You don't get it. Or you don't care."

"Of course I care," Mom snaps back. "But you just got out of the hospital. Do you want to go back?"

"I want to fix this. I want to beat Sullivan. And it means I have to work."

"Fine. Just not today."

"It's all we have. Today. That's it," he slices a hand through the air like he's cutting time in half. And I almost see it, the hours dwindling down to nothing.

"Stop it!" I shout, just loud enough to startle them. And it works. Now they're staring at me. I can't stand the shocked look on their faces, so I turn and quickly walk back to my room and shut the door, trying not to slam it.

I sit on my bed and take deep breaths, then I hold my breath for a moment to listen. I hear Mom and Dad talking again on the other side of the door in quiet voices. I didn't mean to scare them.

Then again, maybe I did.

I try to imagine Dad's face when I tell him I've found what he's looking for, that I've found the real Mary Donovan, the key that will solve everything and put an end to all this stress. I imagine how happy he'll be.

Then I imagine trying to explain it. And the looks on their faces.

What good is it if I can't tell them?

Chapter 29 - Mary

When I open my eyes, the girl is gone, but her words are still in my head.

After you leave Thornwood you wrote books...gave speeches. You went to Europe...

It's those first four words that break me wide open. *After you leave Thornwood.*

I leave. I get to leave here.

It's almost too much. Dizziness takes me, and I sink to my knees in the soft bed of pine needles. All these little markers with no names, all these forgotten people turned into dirt.

I'm not one of them.

I get to leave.

My heart is hammering so fast I feel like I might faint or fly. I've heard stories about people who were about to die, rescued at the last second from the firing squad or the hangman's noose. I wonder if this is how they felt.

And those other things she said...*You wrote books...gave speeches...you went to Europe...* A laugh rises up in my throat. Not because I don't believe it but because, somehow, I do. I don't know why, but I believe it.

Anything feels possible now.

What about Jamie? Does this mean he gets to leave here, too? It must. It has to mean that. If Jamie doesn't get to leave with me, what's the point?

I walk out of the trees and across the field toward the big building looming against the sky. Instead of looking strong and scary like before, it just seems old and weak, like I could push it over with one hand. *You won't last,* I think. *One day you'll be empty and hollow.*

I go inside, no longer worried about anything, like nothing has a hold on me. One of the matrons frowns at me. She must see it on my face, this new feeling inside of me, but I don't try to hide it. I look her right in the eye.

You won't last either, I say to her in my mind. None of this does. I know what happens.

Later at lunch, the laughter I felt rising in my throat earlier comes bursting out. I take a quick look around, but no one notices. In this place, people laugh for no reason all the time, and no one thinks it strange. No one except for Kathleen. I spot her staring at me from the far end of the table. Later, when we're washing up in the kitchen, she walks over and stands beside me.

"What's going on with you?" she whispers.

"What do you mean?" I ask. Even now, I can't hold back the smile inside of me.

"I mean *that,*" she whispers. "The smiling. And the laughing."

"What's wrong with laughing?"

"Jesus, Mary, you're not the laughing type."

A hand falls on my shoulder. I turn and look into the stern face of one of the matrons. *What have I done now?* The thought of it makes me want to laugh even louder. It's ridiculous, all of this. None of it matters now.

"Come with me," she says. "Doctor Blackwell wants to see you."

Doctor Blackwell. It feels different to hear that name now. The heaviness of it, all the dread, suspicion, and resentment that came with it has faded like something in a dream.

We reach the office door, the matron knocks and I hear Blackwell's voice from the other side telling us to enter. I wonder if Blackwell will be able to see the change in me. When the matron pulls the big doors open, I stifle a gasp.

A headless woman stands in front of me. Not a headless woman. A dress. A woman's dress on a headless mannequin. The dress is simple and black but well-made with long sleeves and white trim. What's it doing here? It stands in front of me like a guard barring my way.

I see a movement from the corner of my eye. I tear my eyes away from the dress and find Blackwell standing against the bookcase, his hands clasped behind his back.

"Come forward, Mary." He steps toward the dress and points to a place on the floor directly in front of it. "Stand there."

"What is this?" I ask.

"You can see what it is as well as I can."

"*Why.* Why is it here?"

"It's for you."

I automatically turn and look toward the matron standing behind me. There's an expression in her eyes I can't quite read, and she looks away before I can decipher it.

"Step forward," Blackwell says again. "Come closer." Still, I don't budge.

"Why?"

"For your fitting," he says. He nods once toward the matron standing behind me, and I understand why she's still here. "You are going to participate in a presentation. So you need to be…presentable." A flicker of a smile passes across his face, and I realize he thinks he's made a joke.

"Presentation? What kind of presentation?"

"We will appear before a group of fellow physicians, colleagues, and benefactors. To discuss the work that I've been doing."

I try to take his words apart in my head. I glance again at the long black dress. Then I understand. The "work" he's talking about is *me*.

"What…" I pause and search for the words. "What is it you expect me to do?"

"I expect you to behave like a well-mannered, intelligent young lady. Because that is what you are now."

I try to picture it. My face above the long black dress. All those other strange faces out there looking at me. Examining me.

"Why are you doing this?" I ask. "Why do you want to show me off to these…people?

"You've done well here, Mary," Blackwell says. "When you first arrived, you were quite different. Unmanageable, frankly. Since then, you've shown great improvement. Wouldn't you say that's true?"

I don't answer, but the anger starts boiling inside me. He thinks it's him who's done this. *Improved* me.

The word bursts out of me before I realize it. "No."

He looks up at me, more confused than angry. "What did you say?"

"I won't do it. I won't be put on display. Not like that."

"And why not?" he says. "You don't believe you're worth that? Aren't you worthy of the attention and respect of other people?"

The word makes my lips curl with disgust. *Respect.* Whatever this is, it's got nothing to do with respect. Suddenly, all the care I've been taking to watch my tongue falls away.

"This isn't about me," I say. "It's got nothing to do with me. It's about *you*. I won't do it. Dressing me up like some kind of doll, dragging me out in front of a bunch of people to gawk and stare…I won't do it! I'm not your fucking show pony!"

I hear the matron behind me make a small, uncomfortable noise in her throat. Blackwell must have heard it, too, because I see him glance in her direction and then nod toward the door. "Leave us," he says.

I hear the matron's skirts rustle and the door shut. Blackwell turns his attention back to me. And now the anger comes. It starts slowly, like it always does, like the sky darkening before a storm.

"I'm not going to threaten you, Mary," he says in his slow, deliberate voice. "You're not the type of person who responds to threats. You see, I've learned that much about you. In our time together."

Our time together. The words make my skin crawl.

"Instead, we're going to make a bargain, you and I. I will take you to see your brother. In return, you will do this presentation for me."

For a moment, I feel faint. My hand finds a chair behind me, and I sink down into it. The room around me is threatening to spin.

Blackwell sees the effect his words have had on me. I can see the slight smile twitching at the corner of his mouth. He's going to dangle Jamie in front of me like a carrot on a stick, and I hate him for doing it.

"So," I say, "You're trying to bribe me."

"No. Not a bribe. It's a bargain. Between two civilized individuals." He pauses and looks at me carefully. "So. Do we have a bargain?"

"When? When can I see him?"

"You can see him now," he says. "Is that soon enough for you?"

A minute later I'm walking down the hallway with Blackwell on one side of me and the matron on the other. It's like moving through a dream, like I'm hardly walking at all.

It's not until we pass through another set of doors into a large, dim room that reeks of sickness that I realize where we're going—the infirmary. I quickly scan the rows of wooden beds, some with huddled, shrunken forms, others empty.

When I see Jamie, I break into a run and go to my knees next to him. His eyes are closed, and his breathing sounds bad. When I kiss his forehead, it's so hot it burns my lips.

"Jamie," I say to him. "Jamie, it's me. It's Mary." His chest rises and falls, his breath weak and ragged, but his eyes don't open.

"What's wrong with him?" I ask.

Blackwell doesn't answer right away, and in those few seconds, I realize how bad it must be.

"Consumption."

The word stabs right through my heart like a knife. "What are you doing to help him?" I ask.

"All that can be done." The heaviness in Blackwell's voice crushes the breath out of me. And I understand now why they've brought me here so quickly.

The rage starts to fly up inside of me. I want to scream and break something, but there's no one to strike out at. Not even Blackwell. The real enemy is inside of Jamie, where I can't get to it.

"Jamie…" I say, stroking the hair back from his forehead. His skin is sweaty, and strands of his hair stick to it. He doesn't respond when I call his name. "Jamie. It's me…" His eyes open, and a smile starts to bloom on his face. He closes his eyes again, and the smile fades.

Tears run down my face, but I keep my back to Blackwell so he can't see. All the things that girl told me, all those promises about my future. What good are they now?

"That's enough," Blackwell says. His words don't make sense. I hear him clear his throat and then speak a little louder. "I said that's enough."

I wipe my tears away quickly and turn to face them. "No!"

Blackwell scowls. "Mary…"

"If you try to make me leave now, I swear to God, I'll kill you. I'll burn this whole fucking place to the ground."

I see him flinch. *Good.* I can almost feel my hands around his scrawny neck, crushing the life out of him. I could do it right now. There's only one thing stopping me. Jamie. What would happen to him then?

I look down at Jamie's flushed face, the dark hollows around his eyes that remain closed. Blackwell and the matron are still standing behind me, keeping their distance. *Why?* Why doesn't he snap his fingers and have me dragged away from here, like all the other times?

Then I realize I have something he wants. Something he doesn't want to risk losing.

"You let me take care of him," I say. "And I get to be with him every day. *Every day.* You do that… and I'll do your stupid presentation."

I can see him trying to decide. It doesn't take long.

"Alright," Blackwell says in a voice so low it's hard to hear. Then he turns on his heel and walks away. The matron stays behind for a moment. Then she turns and follows him out.

I turn back to Jamie, stroke the fine pale hair away from his face, and let myself breathe. I lean down to kiss his burning forehead, then put my lips close to his ear.

"Don't worry, Jamie," I say. "I'm here now. I'm here."

Chapter 30 - Annie

"Have you heard from the ice cream shop?" Mom asks, "When do you start?"

I'd forgotten all about it. Mom thinks I applied already.

"I...I didn't finish the application. I didn't know what to write. Like where I live and references."

"Wait," says Dad. "You're applying to Maggie's?"

I have no idea what it's called, but I nod. How does he know this?

"Cool," he nods and grins. "Maggie's is the best. Let's see the application." I don't like this, but I pull it from my backpack and hand it over.

Mom looks over his shoulder as he scans the items. "Use Dan as a reference. Everybody knows him, and he'll vouch for you."

When it's all done, it hits me: I'm going to start a new job with strangers.

"But when will I have time to help Dad?"

"They can't hire you full-time," Mom says. "So you should have plenty of time to help us both."

They seem so pleased about it, but I'm having second thoughts. Working with strangers, all those customers asking me about Dad, since everybody here seems to know him. But now that I've told Mom and Dad, I can't back out.

Before heading out to the ice cream place, I check my clothes and face. For the first time since this started, I think about how I look.

Don't let them see you like that. Mary's words, the way she stared at me like I was naked. I look through my clothes—I didn't bring nearly enough. Still, I find clean shorts and a tank top of Mom's covered in swirls of bright colors. I change my earrings from large hoops to small studs, put on eyeliner, and pull back my hair into a clip. Staring at my reflection, I suddenly feel more like myself. *Armor*, I think.

Maybe I'll like this job. The money won't hurt. It's been all about Dad for the past few weeks, and maybe, just maybe, I'll have a chance to talk about something else. Maybe even make some friends.

There's a long line in front of the small shack. The same girl is there by herself, her arms a blur as she scoops and thrusts cones into waiting hands, then goes back to scooping again.

When she sees me, she waves me to the front.

"Tell me you're applying for the job. Please?" When I pull out the application, she gives a loud *"Whoop!"*

"Hold on a sec." She rushes through another cone, the exchange of money, then pulls out her phone.

"Hey, we got one. Get down here. I need help." She looks at me. "Can you start today?"

I stare at her for a moment. No training, no prep? I'm scared. Then I look at the line. A couple of kids are crying and pulling on their mother's hands. "I want ice cream!" Adults glare at me for holding them up.

"I guess..." I say.

"Tie your hair back and wash up," she says before turning back and handing a customer a tiny spoon with a bit of blue ice cream.

I find a sink and wash my hands. My hair clip is hanging off my hair, so I pull everything back and clip it again. She hands me a red and white striped apron, and I put it on.

"I'll handle the money," the girl says. "You help serve." She turns to the window. "What can I get you?"

Once she has the order, she hands me a scoop. "You do the cookie dough. Watch me..." She starts rolling up a ball of chocolate with the scoop, plops it on the cone, and then does one more. "Easy peasy."

I pull the scoop through the ice cream like she did, making a ball, and put it on the cone.

"How long am I… How long do you need me?"

"You mean today?" She sighs. "My shift ends at five. Can you stay that long?"

I have no idea, but I nod. I'll text Mom when it slows down.

After about an hour, my feet start to hurt. A man barely older than the girl stops by to get my application and make me fill out more forms. Something about taxes. I don't stop to read them, I just sign where he asks me to.

"We're closed on Mondays," he says. "Can you come back Tuesday, 10 a.m.?" I nod. "We'll set your schedule when you come in." Then he's gone.

A car pulls into the lot and a family gets out. I pick up a scoop, but the girl says, "I got this. See ya Tuesday." I put the scoop down, pick it up, bring it to the sink, and clean it.

I take off the apron and hang it up. On my way out, I stop and call out to the girl, "See you Tuesday."

At dinner, all we talk about is the job, how quickly I was hired, did I like it, and when am I going back. I answer, but I'm thinking about Mary.

After dinner, Dad heads toward his office and I follow.

"I'm sorry, kitten, I've got some work to do."

"I know. I want to help." *You need me to help,* is what I want to say.

"Okay. I can use it." He points to some boxes on the floor. "Dan brought these from the museum. Intake records. First we look for Mary Donovan."

I see the girl so clearly in my mind, her angry face with two bright spots of color on her cheeks. A shiver runs down my back. I don't have to look for her. I know where she is.

Dad hands me a box. "Let's get started."

"Dad?"

He looks at me, putting the second box on his desk.

"What happens when we find her?"

He smiles. "That's the start. We can apply to the Massachusetts Historic Registry with that information. If they accept the application, we'll have a leg up at the national level."

"So, what do they need? To save the building?"

"Historic significance. Basically, we need to prove that something important happened here. That she met someone, did something, or wrote something while she was in Thornwood. It just might be enough."

"So, if we find her here," I point to the box, "what's next?

"Then we pour over any and every document written by or about her. Look for surviving family that might have letters she wrote." He opens the box on his desk and looks inside. "Come on, let's start."

I open my box and pull out the first old crumbly binder. I open it to find rows and rows of cramped handwriting. "How can you read this?"

Dad chuckles. "Takes a little getting used to."

Thankfully, there are columns, and the names are broken out on their own. As I keep scanning through, I find it easier to make out the loopy script.

"Jeez, are they *all* Irish?" I've searched several pages of 'O's; *O'Henry, O'Shanahan, O'Leary, O'Reilly*. There are also Ryans, Brians, and Donahues. The first Donovan I find is *Hanlon*. I go for several pages before seeing another one, but it isn't Mary. Or Jamie.

I finish the book and reach for the next. I hope we find the record, but I don't need words on a page to prove that Mary was here. I believe my eyes. She was here. And for some reason, she's still here.

"Did you ever see a…" I stop. She isn't a ghost, so I'm not sure what to ask. "A spirit? Something that's not supposed to be there?"

He looks up. "A ghost? Or a hallucination?"

"Well, yeah. Either one."

He's quiet for a long time. Finally, he says, "No, I guess not. Have you?"

I want to tell him so badly. But the only way would be if he could see her too, so he'd know I wasn't going crazy.

"No," I say. "Me neither."

I've gone through the entire box with no Mary. But there's one more binder, and halfway through, I see her name.

"Dad!"

"What? Did you find her?"

"Mary Donovan," I read, "April 28, 1856, age 15, slight cough, surrendered by family, indigent."

Dad leans forward, eyes bright. "I knew it! I knew she was here!" He reaches for the book. "Fifteen in 1856.. that sounds a little young, but these records frequently have mistakes. No record of release date…" He flips through the pages. "Well, what's important is she's in there. She was here!"

I picture Mary, her vitality, her anger. And then I remember something.

"Relatives. You said to check with relatives. Do you know who they are?" Her grandchildren, great-grandchildren. How old would they be? Would they look like her? That same dark hair, those passionate eyes?

"She had no children of her own," Dad says. "I think there was a stepson."

No children… Then I remember.

"What about her brother?"

"What's that?" Dad looks up from the book. "She had a brother? Where did you see that?" His eagerness nearly kills me. What am I supposed to say now?

"I…I don't know. I saw it somewhere."

"A brother…that could be perfect! If he had children and grandchildren, they might have some of her writing. We've got to find him."

It's what Mary asked me to do. *Find Jamie.* Find out what happened to him.

"You don't happen to remember his name?" Dad asks.

"Jamie."

"Jamie...James... Alright, let's see what we can find."

He puts all the books away but the one with Mary's name and closes the boxes.

"I'll get marriage, birth, and death records from that time in the area and look for James Donovan. You find everything you can on Mary. Make a timeline with every event you find. Write down anything you see about relations, that stepson, her husband's other relatives."

Then he draws a hand across his face and yawns. "I'm beat. What about you?"

"Yeah, what time is it?"

"It's only ten," he says, staring at his watch in surprise.

There's a knock on the door, and Mom pokes her head in. "Gettin' late. How are you doing?"

"Great! We found the intake record! We're on our way..." he breaks off with another yawn.

"Great," Mom says, then comes in and puts a hand on Dad's shoulder. "Looks like it's bedtime for Bonzo."

Dad makes one of his funny faces. *"Bedtime,* she says," he whispers, then grabs and kisses her hand.

"I'm outta here...." I make a face myself, but inside, I'm glad. They look happy.

The next day, Mom comes back from the hospital without Dad. At first, I'm worried. Then she explains.

"Your dad's at Dan's talking over what you guys found last night. He should be home in a couple of hours."

"Everything okay?" I still don't know how to talk about his illness.

Mom smiles, "So far, so good."

She goes into her office and I follow. "How's the show coming?"

"So-so. Wanna hear what I have so far?"

I nod.

"They still want a haunted house tour, a bunch of people dressed in hospital gowns doing jump scares."

"Yuck," I say. "So, what are you going to do?"

She sits at her desk, opens her laptop, and turns it toward me. On the screen is a floor plan for the museum.

"I'm thinking of setting up individual tableaux in each of the main rooms, then have them come to life as each tour group enters. Make it immersive. Have the guests be treated like patients." She looks at me expectantly. "You like?"

I nod. "Sounds creepy. But great."

She points to a place on the floorplan, "They'll enter the lobby here, and some actors dressed as nurses will fill out intake records for each one. Then they'll move here..." Mom points to the space marked *laundry*. "This room will be set up with a sorting table, a big tub full of soapy water, a line for drying, a mangle."

"What's a mangle?"

"It's for wringing out wet laundry," she clicks on a different screen and pulls up a picture of a device with two rollers and a big handle.

"Will there be actors dressed as patients? Will you put the guests to work?"

"Yes… and maybe. I haven't decided yet."

"But not scary, right? You said they wanted 'haunted'."

"I'm going for educational," Mom says. "What was actually done to patients in that time is scary enough. Then they move into this space." She points to the wide hallway leading to that isolation box. "We'll stage some kind of altercation, and someone will get put in the box."

It's easy to imagine. The actor struggling and shouting, getting dragged inside the box, the heavy door slamming shut.

Mom runs a hand across her face and shuts her laptop. "I'm not sure what's next, but I know I want to end it in the cemetery. Do something really big."

I feel a chill at Mom's words. All those people in that quiet place, the same place where I see Mary. All of them tromping around and making noise. Will they see her? Will it frighten her away? Maybe forever?

Mom looks at me, her eyes hopeful. "What do you think?"

I want to tell her, but I can't. I swallow, then answer.

"Sure, Mom. Sounds great."

Chapter 31 - Annie

I lock my bike at the trailhead and enter the familiar path. It's dusk, and fingers of light stretch from the field on the other side of the tall pines, reaching toward me. The cemetery looks different. The grave markers leave long shadows, and for the first time, I can imagine them as what they should be; actual headstones of people who were loved, missed.

Looking around at the tall, dark trees and down at the markers, I try to picture Mom's show. Crowds of people holding candles while actors dressed in — what? Sheets? Shrouds? — play out their stories. I shouldn't have been surprised when Mom said she wanted to end the show here. What if Mary showed up? Now, *that* would be a finale.

"What are you laughing about?"

I spin around, and there she is. As if I'd conjured her with my thoughts. I cover my mouth. It's like I've dishonored her by laughing, by imagining the show here. Then I notice the tears on Mary's face. She looks wretched. Her eyes blaze with the anger I've seen before, but now there's something else—something broken.

"What is it? What's happened?"

"Did you find what happened to Jamie?"

"Not yet. But we will."

"We?"

"Dad and me. We think Jamie's family might have letters or journals from you that mention Thornwood. Something that will stop the developers from tearing it down."

"You're just like him." The words snap between her teeth.

"What?"

"You're using me. You don't care about me. Or Jamie." She turns away, and I'm afraid she's about to leave. "What's the use of this? Any of it? Why are you here? Why do you torture me?" Even as the angry words fly from her mouth, she's crying, and I want to hold her.

"Tell me what happened."

"He's dying. Jamie's dying. You didn't find him...because he never gets out." The last word ends with a sob, and without thinking, I cross the space between us and pull her into my arms.

Her body stiffens, and she tries to pull away, but I hold on tight, and then she gives in, burying her face against my shoulder as her body is wracked with sobs. She's warm and real, and solid. I feel her grief enter me, a thick dark cloud of pain, and now I'm crying, too.

Something snaps, and she pulls out of my arms and wipes her face.

"Why are *you* crying?" she throws at me, the blaze of her anger making me flinch.

"Because it's sad."

She sways, and I'm afraid she's going to faint, so I take her arm, lead her to the bench, and sit her down. "When was the last time you ate?"

She shakes her head. "It doesn't matter."

"Of course it does. How can you help your brother if you collapse?"

She looks at me. Her grief is overwhelming, and I have to force myself to keep her gaze.

"I can't help him." Her voice cracks. She takes in a shuddering breath as more tears trail down her face. Her despair is contagious.

"What does he have?"

"Have?"

"He's sick. With what?"

She sighs and bites her lip before saying so quietly I almost miss it, "Consumption."

Consumption? It takes me a moment to remember what that is.

"Tuberculosis! But...that's curable. All you need is antibiotics."

She looks up at me, the hope in her face laced with fear and anger. "What… what is that? What did you call it?"

And that's when I remember something else, and my heart sinks. She must see it in my face because she grabs my wrist. "What? Tell me!"

"It's medicine. It's strong medicine, but…" There's a pain in my chest; it's like I'm giving Jamie a death sentence. "It's not invented yet."

She lets loose with a sound half-growl, half-scream. "Of course it isn't! WHY ARE YOU HERE?" Her hands fly up as if to strike me, but she holds back and drops them into her lap, her eyes gleaming hot in the dimming light.

I pull out my phone and type quickly, *mid-1800s tuberculosis treatment,* and scan the results.

number one killer…

no reliable treatment…

cod liver oil, vinegar massages, inhaling hemlock…

"What are you doing?" Mary leans over to look at my screen, but I pull it away.

"I'm looking up treatments. Something you can do for him."

I find an article on sanatoriums and see an old photo of people bundled up in lounge chairs, spectacular mountains rising behind them. "Fresh air!"

"What?"

"He needs fresh air. Is he near a window? You need to open it, get a fan, circulate the air."

"He's in the infirmary. I don't remember windows. I don't think they'll let me open them."

"Can you take him outside? Get him some fresh air every day?" I'm still reading. "And you need to wear a mask. It's really contagious."

"Mask? What are you talking about?" I look up, and she's staring at me, a frown creasing her brow.

"A paper mask for your mouth and nose. It filters the air so you don't get sick. Can you get hold of one?"

Her face is screwed up in disbelief. "I don't care about me. What does your magic light tell you about helping Jamie?"

I change my search to herbal remedies for tuberculosis.

"Garlic, mint, coneflower," I read, then look at Mary. "Give him fresh garlic in his food and make him mint and coneflower tea. Can you get hold of them?"

She looks skeptical. "It says they'll help?"

I nod. "How long has he been sick?"

She looks away. "Don't know. They kept me from him. Blackwell let me see him as a bribe."

I stare at her, chills running through me. "Bribe? For what?"

"He wants to make a big name for himself. He wants me to do some kind of presentation and show how he works *miracles* with his patients."

I'm starting to see it. Mary displayed before a group of doctors and rich people.

"So…what are you supposed to do?"

"Wear a fancy frock. Keep my mouth shut. Speak only when spoken to and only words he's fed me."

My phone buzzes and I see a text from Mom. *Dinner's at 7:30. Will you make it?*

It's 7:15. I text back, *I'll hurry. May be a few minutes late.*

When I look up, Mary's staring at the phone. "What does it say?"

"It's Mom. She wants to know when I'm coming home."

She frowns and wipes her face. "I thought you were looking to help Jamie."

"She texted me just now." I realize she doesn't know what that means. I look at the last search result and read everything quickly so I can try to explain it to her.

"Jamie doesn't have to die from this," I say. "In my time, there's almost nowhere on earth with tuberculosis, and no one dies from it. You can help him fight it."

Her eyes are suspicious, but I see a glint of hope. "If you're lying, I'll kill you, I swear I will."

"It's true. He can fight it. He just needs to get strong. Food and fresh air. Exercise. Mary, he doesn't have to die."

Her eyes soften, and I understand what's at stake for her. If I'm lying, she's just been dragged through hope and despair like a used toy. If I'm telling the truth, she has a mission. "Just try," I say. "Please? You won't be sorry."

"I'm scared."

It's like she's kicked me in the stomach. But I pull her into my arms and squeeze her tight.

"Of course you are. But that's okay."

I hear her say *Thank you*, but she's turning liquid, and then into fog. Then nothingness.

I'm holding air.

Chapter 32 - Mary

As soon as it's light, I take a basket from the kitchen and head out to the big meadow. The high grass is wet with dew and soaks through my dress, but I don't care.

I'm out here looking for miracle cures, but instead of setting my eyes on what's above, I'm looking at the ground, trying to find a flash of purple in all the green.

I spot a bit of purple across the meadow, walk toward it, and find more and more hairy purple stems standing up in the morning light like they've popped up out of the earth just for me.

By the time the rising sun is hot on my neck, I've got a full basket. Coneflower. Garlic. Woodmint—that's what she told me to look for. That girl with her magic lantern and her big, earnest eyes.

I can't get her words out of my head. *Jamie doesn't have to die.* I want to believe her. I have to believe her.

I'm on my way to the kitchen to brew Jamie's tea when I see those girls walking toward me, watching me with their narrow, hateful eyes. I know how it must look to them, how I come and go freely now in this place with Blackwell's blessing. One of them, the leader, steps out of the pack and puts herself before me.

"Hey, Little Red Riding Hood…what's in the basket? More treats for the Big Bad Wolf?"

I say nothing and try to step around her—that's when she takes a swing at me. The basket flies from my hands and the wood-mint scatters across the floor.

Their laughter claws at my nerves. I want to bash their stupid heads in, but I can't afford any punishable offenses, not now that I'm on Blackwell's good side. I drop to my knees and start picking up the wood-mint and shoving it back in the basket. I can hear them walking away, their cruel laughter fading down the hall. Then someone is standing over me. I brace myself for a kick or a blow—then I see it's Kathleen going down on her knees beside me, picking up the woodmint and putting it back in the basket.

"Thanks," I say.

She pauses to look at the furry stalks with their purple flowers in her hand. "So…what's all this?

"For Jamie," I say.

"Yeah? So what do you do with it?"

"Put it in a tea."

Kathleen keeps staring at the purple flowers. "And that's supposed to help him?"

"Maybe," I say. "They're moving Jamie to the roof today. Fresh air's supposed to be good for him. Good for his lungs. They're putting a bed out there for him…"

Kathleen's face grows hard. She drops the flowers back in the basket, stands up, and wipes the dust from her hands, glaring down at the basket like it's done her an injury.

"So I suppose they'll be giving him breakfast in bed, too, will they?" Her voice is hard and cold, and it hurts to hear it.

"What are you going on about?"

"Why should they be doing all that for him? When there are so many others here just as sick as he is, or worse?"

I know she's right, but I'm too angry to admit it. "What's the matter with you?" I ask. She looks away, her lips tight, like she's trying to hold back the words inside her. After a while, she speaks in a low, hard voice.

"My sister…she had the consumption when we came here. My family couldn't pay for a doctor. I knew they had doctors here. Doctors and nurses. I was thinking they could help her. That this might even be a good place for her…" I see her clench her jaw and a flash of anger in her eyes. "They kept her put away in that stinking infirmary…like a dog in a kennel. I tried to see her. I begged them, but they wouldn't let me. Tried to force my way in there, same as you. Spent two days and nights in the box for it…"

She stops and swallows, then begins again. "By the time they let me out…she was gone."

Kathleen wipes her eyes angrily with the back of her arm. I remember her taking special care with one of those little graves out there under the trees. Now I know why. I don't know what to do for her, so I reach out and lay my hand on her foot.

"I'm sorry…" I say. "About your sister and all. But…you can't blame me for wanting good things for Jamie."

"I don't blame you for that," she spits the words. "I'd be doing the same as you. It's just…it's not fair, that's all."

She's right. It's not fair. None of it.

We're both silent for a while. Finally, I gather the last stalks of wood mint from the floor and stand up.

"Well," I say, "Thanks again."

"Listen, fuck those girls," Kathleen says. "You're better than a hundred of them."

Her words move me, and I turn my face away so she won't see it.

"Alright…" I say, "See you later, then."

In the kitchen, I put the kettle on, brew the tea, and put it on a tray with a tin cup. I climb the stairs to the rooftop where the nurses have moved Jamie's bed. I balance the tray with one hand and push open the heavy door, careful not to spill the drink I've made for him.

It's cold out here on this roof, but that's fine—the cold is good for Jamie's lungs. I sit on the wooden cot next to him and watch him sleep. After all these weeks without seeing him, it's strange to finally have him next to me. I reach out and put my hand on his brow. It's warm, but not as hot as it's been.

Jamie makes an uneasy sound and turns away from me, trying to gather the blanket around him. He mutters a word I can't quite hear.

"What?" I ask.

"Cold…"

"I know, I know, Jamie boy. It's good for you, though, the cold air." He makes a grumbling noise. "I made something for you," I tell him. "Mint tea. With honey." At the word *honey*, his eyes fly open, and he struggles to push himself up on one elbow. Jamie loves honey. I put in a little extra to make sure he finishes what I give him.

I help bring the tin cup to his lips. "Here," I say, "This'll warm you up." Jamie takes a sip, then lowers the cup. "No, leave it here," I tell him, trying to hold the cup close to his face so he can breathe in the good, minty steam. He coughs and tries to push the cup away again. I struggle to hold it near his face, and it tips, spilling hot tea all over the blanket.

"Damn it, Jamie…!" I say. I'm afraid he's burned himself, though it looks like the blanket caught most of it. Still, it shows he's got some fight in him, and that's a good thing.

"I'm gonna get you a dry blanket," I say, standing up.

"No," he says, reaching up and grabbing my arm. "Where were you? Where did you go?"

"I'm right here," I say. "I just went down to get you some tea…"

"No!" he says again, almost shouting, and I can see how upset he is. "I woke up and you weren't there. I didn't know where you were. I called for you but you didn't come." And now it hits me in the chest like a blow from a fist—he's talking about all the days before this one—all those terrible days and nights.

I go down on my knees beside him.

"I was here, Jamie," I say. "I was always here."

"No!" he says again, "I called for you. I kept calling for you and you didn't come. Why didn't you come?"

"I couldn't. I wanted to come, Jamie, but they wouldn't let me. I tried. I kept trying and trying, but they wouldn't let me…"

I don't know I'm crying until I see Jamie's eyes widen with surprise and concern. Then he's reaching for me with both arms. I let him pull me in, and I rest my head on his thin chest. I can hear his heart beating under my left ear.

"I'll never leave you, Jamie," I whisper. "I'll never leave you again."

Chapter 33 – Annie

Mary's sadness is inside me. Like it's my brother who's dying.

I have trouble standing, moving toward my bike, and riding home. I have to find a way to help her, to help them both. I have to.

Mom zeroes in on me the second I'm in the door. "What's wrong? Did something happen?"

I should have taken more time to compose myself before coming in the door.

"Annie?" Dad walks in from the kitchen, oven mitts on both hands, the sight so familiar and comforting I almost burst out crying.

"Nothing. I'm just sad." I've never been good about keeping secrets, particularly from these two. "I passed the hospital just now, and I was thinking about the patients, you know, from a long time ago."

Mom strokes my hair. "I think I know what you mean," she says, her fingers finding their way to my scalp and massaging there. It brings up a memory of her doing this whenever I was sick at home. How it eased whatever pain I had, how I would sometimes long for illness just so she would do this.

Dad hugs me, pressing the mitts into my back, then slips back into the kitchen, saying, "Hope you're hungry."

After dinner, Dad excuses himself to do some work and I follow him. I'm afraid to ask, but I say, "Any luck finding Jamie Donovan?" I see Mary's tear-streaked face and cross my fingers.

He shakes his head. "I'm *finding* tons of them. But getting one to match, proving he's Mary's brother, and finding living relatives… that's another story."

Consumption. The words I'd found on my phone come back to me. *Number one killer.* Maybe Mary's right. Maybe we can't find Jamie because he never grew up.

I peer over Dad's shoulder. On the pad beside him are several scribbles, a drawing of a woman who looks like the old pictures of Mary, and some words written with such force that the paper is ripped.

He shuts his laptop and yawns, and I notice blue shadows under his eyes.

"Bedtime?" I ask. When he starts opening his laptop again, I put my hand out to stop him. "At least an eye break, okay?"

I return to my room and Google Jamie, Thornwood, Mary, and Blackwell. Jamie gets a lot of hits, but none of them are the one I'm looking for. More and more, I believe he died in Thornwood, that his is one of the markers I trip over every time I go there.

I follow another thread of Thornwood hits and find a strange drawing. I recognize the building, Thornwood under a dark, threatening sky. The style is realistic, hashmarks in shaded areas, but there's something off. The scale is skewed, making the tower loom large as if about to fall on the viewer. Something about the image is both terrifying and intriguing.

The website gives no attribute, so I copy the image and put it into Google. There are lots of hits with similar pictures. Most are other buildings, but none of them in this particular style. I click on the few images that match the first drawing, and after several tries, there it is:

Jamie Donovan, 1868, 'Facade'.

I can't take my eyes off the name and the drawing, which is so clearly of Thornwood. He made it! He's real! It's all real.

I shut the laptop. 1868...he was an adult, several years out of Thornwood, but still drawing the building. I can imagine the terror of a child being thrown into that place, sick and separated from his family. It wouldn't leave you.

I start to shake. Now that I've found Jamie and can tell Mary that he made it, now that I'm closing in on what Dad needs to save Thornwood, will everything be better?

There's a light tapping at my door. "Just a minute..." I'm not sure if the shaking has stopped, but I open my door a crack and put my head out.

Mom's standing there with that look on her face, calm but thoughtful. "Can I come in?" she asks.

I open the door wide and step back into the room. She enters and closes the door behind her, making me nervous. "What's up?" Keeping my voice light.

She crosses to my bed and sits, patting the space beside her. "Come."

"Am I in trouble?" I try to make it jokey but fail. Mom shakes her head and pats the bed again. I sit beside her.

"How does he seem to you?"

I remember the shadows under Dad's eyes, but say, "Fine. Good. He's excited about finding that intake record for Mary Donovan." *Wait till he hears about Jamie!*

"He's had some highs," Mom says, "Maybe just a bit manic. Have you noticed?"

"Of course, he's high. He's been working at this for months..."

"I mean...otherwise. It seems he's been talking faster, interrupting when we talk. I just wanted to know if you'd noticed it."

I think about the way he's been these past few nights. The image of that pad of paper beside his computer with drawings of Mary, how the writing tore the paper. And suddenly I'm angry.

"People get happy, sad, and talk fast sometimes. It doesn't mean anything's wrong."

"Just tell me if something he does makes you uncomfortable."

"Like what?" I glare at her.

"Like talk over you. Or get depressed. You know what your dad was like. Look for differences."

I don't say anything, but when she pulls me in, I let her, and her chin comes to rest on the top of my head. "Don't worry about it. He's better."

Something about her words, *Don't worry, he's better,* make me remember Jamie. And Mary.

Mary doesn't know that Jamie made it out.

I have to tell her!

"I... I left a book at the ice cream shop. I have to get it, okay?" I stand up. "I'll be right back."

"I can drive you," Mom offers.

"That's okay. I want to walk."

The sun is almost gone, but the sky is filled with pink-orange, and everything glows. I'm too wound up to walk, so I run to the cemetery, my heart bursting with my news.

"Mary?"

The pines shush me as a breeze ripples through the canopy.

"Mary?"

There's no reply. I go to the bench and sit, catching my breath and smiling.

"Mary... Jamie lived!"

I wait for the suction of air and the sound that happens just before she appears. But there's still nothing.

"Come on. Please. Come on!"

She has to come. She must. The woods grow still, and I hear the sound of tires on asphalt as a single car goes by, reminding me how close the road is.

"Mary, I can't stay. Please come. Jamie makes it! I found him!"

I wait, holding my breath. I want to tell her.

But she doesn't come.

When I get back home, Mom's on the couch, her laptop open. "Hey," she says. "Check this out."

I sit beside her and look at the screen. It's a video, black background with a painted image of a man and a horse in the center. She presses *Play* and the image shakes a little like it was filmed with a hand-held camera. Then, the horse moves. Its head goes down into what could be hay in a trough, eating with jerky, puppet-like movements.

"What is it?"

"A magic lantern show! It was created using a candle or lantern and glass slides. It was used in the 1800s in some of the asylums as treatment and entertainment. I'm going to find one and use it in my show!"

The video is still playing, though you can hardly tell. There are long portions with nothing but black. Then a hand-painted glass image appears, remaining still for several seconds before something in the image moves. I don't want to tell Mom, but this is boring. Not a good way to engage an audience. But then I think of Mary's face, the light from the screen barely illuminating her, and how she called my phone a 'magic light.'   What would it have been like before smartphones, TV, and movies? These projections would have been charming, delightful, even. And as I think this, eyes on the video, I'm pulled into the simple story being told.

"It's wonderful," I say. "Will you make new slides or try to find ones like these?"

"Both, I hope. Let's see what I can uncover. Did you find your book?"

I'm not sure what she means, then I remember. "Oh. It wasn't there. Must be in my room. Where's Dad?"

She jerks her head toward the office. "Where else?" But she doesn't sound upset, so I go into my room, grab my laptop, and knock on Dad's door before opening it and peering in.

"Dad?"

He's sitting at his desk, scribbling hard on a pad of paper. His laptop is open, and I see the screen filled with YouTube, with orchestral music playing. He writes a few moments longer before looking up. "Hey."

"Can I show you something?"

He waves me into the office. I pull up a chair close to him, open my laptop, and press a key to wake the screen.

The image of Jamie's drawing is there, large and unmistakably Thornwood.

"What's this?"

"I found him! Mary Donovan's brother."

Dad pulls my laptop close and studies the image for several moments in silence. "This is his?"

I nod.

"*1868*," he reads the date on the image. "So he did this sometime after being incarcerated there." He looks at me, eyes bright. "You found him! That's great." He studies the drawing. "Interesting perspective. Creepy. Did he study art, or is this all self-taught?"

I shake my head. "I don't know."

He turns back to look at his own writing. "Now we need a living relative." I look at the pad. His writing is dense, scribbled. I'm not sure how he can read it. "Where did you find that she had a brother? We'll need that, too."

My stomach sinks. "We need that?" I imagine Dad's face if I told him the truth. *Mary told me.* It almost makes me laugh.

"Yeah, of course we need it," Dad says. "Nothing I've found mentions a brother. I'm working on the narrative for the history preservation application. Every little bit helps."

Every little bit. I imagine telling Mary about her brother. The joy it will bring her, and it makes me smile.

"If only we could ask her," Dad says, and I practically jump out of my skin.

"What?!"

"You know, time travel, ask her what she did there, where she kept her writing. Stuff like that."

It's hard not to stare at him.

"Ask Mary...?" I say.

"Mm-hmm," he responds, still studying his own writing.

"So..." I pick my words carefully. "If you *could* talk to Mary, what would you say? Like, what would you want from her to make this application strong?"

He puts the papers down, leans back in his chair, puts one hand to his head, and runs the fingers through his hair. "I'd ask where she kept her journal... no, wait!" He sits up straight. "I'd ask if she wrote this."

He pulls his laptop closer and types until the screen fills with the title page of a book. Dad reads it aloud, *"On the Organization of Hospitals for the Insane, by Jonathan Blackwell."*

A chill runs down my spine. I don't know why hearing Dad say his name hits me so hard.

"What do you mean if *she* wrote it?!"

"They say she began to formulate her mental health reform ideas when she was in Thornwood. Some of the writing and ideas in her work are nearly identical to the writing in this book. There were rumors that this doctor, Blackwell, stole her ideas."

"Bastard," I mutter. But then I think of something. I don't want to believe it, but I have to ask. "Could it be the other way around? I mean...if she did work with him, could it be that she copied it from *him?"*

Dad looks at me, a smile forming slowly. "That's exactly why she never said anything about it." He tapped his screen. "Who would believe a young woman over this famous doctor?"

"So...did he make the improvements she suggested?"

Dad shakes his head. "That's just it. He didn't implement any of it. In fact, shortly after the publication of this book, the governor of Massachusetts sued the management of Thornwood for patient abuse. Blackwell disappeared before he could be prosecuted."

Patient abuse. Like with Mary. And Jamie. "At least they got out," I say. "Mary and Jamie, right?"

"Right," Dad says, looking at my laptop and writing something down. "Let's hope your Jamie has living relatives who kept some of his stuff. Let me know what else you find." He turns back to his computer and picks up his phone. "Gotta make a call... "

I take my laptop back to my room and lie across the bed, squishing a lump under the covers that turns out to be Gremlin. "Sorry, baby," I say, pulling him out and putting him on my stomach, where he promptly curls up, purring.

I try to picture Mary's face when I tell her about Jamie, but I can't. She's so odd. She might smile—that would be a change. She might cry.

I know I would.

Chapter 34 - Mary

"Paper," Jamie says. "I want paper."

I know what this means. He wants to draw. That's how much better he must feel, and my heart leaps inside my chest. Sure, I'll bring him paper—I'll bring him all the paper in the goddamn world.

I go to the only place where I know I'll find it—Blackwell's office. I find him behind his desk, as usual. He looks up at me with a startled and slightly disapproving look. It's not my normal time to be here.

"Can I have some paper?" I ask.

"Already?" he says. "You must be making progress."

I wonder what he means. Then I realize—he thinks I want it for the writing I'm supposed to be doing.

He reaches into his desk, pulls out a short stack of blank pages and holds them out to me. I try to take them from his hand, but he holds on tight, not letting go. "When can I see it?" he asks.

"Soon," I tell him.

He keeps peering up at me for a moment, then loosens his grip on the papers, and I pull them away into my hands.

I bring the sheets of paper up to the roof where Jamie is waiting. When he sees the paper in my hand, he gets excited and struggles to sit up. I hand him one of the sheets and the stub of pencil from my pocket. He takes the paper from my hand slowly and reverently, like it's something holy, then grabs the pencil nub like a hungry child grabs at food. Then he places the paper across his knees and starts drawing eagerly.

I wonder, what will Blackwell do when he finds out that Jamie's better? He's sure to hold me to my promise and make me stand up in front of those fancy people and show me off like a prize pony.

Don't you think you're worth that? I can hear the words Blackwell said before. Trying to make me feel special so he can get what he wants.

But I *am* special—that's what that girl, Anne, told me. I'm special and bound to do great things in this world.

Blackwell has no hold over me. He doesn't know that yet, but I know it. All I have to do is wait.

Jamie suddenly cries out, his mouth twisted in an ugly grimace. I see that the pencil point has torn a hole in the paper. I grab the tray and lay it across his lap with a fresh sheet of paper, but he pushes it away, too upset to see what I'm trying to do for him.

"Jamie, stop it…" but he won't stop. He shoves the tray away again, and it falls, clattering to the floor.

Anger flies up inside me, and I turn and walk away. I can still hear him yelling while I run down the stairs to get away from that sound.

I push open the kitchen door and walk outside, and then there's that quick burst of freedom in my chest, like the last time when I was ten. I was supposed to be taking care of Jamie. He was having one of his fits and something just snapped inside me. I walked out the door and listened to his yelling, getting farther and farther behind me. I ended up leaning against a tree with my eyes closed, listening to the sound of my own heart beating. I was ashamed and thrilled by how good it felt to get away.

That's when I heard my Da's voice. *What are you doing?* I opened my eyes and saw him standing with the sun at his back, looking down at me. *You run away once,* he told me, *that makes it easier to do it a second time. Each time you do, it just makes it easier to do it again. Till one day that's all you know how to do.*

I know I should turn around and go back now, but somehow, I find myself moving across the open field and toward the trees, toward the place where that girl is waiting. How do I know she's there? I'm not sure. I only know that she is.

I move deeper into the trees and find her standing by the bench. The happy look on her face nearly blinds me.

"Mary!" she calls out. "I found him! I found Jamie!"

Found Jamie? She must see the confusion on my face because she comes nearer and pulls that strange picture-light out of her pocket. "You wanted to know what happens to Jamie... I found it! Look..."

She thrusts the picture-light toward me. It takes a moment for my eyes to focus on what she's trying to show me. Then I see it. A photograph of a drawing, the walls and towers of Thornwood. I've never seen this drawing before, but I'd know it anywhere—it's Jamie's.

"Where did you get this?" I ask.

"I searched for him and I found this. There's more..." She reaches over and moves her thumb across the picture-light, and the picture changes to a drawing of horses standing in a field, then the steeple of a church, then the face of a child. All drawn by Jamie's hand, I can tell.

"Here's a whole article about him," she keeps talking, almost out of breath. "It says he became a professional artist. He illustrated books and magazines, and his pictures sold in art galleries..."

She's still talking, but it's hard to hear what she's saying. All I can hear are these words in my head. *He gets out. He gets well. He lives.*

Jamie lives.

I fall to my knees in the grass. A pair of hands lift me up, then two arms wrap around me. But it's too much, and I push her away.

"Wait," I say. "How do you know all this? How do you know it's true?" I want it to be true, of course. More than anything. But I'm afraid to believe it.

The girl stares at me with a startled look, some of the excitement she greeted me with fading. "It..." she stammers, "It's not just one article. I found two more…" She takes the picture-light and runs her finger over it, the glow lighting up her face. "See? Here's another one. 'Jamie Donovan … Former inmate at Thornwood Asylum⋯ Overcame great odds … to become a sought-after artist and illustrator…' Mary, it's him! He's okay! He's going to be okay!"

It hurts to cry. It always has. The sounds animals make when they're giving birth, when something too big inside them is trying to come out—those must be like the sounds coming out of me now.

"Are you okay?" Anne asks, her eyes wide with surprise and concern. "I…I thought you'd be happy…"

She moves toward me and I raise my hand, palm facing her, and shake my head. When I can speak again, I take a deep breath.

"Give me something…"

"What?"

I swallow hard and try again. "Give me something I can do. For you." I'll never be able to pay her back for what she's just done for me. But I can start trying. That's all I need right now—just a start.

I can see her looking for something to say. Finally, she speaks.

"I asked my dad what he needs. To prove you were here. To save Thornwood…"

Save Thornwood?

"Why…" I stammer, "Why do you want to save this fucking place? Don't you know what they do to people here?"

"I know," she says. "I've read about it…"

"Oh, you've *read* about it, have you?" I say, and now the anger's starting to come back. "You *don't* know! You've got no idea what it's like!"

She hangs her head for a moment. "I'm sorry," she says. "You're right. But…it's different now. Things have changed. They don't do those things anymore. They help people now."

"Blackwell thinks *he* helps people," I say. "What's the difference? Those doctors, the ones in your time. Maybe they're wrong too. Did you ever think of that?"

"Okay," she says, "Maybe it's not perfect now. But it's better. It's better than it was. And maybe one day it'll be even better."

"How do you know that?"

"Because," she says, "That's how things work."

"No they don't," I say. "Things get worse. That's all I've ever seen. I don't think I've ever seen anything get better."

"But…" she takes a step closer, "You don't really think that. How could you? I mean…if you think nothing ever gets better, why would you keep going?"

I stop and wonder. Why *do* I keep going? Because of Jamie. Because of my promise to our Da. I think of everything this girl has told me about what will happen to Jamie in the future. And to me. It's too good to believe, too much.

But I believe it. I don't know why, but I believe it. I'm just not used to it yet.

"So…you want me to help you save Thornwood," I say. "Save it from what?"

"These people," she says. "They're trying to take it over, turn it into fancy apartments and shopping places."

"What people?"

"Developers."

I've never heard the word before—then I understand.

"Rich people," I say. "You mean rich people." She nods. "So they tear it down and turn it into apartments and shops and such," I say. "Where's the harm in that?"

"It's the patients," she says. "Like you and like Jamie. Like my dad. Where are they supposed to go? A lot of them are just going to end up on the street. It's not fair!"

Save Thornwood. The whole idea still sounds insane to me. But now I know—this has something to do with her father. I can tell by looking at her face. It's important to her. As important as Jamie is to me.

"Alright," I say. "What do you need?"

I can see her face grow brighter. "Anything that you write while you're here. Like a journal, maybe. A diary."

I think of the pitiful scribblings I've started for Blackwell, no more than half a page, and my heart sinks.

"Why?" I ask. "Why does that matter?"

"Listen," she says, fixing me with a serious look. "Blackwell writes a book, a book about how to treat the mentally ill. He gets famous for it. Some people say he stole it from you. That you're the one who really wrote it."

"Fucker..." I growl under my breath—like I need another reason to hate him.

"No one's been able to prove it. But if there was something that you wrote while you were here, maybe some kind of rough draft, just some notes. That could prove it."

"Wait," I ask. "How does that stop those people from tearing down Thornwood?"

"Because," she says, "If we can prove you wrote that book in Thornwood or started to write it, that proves something important happened there. Something...historic."

"Alright," I say. "What can I do?"

"Have you written anything?"

"Only a little..."

"Okay. That's a start. So...just keep going. Keep writing. As much as you can. As fast as you can. Then, when you're done, you can give it to me."

"When I'm *done?* How will I know when I'm done?"

"I guess...when you've said what you want to say."

"That's no help!" I say louder than I mean to, because I see her flinch. "How do I know what I'm supposed to say?"

"Well...whenever I had to write something for school, and I didn't know what to say, my dad would tell me to say one true thing. Just one true thing. Then another. He told me that if I just kept doing that, I'd be fine."

Some of the calm in her voice has gotten into me. I'm still not sure what to do, but it no longer seems so impossible.

Suddenly, I remember.

"Jamie… I've got to get back to him." I turn to go. "I'll be back." I don't say when, and she doesn't ask. Somehow, I know we'll find each other.

I run all the way across the field and up the stairs, trying to get back to Jamie as fast as I can, afraid of what I might find. But when I open the door and step out onto the roof, he's sitting up in bed, drawing away as calmly as you please, like he barely even noticed I was gone.

I see that he's pulled the tray onto his lap and is using it to rest his paper on. He didn't need me to come back and do it for him.

"Look," he says, holding up his drawing for me. I can tell it's one of me. Jamie's always liked drawing me. I look closer and see he's drawn dark shadows around the eyes, making my mouth look grim and hard at the corners.

"What's this?" I say, pointing at the dark shadows he's drawn around my eyes. "You make me look like a raccoon." I hand the drawing back to Jamie. "That doesn't look like me."

Jamie glances down at the drawing, then reaches up and touches my face, tracing his fingertips across the soft flesh under my eyes.

Then I understand. He's not trying to hurt or make fun of me— he's just drawing what he sees. It's like what that girl, Anne told me. *One true thing.*

I look at Jamie working away at his drawing, and a surge of pride rushes through me. Jamie can do more than draw well. He can tell the truth. With just pencil and paper, he can tell more truth than most people can with all their words put together.

I remember what Anne had just told me about Jamie and the good things the future holds for him. Maybe he doesn't need me as much as I think he does. Maybe he *can* survive without me.

That should make me happy, shouldn't it?

"Jamie," I say, "You're going to be alright. Do you hear me? You're going to be alright."

Jamie doesn't answer. He just keeps drawing.

Chapter 35 - Mary

Today's the day that Blackwell is going to prepare me for his presentation. I don't know what to expect. I imagine there'll be some reading aloud like a schoolgirl, a few warnings to behave myself, *stand up straight, speak clearly.*

Two matrons arrive to escort me to Blackwell's office. Before we get there, they stop at a door, unlock it, and usher me inside. Standing alone in the center of the room is the mannikin wearing the fine black dress I've seen before.

Before I know it, their hands are all over me, pulling at my clothes. I shake them off and turn to face them. "I can dress myself!" I snap at them. I wait for them to leave, but they don't—they just stand there with their grim faces and their hands folded in front of them, waiting.

I see a fresh white slip and a pair of snow-white bloomers laid out on a bench. "All of it," one of the matrons says, the first words I've heard her speak.

I could refuse, but it doesn't seem worth the trouble. I know the truth—I get out of here. They probably never do.

I turn away and start to strip down. The bloomers and slip are cool and soft against my skin, softer than anything I've ever felt before. Then I look at the dress—so many buttons, I'm not sure where to start. The matrons step in to help me, and this time I let them. Their hands move more quickly and surely than mine, fastening me in, and before I know it, they're finished.

One comes forward holding a handsome pair of lady's dress boots. She kneels in front of me to slip the first one on and fasten it. For a moment, it's like we've switched places as if it's she who's the servant and me who's the master.

Before we leave, they sit me down in a chair and take a brush to my hair, then pull it back and fasten it behind my head with pins and a lacquer comb. When they're finally done, they both stand back and look at me, their faces grim, like it pains them to see me like this.

"Come on," one of them snaps at me.

We leave the room and walk the rest of the way down the hallway, the new sound of my lady's dress boots *clip-clopping* off the walls. I'm a little unsteady in them at first, but I'm getting used to it. We pass a couple of girls I recognize from the laundry room who stop and stare as we pass.

When we reach Blackwell's office, the matrons open the door for me but stay behind in the hallway. I step across the threshold and look around. Two large objects I've never seen before catch my eye, tall metal poles with what look like large lamps on top.

Blackwell steps out from behind his desk, hands clasped behind his back and slowly paces back and forth in front of me, gazing closely. The warm blood rushes to my face. I hope he doesn't notice it, but I know he must. I've had men look at me closely before—this is different.

"Good," he says, "Very good."

I say nothing and wonder what he's praising me for—I haven't even done anything yet.

"Stand here," he says. I do as he directs and find myself facing those two tall lamps. The room grows darker. I turn and see Blackwell walking from window to window, closing the heavy drapes. There's a sudden metallic click, a soft hissing sound, and the smell of gas. Then, a soft *whomp*, and I'm blinded by a bright blazing light in my face.

"Jesus..." I cry out, "Turn it off!"

"Wait for a minute," Blackwell says. "You'll get used to it."

I try to open my eyes, but I can't. "It's too bright," I tell him.

"Give it a moment," he says. I try to open my eyes again. This time I find I can keep them open a little longer.

"What is this?" I ask. "Why are you doing this?"

"We're trying to replicate the circumstances under which you'll be doing your presentation," he says. "The lights onstage at the theater will be at least as bright as these. You'll need to be used to them when the time comes."

The theater? Am I supposed to dance and sing?

"Here," Blackwell says, his voice right next to me. "Take this." I hear the sound of paper crinkling, reach out, and take hold of the page he's thrusting toward me. "Read it."

My eyes still aren't quite used to the bright lights, and I squint to make out the words written on the page in front of me. "Out loud," he says. "Read it out loud."

I hold the paper closer to my eyes and begin.

"Ladies and gentlemen, my name is Mary Donovan..."

"Stop," Blackwell interrupts sharply. "Hold it lower. Don't cover your face."

I do as he says and begin again. "My name is Mary Donovan. I wish to thank you for the opportunity to address you this evening and to share with you my experiences at Thornwood Hospital under the care of Doctor Jonathan Blackwell..."

I stop and look up. These aren't my words. They're his.

"You want me to read this?" I say. "This isn't me."

"You will read it as it's written," he says. I can't see his face beyond the glare of the lamps. "Continue."

I look down at the paper and keep going. "...under the care of Doctor Jonathan Blackwell and his skilled and compassionate staff..."

Skilled and compassionate staff... I almost choke on the words. I swallow back the anger rising in my throat, take another deep breath, then continue.

"...under the care of Doctor Jonathan Blackwell and his skilled and compassionate staff..."

"Stop," Blackwell interrupts again. "Now you sound angry."

"This my voice," I say. "It's how I speak."

"Not anymore. Remember, you are no longer an angry person. You now speak like someone who is under complete control of their emotions. *Complete…control."* He says the two words very slowly. It sounds to me like someone talking in their sleep. I take a deep breath and try again.

"…under the care of Doctor Jonathan Blackwell and his skilled and compassionate staff, I have made significant improvements both in my symptoms and in my quality of life…"

The hot lights are starting to make me sweat. I wipe my brow, then keep reading.

"Imagine, if you will, the worst moment you have ever had, when anger, sadness, or fear rise up like a great flood and threaten to drown you. Now imagine that single moment lasting a full hour, then two hours, then three. Now imagine it lasting an entire week, or a month, or even a full year. Then perhaps you can imagine what life was like for me, and for others like me, for whom hope and peace and happiness seem forever out of reach…"

I stop. There's an aching tightness in my throat. The words on the page in front of me blur and swim, and I reach up and wipe away the tears that have taken me by surprise.

I know two things. I know that these words were written by someone who truly *sees* me. And I know that Blackwell could never have written them.

When I can speak again, I ask, "Who wrote this?"

Both blazing lights are suddenly extinguished, but I still see them dancing in front of my eyes as Blackwell answers.

"Why, *you* did, Mary." I hear a strange smile in his voice. "You did."

Chapter 36 - Annie

A mosquito buzzes in my ear as I stare at where Mary was, empty now, pine trees looming and grave markers barely visible in the fading light. I remember the first time I saw her vanish. Back then, it terrified me, and I was afraid I was going mad. *Funny how you can get used to anything*, I think. Even vanishing 19th-century girls who are long dead.

"Justin! Don't go!"

I spin around and see two figures between the trees. How long have they been there? Did they see us? Slowly, I move behind the nearest tree I can find.

"Why?" the other boy says.

"I want to explain."

I peer slowly around the tree and recognize the first speaker. It's that boy from the hospital. Carson.

"You don't have to," the other boy says.

"Yes. I do."

They're silent for several moments. I don't know what to do. Should I walk out like I just got here? Or wait till they leave?

"Well. What is it? You asked me here. You say you wanna talk, but you don't say anything."

"Wait…" Carson's voice wavers like he's about to cry. "Maybe this was a bad idea."

"Uh…duh." I don't like the other boy's tone. It's nasty.

"It's just…" again, the waver, but he takes a deep breath and continues. "I want you to understand."

"What? I knew you had issues, but this?" He points to Carson's arms. "They should lock you up. Loony."

"Don't say that."

"Why? Not p.c. enough? Then how's this...Death-obsessed? Or just Obsessed. Jesus."

Carson moves to touch the other boy. "Justin…"

"Don't." The boy shifts out of reach. "Look where we are. Dead people all around. Christ."

"It's quiet here."

"No shit."

"Justin…"

"It's not my fault. You want too much. I couldn't take it. But this," he looks again at Carson's arms. "You can't guilt someone into being close."

I gasp, remembering what Bess had said to me. *You always want too much.*

"That's…" Carson's voice breaks, but he continues, gulping air the way I do when I'm trying not to cry. "That's what I've been trying to tell you. I didn't do this because of you."

"No?" Justin sneers. "I tell you to get lost, and next thing I know, Mom's crying and telling me you're in the hospital."

"I'm sorry. I'm so sorry…" Carson takes a breath. "I've been depressed. A long time. Before you and me… before we…"

"Everybody's depressed."

"Not like this."

"Oh, boo-hoo."

I want to punch him.

"I wanted you to know," Carson continues. "It wasn't you. It was never you."

"I don't care. You don't belong there," he jerks his head toward the newer hospital up the hill. "You belong there," he indicates the old building. "Locked up with the other loonies."

"Don't!"

"What are you going to do, hit me?" Justin puffs out his chest and steps forward.

Carson surprises me. He steps into that space, Justin's personal space, leans in and kisses him on the mouth. I look away, but I think Justin kisses him back. Then I hear a sound of disgust and look to see Justin holding Carson at arm's length, then wiping his mouth. "You taste disgusting."

Then he turns and walks toward the open field, thankfully away from me.

Carson looks after him for several seconds, his mouth still in the shape of a kiss, before his face crumples and tears start coursing down his cheeks.

I want to slip away, leave him alone, but I'm scared. What if he tries to kill himself again? I left him alone here once; I'm not going to do it again.

I step out and start walking toward him, calling his name softly. "Carson?"

His head jerks up and he stares at me, frowning. "What are you doing here?"

"Are you okay?"

"Go away."

I stand still. Part of me wants to do what he asks. But I stay.

"I heard some of that," I say. "Sorry. I didn't mean to, but you guys were just there."

He glares at me. "You…you saw…"

"He's an asshole."

Carson looks away. "Maybe."

"He is. I know. My girlfriend is an asshole too."

The minute it's out, I know it's true. Bess hasn't been my friend, hasn't really cared about me, for a long while. Tears burn my eyes.

He continues staring at me, his mouth falling open. Then he says, "Don't tell anyone."

"What? That you broke up? That he's mean to you?"

"That I'm … we're… I'm…"

"Queer? So what? I think I'm queer too."

The minute it's out, I stop talking and have trouble catching my breath. Why did I say that? But the truth of it fills the space around me. So I keep talking.

"I kissed my best friend. She kissed me back, I know she did. Then she changed, and now she doesn't want to be friends." My voice breaks. I'm not sure why I said all this to this strange boy.

"Why are you telling me?"

"You're not alone."

"Yeah, right."

"You're not!"

"Stop it!" He looks angry now. "Why do you treat me like I'm an idiot?"

"I'm not! I don't mean…"

"Everybody thinks I'm going to kill myself. You think I'm going to try again, don't you?" He glares at me, waiting for an answer. I can't hold his gaze. "See? I knew it! Everybody's tiptoeing around me. Everybody but Justin."

"Justin only cares about himself."

"You don't know."

"I know what I saw."

"Go away!" Carson folds his legs and sits on the forest floor, putting his head in his hands.

I feel stupid, but I don't leave. Finally, I sit down, too.

He looks up at me, "Really?"

"Do you wanna talk to someone else? My dad, maybe?"

He sighs. "You're really not going to go away, are you?"

"In a minute."

"What were you doing here?"

"Visiting a ghost."

We say nothing, and slowly, the silence of the woods fills up the spaces between and around us. I look up and see small patches of blue between the tall pines.

"Do you ever wish," I say, breaking the silence, "that someone from the future could tell us how it all works out? That it's gonna be good, maybe better than good."

Carson doesn't answer, and when I look at him, I see he's considering the question. "Does it have to be us?" he asks. "The future person. Or can it be someone else?"

"Not us. Someone else. Maybe from after we're dead. But they know about something we did. Something good."

"Like what your dad is doing."

I think about Dad saving Thornwood, the hospital and mental health facilities rescued, improved, expanded. I picture myself as a ghost or time traveler visiting a future me. She tells me how my dad is honored and respected—how it all worked out. This could be his legacy. Maybe mine, too. I look at Carson.

"Maybe you'll be part of it," I say.

Carson cringes, shakes his head. "I like what your dad is doing. I'd like to help him. Do you think he'd let me?"

My chest grows tight. *That's my job*, I say to myself. But the hope on Carson's face moves me. Maybe he *could* help Dad. Maybe that would help him, too.

"Sure. I'll ask. Gimme your phone number," I say, standing up and taking out my phone.

He looks surprised but stands up, too. "Thanks, Annie."

"I prefer Anne."

"Thanks, I-prefer-Anne," he says with a smirk. And I have to smile. I turn to walk out and he follows me.

"Don't you have to get back?" I ask, jerking my head in the hospital's direction.

He shakes his head. "I'm out. Home."

"Your folks let you come here?"

He stops and glares at me. "Why, because I have to be 'watched'? If I wanted to be dead, I'd have done it right the first time." He walks away from me, fast.

"Wait!" I don't want him to leave like this. "I'm sorry." He's right. It's easy to be scared of what someone will do after they've done something scary. Like Dad. "It's all...new stuff. I don't know how to handle it." I feel tears coming and swallow hard. "Dad...moving here...this place. I'm sorry."

He stops but doesn't turn around. When I reach him, he starts walking again, and we quietly exit the cemetery. I see a bike in the rack next to mine and say, "Yours?" He nods, and then I say, "Dad was home when I left. Wanna come back with me and ask him? About helping?"

He looks surprised, then frowns, but unlocks his bike and pulls it off the rack. "What time is it?" But he's already pulling out his phone to check. "The Carriage House, right? It's close." He mounts his bike. "You think he'll mind?"

I pause. "He won't," I say. The old dad wouldn't, but I'm not sure about this one. I mount my bike, and we're off.

Dad's outside when we get there, pulling a bag from the car. When he sees us, he grins. "Carson! Annie! Wait...do you two know each other?"

I shrug and Carson says, "Hey Jackson. How's it going?"

"Good, good. How are you? When did you get out?"

"Yesterday. Seeing Dr. O. later today."

Dad nods, his smile fading a little, then coming back strong. "We're going to the pool in a bit. You know, Dan's house. Wanna join us?"

I realize how hot I am and think that a pool is heaven. Then I wonder, *Will Carson come with those scars?*

Carson's shaking his head. "Can't, thanks. But, um, I was wondering. And Anne... she said you wouldn't mind..."

"Wouldn't mind what?"

"Me helping you. I mean, I don't know what I can do, but if you could use some help with Thornwood, I'm your man." He stands up a little taller and grins nervously.

Dad's face transforms. He looks amazed and moved. "Really?

You want to help me?"

Carson nods.

Dad steps close to him and takes his hand, shaking it vigorously. "Well that's just fine. That's great. Sure. I can use all the help I can get. When can you start?"

Chapter 37 - Mary

I need a place to write.

Privacy is hard to come by in this place. They make sure of that. We eat together, we wash and clean together, we sleep together. And even with all that togetherness, there's still so much loneliness.

I've got to remember that. *Even with all of that togetherness, there's still so much loneliness.* That sounds like something that came from a book, doesn't it? I've got to write that down.

I take some of Jamie's drawing paper and the stub of a pencil and walk across the field to the woods, where I can be alone for a while, but the birds chirping and the wind whispering in the pine needles distract me. And I keep expecting to see that girl, Anne. She doesn't appear, but I keep seeing her out of the corner of my eye, so I gather my paper and head back to the big building without writing a word.

I enter through the kitchen, but it's crowded with girls hurrying back and forth, tending to the big steaming kettles of watery soup. I go to the dorm where a few girls—the ones who never leave—are still in their beds. Some are sitting and staring into space, some hugging themselves and rocking, and others curled up on their sides. I can't write here. Just a small room. That's all I need. Some place where I can be alone.

I'm heading back through the kitchen when I notice the pantry door standing open. *The pantry.* It's small enough. And tonight, once supper is over, there'll be no one there but me.

I bide my time until things are quieter, then I take my few sheets of paper and pencil and walk down the hallway. The kitchen is silent and empty at this hour. I go to the pantry and open the door. When I see how dark it is there, I strike a match, light a candle, and place it on a shelf above me, then look around for a place to sit. I find a big bag of flour, drag it closer to the candle, and sit—it's more comfortable than I expect it to be. I pull a heavy wooden crate in front of me and spread the papers on it.

All those blank, white pages…

Panic comes over me. What am I supposed to write? What was it Anne told me? Whatever she said that had made so much sense to me before, it's gone now. And those smart-sounding words I'd thought of just a few minutes ago. They're gone, too.

Why am I doing this? I try to remember how Anne explained it…I have to write a book so that Blackwell can steal it, so Anne can find it and prove Blackwell stole it, so her Da can save Thornwood…? It all makes my head hurt.

Then I remember the part about Blackwell being found out, exposed as a thief and a liar, and my blood runs hot. I like that part. I like it a lot.

I look down at the paper in front of me. Still empty. I pick up the pencil nub, take a deep breath and blow it out. The candle flame flickers, shadows dance around me. Then everything settles and turns still, and I start to write.

My name is Mary Donovan…

What to say next? Now I remember what Anne told me. 'Just say one true thing'…

I keep writing.

… and I am afraid.

I read the words on the page in front of me, and something moves in my heart. The pencil keeps moving.

I am afraid that these words I am writing do not matter. I am afraid that I do not matter.

The room around me is starting to go away. There's just a pencil, this paper, and these words in front of me.

Some people do not worry whether they do not matter. People who have money. People who tell other people what to do and what not to do. They never worry whether they do not matter because they have nobody looking down on them.

My heart is beating harder in my chest. It's like I can hear it echoing off the walls in this tiny room.

I think that those people are wrong. People who have money do not matter more than people who don't. They are just richer. People who tell other people what to do or what not to do are not more important. Either everyone matters, or no one matters…

I hear the pantry door click open, then a familiar voice.

"What the hell are you doing in here?"

Kathleen is standing in the doorway, just a tall, slim shadow.

"Shut the door!" I hiss at her. She slips inside and closes the door behind her. She moves closer, and I see her face better in the candle-glow, scowling, confused, and concerned.

"How did you know I was in here?" I ask.

"The candlelight," she points at the flame. "You can see it under the door. Anyone can. You're lucky it was me." She takes a step closer, looking down at the paper in front of me. "What are you writing there?"

I put my hand over the paper and pull it closer to me. "Nothing," I say.

She takes a step closer. I grab the paper off the box and press it to my chest. "Jesus," Kathleen says, "You don't have to hide it from me."

"Why not?"

"Because *I can't fucking read,* Mary, that's why not. Is that good enough for you?" She looks away for a moment, and I realize how much it must have pained her to say that. "So…" she finally says, "Jamie…how is he? Is he better?"

"He is. He's better. He's drawing now and everything." I pull Jamie's drawing of me from under the stack of papers and show it to her. Kathleen's eyes grow wider.

"Jesus," she says, "Your Jamie drew this? It's good, isn't it?"

A warm rush of pride goes through me. "Yeah. It is."

"So," she nods at the pages in front of me, "You're writing this for Blackwell, are you?"

What am I supposed to tell her? That I'm writing it for a girl who hasn't been born yet?

"Yes," I say, because that's easier. "He wants me to do a presentation."

"A what?"

"He wants to stand me up onstage in front of a bunch of doctors and rich fuckers. He wants to show them what a great job he's done with me. You know…what a fine, brilliant doctor he is and all that."

"Christ…." Kathleen mutters. "So…" she nods toward the pages again, "Are you supposed to give some kind of speech or something?"

At the word, my heart tightens. I think about all those faces out there, watching me, waiting for me to make a mistake.

As if she can read my mind, Kathleen says, "You'll do alright. I know you will."

Some of the tightness around my heart loosens its grip. I didn't like it when Kathleen found me here—now I'm glad she did.

"Be careful, though, Mary. Whatever Blackwell's telling you, there's a lot more he's *not* telling you. You can count on that."

"What do you mean?" I ask.

Kathleen comes nearer and lowers her voice. "You remember that girl, the one I told you about? The one Blackwell was making over and bringing to his office every day, like you?" I nod. "Word is, he was training her, getting her ready for something important. And right before it was supposed to happen, she disappeared."

"What happened to her?"

Kathleen shrugs. "Some girls say she ran off. Some say Blackwell got rid of her."

"You mean…"

"I don't know," she says. "But there's part of this place most people don't know about or have never seen. Down under the ground, like a dungeon. Some say she's down there…"

A dungeon. I try to picture it— cold, wet stone walls, manacles and chains.

"So…" I ask her, "Do you believe all of that?"

"I don't know…" she says. "You just be careful, alright? Watch yourself."

"I will."

"Promise me," she says.

"I promise."

"Alright then," she says, backing toward the pantry door. "Just don't let them find you here in the morning." She steps out, closes the door behind her, and I'm alone again.

I look at the words I've written and don't recognize them. It's like they were written by somebody else. For a moment, they almost frighten me. I hear a sharp voice in my head. *Who do you think you are?* It's my Aunt Bridget's voice, and every other voice that's tried to put me in my place.

Then I hear another voice. One I haven't heard for a long time.

You'll do great things one day, Mary. Great things. I see it in you.

My Da used to tell me that. I wasn't sure I believed him, but I wanted to. What child doesn't want to do great things? Some of the saints were children, I remember. They never made it past ten or twelve, but they still did great things with the time they were given. Things they're still remembered for.

What will I be remembered for? And who will remember me?

I pick up the pencil nub and keep writing. I'm going to keep going for as long as it takes.

Chapter 38 - Annie

"Would you like a ride to work?" Mom asks. "It's pretty wet out there."

I shake my head—I want time alone to think.

The minute I'm outside, I regret it. The rain is steady, and I'll be wet by the time I get to the ice cream shack, even with the umbrella Mom gave me. But I set out on foot anyway.

If all goes well, I'll see Mary today. Maybe she'll have news. Will she be able to write something? For the first time, I wonder how she'll get paper and pens. And where is she supposed to write? In bed at night? With no candle? Will she have trouble getting started? How long will it take?

Suddenly, it hits me...

The writing we're looking for, the kind that we need—she can't do it. It's too soon. She doesn't have what it takes to write it. She hasn't learned enough, *lived* enough yet. In a few years, maybe. But not now.

We have to wait.

But we can't wait. We don't have time.

I want to sit down and weep. Why did this happen to us? Why did we meet? Was it just so I could help Mary, tell her about Jamie, and give her hope? What about my Dad? What about *his* hope? What's going to happen when that gets taken away?

Before I know it, I'm standing in the rain in an empty parking lot in front of the ice cream shack.

"Anne! Thank God! I can't keep up." The girl gestures to the empty space in front of the window and furiously mimes scooping.

She laughs, and I realize I don't know her name.

I duck inside and shake off my umbrella. "This may sound dumb," I say, "and I'm sorry if you told me, but what's your name?"

She stares at me a moment, then smacks her forehead with her palm and smiles. Instead of answering, she turns her arm face up and points to one of her bigger tattoos. It's a woman transforming into a tree and it covers her entire forearm. It is quite beautiful.

"Wow. Who is it?"

She grins and points to her chest. "Me. Daphne, the Naiad. She became a laurel tree to escape Apollo...the bastard."

I remember it somewhere deep in my brain. "Bad gods. They were always chasing and raping women."

"Yup. But Daphne got away."

"It's beautiful." I'm still looking at her ink.

"Took three sessions. Hurt like bloody hell. Took most of my savings. But it was worth it, right?"

I nod, then look out at the rainy day. "Has anyone been by today?"

"A couple of people, but yeah, it's pretty dead." She turns to look at me. "Hey, I hear Carson's at your place a lot."

I stare at her. "You know Carson?"

She laughs and gestures to the street. "Welcome to small town USA."

Does she know about Carson's attempted suicide? Does everyone? "Are you a friend?"

She cocks her head and squints. "Yeah, I'm a friend. Why would I be asking if I wasn't?"

"Well, why don't you ask *him* what he's doing?"

She looks away. "He's not answering texts."

"How do you know where he's been?" I want to believe she cares for him, but I can still picture the sneer on that other boy's face when I saw them in the cemetery. I'm not sure why, but I want to protect him.

Again, she waves her hand toward the street. "Small town. So, what's he doing there? You two hooking up?"

"What?!" I give a harsh laugh. "No! Not likely." Then I remember Carson asking me not to tell. "Wait, are you into him?"

She's looking at me in a way that makes me worried. What does she see? "I was," she says, "A few years back. But now I'm pretty sure he's gay." She grabs my arm. "Don't tell him I said that. He's not out, so who knows."

"He's helping my dad. Getting background material to save Thornwood."

Her eyes light up. "He is? That's great. I mean, it's perfect. He needs to get his mind off… you know." She looks away, but not before I see the sad look in her eyes.

A car pulls up, and someone opens the car door, but just then, the sky lets loose with a serious deluge. A mom gets out with an umbrella and runs to the window.

"Two Cookie Monsters in cones, please. And one scoop of Chocolate Death in a cup."

It's still raining when I get to the cemetery. The ground is squishy; water enters my sneakers, soaking my socks.

I see Mary before I step into the circle, and the relief is overwhelming. I pause to catch my breath as hope blots out my soaked feet, my frizzy hair, everything but the vision of Mary waiting for me.

She's staring at the umbrella so hard I wonder if they existed in her time.

"Umbrella," I say as I get closer. "Hi."

"Umbrella to you," she says, frowning. "What are you doing with it?"

"Keeping the rain off, what do you think." I shake off some of the water.

She stares at me before stepping up and examining the umbrella.

"It's not raining..." She studies my hair, my shoes, touches the umbrella, and then stares at the water on her hand. "How?"

That's when I realize—she's dry. Nothing on her is touched by what's clearly still coming down on me. I start to laugh.

"You're dry, I'm wet...and none of this should be happening."

"'Tis happening. You can be sure of that. For once, I'm glad to be on *my* side of this." Then she starts laughing, too. It's a wonderful thing to see. All the worry lines vanish as her cheeks lift and her eyes look clear. Delight makes her a stranger to me, but I like this new Mary.

Then I remember what I've come here to ask. Maybe it doesn't matter that she can't write a lot yet. Something, anything, has got to be better than nothing.

"Did you write anything yet?" I ask.

She shakes her head. "Maybe. Yes, a little."

I can't hide my disappointment. *Two weeks.* That's all we've got to have something for the historical preservation board, or Thornwood will be bulldozed.

"Something strange happened to me," Mary says. "The doctor, he had me practicing for the presentation..."

"Okay..."

"The matrons dressed me in fine clothes and pinned up my hair. And the boots…" she looks wistful. I glance down at her feet and see scuffed and worn shoes. The soles look thin.

"He had me under these hot lights," she continues. "I could barely keep my eyes open. Then he gave me something to read." She stops.

"Read?" I say. What was it?"

She doesn't look at me but studies something off in the distance. "Words. The most beautiful words." She fumbles at her dress and pulls a sheet of paper from her pocket. On the back of it is a rough pencil sketch whose style I recognize instantly. I reach for it.

"Is this Jamie's?"

She turns the sheet over and stares at it. "Yeah…. I just grabbed the first thing I saw so I could copy what I remembered. Here, listen..." She turns the paper over again and starts reading haltingly.

"Imagine the worst moment you have ever had, when anger threatens to drown you. Now imagine it lasting a full hour, two, three. A week, a month, a year. Then perhaps you can imagine what life was like for me," her voice gets wobbly. She stops for a moment, taking a deep breath before continuing. "...and for others like me, for whom hope and happiness seem forever out of reach..."

"That's beautiful," I say.

Mary touches the paper, running her fingertips over the words. "'Tis," she says. She looks up at me, blinking away tears, and shakes the paper at me. "How did they know?"

"I don't know. Who wrote it?"

She scowls, the frown lines returning in full. "Blackwell wouldn't tell me. He said that *I* wrote it," she spits the words. I can see her hand turning into a fist, about to crumple the paper, so I gently take it from her.

"How's Jamie?" I ask.

"He's grand. How's your da?"

I grin. "He's grand." I try to say it the way she did but fail miserably. Then I wonder if it's true. "He's good...as long as he thinks there's hope."

She looks sad, then thoughtful. She glances at the paper one more time before folding it and returning it to her pocket. "What can I do?"

I want her to help, but I'm so afraid she can't. I look away for a moment, hoping she can't see the doubt on my face.

"For now, just keep writing. Maybe...about what's going on inside Thornwood. How the staff and doctors treat you. Things you'd like to change. Blackwell's going to act like the big reformer, but he's not going to change anything. *You're* the antidote to that."

"I'd like to be his poison," she says bitterly. After a moment, she says, "I think I can write about what's going wrong, starting with the food."

"Okay, that's good. It's a start."

"This is supposed to be a home for the poor, but we ate better at my aunt's house, even with her complaining over every penny spent. I'm tired all the time, hungry too."

I study her for a moment, thin face and arms, the loose dress. She looks ill. "Are you…are you sick?"

She shakes her head firmly. "Nah, just starving, that's all."

I have to let it go. I'd feed her if I could, but I'm pretty sure whatever I give her in this space will disappear when she leaves it. Then I realize something.

"We have another problem," I say.

She looks wary. "What?"

"We've got to figure out how you give me the writing when you have it."

"I'll bring it with me, like this," she pats her pocket, "Easy."

I shake my head. "No. Remember the food you brought me? I could hold it. I could smell it. But when you left and when I left here, it vanished."

She stares at me for a moment before speaking. "Vanished?"

I nod.

"So if I handed you this paper and you walked out there, somewhere…"

"It would disappear."

She puts both hands over her pocket as if to keep the paper safe. "So…how am I supposed to give it to you?"

"I don't know. We have to figure it out." I start pacing. I feel like crying, but I can't. It won't help. We have to solve this.

"Anne," Mary says, "Have you ever… has this ever happened to you before? Is this a common thing where you're from? Visiting someone in the past?"

I shake my head, "No. Never. I don't know anyone it's happened to. People write fiction about it, and science says it may be possible. But no one knows how to do it yet."

"Yet," she repeats, laughing a little.

"How about you? Have you ever met someone from the future? Or the past?"

She shakes her head. "My Da said his da came to him after he died. Told him to fetch in the milk."

I smile. "Not quite the same."

"So, how does it work? And why?"

I shake my head. "I think the *why* is to help each other. At least…me helping you."

"Well then, I damn well better help you back!" She puts both hands on her hips and glares at me. This is the Mary I know. "But… how *does* it work?" she says. "I came here a few times, and you never came."

I remember the times I've looked for her, the desperation I felt when she didn't come.

"Remember the first time you saw me?" I ask.

"I'm not likely to forget that."

"Why were you here?"

Something happens to her—her chest caves in a little like she's been punched, then she lifts her chin up and says, "Jamie. I'd just found out he was sick. I thought he was dying." She inhales sharply, lets the air out slowly. "Why were you here?"

I remember Dad's head lolling on his neck, the orderlies rushing him to the E.R. "My dad nearly died."

The turmoil and depth of our unhappiness fill the air between us. "Maybe that's why," I say.

"Why?"

"We were hurting. Both of us. We needed help. Maybe that's why it happened."

We're both quiet for a moment. It feels like I've just caught a glimpse of something. Something so big I can barely fit it all in my heart. Does she feel it, too?

"Okay," I say. "Let's figure this out. How can we get your

manuscript to me?"

We both think for a few minutes, then Mary speaks, eyes filled with excitement. "I could bury it! Not here, but a little ways out, in case the magic only works in the circle. Anything I bury now could be dug up in the future, could it not?"

It only takes a few seconds for this to sink in—the beauty and simplicity of it. "Yes! That's it! Mary, you're a genius!"

I hug her, and she allows it for a second before pushing me away. "Yeah yeah. Me, the great genius reformer and all."

"Let's test it."

"Now?" Mary's studying the ground and says, "I can't." She looks at me with terror in her eyes. "There's corpses everywhere."

I shudder. "Okay. Maybe further out, in the field…"

"The garden? It's plowed up all the time. Nothing will stay."

"There must be another place…" I stare at the soggy ground. I can't imagine paper surviving there. We pace for a few minutes before Mary stops and points in the direction of Thornwood.

"In there," she points to the old building. "You've been inside, right? You told me you were. I'll find a hiding place so good, you're sure to be the first one to find it!" Her eyes gleam as she turns to me, and somehow, I know she's about to vanish. "Don't give it another thought," she says.

And then she's gone.

Chapter 39 - Mary

Walking back across the open field, I can see the walls and towers of Thornwood turning black against the reddening sky. All those rooms inside, all those twisting, turning hallways. So many dark corners. So many places to hide something.

I go straight to the dorm, to my bed. I look around to make sure nobody's watching. I reach under the mattress, pull out the thin stack of paper, and flip through the pages, marveling at what I'm about to do—send a message across all those years to a girl who hasn't been born yet.

What if it works?

I think of Blackwell. What I'm about to do—what *we're* about to do, will destroy him. As sweet as that promise sounds, it's one I won't live to see. And neither will he. It burns, the unfairness of that.

Then I think of the girl, Anne, and what I owe her. Jamie's life. That's enough to put me in her debt forever. But it's a debt I can live with. Gladly.

I pull out a blank page, pick up the little nub of a pencil, and wonder—what should I write? I picture Anne finding this piece of paper a hundred years from now—then it comes to me. I smile and write one word, big enough to cover the whole page:

HELLO

I fold the paper in half, tuck it inside my dress, and start walking, looking for someplace safe. Someplace nobody goes.

Where?

The pantry where I've been doing my secret writing by candlelight? No—too many pairs of eyes going in and out of there during the day, too many hands searching through the shelves and cupboards.

I close my eyes, and my mind flies up like a bird looking down at Thornwood, all its walls and rooftops and towers, all its twists and turns like a maze or a puzzle.

Then I see it in my mind —iron bars bent like tree branches and a glint of glass. The greenhouse! It was half-dead when I got here, empty and neglected, and it's sure to be the same now.

I go through the kitchen door and walk all the way around to the back of the building. And there it is, sitting on its own like something strange that fell from the sky, all its little panes of glass catching the last of the evening sun.

I'm worried it's locked, but the door opens easily at my touch, and I step inside.

The air here smells of old dirt and living things left alone too long. That smell of dirt makes something turn over in my mind. I'm suddenly walking through the plowed field with my Da, big clods of earth rolling under my little shoes, enough to make me trip and fall if it wasn't for his big, warm hand holding onto mine.

Then I'm kneeling in the rows of fresh-turned earth. Da hands me a plug of potato, the green, knotty shoots already breaking through the rough, gray skin. *Put it there,* he says. *Right there.* I lay the plug in the deep groove in the ground. It looks lost and unprotected. *Now cover it.* I reach down, scoop the cool black dirt with my small white hands, and cover the potato. It's like I'm tucking it in so it can be warm and dream nice potato dreams. I know what happens next, and I want to see it.

How long? I ask my Da. *How long before it grows?*

Not long. His bright white teeth flash at me from the dark thicket of his beard. *Too long to stand here and wait for it.*

I don't want to wait, I tell him.

I know, he says, his voice even gentler than before. *I know you don't. But sometimes you have to. Sometimes waiting is the only way.* His big hand comes to rest on the top of my head, warming me.

Patience, Mary, he says. *A little patience is a good thing.*

I feel the pull inside my chest, the struggle between the person I am and the person he wants me to be. I scoop the last of the dirt over the little mound I've made and pat it down. Then I stand up and brush the dirt from my knees.

Good, he says. *You did well, Mary.*

The last of the evening sun streams through the glass in the greenhouse roof, making this place look like a church, just as still and quiet.

I walk along the rows of long tables bearing clay pots that hold the remains of twisted plants, dead or dying, until I reach the far end. A wall of drawers and cupboards all made of tin, I'm glad to see. Nothing to rot or fall apart.

I go down on my knees and open one of the bottom drawers—empty. Good. Then I wonder. Might someone come back here and find it before Anne can? A hundred years is a long time.

I pull hard on the drawer until it comes out of the wall and clatters to the floor. I take the paper out and lay it gently where the drawer was. I pick up the drawer and carefully slide it back in, covering the paper like it was never there.

I look up at all the iron and glass around me. This place is built to last, to keep the elements out for years and years to come.

I stand up, dust off my knees, and walk out into the evening air, trying to hold back the big smile that wants to spread across my face.

It's going to work. I know it.

I've done well.

Chapter 40 - Annie

I'm emptying the trash. For a small house, there are so many trashcans. The one from Dad's office is nearly empty but rattles when I lift it. Inside are pens, ten or twenty of them. The kind Dad likes, with the skinny felt tip.

I show it to him. "Dad, what's all this? You killed a lotta pens…"

He looks into the can and then turns away from me. "Switching to pencil," he holds up the one in his hand and finally looks at me with a goofy grin. Even as I watch, the grin breaks up, and his face falls into something sad, something I don't recognize. "I had to stop it somehow." He looks down at his hands.

"Stop what?"

He shakes his head. "The, um, compulsion, I guess. To write everywhere."

Fear seizes my chest. I look around his office, but the walls are empty.

"I haven't yet. Don't worry," he tells me with a lifeless laugh. "Pencils seemed like a good idea." He goes back to writing, so I leave the office.

I don't know what to do with the pens, so I stash them in a drawer in my room and wait for Mom to come home. Surely it's a good thing he noticed he's taking steps to help himself, isn't it?

When Mom gets home, she notices right away. "What's wrong?" Her voice is firm and should reassure me, but her eyes are worried. I gesture toward my room, and she follows me inside and closes the door.

"Dad's worried about writing on the walls. He threw away all his pens. Said he's switching to pencil."

"He told you this?"

"I found the pens. In the trash."

She's quiet for several moments. Then, "But he said that? About being afraid?"

"He called it *the compulsion.*"

She takes a few steps around the room before stopping in front of me and pulling me into a hug. "I'm sorry. I'll talk with him." Again, her voice reassures me, the confidence there, but after she leaves my room, I can hear her sigh.

I go back to my chores. When I'm done, Dad is cooking, and Mom is setting the table; all normal. After we eat, but before we clear the table, Mom takes my hand and says, "How would you like to come with us tomorrow to see your dad's doctor?"

Dad takes my other hand. "We want you to be part of this. Part of…" He gestures with his other hand but doesn't continue.

"Part of your dad getting better," Mom fills in.

"Okay," I say. "But nobody gets angry this time, okay?"

I look at Mom and she looks down. I look at Dad and he gives me a grin.

"Agreed."

The doctor—Dad calls him *Doc O.*—is all smiles when he sees us, quickly moving files off one of the chairs so we can all sit. He shakes our hands one at a time and his fingers are small and damp.

"Welcome. Welcome. So glad you could all come today." He moves back behind his desk and sits, folding his hands together and blinking at us. "So," he says, "How's it going?"

Dad clears his throat. He's smiling, and I see he's holding Mom's hand. "Great. Good. I love the carriage house. Deceptively roomy."

Doc O. nods and smiles but says nothing.

"I think we're getting close," Dad says, leaning forward and smiling. "I reached a relative of Mary Donovan's stepson who said she'll look in her attic. Says she has–"

I look up to see Mom's hand on Dad's arm. "We're not here to talk about that," she says, looking at the doctor. "We want to know if…if you should be adjusting Jack's treatment."

The doctor blinks at her. "We can, of course. What is it you're concerned about?"

She looks down for a moment, then at Dad. He speaks. "I'm, uh," he looks at Mom. "I guess…jittery. Anxious. Writing too much."

Doc O. leans forward. "Too much?"

Dad puts up his hand. "No walls. Just paper. But I can see it sometimes, the writing on the walls. And...it makes sense to me."

"How about sleep? Are you sleeping well?"

Before Dad can speak, Mom says, "No. He's up several times in the night. Sometimes going to his office to work."

Why didn't I know this?

"Are you taking the sleep medication I gave you?"

Dad looks down, shakes his head. "I was, but it made me too groggy. Took hours each morning before I could do much of anything."

The doctor studies him for several moments and then turns to me. "How about you, young lady? Is there anything about Dad that concerns you?"

Young lady? I didn't trust him before and don't trust him now. But I say, "I found a bunch of pens."

"Pens?"

"Good ones he'd thrown away." Why are they making me do this? "He told me he switched to pencil."

The doctor turns to Dad, "Did you tell her why?"

Dad nods slowly, sheepishly. "The work, it's going so well. I didn't want to stop and call you. But yeah, I didn't want to damage the property." Everybody's silent, and Dad says, "Do you think it'll hurt the project? My being… this way? Will it damage the veracity of my reports?"

The doctor's face goes gray for just a second. "Of course not." It sounds like bullshit to me. "As long as you can back up your hypothesis. If you have evidence, that's all we need."

Relief pours over Dad's face. "That's great, Doc. Thanks."

"But…" the doctor continues, "I'm going to change your medication and see if that reduces your compulsions. And you have to take a sleeping aid until you can sleep on your own. I'll have you try something that might make you less groggy."

On our way home, I can't stop thinking about the proof Dad needs. I don't have to look at the calendar to know how little time we have.

At home, I follow him into his office. "Reporting for duty," I say, giving a weak salute.

Dad studies me for a moment like he's forgotten something before smiling. "That's great, but I don't need you right now. Have some calls to make, okay?"

"Sure." I leave his office, closing his door quietly.

All this time, I've been acting like the solution to everything is saving Thornwood. What if we can't? What happens then?

I picture Mary in the cemetery, The way she asked what she could do for me. How important it was to her. To be able to help me.

We can't stop now.

The ride to the cemetery is familiar now, like I've been coming here for months instead of weeks. And Mary, her pale, freckled face, dark hair, eyes that could burn steel; she's so clear in my memory that it takes a moment for me to realize I'm actually seeing her, standing in our magic circle, waiting for me.

I've never been so happy to see someone in my life. She looks excited, so I know it's done. She's found a place.

"Hey," I say, breathless.

There are two spots of color on Mary's cheeks, and her eyes glitter. "How's it goin'?"

I want to laugh. I want to shout, *Where is it? Where'd you hide it?* But all I say is, "Good," and grin.

We stand there grinning at each other as the silence of the place fills my ears. I listen for traffic, for birds, for wind, but I hear nothing.

"Well?" she says suddenly, crossing her arms and glaring at me.

"You found a place."

"Yes!" She nods vigorously and crosses over to me, "You'll never guess where. It's so perfect." Her eyes shine.

"Where? Where did you pick?"

She shakes her head. "Guess."

"Really?!" But her face is so animated, her eyes lively. When was the last time she played a game with someone? "Okay…the kitchen?"

"Nope, too busy."

"The laundry room?"

"No."

"The waiting room."

"Nah. I found a better place."

"Where?"

"No more guesses?" She sounds disappointed, but she doesn't wait for me. "The greenhouse!"

"What greenhouse?"

Her face falls. "The one behind the building, next to the barn. Don't you know what I'm talking about?"

What barn? "Okay. I haven't been there. Behind the building. So, there's a greenhouse?"

"Yes!" She's shining again, her face bright and happy. "And the cabinets and things are made of tin. Not going anywhere. Not like wood."

A greenhouse! I imagine it, several panes broken but still intact, just waiting for me to find what Mary left me.

"*Where* inside? How will I find it?"

She grins. "There's only the one door. Inside, go all the way to the back. On your left, almost to the back wall, is a table with drawers. D'you follow?"

I nod, picturing myself walking into the building, an iron framework rising against the sky. "Which drawer?"

"The bottom one."

I frown. "What if someone looks there?"

She puts her hands on her hips, "Do you think I'm daft? Take the drawer all the way out. I left it underneath."

"It's brilliant!" I go to hug her, but she side-steps me.

"None of that." She's smiling, though. "I thought it a good place."

"It's a very good place," I say.

"Alright then, go on," she urges. "I'll wait."

"Wait? For what?" Then I understand—she wants me to go there now. She's just as impatient as I am! "What if it doesn't work?" I say. "I mean, what if you're not here when I get back?"

Her mouth screws up, but she says, "Then I guess I'll have to come tomorrow."

I nod, itching to see if it worked. Afraid to go.

"Well," she says, "What are you waiting for?"

I head out of the cemetery directly toward the old building. I veer left so I can approach it from behind, but as I draw near, I see barriers and work trucks, men wearing hard hats, standing around smoking. One of them is holding paper and gesticulating. No one seems to be working.

I can't see past their trucks and piles of building material, so I walk up the hill and look for a way around it all, but fencing rises up and blocks my way.

"Hey. Hey you!" A voice behind me shouts, and I turn around. "Can't you read?" There's a man a few yards away, standing between me and the parking lot and gesturing toward a 'no trespassing' sign.

"Sorry," I say, hurrying past him, cursing that I've been seen.

How am I going to find Mary's hiding place now?
I go back to the cemetery to let Mary know.
But the circle is empty.

Chapter 41 - Annie

Back home, I find Mom staring at the invitation list for the fundraiser, and she doesn't look happy.

"You'd think they'd never had a fundraiser before," she complains. "No politicians, only a couple of doctors… What were they thinking? And anyone who might have a relative in that cemetery. I *told* them to go after those people…"

"The invitations came out good," I say, holding up the glossy cardboard tri-fold. The outside is a black and white sketch of the original Thornwood. The folds in the front meet at the door, and when you flip it open, the inside is brilliant with greens and blues, a painting of the grounds with Thornwood rising above it, red brick and white wood shining. "Who did the painting?"

Mom's still staring at the list. "Mabel Humphries, a local. There are fifty accepts, and you know only half will show up. All this for twenty-five people!" She throws down the list.

"What about a lottery?" I say. "I know it's a fundraiser, but what if you offer it to the town? Buy a ticket, get one free?"

Mom frowns at me for a moment, then smiles. "You have something there." She reaches for her phone. "But first, the deep pockets." She presses a number on her phone, then says, "Brenda? I'm sending you a list to invite, but your people need to call your representatives, anybody with a connection, local, state, and federal. Make sure they understand how this can impact their voting base." She smiles at me, listening. "Everybody's busy. So let me ask you…how important is this to you?" She nods a bit, her smile disappearing, then reappearing more broadly. "Of course. Great. And another idea, my daughter's actually. Offer buy one get one free tickets to the town. We'll need locals for the video telling the world why this is important. The list I'm sending is people who may have relatives buried in that cemetery. Former patients." She pauses, then shakes her head, "I know, I know, but there's a flip side to guilt. And if they see what we're trying to do… Check your email for that list…"

She hangs up, looking happier than I've seen her in a while. "It's good to have a plan."

"What can I do?"

"You think your boss would let us put up a sign?"

"I'm not sure. I'll ask."

"Wanna help me design it?"

We spend a little time creating the sign. In the end, it looks fantastic.

Come to the event of the year!

**An immersive theater experience
at Thornwood Asylum!**

Buy one, get one free!

**This offer good for Pineville
residents only.**

**All proceeds will go towards
saving the medical center.**

"Can you keep some of these on hand at the ice cream shop?"

I have no idea, but I nod. "How many posters will you print?"

"How many do you think? Where else can we put this?"

"Everywhere. The library. Diner. Hair cutter."

"That's good," Mom's scribbling them down. "Very good. Can you help?"

"Sure," I say, although the thought of approaching owners in all those places makes me cringe.

"I'll start with thirty." She presses a few keys on her computer. "Done." Then she leans back in her chair. "They should be ready in an hour."

Mom drops me off at work after picking up the posters from the local print shop. I take one and a handful of invitations inside the ice cream shack.

"Morning," Daphne says, counting out money.

"Mom wants to know if we can put this up." I unroll the poster.

"Cool!" Daphne reads the text. "That's the fundraiser, right? How much are tickets?"

I pull out the invitation. "$75."

"Ouch."

"But that includes finger food and the show. It's really cool, what she's doing. A different experience in each room at Thornwood, ending in the cemetery. From the viewpoint of patients through the years. You gotta come."

"Too steep for me."

"Even if you split it with someone? $37.50 for a show and food?"

"Hmmm…" She looks at the poster again. "Maybe. Then she opens the door and steps outside. "Let's find a place for this."

We post the flyer next to the daily specials, and people comment on it throughout the day. Not all the comments are positive. One woman with dyed red hair frowns at it, and I hear her talking to her friend, "These people don't know what they're doing. The development will bring in jobs, increase money to the schools…"

I have arguments ready, but Daphne beats me to it.

"Really?" Daphne says. "That old *jobs and schools* thing? What about the jobs we'll *lose?* Ninety percent of the people working at the medical center live here in Pineville. Not just doctors and nurses. Maintenance crews, cleaners, receptionists."

"Development creates jobs…" the woman tries to interrupt, but Daphne's not having it.

"Yeah, but for who? It's one thing to promise jobs, another to come through. My uncle told me about the development near him over in Framingham. Townsfolk weren't *qualified* for most of the jobs offered, so those jobs went to people outside the community."

"That doesn't…" the woman starts, but Daphne keeps going.

"You want to talk about the schools? Look at the proposals posted by the town. You'll see Pineville offered a big fat tax *break* to the developers. That's not *more* money for the schools. That's *less.*"

The woman harrumphs a little, but I can see Daphne's words taking hold, doubt seeping past the righteousness.

"Oh yeah," Daphne adds, "And speaking of the schools, most of the high school students here get their community service credits volunteering at that hospital. You think they can get that from Walmart?"

The woman is silent now. She stares at the poster as her ice cream drips down her hand. Daphne hands her a wad of paper napkins.

"Here, sweetheart," Daphne smiles. "You're dripping." The woman takes the napkins, mutters thanks, and heads back to her car.

"Oh my God," I laugh. "You *smoked* her!"

"Yeah, well I'm thinking of going for a double major," Daphne says, scooping out another cone. "Economics and poly sci. My mom's big on knowing what you're voting for. Having a voice. So…I read things."

The next day, when I wake up, the weather's worsened.

"Raining?!" I moan, pouring granola into a bowl and watching sheets of water stream down the windows. I picture the construction barriers behind Thornwood, how wet and muddy it will be.

Then I realize—the workers will be gone! There'll be no one to stop me from getting into that greenhouse this time.

"I can drive you," Mom says. "I have a meeting in town anyway."

I look up in shock. How does she know where I'm going? Then I remember I'm supposed to work today. "Damn. I forgot. Do I have to go? No one's going to be out buying ice cream in this."

Mom looks out the window for a moment before smiling a little. "You're probably right, but yes, you have to go. A job is a commitment. You know that."

My eyes start to roll, but I manage to stop them. My shift isn't that long. And maybe the rain will stop soon. Then I can go look for what Mary's hidden.

There's no one at the ice cream shack when we arrive, but Daphne comes screeching in and parks behind the shack. The passenger side window of her car is covered in clear plastic and flaps in the wind. She gets out and dashes for the door, waving me in.

"See ya later," I tell Mom, grabbing my backpack and launching myself out of the car.

Daphne shakes out her hair and hangs up her rain poncho. "Nice day."

"Yeah. What happened to your window?"

"It's stuck. My brother promised he'll look at it."

"Must be nice."

"What?"

"Having a mechanic for a brother."

She frowns for a moment, then stares at me. "You're an only?"

I nod.

"You have no idea," she shakes her head. "Frank and me, when we're not fighting, we don't speak. Water and oil." She looks out at the empty lot.

"I used to beg for a sister," I say. "I thought we'd be best friends. But my folks were too busy, didn't make enough money, blah blah blah."

"So you asked for a dog, right?"

I nodded. "After the pony idea didn't fly. Ended up with a cat, though!"

"Sweet! Got pics?"

I pull out my phone and scroll to some pictures of Gremlin.

Daphne takes the phone and scrolls through them. "He's a cutie, all right." She suddenly stops scrolling. "Where the hell is this?"

I take my phone and look. It's the cemetery at Thornwood, a picture I took of the graves where Mary stood. "It's nothing. Just a place I fou—"

"I know this place," she grabs my phone. "That park by the hospital… something Pines, right? Where they buried all those people."

"Yeah." I manage to take back my phone and shove it in my pocket. "Kinda cool."

"Kinda creepy, you mean." She gives me the once-over like I'm a science specimen. "I'm pretty sure my great-great aunt is there."

"What?"

"Everybody in town's got someone in there. And the records suck, so nobody knows who's buried where." She pulls out the cash drawer and starts counting bills. "Can you imagine being dumped there when you had family in town that could have taken care of you?" She closes the cash drawer with a slam and glares at me. "Why did you go there?"

"I'm sorry. I don't know. I wanted to be alone."

"Well, guess what. You're not alone there."

The bitterness of her words sting.

"Look, I'm sorry," Daphne says. "I got a little hot, I know. It just bugs me what those people went through, and nobody cares. Kids go to the cemetery to get high all the time. I hate it." She grabs clean scoops and puts them on the counter. "I heard the Boy Scouts cleaned it up."

I picture the thick layer of pine needles and ivy covering the ground and wonder how long ago that was, but I say nothing.

"This town," she says, shaking her head. "We have a lot to make up for." She looks at me. "Can your Dad save the property?"

"Yeah, we're working on it. I think he'll have something soon."

"I hope so. Last thing we need is another mall." After a moment she says, "Have you been to the old building?"

I'm so grateful she's no longer angry, I blurt, "Yeah, it's amazing. And creepy. That box…"

She sits up, "The Box! Do they still show that thing? Do they let you go inside?"

I shake my head. "But I did anyway. When everyone was in another room."

"That was brave. Or stupid. What was it like?"

I remember the words scratched into the door. *Help me Anne.* "Terrifying."

"The school sends kids every year," she says. "We went in 6th grade. The box was locked. But Frank told me that in his time, it was open, and kids were always locking other kids inside, making them scream. There was a greenhouse too…"

"What?!"

"Yeah, beautiful place. Most of the glass was gone. I knocked out a few panes." She mimes pitching. "Good arm."

"What… what was it like?"

"There were benches and cabinets, bits of old pots. Great for hide-n-seek."

I remember Mary's words. *On your left, almost to the back wall, a table with drawers.* I picture myself leaning down, pulling out the drawer…

"Maybe I'll check it out." I look outside, "If this rain ever stops."

"It's gone."

"What's gone?"

"The greenhouse. Demolished. A few years back. They put a wall around it, but someone's kid got hurt, so they tore it down. Hey, are you okay? You look like you lost your best friend or something…"

I look away and try to pull myself together. I can see Mary's face so plainly, the excitement there. *Do you think it'll work?* So much hope. All gone.

A loud banging makes both of us jump. Someone's at the

window. Daphne slides it open.

"Good morning, Mrs. Petrie. The usual?"

Chapter 42 - Mary

On my way to the graveyard, I try to quell the fluttering in my stomach, but I can't. When I get to our spot in the woods, that girl, Anne, is already there waiting. The closer I get, I can tell something's wrong. It's the look on her face, all tense and worried.

"Did you go?" I ask her. "Did you find it?"

"No," she says. "It's gone."

"Are you sure? Did you look under the drawer like I said?"

"No," she shakes her head, "I mean the greenhouse. It's gone. The whole thing. They tore it down."

"Jesus…" All that iron and glass, gone. I can't believe it. "So, we just think of another place, right? One they're not gonna tear down."

"There's the building," she says, "It's still there."

"Listen," I say, "You've been inside the place, right? What are some of the places you've seen?"

"Well…" she frowns, "There's this long hallway…"

You can't hide something in a fucking hallway, I almost say, then think better of it.

"There's a kitchen," she says, "And…and a laundry room…"

"No," I say. "Too many people. And all that water. We need someplace no one's gonna bother."

"Then…there's this fancy room I saw once. With an antique desk and big bookshelves full of old books. The doctor's office…"

"*Blackwell's* office? You've been there?" It's strange to think of this girl nosing around in there, standing where I've stood. "You sure it was *his* office you were in?"

"Yeah. It's even got this big, scary-looking painting of him hanging on the wall…"

"That ugly thing? It's still there?"

"Yeah. Right there in the middle of the room. Kind of feels like it's watching you…"

I think of it, the portrait of that bastard, still hanging in the same spot all these years. Then a thought comes into my head, a wild, crazy thought. A laugh bursts from my mouth. I raise my hand to stop it but I can't, and soon I'm laughing harder.

"What?" Anne asks. "What's so funny?"

I take a few deep breaths before I can get the words out. "Oh Jesus…fucking hell…it's too good. It's too fucking good…"

"*What's* too good?"

"The painting," I say. "What if I hide it in *there?*"

"In the painting? How?"

"In back, you know. *Behind* the painting, inside the frame! My Aunt Bridget, she used to hide money inside this old picture of her grand da…Oh fucking hell, it's too good…" and another wave of wild laughter carries me away. It must be contagious because I see Anne's eyes brighten, and now she's laughing too.

"Are you serious? Oh my God…oh Mary…you've *got* to do it!" She stops laughing, and a serious, practical look comes over her face again. "We've got to test it first."

"I'm going there today," I say. "The presentation, the one I told you about. It's tonight. Blackwell wants me in his office at noon. I'll hide it while I'm there."

"How? How are you going to do it if he's there too?"

"I don't know. I'll think of something…" I look up at the daylight growing brighter through the trees above. "I've got to go," I say. "Meet me back here tomorrow. Let me know if it works."

She nods. "Be careful," she says. Then, "Good luck."

I wonder, *is she wishing me luck with hiding the note?* Or with the presentation tonight? I can't ask because I'm already walking out of the trees into the open field. When I see how high the sun is, I start running.

"Where have you been?"

Blackwell glares at me when I enter his office. He looks different. He's always looked a little dressed up to me, but now he looks like some kind of fancy gentleman with a long black dress coat, and that white kerchief I see sticking out of his breast pocket has got to be silk.

"Did I not explain to you how important tonight is?" He's angry at me for being late, but something else in his voice is new to me. He's nervous. It tickles me. The great Doctor Blackwell, nervous.

"What are you smiling about?" he asks. Before I can wipe the smile from my face, he continues. "The matrons will be here shortly to prepare you for the presentation. Before they arrive, I want to review our itinerary so you'll know what's expected of you. Once you are dressed and ready, you will be taken to a carriage and escorted to the theater."

"By you?"

"No, of course not. I will be traveling in a separate carriage. One of the matrons will ride with you." Nervous as I am, something relaxes inside of me. I don't like the matrons, but sharing a three-hour carriage ride with Blackwell is something I'm glad not to be doing.

"When you arrive at the theater, you will be escorted inside, where you will wait backstage. First, the Chairman of the Massachusetts Association of Hospitals for the Insane will make a few introductory remarks. I will then address the audience. When I am through speaking, I will introduce you. Then you will come out onstage and deliver your speech."

I try to picture it, the blazing hot lights, all those faces out there in the dark.

"When you speak," Blackwell continues, "You will say only the speech as written. You will not depart from the speech or make any extraneous remarks..."

I don't know what *extraneous* means, but I'm guessing he doesn't want me to say anything that will embarrass him.

"What if they ask me something?"

Blackwell looks at me strangely. "Who?"

"One of the people in the audience."

A smile breaks across his face, and I don't like the look of it. "That's not likely to happen," he says.

There's a soft knock at the door. It swings open slowly, and two matrons step inside. One holds the long black dress, cradling it like a sleeping child. The other is carrying a bundle of clean white undergarments and a pair of dress boots.

"Notify me when she is ready," Blackwell says, then turns and practically flees from the room.

The two women stand looking at me for a moment, then take a few careful steps toward me. It almost makes me laugh, their uncertainty. A few months ago, they would have tackled me and thrown me to the ground like a wild animal. Now they don't know what to make of me, of this new thing I've become.

Good, I think. I can use that.

"No!" I shout. They both freeze in their tracks. "I don't need your help. I'm a young lady, not a child. I can dress myself."

They both hesitate and glance at each other, unsure what to do.

"Just leave it all there," I point toward a chair. "Go on, now. *Go on!*" I take one step toward them, and they practically throw the clothes on the floor in their hurry to get out. The two dress boots tumble to the ground with an awkward clumping sound.

I follow close on their heels so they won't think twice and slow down. Once they're outside, I close the door and lock it.

Then I go about my work.

I cross the room and approach Blackwell's portrait, trying not to look up at that hateful face. I reach up, take hold of the thick, gold-painted frame, and lift it from the wall. It's heavier than I thought.

I lay the big painting face down on the floor and have a look—thick-looking brown paper fastened to the frame with little iron nails.

I could cut a hole in it, but someone might notice that.

I go over to Blackwell's desk and find a bronze letter opener that looks like a dagger. I drop down on my knees and work the blade's edge under the head of a nail, twisting and prying until it finally comes out—a little bent, but I can still use it. Two more nails out, and now I can slip my hand under the brown paper into the dark space inside.

I reach into my dress and pull out the piece of paper with the single word I've written—HELLO. I slip it inside the painting. Then, as quickly as I can, I put the little nails back into their holes one by one, pressing them in with the hilt of the knife until it looks the same as before.

I hear voices in the hallway, so I pick up the painting and hang it on the wall. I step back to make sure it's not crooked and move it until it looks right.

There's a knock at the door and a woman's voice. The matrons. They're back. And I haven't even dressed yet.

"Give me a minute," I shout at the door, then start pulling off my clothes as fast as I can. The petticoats give me some trouble—it's like trying to pull a circus tent over my head, but somehow I manage. Then the long black dress and all those damn buttons. I'm halfway done with them when I hear that knock again, louder this time.

"Just a minute!" I shout again. I finish the last few buttons, then unlock the door and open it. Both matrons are standing there, their faces flushed and impatient.

"I'm ready," I say, a little out of breath. I see one of them gaze at my feet, a puzzled look on her brow. I know without looking—my feet are bare.

Warm blood rushes to my face. I want to look away and hide it. Instead, I pull myself up straight, lift my chin a little higher, and say the first thing that comes to mind.

"You may help me with my boots."

Chapter 43 - Mary

This carriage rattles my bones. By the time I get to Boston and this fancy theater they're taking me to, my poor backside will be black and blue.

The matron sitting across from me is suffering, too, but she's trying to hide it, her face stiff as a mask. But I can see the veins standing out on her hand as she clutches the door handle, trying like me not to be pitched to the floor.

The beat of the horse's hooves and the bounce and roll of the carriage remind me of that first night when Jamie and I were brought to Thornwood—how many weeks ago? *Funny,* I think. I was brought here in a wagon but never dreamed I'd leave in a carriage.

The woman across from me won't meet my eyes but I catch her glancing at me, running her eyes over the long black dress I'm wearing, with its bright pearl buttons, and the ivory combs in my hair. She doesn't know what to make of me.

After a while, the road beneath us smooths out, and the carriage stops its mad bouncing. I gaze out at the big pine trees passing by in the moonlight. The strangeness of it all hits me—being outside the walls of Thornwood after all this time, dressed like a fine lady. And the grand new life I've been promised by a girl who's not even born yet…

I must have fallen asleep because when I open my eyes, the pine trees and moonlight are gone. Instead, I see great stone buildings all in a row, tall poles with blazing lamps. I see other carriages moving past, more than I've ever seen before, with men and women in fine-looking clothes, top hats, and fur stoles, many of them moving toward one huge building with big, beautiful windows lit up from inside, the glass glowing a golden honey-color.

The coachman takes us past all those fancy people into an alley along the side of the great building, where we finally stop. The matron climbs down from the carriage and stands there waiting for me. "Come on, then," she says, the first words she's spoken to me since we left Thornwood.

I can still feel the carriage rolling and swaying under me when I step down onto the cobblestones. I find my footing and follow the woman to a door that opens to her knock. A man appears, and they exchange a few words. We walk down a long hallway with beautiful woodwork and fancy carpets under our feet. On the walls in gold-painted frames are pictures of important-looking men with high collars and long beards.

We pass through another door, and everything suddenly opens up around us and seems larger. I look around, stunned by what I'm seeing. Rows and rows of seats, hundreds of them, all facing a raised platform with giant red curtains on either side. It's like a church, except there's no Jesus on the cross, no statues or pictures of saints––just shadows and light and a single wooden pulpit.

"You're here." Blackwell's voice echoes from somewhere in the shadows. He steps out from behind the curtain on the left and walks to the edge of the platform, waving one hand for us to come forward. There's a set of wooden stairs at one end of the stage. I pause, then climb up and walk toward him. He peers at me closely, takes off his spectacles and wipes them with his silk kerchief, puts them back on, and looks at me again.

"Well then," he says. "Come. Over here." I follow him to the tall wooden stand. "Here," he says, tapping the stand with one hand. "This is where you will stand. Your speech will be waiting for you here. You won't need to hold the pages, so your face will not be covered, and the audience will be able to hear you."

And see you. I recall the way he looked at me a moment ago when I first stepped out onstage, his eyes wide and raking over me. I think of that look coming from a hundred pairs of eyes, and for a moment,

I get the urge to run.

"Remember to speak clearly. Loud, but not too loud. And slowly. When you have finished, you will return to your seat and wait until someone comes to get you."

"Where?" I ask. "Where am I to sit?"

Blackwell steps toward the red curtain and pulls it aside. There is a single wooden chair, sitting all alone. "You will sit here until I call for you, then you will return here when you are done."

I hear doors opening and closing somewhere, other voices speaking.

"Come," Blackwell says, taking me by the arm and guiding me to the chair behind the curtain. "Sit here until I call for you."

I sit down and he leaves me there. The voices I heard before are louder and closer. I hear Blackwell talking with someone, a man, maybe two men, on the other side of this curtain, though what they're saying, I can't tell.

This chair feels hard and uncomfortable, and I realize I have to piss. I wonder if I can hold it, but I feel like I might explode, so I get up and go looking for a place to relieve myself.

It's dark back here, so I have to go by touch, my hands getting tangled in long ropes, my feet blundering into things I can't see. Finally, my hands find a door-latch. I twist it and push, and cool night-air pours in.

I step outside and find myself in a narrow alley. I see no one, so I walk a ways and hitch up the long dress. It takes forever to wrestle with the giant petticoat and bloomers, but I finally manage and squat down.

Then a chill goes up my spine. Someone else is here. Watching me.

I look around and see a woman standing at one end of the alley, close enough for me to see her gaunt face and ragged clothes. She's standing by a pile of trash she must have been digging through—there's still some of it in her hands. The look on her face is part shock, part amusement.

"Jesus…" I hear her say, and in her voice, *Jaysus,* I can immediately tell where she's from. "Well, I never! Fine lady like yourself. Having a piss in the street…" She cocks her head to one side like a curious bird and takes a step closer. "What's the matter, darling? Did you get locked out? Or did they *put* you out?"

I stand up quick as I can, straighten the bloomers and petticoat, and tug the long dress back into place. I don't say a word—the moment I open my mouth, she'll know what I really am. Her curious smile starts to fade, and she takes another step toward me.

"Where did you get that dress…?"

I turn and walk quickly back inside the building and pull the door shut behind me. I stand there in the dark with my hand holding tight to the latch, waiting for it to twist and shake, but it doesn't.

When I'm sure the woman outside has gone away, I let go of the door handle and walk back to my chair behind the curtain. I wonder if they've missed me, but there's no one there looking for me, no Blackwell glaring, demanding to know where I've been. Just that bare wooden chair, all alone.

I sit down and wait. It's begun, I can tell. There's a man's voice on the other side of the curtain, speaking loudly, saying a load of things I only half-understand. Blackwell's next, I remember.

Then me.

Who do you think you are? It's Aunt Bridget's voice, all the times she said that to me. *Who do you think you are.* It's the kind of question asked by someone who thinks they know the answer.

It comes over me again, the sense that none of this is real, that the whole thing is some kind of dream I'm going to wake up from. But this chair is real underneath me, and this dress binds me tight like a fist squeezing the breath out of me. That's real. I reach up with one hand and touch my fingers to my cheek. That's real, too.

Who do I think I am?

I am Mary Donovan. Daughter of Martin Donovan of Ulster

County. Sister of Jamie Donovan. Prisoner at Thornwood, but not forever. I am more than all of that. I am the girl who speaks with angels. I am the girl who goes on to write books and make speeches, and change laws to protect people like myself. I am ready. Ready to set the future in motion.

Blackwell is talking. I can hear his hateful voice droning on from the other side of the curtain.

"...humane conditions and physical improvements for the comfort and safety of the men and women under our care..."

Comfort and safety? I'd laugh out loud if I didn't want to scream.

"...but these are merely the externals," Blackwell drones on, "The pot in which the flower is planted. For the flower to blossom and flourish, it is the plant itself that must be tended to and nourished..."

I choke back a laugh. So I'm a plant now, am I? A flower? I wonder what kind of flower he thinks I am.

"The subject who you are about to meet," Blackwell says, "is a very different individual today than when she first came under our care. Uncooperative. Uncontrollable. Violent. The kind of patient who, just a few years ago, would have been put away and clapped in irons. Instead, we have provided her with every advantage. Freedom, fresh air. Exercise for the improvement of her body. Fine books to read for the improvement of her mind. But enough. Allow me to bring her out before you now so that she may speak for herself."

A hand, Blackwell's hand, pulls back the curtain a little. A harsh white light shines into my face. I rise up and walk toward it.

Blackwell steps away from the wooden pulpit. I stand behind it, gripping its edges. In front of me I can only see those bright white lights blazing like two suns in the dark. I can't see the people behind them, thank God, but I know they're out there, watching and waiting. I can smell them, too, the traces of ladies' perfume and the lingering scent of cigar smoke clinging to gentlemen's clothes.

In front of me are the handwritten pages Blackwell has left for me to read. Just two pages in his tiny, crabbed hand. I've been over it with him so many times now, I can say it with my eyes closed.

"Ladies and gentlemen," I begin, my voice strange and ghostly-sounding in this huge place. "My name is Mary Donovan, and I thank you for the opportunity to address you this evening. My thanks to the Association of Massachusetts Hospitals. Most of all, my thanks to Doctor Jonathan Blackwell, without whose expert guidance and support, I would not be standing here today…"

A wave of sickness rises up inside me for a moment, and I have to pause and swallow it back down. Do they think I'm moved by these words? Overwhelmed with gratitude toward my great mentor? The thought of it makes me want to laugh, and for a terrible moment, I almost do.

"Under the care of Doctor Blackwell and his skilled and compassionate staff, I have made significant improvements, both in my symptoms and in my quality of life. But that was not always the case…"

I look down at the page in front of me, and the tightness in my stomach starts to relax because I see them coming, those words that moved me so much before, the words that are not his.

"Imagine, if you will, the worst moment you have ever experienced, when anger, sadness, or depression rise up and threaten to drown you. Imagine that moment lasting a full hour, then for two hours. Now imagine it lasting for an entire day, or a month, or a year. Then, perhaps, you can imagine what life was like for me, and for others like me, for whom peace and hope and happiness seem forever out of reach…"

The words have me by the throat again. They're an island of truth in an ocean of lies, and they give me the strength to do what I do next.

I reach into the top of my dress and pull out the folded piece of paper I've been keeping there. I unfold it, smooth it out in front of me, look down at my handwriting, and begin to read.

"They say that people like me, people like us, are not important. The people with money, people who can tell other people what to do, they think they're the important ones, because no one is looking down at them. But if you take away their money, what happens to them? Now they're not so important anymore. Real importance isn't like that. It's not something you can buy or take away. Either everyone is important, or no one is."

I reach the end of my page. My heart is pounding louder than ever. I go on and say the last few words Blackwell has written for me to bring this thing to an end, but I barely hear them. I'm remembering what my Da once told me, that just one lie can spoil a hundred truths. I'm wondering if for once, just this once, it might work the other way, too.

I've come to the end of it. There's a change in the room, a change in the air. A silence so deep I could fall into it. I hear a sound I don't recognize at first, a sharp slapping sound joined by another, then another, until it sounds like a hard rain pattering down. The sound of hands clapping. I don't quite know what to make of it, and I just stand there, letting it wash over me.

A hand grips my arm, Blackwell's hand, guiding me away from the pulpit, out of the light, and back into the shadows. He steps back to the pulpit and says a few more words to the audience—mostly about himself, I notice. There's that sound of hands clapping again. A smiling, white-bearded man comes and touches Blackwell on the shoulder and guides him toward the steps at the side of the stage where people are already gathering. Then he turns and smiles at me.

"Miss Donovan…" he says, then points his elbow at me. At first I don't understand what he wants. Then I step toward him and awkwardly loop my arm through his. And now we're moving down those steps and into the crowd waiting there, looking up at us with expectant faces.

I see Blackwell standing several feet away, deep in conversation with three large men in fancy suits. He's working very hard to hold their attention, waving his hands around to make some kind of point, drawing pictures in the air.

The nice man with the white beard lets go of my arm, and now I'm just floating free in this crowd of wealthy-looking strangers. Some of them catch my eye, smile and nod. Others carefully look away. Like everyone, I suppose, they're not sure what to make of me.

I notice a man and woman standing nearby, looking at me closely. Unlike the rest of this crowd, they're both dressed in plain, drab-looking clothes, all brown and gray. The man wears a black broad-brimmed hat, and the woman's head is covered with a plain-looking bonnet. It's she who steps closer to me and smiles.

"That was a fine speech thee made, Mary Donovan."

Up close, I can see she wears no jewelry, ribbons or lace anywhere, but I can tell that her clothes are made of fine material, probably silk and satin. "My name is Dorothy Allen," she says, then nods toward the man at her side. "My husband, Richard Allen." The man nods respectfully but doesn't remove his hat. "How long has thee been under Doctor Blackwell's care?"

"A month or two," I say.

"And where did thee take thy schooling?"

Her words are strange to me, and I need to think for a moment to guess her meaning. When I understand what she's asking, the blood rises to my face. She sees what her question has done, then smiles again, the gentlest smile I've ever seen. "No matter, then," she says. "It was a very fine speech. Thee speaks my mind, Mary Donovan." They both smile and nod, then disappear into the rest of the crowd, two plain birds mingling with a flock of colorful ones.

Blackwell takes hold of my arm again. "Those people," he says in a low voice, "What were you doing talking with them?"

"They came over to me," I say. "They wanted to talk to me." Blackwell sniffs as if he doesn't believe me. "Are they Quakers?" I ask. I've heard the name before, heard stories, but I've never seen one.

"Yes," Blackwell says, peering into the crowd like he's trying to catch a glimpse of them.

"Are they poor?"

"Poor?" Blackwell sniffs. "They're more wealthy than anyone here. What did they say to you?"

"They said they liked my speech."

"*Your* speech…" Blackwell growls under his breath. "What on earth made you…Why did you not do as I told you?"

"I said everything you wanted me to say. Not one word less."

"And everything *you* wanted to say."

"Yes." I look him in the eye. He looks angry, but shaken too.

"Well-well…You're quite the little Quaker yourself, aren't you?"

The man with the white beard is suddenly at our side again. Blackwell twists his face into a smile and talks with him a while. But the crowd is thinning out, and in another minute, I'm being led out to the street and into the carriage that brought me here.

The matron sits across from me again, fixing me with a cold stare. I look her right back in the eye until she turns away. The carriage rattles and sways beneath us, and I look out the window at the tall buildings passing by, all lit up from the inside.

It's already like a dream, but it's one I don't feel quite ready to wake up from yet.

Chapter 44 - Annie

I'm walking as fast as I can toward the museum. Even though I know it's closed, I can't stay away.

Did she do it? Was Mary able to do what she promised?

As I walk up the driveway, I see two men walking toward me. One of them is Dad. The other man is Dan Michaels. They look angry and don't notice me right away.

"Dad?"

He looks up and frowns before smiling. "Hey. What are you doing here? Did your mom send you?"

"Nope. Just walking. Why are you here?"

His face grows dark. "I had to show Dan what those bastards are doing."

Dan puts a hand on his arm, looking at me. "Let's go back to my office. I'm sure Annie isn't interested."

Annie is very interested. "What's going on?"

"They're starting demolition. There's a ban on work until mid-August, but they've started anyway."

A chill rips through me and I start to shake. "Where?"

Dan answers, "They're starting with one of the outbuildings. Originally used as the women's ward."

"But…how can they? Can't you stop it?"

"I'm heading downtown to do just that," Dan says. "They claim it's a public safety issue, building could collapse at any time."

"Bullshit," Dad says.

Dan looks at him before saying, "I'll let the County building office and state police decide that. We'd better go, Jack."

"Don't go around back," Dad warns me. "That's where the

demo's going on. You could get hurt."

"I won't." But of course, the minute he and Dan drive away, I head around the building to the back.

There are more workmen than before, all hanging out like they're on break. Huge yellow tractors are at the edge of a half-demolished building, some with buckets, some with drills. In front of them is a pile of cracked wood and brick.

There's a great groan of creaking wood, and someone shouts, "Watch out!" The workers closest to the pile leap up and run backward as part of the nearest wall gives way. I can't take my eyes away. It happens so slowly; first, the middle buckles, then the top half starts to fall. When it hits the pile, debris flies up and scatters, some of it pinging off the hardhats of the nearest men. A dust cloud follows, spreading up and out and making the building vanish. One of the tractors is partially buried, and for some reason this makes me glad. No one appears hurt, so I slip away before anyone can see me.

My legs are wobbly, and I realize I'm shaking. So that's what happens when they destroy buildings. I can picture Thornwood coming down like this in a cloud of dust, and I shiver.

I've reached the front of the building and look up at the wooden tower and below that, the brick and stonework of the walls. It looks completely stable. But then I imagine a wrecking ball swinging like a great pendulum, knocking a giant hole in the side of the building. I can picture the tower falling slowly to one side, and I shut my eyes.

That's not going to happen. We'll stop it, Mary and I.

Early the next morning, I'm standing at the museum door, waiting for it to open. A woman walks past me, giving me a quick nod and pulls out a set of keys. I recognize her as the tour guide from when Mom and I came. She opens the door and goes inside without another glance at me.

I wait a few moments before following her. The entryway is empty, a placard on a table with the word 'Museum' and an arrow pointing down the hall. Blackwell's office is down there. I picture Mary on her way there to plant her message, and for an instant, I'm afraid. What if she didn't do it? What if she didn't have time?

I hear footsteps and see the tour woman walk out of one room and down the hall from me. I'm pretty sure the room she left is Blackwell's. I hurry as fast as I can without making noise and slip inside.

Lights are on and the curtains are open, but still it is a dark room. The desk is large, dark wood, and looks heavy. I wonder if it was Blackwell's, and take a picture to show Mary later. Behind the desk hangs the portrait.

Blackwell's eyes seem to follow me as I come close as if he's daring me to do this thing I've come to do. I put both hands on the frame to lift it from the wall—then I hear footsteps approaching. I let go of the frame and move quickly to the center of the room, forcing all guilt from my face, hoping I've succeeded.

"Oh," the woman says, stopping and staring at me. "Did you come for a tour?" She doesn't wait for my answer but moves behind the desk and opens a drawer. "There are some people coming at one. You can join that tour if you like."

I shake my head. "I just wanted to look around here. If that's okay."

She frowns, studying me for a moment. "You're Jackson's kid, right?"

I should be used to this by now, but it still takes me by surprise. "You know my Dad?"

She laughs, "Doesn't everybody? He's in here a lot. And I'm on the committee, so I see him in meetings. Annie, right?" I nod.

"Okay then," she continues. "you're free to look around here or any of the front rooms, including the gift shop. I'll be in here if you need anything."

I try to smile, but my stomach is tight. I have to wait till the tour starts. The second she's out with them I can take the picture down.

I look around the room, reading notes under the photographs, studying the various devices in the glass case I remember from last time. I end up staring at Blackwell's portrait, imagining his face in motion. I picture Mary standing before him, taking whatever he's dealing out.

I must have made a sound because the woman says, "Everything okay?"

"Fine. Everything's fine," I say and move down the hall into the gift shop with the requisite mugs and tee-shirts with an image of the building. Above the image are the words 'Thornwood Lunatic Asylum'. *Who the hell would wear that?*

I listen for footsteps, voices, willing the tour people to come. It seems like ages, but I finally hear the door squeal open. There are loud voices and laughter followed by shushing and footsteps.

"Welcome to the Lunatic Asylum! Don't be scared. There's nothing here that can hurt you. I hope…" It's the museum woman. I recognize her spiel from our tour. Same fake scary voice. And the group reacts with the same nervous laughter.

"Go on. Go on!" I say under my breath. Finally, they move down the hall, and my way is clear.

I enter Blackwell's office quickly and close the door. I cross to the painting and lift it off the wall. The desk is covered with various items, so I lay it face down on the carpet. *Lower left corner,* I remember. Then I see the nails. "Damn."

I rush over to the desk, hoping for a screwdriver, but all I find is a metal ruler. I go to the painting and try to pry up the first nail. It doesn't budge, and the corner of the ruler digs a small hole in the paper. "Fuck!"

Moving more slowly, I try again. This time, the nail comes out. Two more and I should be able to see if there's anything here.

My heart is beating erratically now. The next nail is easier, but the last one is a bear. I manage not to tear the paper, but the ruler starts bending. I get under the nail head with my fingers, and one of my fingernails breaks, but the nail loosens, and I'm able to pull it out.

I sit and stare at the paper, old and brown, very brittle, and realize I'm terrified. What if there's nothing here? I know someone could find me here any moment, that I have no time to waste, but now that I'm ready to lift the paper and look inside, I can't do it. My arm and hand won't comply.

I finally break the paralysis and lift the corner of the paper. I instantly see it, a yellowed and brittle rolled up piece of paper. Real. Tears are forming in my eyes, but I have to see. I pull it out and carefully unroll it.

A single word in pencil.

HELLO.

Oh, Mary!

I stand outside the ice cream shack, facing a surprised Daphne.

"What happened?" She asks, staring at me.

"What do you mean?" I wonder if she can tell I've been crying. Everything after reading Mary's note is a blur. I somehow closed up the painting and hung it, left Thornwood, and came here.

"You look… happy."

I laugh. "I am. Very."

"Did you find Mary?"

That stops me. "What?!"

"Mary Donovan. Did you find something to help your dad?"

"How do you know about that?"

My mind twists between the paper with Mary's note in my pocket and the words 'Help your dad.'

"Carson. He came by," she smiles. "Told me what you're working on. I thought maybe you found something."

If you only knew, I think, smiling. "Not yet," I say, remembering what I came here for. "Can I have two cups, two scoops each…" A car door opens behind us and several squealing kids run out and stand behind me.

"Come on in and make it yourself, if you don't mind," Daphne says. "And you should laugh more. It looks good on you."

I slip inside, make the cups with four flavors, put them in a paper bag with two spoons, and leave.

I walk half-running toward the cemetery, hoping Mary's there. As soon as I get close, I can see her pacing. A ripple of excitement courses through me.

"Mary!"

She looks up, frowning, but almost immediately says, "It worked?!"

I nod. I pull out the paper and show it to her. "Yes!"

"Jesus it's old…" She takes it from me, studying the paper, shaking it. Then she looks at me. "Why are you crying?"

I wipe my face with my free hand. "I don't know. Just happy, I guess." *It's going to work out,* I think. *Everything's going to work out.* Then I remember what's in the bag.

"Here." I open the bag, hoping the ice cream is still frozen. I pull out a cup and hand it to her, then I pull out a spoon.

"Ow, it's cold! What is it?" she says, then takes the spoon, looking at it as if it was dangerous.

"Ice cream!" I point to the cup. "Have you ever had it?"

"Ice cream…" she repeats reverently. "Yes, once." She closes her eyes. "It was heaven."

I take out the other cup. "Vanilla, right? Maybe chocolate? Wait till you try these."

"Chocolate ice cream? Is there such a thing?"

"Here," I take the lid off her cup. "This is cookie dough, and this is black raspberry," pointing to each scoop.

"What?" she stares at the ice cream, then again at the spoon. "And whaddya call this? Looks like a spoon, but what kind of spoon is purple and so light?"

I laugh. "Plastic. Try the ice cream!"

She dips the spoon into the black raspberry and brings it to her mouth. Again, her eyes close. "That's sinful, that is," she finally says, opening her eyes and going for another bite. "What's in yours?"

"Chocolate Death and Birthday Cake."

"*Cookie dough, birthday cake!* How can it be ice cream?" Her words slightly garbled around the black raspberry she's now shoveling into her mouth.

"It's vanilla ice cream with bits of chocolate chip cookie dough in it. Didn't you ever eat cookie dough?" She shakes her head and stares at the cup; nothing but a purple puddle where half her ice cream was. "Go ahead, try it."

She dips her spoon and brings it to her mouth. As soon as the spoon leaves her mouth, she frowns and her mouth works. I'm guessing she encountered the cookie dough. She peers into my cup. "Not my cup of tea. You can have it." Her eyes never leave my cup.

"Here," I hand it to her and take her cup. I salute her with my spoon before diving in.

She tries the chocolate first. Again, her eyes close as she holds the ice cream in her mouth. She sighs. "I wish I could bring this to Jamie. Are you sure it would disappear?"

I nod. "Anyway, it's melting already. I'm not sure if it would last."

She stares inside the cup. "Well then. Wouldn't want it to go to waste," and quickly finishes both scoops. "Are there more flavors?"

I nod. "Do you like caramel? Coffee? Or maybe sorbet? Lemon, rainbow?"

"Stop, stop," she's laughing now, holding up a hand. "Coffee? And what the hell is *sore bay*?" Her laughter dies down. "The ice cream was wonderful. Thank you."

Something in her voice moves me. Bringing ice cream was nothing to me, but means so much to her. It makes me want to do more.

Then she stands up straight. "The presentation was last night."

"Wow." I'd forgotten, with all my excitement over finding her note. "How was it?"

"Thrilling." Her face is sober, thoughtful. "I was scared, but it was those words, you know the ones. *Her* words. Just saying those words to a group of people I couldn't see because of the lights, but… I felt them out there, listening…" She stops and stares off into the woods.

"So, it went well?"

She blinks and looks down, a flush creeping into her cheeks. "I did something. Something I wasn't supposed to." She looks up at me, eyes glittering. "The writing you wanted me to do? I did it. And I read it."

"What?"

"They clapped, Anne. They clapped for me." I can see the color rising on her cheeks, her eyes shining.

"Sweet!"

"There was this one couple. Simple clothes, simple manner, but folks treated them with respect. Called themselves 'Friends'. I liked them. The woman was so kind. She told me she liked what I had to say."

Her happiness moves me. I'm proud. Proud to know her.

She smiles wider and, for the first time, takes my hand and squeezes it. "So. What do we do now?"

"How much did you write. Can I see it?"

"Not much yet. It's a few paragraphs. But I'll keep on. I promise." She looks at me closely. "How's your da? Is he okay?"

And just like that, the tightness returns around my heart. I think of Dad, growing angrier every day as the deadline looms. Of Mom, so busy with her production that she doesn't notice. All she wants is an end to our being in Pineville, going home, picking up our lives. She's not thinking about what'll happen to Dad if we can't save Thornwood.

"He's… doing okay. But we need your writing, and soon."

Mary's frowning, studying me. "How much time do I have?"

"For what?"

"To write the thing?"

"Three weeks, give or take. We have to submit it to the historic preservation society before they go on vacation so they can extend the work stoppage. Those developers are chomping at the bit to tear everything down."

"That's it? Three weeks…" She trails off.

If only we had more time… And then it hits me. I may only have three weeks, but Mary has as long as she needs.

"Wait! You don't have to get it done in three weeks. You can take a year or two. However long it takes until you have something to give me. It doesn't matter *when* you hide it."

She's frowning and shaking her head. "I don't know what you're saying."

I catch my breath and start again more slowly. "Let's say you write for eight months."

"Eight months!"

"Or three, say three or four months. You write as much as you want. You sign and date the document and slip it in the painting."

"But they'll be tearing down the building long before then. You said three weeks!"

"I know, but *your* three months, or two years, all of it has already happened. Don't you see? Your future is already my past. In my time, you've already written it all."

"And now I'm dead."

That stops me cold. I look at her face, flushed, eyes full of life. How can she be dead?

I take a deep breath. "What I'm trying to say is that the manuscript will be there, in the painting, the next time I look."

"But it wasn't there when you found my note."

"Because you didn't know to put it there yet. Because we were still testing it. Now that you know, you have plenty of time to write something and hide it there. One month, three months, a year. As long as you need."

"And you'll find it *now*?" she says slowly.

"Yes!"

"And you can come back and tell me. Tell me it worked?"

I hesitate. It makes my head ache. But then I picture Dad's face when I show him the manuscript; other faces, Carson, Mom, that guy Dan Michaels, everyone cheering…

"It'll work," I say. It's got to."

"Okay then. I'd better get down to it," Mary says, turning as if to leave. She turns back. "D'you think you might bring a bit of ice cream again?"

I grin. "Absolutely. Chocolate Death?"

"Chocolate Death."

Chapter 45 - Mary

There's a strange smell in the air today, one that's familiar, but I can't quite place it.

I walk into the main room and see dozens of girls on their knees, scrubbing the floor with wet rags, big buckets of steaming, soapy water at their sides. The matrons stand over them, not lifting a finger, of course. I recognize one of them, the one who rode with me to Boston. She glares at me.

"So, Miss Fancy Pants," she says. "Are you too good to pick up a rag?" She reaches into a bucket near her feet, pulls out a dripping rag, and throws it at me. I step aside and let it slap against the wall behind me and slide to the floor. I'm all set to give her a good cursing, then notice the other girls on their knees, their dresses wet, their hands already raw and red. They're looking at me, waiting to see what I will do next.

I see Kathleen among them, looking at me, her dress all wet down the front and a rag in her hand. Her eyes lock with mine, and she shakes her head, so I bend over and pick the wet rag off the floor, go down on my knees, and work like the rest of them.

It's cold in here. I look around and see why. The windows are all open and cold air pours in from outside. That's a smell even more foreign here than soap and water—the smell of fresh air.

When I get closer to Kathleen, I ask her, "What's all this?"

"Visitors," she says, her mouth twisting around the word as she scrubs.

"What kind of visitors?"

"Ones that can't stand a bit of dirt, I suppose," Kathleen says. She straightens up and wrings the dirty water out of her rag into the bucket. "You know. Rich people. It's where Blackwell gets his money. It happens every year. All this…" she waves her hand at the room full of girls toiling away. "He wants 'em to think this place is a little bit of heaven on earth."

The work goes on all day. Hallways swept, floors scrubbed, windows washed until the glass shines. Buckets of whitewash are carried in, and grimy dark walls are painted white. The dining hall and kitchen are scrubbed and buffed as close to shining as they can get. At the end of the day, I fall into bed and go straight to sleep with the smell of soap and whitewash still in my nose.

The next day, wagons rattle up to the kitchen door, and men carry in crates full of green cabbage, lettuce, gold potatoes, and bright red apples. The colors almost hurt my eyes. Some of the girls, the new ones, get excited, but not the ones who've been here longer, like Kathleen.

"Don't get used to it," she says to me. "After tomorrow, it's back to cornmeal porridge again."

In the morning, I go up to the roof to see Jamie. I find him sitting up in bed, drawing away. "So, Jamie," I say, "Are you feeling more like yourself today?" He doesn't answer at first—he's too busy drawing—but the color in his cheeks and the brightness in his eyes tell me he's on the mend for certain.

The door to the stairwell opens behind me. I turn and see one of the guards, a big man who helped carry Jamie up here a while ago. He and another guard carry out a cot with a girl in it, a thin young thing I remember seeing in the sick ward. They bring her over and set her down a few feet from Jamie.

"What's all this?" I ask them. The men ignore me and disappear inside. A few minutes later, they're back with another cot carrying a young boy with a thin, wasted face. They set him down, too, and keep coming until the roof is filled with a half-dozen other patients all spread out under the sky.

The door opens again, and one of the nurses comes out carrying a tray. She sets it down and pours from a steaming kettle into six tin cups. I can smell the mint and coneflower tea I've been giving to Jamie. I watch her walk over to the thin boy, raise his head with one hand and lift the steaming cup to his lips with the other.

"What's going on here?" I ask. The men wouldn't answer me, but I'm hoping she will.

"Doctor Blackwell's orders," she says without meeting my eyes.

Blackwell's orders? I remember how I had to fight to get Jamie out of that stinking sick ward, how I had to beg, bargain, and threaten to get the herbs that helped him, the same ones the nurse is giving to the others now.

Then I realize. It's like all those bright-colored vegetables and whitewashed walls—all for show. Or is it? I mean, it's one thing to whitewash a dirty old wall, but to start nursing sick children back to health and then take it away—not even Blackwell can be cruel enough to do that.

Early in the afternoon, the matrons bring me a new dress. Not the fancy one I wore to the presentation, but a lovely dark grey gown with a white collar. They let me dress myself this time. When I'm done, one of them says, "Blackwell wants to see you."

When I get to his office, Blackwell is dressed in that same fancy black suit I saw before. He's holding some kind of white flower in his hand. For one crazy second, I wonder if it's for me. He looks me up and down like I'm some kind of prize pony. Then he turns to a mirror on the wall and starts to pin the white flower to his coat.

"We are going to have visitors today," he says, still gazing at himself in the mirror as he struggles with the flower and the pin. "Important visitors. I need you to help with them."

"Why me?" I ask.

A scowl comes over his face. I can see it over his shoulder in the mirror. "The Allens. They've asked to see you."

The name means nothing to me. "Who are the Allens?"

"You met them," he says. "At the presentation. The Quakers."

Of course. I remember the woman, especially. Her kind words

and gentle eyes.

"Why do they want to see me?"

"Apparently, you must have impressed them somehow." He sounds annoyed. Didn't he want me to impress those people?

"They are interested in the improvements we've made here," he says. "Particularly our new outdoor clinic for consumptive patients."

"You mean…the roof, where Jamie is?"

"Yes," he says, twisting his face into something like a smile. "That was your idea, wasn't it? Don't you want to take credit for it?"

My mind is spinning. This is the same man Anne says will one day steal my ideas and take credit for them. What game is he playing?

"What do you want?" I say.

"I want you to accompany the Allens during their tour. Show them what they ask to see. Answer any questions they may have."

"You want me to tell them we've been having dance parties with tea and cakes?"

Blackwell sits behind his desk with a sigh, removes his spectacles, and looks at me.

"You disappoint me, Mary. You assume that because something hasn't happened yet, it will never happen. That's not how the world works. Things change. Look at your brother and what I've allowed you to do for him. All the things you must have thought would never happen. And yet they did. Think of how much more can happen, even if you can't imagine it now. How can you say it won't happen? Can you see the future?"

Yes, I can see the future. I've had it shown to me. I know who you are and what you're going to do.

"I won't lie for you," I say.

"I'm not asking you to lie. The truth is that things *are* changing here. Look around. You can see it, can't you? That's all our visitors need to see and all you need to tell them."

I watch him glance down and adjust the flower on his lapel. "There is one more thing I'd like you to keep in mind, Mary. Your brother. The special treatment and good care that he enjoys and your ability to spend time with him are because of the trust that you and I have in each other. You trust me to continue to provide you with these things, and I trust you to take my wishes seriously. Do we understand each other?"

And just like that, the world makes sense to me again. This is the Blackwell I know. *Thanks,* I think, *for showing me who you really are.*

"Yes," I say. "We understand each other."

I hear the sound of horses' hooves and carriages rattling up the long drive outside. Blackwell hears it, too.

"They are here," he says, rising quickly from behind his desk. "Come."

We step outside just as two carriages roll up. The guards step forward and tend to the horses while the drivers climb down and open the carriage doors. The people who emerge look familiar, white-bearded men wearing waistcoats and fine leather shoes, women in beautiful dresses.

The last two to step down from the coach are the Quakers—*the Allens,* Blackwell called them. They look plain and colorless as the last time I saw them, dressed in brown and grey, with no ribbons or frills, almost like poor people. But they don't carry themselves that way. Something about the way they move, especially the woman, demands attention and respect.

Blackwell greets the visitors one by one as they file past us and into the building. The wealthy-looking men and women give me a polite nod or ignore me as they pass by. The Quaker woman returns Blackwell's greeting, then pauses, smiling down at me.

"Mary Donovan," she says. "I am pleased to see thee."

I don't know what I should say. I'm pleased to see her, too, but it doesn't seem like a proper thing for me to say out loud.

"Thank you," I say and give a little nod.

Blackwell leads the group into the great room. Traces of soap smell still linger from the all-day scrubbing we gave it. The whitewashed walls catch the sunlight streaming through the newly clean windows, making everything brighter. Vases of flowers have been set about on little tables that weren't there yesterday. Daisies, marigolds, irises.

A sudden burst of sound startles me. I turn to see a little man in a dress coat playing a fiddle. The girls sitting around the room stare at him as if they've never seen such a thing before. Blackwell is smiling and saying things about *the therapeutic qualities of music.* The rich visitors nod and stroke their beards, the fiddler plays fancy tunes I don't recognize, and the bright, hot sun shines on us all. *Madness,* I think. *This is what real madness is.*

"Mary," I hear Blackwell call my name. "The Allens would like to see our new outdoor clinic for consumptives. Would you be so good as to accompany them?"

I lead the Quakers away from the great room, away from the smell of soap and flowers and the whining of that damn fiddle, down the hallway where it's darker and cooler.

"I trust thee is well, Mary Donovan?" the woman says.

"Yes."

"I am glad to hear it." We walk in silence for a moment. "The flowers, and the musician. How long have they been here?"

My heart beats faster. I don't know what I'm supposed to tell her.

"They're new," I say, hoping that will be enough.

"They're new…" she repeats. I think I see the beginning of a smile at the corner of her mouth. "I see…" she says.

I lead them to the stairs, and we start the climb. Halfway up, the woman asks, "Does thee like working with Doctor Blackwell, Mary Donovan?"

A thousand thoughts and words come rushing up inside me, but I bite them back.

"It's…" I struggle for a word. "It's interesting."

"Yes," she says, "Yes, I imagine it must be."

We reach the top of the stairs, I push the door open, and we step out into the fresh air and sunlight. It still surprises me to see the other beds and patients here, the nurse moving about with her pot of steaming hot tea.

Jamie sees me and starts to call my name, "Mary…Mary…" He's holding a piece of paper, a new drawing he wants to show me. I go over to him and take it from his hand. It's a drawing of the hills and treetops I can see all around us. I hand it back to him.

"I see that this one must like thee," the woman says, gazing down at us.

"He's my brother," I say.

"Is he indeed?" she smiles. "May I know his name?"

"Jamie."

"I am pleased to meet thee, Jamie Donovan," she says. Jamie doesn't answer. He looks up at her face, then holds his drawing out toward her. She takes it and looks at it for a long time.

"He has more," the words burst out of me. I reach for the stack of drawings on the table next to him, but Jamie reaches them first and hands them to the woman. She takes them and gazes at the first few.

"Will thee leave us here, Mary Donovan?" she says. "I would like to sit with thy brother a while."

I hesitate. I don't believe anyone has ever asked to talk with Jamie before. The woman's husband comes nearer and speaks to me.

"Come, Mary Donovan," he says. "Show me the things thee has done here. All these beds, out in the fresh air, where did thee get this idea?"

"It's good for the lungs, the fresh air," I say, "It's no good to be shut away."

The man nods. He goes over to the nurse's tray, picks up one of the steaming tin cups, and raises it to his nose.

"Coneflower?"

"Yes."

He nods again. "We use it as well." He must see the question on my face. "My wife and I have a small hospital near Medford." He gazes past my shoulder and says, "I believe my wife is ready to speak with thee now."

The woman rises to her feet as we draw nearer. "Will thee walk with me, Mary Donovan?"

I follow her away from the beds and around the other side of the tower, where we are alone, and the treetops rise around us on the horizon.

"Tell me, Mary Donovan," the woman says. "Does thee like being here, in this place?"

Her question startles me. I don't know what I can say that will be enough. "I…I don't know what you mean…"

"Is thee happy here?"

Happy. The word damn near undoes me. I bite my lip. Then I feel her take my hand in hers, and we just keep walking along that way for a while. Her hand is warm and strong. It's the most comforting thing I've felt for a long time.

"My husband and I have been talking," she says. "We operate a hospital. A home, really, for people such as the ones who live here. We have a school where we try to teach our people things that can be useful to them in living their lives. If you agree, we would like thee to come and work with us there."

The world seems to stop. I can't believe what I'm hearing.

"You mean… leave here?"

"I understand the place may seem strange to thee, as all new places do at first. In a while, though, thee will come to know it and feel at home there."

My heart is pounding so hard I think it might burst through my chest.

"My brother," I say. "I won't go without him."

"Of course. We would not ask thee to leave him behind. It is not our way."

The sun is just now starting to touch the treetops around us and turn them gold. It seems like the most beautiful color I've ever seen. I realize I'm still holding her hand, and I'm afraid to let go of it.

"You mean…you want me to teach? I'm no teacher."

The woman smiles. "Ah, because thee does not have a piece of paper that says thee are? Some of the worst teachers I've known have that piece of paper, and some of the best do not. It is like thee said. Either everyone is important, or no one is important. I believe thee has a great deal to teach others."

The world seems to stop again. No one has ever quoted my own words back to me. No one has ever cared enough to remember them.

"When..?" I start to ask.

"My husband and I will need to discuss it further and make arrangements. We will write to Doctor Blackwell and make our request. I am certain he will see the good of it."

I wish I was as certain as she seems. But her confidence and calm are contagious.

A bell rings below—it's time to bring the visitors back to their carriages for their long ride home.

When we reach the courtyard, Blackwell is already saying goodbye to the other guests.

"Goodbye, Friend Mary," the woman smiles. "I will see thee again."

I watch her husband help her into the coach and follow her inside. The driver closes the carriage door behind them, climbs into the seat, and calls out to the horses. I stand and watch them ride away, wishing I could be with them in that coach more than anything.

"So," I hear Blackwell's voice beside me. "I trust that your time with the Allens went well?"

"Yes," I say, keeping my eyes on the coach. "It did."

That's the way we're going to leave. Jamie and me. The next time. I stand there and watch the coach grow smaller and smaller until I can't see it anymore.

Chapter 46 - Annie

Watching Mary dissolve no longer frightens me; the beauty of it, girl fading, becoming transparent, then gone! I stand there too long, looking at the space that held her, still seeing her in my mind's eye, that happy face, traces of chocolate ice cream above her lip.

If what I told Mary is true, it means she's done it. She's written her book, and it's waiting for me now behind the painting in Blackwell's office. Our plan is going to work. I know it. Just the thought of it fills me with light.

I'm halfway to the museum when I think to check the time. 3:55! I run towards the door, but the lady from the museum is already outside, turning a key in the lock.

"Wait!" I say, pulling up short and pocketing my phone. "I left something. Please, can I go in?"

She frowns at me for a moment, then slowly turns the key. "What is it? I can help you look…"

"My phone. I know where I put it down. I'll just be a sec…"

She pauses, one hand on the door. "Your phone."

I nod, moving toward the door, hoping she'll let me pass.

"The one you just put in your pocket."

I freeze. Then I pat my pocket, pull out the phone, and laugh. It sounds fake, but I say, "Oh. Yeah. What a dolt!" I shake my head, but she's not buying it.

"What are you looking for?" Her tone is even, with no anger that I can hear.

"What?" I realize there's no way I'm getting back inside today, but I'm not about to tell her the truth.

"You barely looked at the gift shop. I know you were snooping around the office. I know you looked under the carpet. There was a corner lifted, I tripped on it. What is it you think you'll find?"

The carpet? Then I remember moving it to protect the painting when I took it down.

"This is a museum of public health. Not a place for scavenging. I'd expect more from a kid of Jackson's. Really!" She turns to lock the door again, then faces me. "Are you going to tell me what you were looking for?"

I remember two things; the innocent always look guilty, and a half-truth goes a long way. I take a deep breath and look down at my feet.

"I'm sorry I bothered you. I thought I left my phone. There's a lot going on at home. But I *was* looking for something earlier." I look up at her and say the truest thing I can. "I want to help my dad. I thought there might be something here that would help."

She studies me firmly, and then her eyes soften. "Well, for goodness sake, why didn't you ask me? Of course, you can look around all you like, but I doubt you'll find anything. Half the town's been through here, not to mention how many times Jackson's been by. Come back Thursday when we open. But don't leave the carpet all messed like that. What did you think you'd find, a trap door?"

Thursday?! I have to wait two days to find out if our plan worked? It's unbearable, but at least the woman won't shoo me away.

"Thank you."

On the way home, I wonder how hard it would be to break in. And how bad it would be if I was caught. I can't risk that.

I'm at the front of the house, hand on the doorknob, when I hear Dad inside, shouting, "You don't understand!"

"*You* don't understand," Mom's voice is raised, but several decibels lower that Dad's. "I want you to call your doctor."

"No you don't. You hate him. I can see it on you every time you mention him. You don't trust him any more than you trust me."

I open the door and slam it shut behind me. Dad's standing in the doorway to his office, Mom facing him. Worst of all, Carson's standing in the kitchen with the Britta pitcher in his hand, like he's forgotten what it's for.

Their three heads turn to me, and we stand there.

Dad breaks the paralysis, crosses over to me, and grabs my arms. "Annie will solve this," he says. He looks into my face, his eyes bloodshot and intense, "Sweetheart, you have to tell me where you found the connection between Mary and Jamie. I want to contact his relatives, but I have to have that citation." His hands tighten, and I'm afraid he's about to shake me.

"Jackson, let her go." Mom's voice is so calm, but her eyes are not. Is she afraid of him?

"Annie?" Dad's grip is tighter and I start to stammer something, but Carson reaches us first. He puts a hand on Dad's and gently pries it off my arm. Dad looks at him, his face morphing from anxiety to confusion.

"Look," Carson says, "I've got Doc O right here." He shows his phone to Dad. "Let's go back in the office and talk, okay?"

Dad studies his face for several seconds before nodding slowly. He turns to me, "I'm sorry, kitten. You can tell me later." He turns to Mom. "Caro…" he looks down. "I'm sorry." He walks into his office, Carson close behind.

As Carson passes my mom, she softly says, "Thank you." Carson nods, follows Dad, and closes the door behind them.

Mom crosses to me and pulls me into a hug.

My mind is spinning. But Mom is holding me tight, stroking my head with one hand, making circles on my back with the other. "I don't think he's sleeping enough," she says.

I pull myself away from Mom as gently as I can. "What about the sleeping pills?"

"They knock him out for a while, but it doesn't last all night."

"You have to make him sleep. You've got to." I take a deep

breath to push back the tears. "We'll be okay. We're really close to finding what he needs. He just has to hold it together."

"I just want to go home." Mom's voice is weary, and her eyes red.

"He needs sleep. Maybe Carson can convince him."

Mom looks at me, and a half-smile appears. "You may be right. He did good just now."

I don't tell her how much I hate it. The idea of someone else, someone outside our circle, helping Dad. I guess I should be grateful, but mostly, I'm ashamed.

"I have to find that link, like Dad asked. Maybe that'll calm him down." I give her another squeeze, then slip out of her arms and go to my room.

In two days I'll have Mary's manuscript—I hope. In the meantime, I have to find a link to Jamie. I open my laptop and pull up the screenshot I took, the one with the name of Jamie's relative.

'James Marsh, 1052 Old Town Road, Boxford, MA.'

There's a phone number under the address. Without thinking, I enter the number and press 'call.' The phone rings for a long time before a robotic voice says, "Please leave a message for Jim Marsh."

I have no idea what to ask. What can I say that would make him call me back? I hang up.

I put the address into Maps and look at the directions. It's over two hours by bike, and some roads look crazy busy. Only thirty minutes by car. I wonder if Carson can drive. That would mean taking him away from Dad, and right now, Dad needs him here.

The image of a car with plastic flapping over one window suddenly comes to me. Daphne! I have her number on a sheet from work, so I call, not entirely sure what to tell her. She picks up right away.

"Anne, hey."

"Hey. Are you working tomorrow?"

"Naw. You? You weren't on the schedule."

"Nope."

"Okay. So. What's up?"

I take a deep breath. "Wanna go on an adventure?"

She laughs. "Sure. Where to?"

"Boxford."

She laughs again. "Yeah, because Boxford is such a hoppin' place for adventure. No, really. Where?"

I take another deep breath. "Okay, so. Here's the deal. You know about Mary Donovan?"

"Sure. Big reformer, right? They say she was at Thornwood way back."

"Yes. Well, she had a brother, Jamie. And his great-great-something grandson lives in Boxford. I'm hoping he has papers or something that can help Dad."

"Papers?"

"Writing. From Mary. Something about Thornwood. Jamie was an artist. He painted Thornwood, so we know they were there."

"Wow. That's cool. So, what did Jamie's great-great say about it? Does he have anything from back then?"

"I...I couldn't reach him." The lie comes easily. "I think it's better in person anyway. If he does have something, he can give it to me then."

It takes her a long time to say anything, and I worry she will balk.

"I'd ask Dad to take me," I say, "but if it doesn't pan out, I don't know how he'll react. I want to surprise him when I find it. The proof, you know. I'm going to find it!"

"Easy, cowboy," she says, and I realize with a little shock how loud I am getting. "I'm in."

My heart leaps. "Great! First thing tomorrow?"

"Sure. Have to gas up. How about 10 o'clock?"

I think about the lie I'll have to tell, but I say, "Yeah. That'll be great. And I'll pay for gas."

"Good thing." And then she's gone.

This could go so many ways, and my mind deals out fully fledged images of success and failure. *I grew up on stories about Great-Grand Jamie. Here's a trunk of his stuff.* Or, *I'm sorry, his house and grounds burned down before my great granddad was born. There's nothing left.*

"You know he might not have anything."

Daphne's voice shocks me back into the car, and I watch as the road, shops, and woods slip by. "Not to be a downer or anything."

I nod, holding tight to what I'll find in the painting. That'll be enough, I hope. This is just backup. But then I picture walking up to a door, the door opening, a man—will he look like Mary?—appearing. He welcomes us inside, shows us old photos, and brings us into a room full of boxes, trunks, bookshelves…

The car slows and turns off the highway onto a narrow country road.

"Okay, GPS me," Daphne says.

I stare at my phone and watch the map unspool. "Second right," I say just before my phone says, *"Take the second right."*

We're on that road for a long time, passing fields, the occasional mansion, and horses.

"Fancy parts for your Mr. Marsh."

The road narrows further, becomes dirt and gravel, and then ends.

"Okay," Daphne says slowly. "Where to now?"

I stare at the map and then look around us. Partway through what looks like a field is a mailbox and faint tracks indicating a drive. I peer through the trees beyond and see some kind of structure, but I can't make out what. "There."

Daphne pulls the car into the driveway and drives slowly through trees that crowd us on both sides. The car bounces along until we see a clearing, a barn looming first, then an old farmhouse materializing behind. There are a few cows in a pen next to the barn, and chickens scatter as Daphne pulls up to the house.

"This looks promising," she says, killing the engine and opening her door.

We both get out and look around. The air is scented by manure, hay, and something sweet and sour.

"If we play it right, they'll ask us to dinner," Daphne says, grinning.

We head toward the front door, and I consider how we look, Daphne with her tattoo sleeves and me with my hair all wild. Both of us young. Will he believe us?

A screen door flies open, and two young children dart out, voices high. The moment they see us, they skid to a halt. The younger one's hand comes up to his mouth, thumb sucked inside.

The older one, a girl, looks us up and down before screaming, "MOM! MOMMY!"

A woman comes to the door, steps out, and gives us the once over before crossing to her children. "It's okay. You go on now." The kids sidle past us before running toward the barn and disappearing inside. The woman turns to us. "You lost?"

I was expecting a 69-year-old man. Did we have the wrong place? I look at Daphne, but she's clearly waiting for me.

"Um, I hope not. We're… I'm looking for James Marsh. Does he live here?"

She frowns, "Uh, yeah. Who are you?"

"I'm sorry…" Her belligerence throws me. The elation that carried me here evaporates. "My name's Anne Blake. Are you his…" I'm afraid to make a mistake.

"Daughter. Yeah. What do you want?"

"I'm… I'm looking for a relative of Jamie Donovan, a famous artist from the 1860's."

Her face changes—recognition?—I can't say. Before she can answer, the screen door slams and a man walks toward us.

"These folks are looking for Jamie Donovan," she tells him, then back to us. "What are you, art students?"

"It's been a long time since anybody came looking for him," the man says. "Folks used to come around asking for paintings, drawings, anything. Paid good money for it, too." He squints at me, looks at Daphne, then her car.

My mind is racing. Other people came here and bought Jamie's paintings? And what did he mean by 'anything'? Were there papers or letters?

"He was in Thornwood, the Luna-… the Almshouse," I stammer. "His sister was a famous reformer. At least… I found something that said that. We need proof, though. Letters maybe? Did you ever find a journal?"

"Sister?" Marsh said. "There was no sister."

Even though I know this is wrong, it hurts to hear it. Daphne touches my arm.

"You okay?"

"Sorry we can't help." The man turns away and walks toward the house.

"Wait!" I take a few steps forward, and he turns around. "Did you sell it all? Do you have anything I could look through? Old letters, maybe?"

He shakes his head. "Even if I did, which I don't, why would I show it to you?"

His daughter makes a sound, and when I look at her, her face is pained.

I take a deep breath. "My dad is working to save Thornwood and the medical complex from developers. If they tear it down, these folks have to commute to Boston for their services, mental health services, see different doctors, and be in support groups with strangers. If we can prove historic significance, we can save it all!"

The man appears unmoved.

"I can't help you. My great, great, whatever grandfather was an only child. I'm sorry." He flings open the door and walks inside, letting the screen door slam behind him.

The woman turns to follow, and I say, "Wait!" When she turns back to me, I say, "Do you believe in ghosts?"

I hear a quiet gasp from Daphne, but I keep looking at the woman, looking for Mary's face in hers, and not finding it. Tears are in my eyes, but I don't try to stop them.

The woman's looking at me with a strange expression, so I take a chance. "She haunts me. Jamie's sister."

The woman's hand goes to her mouth, eyes wide. But she doesn't leave us, doesn't tell us to go. Simply waits.

"Please. If you think there's something here," I point to the house, "Can you let me see it? Please? I won't hurt anything. If it's valuable, I won't take it. I just need to see."

The hardness in her face dissipates. She turns to look at the house, then turns back to us. "It's up there," she nods toward the barn. "In the loft, at the back, there's a room. Lots of junk, but find the old trunk. That's got papers and any drawings no one would buy." I move toward her, and she puts a hand up to stop me. "Don't let him see you. But if he does, don't tell him I said anything."

I nod and grin at her, wiping my face dry. "Thanks!"

She jerks her head at Daphne's car. "Park that up the road where he can't see it and walk back. Hope you find something good." And she turns and goes into the house, closing the inside door behind her.

"Are you sure about this?" Daphne asks as I get into the car.

"You don't have to come."

"Oh, so you can have all the fun?" She drives around a curve in the road and parks, and we walk back as instructed.

Inside the barn, it's dark. I can hear the kids deep inside, but it's hard to make anything out. There's a rickety set of stairs leading upwards, so we climb slowly, trying to keep quiet. The loft is mostly bare, with remnants of hay scattered about. A walled-off area and the door she told us about are at the back. We walk across squeaking boards, around a large hole in the floor, and to the door. I turn the knob and pull it open.

There are chinks in the walls where light bleeds through, but it's still dark. I take out my phone and turn on the flashlight. Something skitters along one wall, making us jump. I turn my light that way but don't see anything.

The room is full of dusty furniture, chairs, desks, tables, and boxes. Daphne moves to a dressmaker's manikin, "May I have this dance?" and pretends to tango. I sweep the room with my light and see a trunk pressed against the back wall. I rush over to it and lift the lid.

My heart starts to race. *This is it. Oh, Mary. I wish you could see this!* At first glance, all I see is dust. I reach in and discover there's fabric covering everything. I gently tug at it, and a cloud of dust rises, temporarily blinding me.

Daphne comes over and waves at the dust till it settles down, then peers into the trunk. "So what are we looking for?"

"Anything. Something with *Mary Donovan* on it. Letters, a journal," I reach in and pull out a box. The cardboard is flimsy, and some of it crumbles in my hands.

"Easy," Daphne says.

"I know, I know…" I place the box on the floor and lift the lid. Inside are letters from galleries, art supply houses, and private buyers to James Donovan. Everything here looks to be related to his adult life.

"Hey, this side is newer," Daphne says, pulling out some manila envelopes stuffed with papers. "Maybe stuff the previous folks sifted through." She opens the top envelope and pulls out drawings, sketches in charcoal, and a couple of watercolors.

I take them from her, recognizing Jamie's hand, looking at the dates: 6-5-1862, 1-18-1868, 10-30-1869—landscapes and buildings I don't remember, a couple of portraits of strangers. She opens another envelope, this one full of letters. "See if there's anything from Mary there," I tell her.

I reach back into the trunk, looking for a journal. There are sketchpads and scrapbooks, but most of what's here are loose papers. "There's so much…"

A door slams, and we hear voices from the man and his daughter as they walk toward the barn.

"Shhh!" Daphne holds up one hand, and we pause to see where they're headed. She touches my arm, points to the corner of the room, then quietly moves to a doorway and peers out at me. "Ladder," she mouths and jerks her head for me to follow.

"Wait!" I whisper, gather as many papers and sketchbooks as possible, and stuff them into my backpack. She sighs and comes back to help, using her bag until it's completely full.

We move to the ladder, and she goes first, as agile as a monkey. I look down, the ground so far away it makes me dizzy, but I can hear the man and his daughter inside the barn, so I get on the ladder and ease my way down.

The kids are in the corral playing at something. We both hold still, hoping they don't look up. If we make it across the driveway, there's cover. Daphne sends me first, then follows. Miraculously, we are not seen.

I hold the backpack on my lap the entire drive home, not looking at anything. I just pray.

Please let something be here. Please.

Chapter 47 - Annie

Daphne takes me home, adrenaline buzzing through my arms and chest. I can't remember if we closed the trunk. What will happen if they find out? Did I tell them my name? Would they look up Dad? These questions ping-pong in my head, even as I clearly remember the two of us lowering the lid of the trunk and not being spotted as we made our escape.

As we pull up to the house, I'm glad to see the car gone, and I hope everyone's cleared out so I can have a bit of time on my own.

"Want some help?" Daphne says as I open the car door to get out.

"Thanks. But no. Are you okay? If anybody asks, I'll say you didn't know I took this stuff."

"Easy," she laughs. "No one's coming after us. And that was the best time I've had in a while."

I smile. "Really? You're hired!" And she laughs again as I take the documents she'd stashed in her satchel, sling my overstuffed backpack on my shoulder, and head toward the house.

"Hope you find what you're looking for," she calls to me, then backs out of the driveway and is gone.

There's a note on the kitchen table in Mom's handwriting. *Taking Dad to his doctor appointment. Back by 5. Please take out the salmon in the freezer. Love you!*

The house is blissfully silent. Not even a hum from the fridge. Gremlin is passed out in a sunspot on the rug. He looks so peaceful that I want to curl up beside him and sleep. Then I realize I'm afraid.

What if there's nothing here?

I go into my room, close the door, and put my backpack and the loose envelopes and papers on the floor.

I pick up one of the manila envelopes and look at the handwritten label: "Personal Correspondence: 1875-1895". The one underneath is for business correspondence during a similar period. The earliest date on any of the envelopes is 1866.

I can't remember Mary's dates, so I quickly search on my phone: born 1831, died 1911. If Mary is 15, then it must be 1846 in her time. Jamie's a couple of years younger, so maybe he was born in 1835? I pick up the envelope marked *1866,* thinking Jamie is about 31. *Please let there be a letter from Mary!*

I open that envelope and pull out the few thin papers there. Two of them address him as 'James', and I can't make out the signature. All about things going on at a farm, the weather, so-and-so says 'hello.' Nothing from Mary. Nothing that references Mary.

I go through the other envelopes marked "personal" and have trouble with the handwriting of some of the letters, but in the end, there's nothing here either.

I picture the stacks of papers we couldn't grab, sitting in the loft above cows and goats. What if it's there? How am I going to go back and get it?

I attack the stacks of loose papers, flipping through the sketchbooks in case there's writing, but finding nothing. I come upon another packet of envelopes tied together near the bottom of the stack. These are yellowed, and the ink has faded to nearly invisible. Still, I can make out the addressees as *Friend Dorothy and Richard Allen.* Friend. It means something, but I can't figure it out. Then I remember Quakers calling themselves Friends. Are these Mary's Quakers?

I look first at the return address. It's marked as "Russell Green," so I flip through the envelopes, hoping against hope to find one from Mary.

I see the town before I see who it's from. "Pineville, Massachusetts." I frown and look at the name. *Dr. Jonathan Blackwell.*

I nearly drop the envelope, and then the paper tears in my rush to open it. I stop and take a deep breath before slowly lifting the flap and pulling out two sheets of paper.

Dear Mr. and Mrs. Allen:

Thank you for your interest in Mary Donovan. It is very gratifying to know that one's work has been appreciated by such as yourselves. Mary has, as you wrote, a unique and powerful voice for change. And I am sure she would be an asset to your school. However, I have some reservations based entirely on my unique relationship with her and her limited time at Thornwood.

Since you requested that I deliver your letter to her directly, I have done so and am enclosing Mary's response. While I had no influence on its contents, I am in complete agreement with her decision.

Thank you again for your interest in Mary, as well as your continued support for our work at Thornwood. You have been very generous, and we will continue to use these resources to improve and enhance our patients' lives.

Sincerely,

Jonathan R. Blackwell, MD

Here it is! Proof that Mary was in Thornwood!

I put Blackwell's letter behind the other sheet and look at the letter from Mary. Mary's words. My eyes blur, and I have to pause to wipe away more tears before I start to read:

Dear Mr. and Mrs. Allen:

It was a pleasure meeting you. Thank you for your kind words following the presentation. I shared them with Dr. Blackwell and he was well pleased. Anything you admire in me is a direct reflection on my doctor.

That said, I must refuse your kind offer of employment. I have only been at Thornwood and under Dr. Blackwell's care for a short time. The mood swings and issues for which I was incarcerated here have diminished but not entirely vanished. I am convinced that my welfare is best served by remaining at Thornwood for the next few years. It is not only for myself I speak, but the others whose care I have been privileged to oversee. The reforms Dr. Blackwell has so eloquently written about are still in the early days here. I look forward to helping them come to fruition.

As for my brother, I wish him to remain here with me. As you have seen, the fresh air and herbal remedies we've supplied him have done wonders for him. It is my belief that Jamie will recover completely under our care.

Thank you again for your offer, as well as your kind words. They are much appreciated, both by Dr. Blackwell and myself.

I wish you all the best in your endeavors.

Sincerely,
Mary Donovan

I almost drop the letters. This is not my Mary. It can't be. She would never write such bullshit. What happened? Did he dictate it to her? Is he still blackmailing her?

Surely, there is more. I look at the stack of documents I pulled out. A name on the top page catches my eye: *Thornwood Marble Company.* I pick it up. It's a bill to Jamie for $20 to carve and erect a gravestone *located at area 13, plot 67 in Thornwood Asylum Pines Cemetery.*

My heart seizes. There's something attached to the bill, and I find myself staring at a drawing in Jamie's style. A simple headstone:

Mary Louise Donovan, b. 1841, d. 1857. Beloved Sister, gone too soon. I will avenge thee.

Chapter 48 - Annie

It makes no sense. She can't die. How can she die?

Sixteen. She dies at sixteen. How old is she now, fourteen? Fifteen?

Born 1841. Isn't that what I found? I look up *Mary Donovan* again, and the dates start to swim before my eyes. Born 1831. Ten years before Mary. Died 1911. Not 1857.

My stomach roils and I make it to the bathroom just in time. I heave into the toilet. When the heaving stops, I rinse out my mouth and splash cold water on my face.

It's a mistake. It has to be. I grab the keys, lock the door on my way out, and mount my bike.

The sun beats down and I should be sweating, but all I feel is dread. My arms and legs are stiff with fear. I feel a breeze from cars as they pass, but the sounds are muffled, my mind repeating *mistake-mistake-mistake*.

I look up and see the cemetery. I lock my bike and walk through the undergrowth, looking for section numbers.

I see a post with a faint engraved number at the top; *28*. I scan the area, looking for more posts. I finally find the one I'm looking for; *13*. The ground here is covered by the same undergrowth that obscures almost everything, broken only by the odd grave marker rising through. My hope gets stronger as I zig-zag through the section. Nothing here, nothing here, nothing.

Then I stub my toe on something hard. I look down, wanting more than anything to find a rock, but I see a partly buried headstone. I crouch down and see what looks like the top of an 'M'. *No!* I push away the weeds, pinecones, and dirt, revealing more and more of the engraving.

Mary's grave. The wrong Mary.

"It's about time." Mary's voice, alive, making my heart leap. "I've been waiting for you for ages."

I look up and see her walking towards me, her face filled with happiness. Then I notice the bench where I'd spent so much time waiting for her, and realize where I am. Her grave has been here all along!

"I've news!" Mary says, but her face changes as she sees mine. "What, didn't it work? Wasn't it in the painting?"

"What year is it?" I ask.

"What?"

"The year, what year is it?!"

"What's the matter? Something's happened, hasn't it?"

"Just tell me the year. Please."

"1856. But you know that. You've told me all about myself."

1856. She should be twenty-five, not a teenager like me. "How old…" my throat is so tight I have to force the words out, "…are you?"

"What?" What's happened?"

"How…*old*?" I raise my head to look at her, and she flinches. Then her chin lifts.

"Not that it matters, but I'm fifteen last February."

"Oh God. Oh God. Oh God…" I double over as I start to cry. "I'm sorry, I'm sorry, I'm sorry…"

She lays her hand on my shoulder, fingers gripping tight. "Jesus, girl. What's happened? Sorry for what?"

She kneels down in front of me, close enough to hug. With everything inside me, I want to curl up in her arms and sob. But I don't deserve it. I don't deserve her.

Her voice is gentler now than I've ever heard. "Tell me. Please. It's okay."

I look into her face and see I've frightened her. I gulp air to stop the sobbing. "You're not…You're not the Mary Donovan we're looking for. I made a mistake. You're not her." The tears burst from me, and I cover my face with my hands.

She doesn't move, doesn't speak. When I manage to get myself under control, I force myself to look at her. Her face is pale and expressionless.

"How… how do you know?"

I swallow hard. "The year. She was born in 1831."

Mary sits back on her heels, one hand on her heart, as if I'd punched her there. Her eyes look everywhere but at me as she takes in what I've said, like a trapped animal looking for escape.

"Why didn't you check? Why didn't you ask me before?" She stands up and starts to pace. Her breath is coming fast, her feet snapping through twigs and kicking up dirt with every angry step. "So what if I'm not the *great Mary Donovan*," her words drip with sarcasm. "I have ideas, I have plans. I'm wanted, I am. The Quakers want me to teach in a fine school. Just you wait and see. I'll get out, I'll ruin Blackwell. And I'll do it without your help!"

I moan, bending over again with the pain of it. "You don't get out," the words come out on a long moan. "You never leave Thornwood. You die here. I'm so, so sorry!"

Mary roars and runs at me, putting her face close to mine and yelling, "LIAR! I knew it! Why did I ever stay and talk with you? You're out of your mind! *Girl from the future?* What shite!"

I want her to hit me, knock me out. But first, she has to believe me. "I found a drawing Jamie did," I say, "with a bill for a gravestone. This one." I point to it.

She turns her head, and I watch her lips move as she reads the words and numbers. She stands staring at the stone, shaking her head. "It's not true. The Quakers are getting us out…."

"No, I fucked up. I'm sorry…"

"You're wrong!"

I wish I could be angry like she is. She still has hope, but for me, it's all over. I can't bear it, knowing how Dad will take this. And this girl, my friend, will be dead in a year. "I wish I was dead!" I pound the dirt with my fists. "Fuck it. Fuck me!"

"Stop it! Stop it right now!" I see Mary's shoes in front of me and I look up. "YOU aren't the one staring at a gravestone with your name on it, are you? YOU didn't just find out that everything you thought would happen to you was a lie. What have you got to be sorry about?" She pushes my shoulder.

"It's Dad," I sob. "What'll happen to him?"

"Oh, you poor, poor thing! At least you *have* a dad. At least he's *with* you, getting cared for by a doctor, you said. Not run off and dead or drunk or mad. He didn't abandon you, did he? To a vicious aunt who hated you, beat your brother, and sent you to this fucking place." She pauses for breath. "Stop your moaning, I'm not wasting any pity on you." She's leaning into me, her face inches from mine, and I scuttle backward to get away.

"I'm sorry!"

"Don't you pity me either!" She glares at me. "So I'm not going to be a fine lady, wearing fancy clothes and speaking in fancy rooms. But I've got Jamie. And me and Jamie can make our own mark in the world. Just you wait. Look me up in your magic light, and you'll be amazed. So you were wrong about who I was. But that," she points to the gravestone, "is not me! You're wrong again, Miss Twenty-twenty-two. I wish I'd never laid eyes on you."

This time, she just blinks out. One moment there, the next... nothing.

Chapter 49 - Mary

Everyone lies. But some lies are worse than others.

It started with the flowers. They could have thrown them out when no one was watching. Instead, they let them die right in front of our eyes, fading and withering day by day. There's a kind of cruelty in that. Don't try to tell me there's not.

Then the fresh fruit and vegetables, all those bright happy colors. Once they got what they wanted, they made us throw it all out and watch it rot away to nothing, like the flowers. Like everything.

You're not her, she told me, and I called her a liar, right to her face, even though something inside me knew she was right.

It hurt for a while. I won't lie about that. I even hid myself in the pantry and cried where no one could see or hear me. I cried like a child who's had something beautiful taken away from her.

But you can't take away something that's not real. That bright future, the speeches, the books, the fancy dresses, all she promised me. They were never real. I think I knew that even if she didn't.

The strange thing is, I don't care now. I don't need to be a fine, fancy lady. I don't need to be important or famous.

But to never get out of here... *That* I will not accept. *That* I will never believe. There's no God in this universe cruel enough to let that happen.

She's wrong. I know she is. I don't care what her history books say, or all her fancy words and pictures, even that ugly stone in the graveyard. It's not true. I'm getting out of here. *We're* getting out, Jamie and me.

I can still see the Quaker lady's face and gray eyes, the kindest I've ever seen. She wants me, her, and her husband. They want us both. Jamie and me.

I watch the sunrise over the woods where I've sworn never to go again, the way it lights up the road stretching out in front of me, the same route that'll take Jamie and me away from this place. There's a future waiting for me out there. Not the one Anne dreamed up for me, not someone else's future, but *mine,* the one I'll make for myself.

I feel someone's hand on my shoulder, turn, and see two guards with grim faces.

"What do you want?" I ask, none too gently. That's how free of this place I feel already.

"Blackwell wants you," one of them says. A chill comes over me, but I shake it off. I follow them down the hall to Blackwell's door and start walking right in, the way I always do, but one holds me back while the other steps up and knocks. At Blackwell's command, the guard opens the door and nearly pushes me inside. I turn to glare at him, but the big door swings shut in my face.

Blackwell is standing at his desk, fixing me with a terrible look that could wither all the flowers in the world. He's holding an envelope in his hand. He lifts it up. When he speaks, his voice is low and tight with rage.

"When were you going to tell me about *this*?"

I look at the envelope, trying to make out the writing on it, but it's too far away, and I don't want to move any closer.

Then I understand. It's from the Quakers. It has to be.

"Is that for me?" I ask, lifting my chin and trying to sound strong. "Give it to me."

"Why?" he asks. "You already know what it says."

I almost run across the room and rip it from his hand.

"Actually," he says, "This letter is to me. What they're offering you is quite amusing, really. A chance to waste away on their filthy little farm in the hills, playing nursemaid to a lot of half-dead street urchins…"

The blood is pounding so loud in my head that I can barely hear what he's saying.

"What were you thinking?" he says. "Did you believe I was going to allow this? Let you go with those self-righteous half-wits? After all the work I've done with you…"

"You've got no right…" I choke the words out.

"No!" he shouts, crumpling the letter and stepping toward me. *"You* have no right! You have no right to take all the work I've done and throw it away like this!"

"What have *you* done? Made me sit here and listen to you talk? Dressed me up like a doll in some fancy dress? What the hell have you ever done for me?"

"Everything!" he shouts. "I have poured my heart and soul into you! My heart and soul!" His face is flushed red, and there's spittle flying from his lips. "And you…" he flings the words at me, "You stupid creature. You're no better than a stray dog. I've trained you not to bite but not how to think. But I will. By God, I will."

"I'll tell them what you've done," I say. "I'll write to them and tell them everything you've done."

A strange look comes over his face, something too wicked to be a smile. "Oh, but you already have," he says, picking up another piece of paper from his desk.

He puts on his spectacles, holds the paper higher, and begins to read aloud.

"Dear Mr. and Mrs. Allen, it was a pleasure meeting you. Thank you for your kind words. That said, I must refuse your kind offer of employment…"

A white-hot light explodes in my head. I try to speak, to rage at him, but the words are stuck in my throat.

"I am convinced that my welfare is best served by remaining at Thornwood for the next few years. As for my brother, my wish is for him to remain here as well…"

In three steps, I'm across the room, clawing at the paper in his hand as he tries to hold it out of my reach, backing away from me until he stumbles backward, falling to the floor. Before he can get up, I'm right on top of him, ready to bring my boot-heel down on his throat. The fear in his eyes makes me glad. I don't care about prison. I'm in prison already.

Then I think of Jamie, and I stop.

The door flies open, and the two guards come charging in. They see Blackwell on the floor and pull me away while I curse and kick at them.

"Stop!" Blackwell shouts. The guards stay where they are but don't let go of me. Blackwell gets up off the floor, then bends down to pick up his spectacles that must have fallen during our struggle. When he speaks, he's gasping for breath.

"Your Quaker friends should thank me…for saving them the trouble of finding out what you really are." He wipes his spectacles with his white kerchief and puts them back on. His face is still flushed and red, his voice still out of breath but steadier. "Look at you. Still, the same wild animal you were when you first came here. You may fool your Quaker friends. You may fool the rest of the world. But you cannot fool me."

"Fucking bastard!" I shout at him.

"Thank you," he says, "for proving my point so well."

I can feel the guards slipping the cold, iron manacles around my wrists and snapping them shut behind me.

"So," Blackwell says, "Since you are so determined to go back to where we started, let's do that now, shall we?"

One word from Blackwell and the guards turn me around and hurry me out of the office and down the hall. A few girls stare at us as we go past, their eyes wide and frightened.

We turn a familiar corner. When I realize where they're taking me, I curse and kick at them. The box, the one they had put me in before, is right ahead of me in the dim light, even smaller and uglier than I remember. I thrash and kick as hard as I can, but the two of them are too strong; they force me inside that dark, stinking box and slam the door. I hear the lock snapping shut and their feet walking away. Then nothing.

I don't shout or scream. I don't kick or pound the door. I know all that will do is wear me out.

Blackwell's voice is still in my head. *Did you really believe I was going to allow this?*

He's right. I'm a fool. Why did I think it would be that easy? I know why— because I wanted it. That's what comes of wanting something too much.

I try to picture the Quaker lady's face again, her kind gray eyes, but they're already fading in the dark.

More words from Blackwell come back to me. *The true measure of a person is how they act when what they want is no longer possible.*

I know what I want. I want to kill Blackwell. Not just kill him. Destroy him. Wipe out all the harm he's ever done and ever will do, not just to me but to every poor soul in this cursed place and all the ones yet to come. I want to see him burn like a farmer uproots and burns a weed that's choking the good crops.

The walls in here look closer than before, pressing in around me. *Please,* I think. *Please, help me.* I don't know who I'm talking to. Or who I think will hear.

Then I open my eyes and see what's scratched into the wall right in front of me, three short words that cut right to my heart.

HELP ME ANNE

All of a sudden, I know I'm not alone. This time, it's not a ghost, not an angel or a saint—it's a girl like me. A girl who hasn't been born yet, reaching across time, trying to tell me something.

Find the book. The one he steals and claims is his own. Show the world what he is, a liar and a thief. Take everything that matters to him, his reputation, his good name, set it all on fire, and watch him burn.

I think about the other girl who was here before me. The *real*

Mary Donovan. I see her standing in Blackwell's office, in my place, listening as he tries to twist her mind, stealing her ideas like a crow stealing shiny things. When did she realize what he was doing, what his wicked plan for her was?

The words come to me before I remember where I first saw them.

Imagine, if you will, the worst moment you have ever experienced...

Then I remember—those pages in Blackwell's desk, the ones he didn't want me to see.

Then perhaps you can imagine what life was like for me, and others like me, for whom peace and hope and happiness seem forever out of reach...

Now I know. Those beautiful words in that simple, elegant handwriting.

It was her.

It was her all along.

Chapter 50 - Annie

"Don't go!"

I'm still kneeling by Mary's grave. Even blinded by tears, I know I'm alone, but I say it anyway, as if my wanting is strong enough to bring her back.

The look on her face when I told her—the memory of it breaks me again. Tears keep coursing out of me, an endless fountain of pain. "I'm sorry, I'm sorry, I'm sorry…"

The letter Blackwell forged, telling the Quakers she wasn't interested—I didn't tell her about that. What good would it do? I've hurt her enough already. What good is a ghost from the future if nothing I tell her can give her hope?

My phone buzzes, and it takes me a few minutes to stop crying and look at it. There are two messages, one from Mom: *Where are you? I said, be back at 5.* And the other from Dad: *Hey, any luck? I'm counting on you.*

Having to tell Dad I had the wrong Mary sends ice through my veins, and I start shaking. I force myself to stand, staggering on bloodless legs.

I check my phone again. The three dots indicate Mom is writing something, so I text them both: *Sorry! On my way.*

I rub my face and see my hands covered in dirt and twigs. I walk quickly out of the cemetery, grab the bottle clipped to my bike, pour the warm water on my hands, and scrub my face.

There's no way to cover that I've been crying. What can I say? *I'm crying because I couldn't find the proof Dad needs.* Just thinking it brings more tears.

Mom meets me at the front door. "When I say five o'clock, I

mean five." Her face is tight until she sees mine. "What happened?"

Dad is standing behind her. His face is full of hope. "My girl!" It completely ruins me, and I start crying. He pulls me into his arms. "Easy. It's okay. Everything will be all right."

Mom strokes my back. "Are you hurt? What happened?" Mom's voice is soft, but the edges are hard with worry.

It reminds me of Mary. The kindness and concern before the ax falls. The thought makes me cry harder, and it takes a while for the sobs to subside enough for me to speak.

"Dad," I say finally, then my legs won't hold me, "I have to sit."

The three of us move to the couch, Mom and Dad on either side of me. I look at Dad, then I say it.

"I had the wrong Mary Donovan. The one with the artist brother. I'm sorry."

Dad slumps but puts his arm around me. "Jamie Donovan? Not related? You're sure?"

I shake my head. Mom puts her hand on my head and runs her fingers against my scalp. "It's okay, sweetie. You tried. We'll keep looking."

Dad's leg starts to bounce. "Yes, of course," he says, "We'll keep looking," but he sounds distracted, and when I look at him, he's staring off into space.

"I'm so sorry," I say again. Do I want him to be angry like Mary? That at least felt like hope.

"Jackson, the show's in two days," Mom says. "It will help."

"How?" Dad snaps. "You don't know these guys. I do. They're all about the money. High-income apartments and expensive boutiques. It's all they care about."

"I'm not telling you to stop looking.."

"You're damn right. I won't stop," Dad interrupts, standing. "Don't worry, kitten," he says, "We'll find her. I know we will." And he heads toward his office.

"Jack, it's dinner…"

"I'll eat later."

"Jack!"

He slips into his office and closes the door behind him.

Mom stares after him for a few moments before turning back to me. "You okay?"

I nod.

"Why don't you go wash up and come to dinner?" she says. "Somebody's got to eat it."

"Okay. See you in a minute."

I go to the bathroom and look in the mirror. My face is smeared with dirt, my eyes red and swollen. When I put my hands under the water, they sting, and I notice a few scratches on my palms. I wash my face, soak the cloth with cold water, and press it to my eyes. I think of Mom waiting alone for someone to eat with her, and I dry my face quickly.

"There's a breeze. Let's eat outside," Mom says, holding out a plate filled with roasted vegetables and feta cheese. My stomach rumbles.

On the patio, the promised breeze ruffles my hair and cools my damp skin. I fill my cup with iced tea from a pitcher on the table and take a long drink.

"Are you okay?" Mom asks gently.

"I guess," I shrug.

"Don't worry about your dad."

"I let him down."

"No, you didn't."

"I did! I thought I had something…" I think of Mary's face, red and angry, and how I can never tell Mom about her. How she's just going to disappear…

Mom kneels beside me to take me in her arms. "Easy there," she whispers. "Hush now. It'll be all right."

I take a few hitching breaths to quell the tears and wipe my face with a napkin. "He's not getting better, is he?"

Mom takes my face in her hands and makes me look at her. "Yes he is." Her eyes and voice are firm and should reassure me.

"What will happen if he fails?" My voice cracks on the last word.

She sighs. "We'll deal with that if it happens. For now, we keep on helping him. I'm sure he'll be better when this is over and he's home."

"What if he's not?"

"He *will* be," her voice is low, less assured, but her hands move to my shoulders and squeeze, almost hurting me. I look into her face. "With the right treatment at home and no pressure, it'll be much better than now. I should never have let him stay…"

I hug her. I'm not the only one worried. I have to remember that.

She pulls away and says, "Eat before it gets cold."

I stick a forkful into my mouth and eat. My stomach rumbles again, and I realize how hungry I am. And tired. As soon as I clean my plate, my eyes droop. I'd lay my head on the table and close my eyes if I could.

"Help me clean up," Mom says. "I've got rehearsal in twenty minutes. Wanna come? It's our first rehearsal onsite."

Thornwood is the last place I want to be right now. "No, thanks," I say, and put our plates in the dishwasher before going to my room.

I open the door and see the floor covered with old papers and envelopes, Jamie's drawing of Mary's gravestone on top of the pile. I have to take them all back at some point. For now, I just want them out of sight.

I find a cardboard box, grab the papers and envelopes, and stack them inside until my floor is clear. Then I put the box in my closet and shut the door.

I'm sorry, Dad. I think as I throw myself on the bed. *I'm sorry, Mary.*

There's scratching at my door, so I get up and let Gremlin in. He jumps on the bed and looks at me like, *Are you coming?* I lie down and he curls up with me, purring and rubbing my face with his, lulling me to sleep.

The following two days pass in a blur. It's now the day of the show. Ticket sales were trickling in until a couple of days ago, then a sudden flood. At the final tally, Mom says, "We've sold 319!"

"How are you gonna fit 'em all in?" I ask, looking over the list and picturing the rooms in Thornwood.

"You'll see," she says, smiling. "Get dressed, okay?"

Mom has enlisted me, along with Dad, Carson, and Daphne, to play 'guides.' I put on the costume she rented, a long grey dress with white pinafore, and tuck my hair inside a white cap. It's a little big on me, but the transformation makes me gasp when I look in the mirror. Is this what Mary's matrons look like?

A familiar stab of pain goes through my chest, remembering her fury. *I wish I'd never laid eyes on you.* I quickly leave my room, trying to forget it.

Dad and Carson are in the living room, wearing white collarless jackets and white pants. They smile as I catch my foot in my skirt and stumble.

"Be grateful I didn't make you wear hoops." Mom stands us together for a picture. "Don't smile!" Then, "Now one with smiles…perfect!"

Daphne is waiting for us at the main building when we drive up. Her dress and cap match mine. From a distance, she looks a bit like Mary.

"Annie, you start in the laundry room," Mom says. "Daphne, you're in the parlor. Carson, you get the medical ward. And Jack, you're in the restraint area." She looks at her watch and says, "Showtime!"

We follow her out the front door to the driveway, where a large crowd reaches all the way to the street. A table is set up where Mom asks each person to fill out an 'intake record,' then hands them a letter, assigning them to their group.

Mom waits fifteen minutes after the start time for latecomers. She pulls me to her side and says loudly, "Everyone in Group A, please follow Annie." We wait as several people line up near us, then she nods, and I lead them to the laundry room.

The room is set up with two large wash tubs filled with steaming water and strung with clotheslines holding dripping sheets. A woman in a plain brown dress is scrubbing wet clothes against a washboard. Once we're all inside, a spotlight shines on her, and she looks up:

"My name is Gladys Mayberry. I was brought here by my husband four years ago. After the birth of our fourth child in three years, I became depressed. Couldn't care for the children, my husband, the house… When he left me here, I was pregnant…again." She pauses and stares at the wet clothes in her hands. "I thought I had my hands full at home, washing all those diapers, children's clothes, everything… Here, they make us do washing for the neighboring rich." Suddenly, her face does something marvelous, looking sad but somehow gleeful. She leans forward and whispers loudly, "Don't let Matron see..." From behind and beneath her skirts, she pulls a young child. "She's the reason I stay sane. I'll get her out of here. I've promised her."

The spotlight goes out. Another actor steps close to the group and says, reading from a card, "Gladys Mayberry died trying to escape in October of 1867. There is no record of her child."

Several audience members gasp. Even though I know the script and have seen rehearsals, I get chills. "Come this way, please," I say and lead them to the Parlor.

This is the nicest room. Velvet drapes hang from the windows, and a red and gold rug covers the floor. I walk over to the old Victrola and mime, putting the needle on a record to cue the music. A waltz starts to play, and three pairs of women begin to dance. One of them steps away while her partner swirls around the room. She faces the group, and a spotlight shines on her.

"I'm Harriet Glover. Tonight is dance night. I look forward to this all week." She looks at the dancers. "Edith is the best dancer. Isn't she lovely? She would go on like this all night if they didn't stop her." She returns to dance with Edith and swirls once around the room before stepping away again. Edith continues dancing.

"When I'm in her arms, I feel like I'm on top of the world. There is no pawing with Edith." Her face grows dark, and her hands fidget with her clothes. "No pushing into dark corners and ripping your dress." She pauses to catch her breath and looks at Edith. "I'm safe with her. With Edith, it's all about the dance." She seems about to join Edith, then turns back to us.

"Father was furious, and Mother was deeply ashamed." They wanted me married, but I didn't. So…they put me here." She watches the dancers as a smile comes to her face. "I guess I should be grateful."

Then the music stops, and the spotlight goes out.

I say, "Everyone, please follow me."

The next room is the Medical Ward. The floor is full of beds, and each bed is stuffed to look like there's a body, with plain white masks over wig forms on the pillows. An actor in white clothes takes the spotlight and tells about prevailing illnesses, consumption and influenza being the most common and deadly. He goes on about various treatments over the decades, including malaria fever treatment for syphilis. I can tell the audience is growing restless—then someone unseen starts to cough.

People's heads turn this way and that, looking for the offending party. Slowly, more and more unseen people begin coughing, the sound amplified, growing louder, drowning out the actor. The audience starts to press themselves back, clearly uncomfortable. The sound of coughing fades, and the actor speaks again.

"By the 1800s, one out of seven people in the US and Europe died from consumption. What we call tuberculosis. It wasn't until 1880 that the bacteria causing TB was isolated, and not until 1921 that a vaccine was first administered to a human."

The coughing stops. The spotlight clicks off, then the room lights come on.

"Please follow me." I herd them all into the final room, which is more of a hallway, called The Restraining Room. It's like a museum of horrors; various restraints on dummies, the collar, a straitjacket, a child's straitjacket, and a chair with arm, leg, and head straps that force the patient to sit fully upright. There's also a mannequin in a tub full of water.

"Hydrotherapy." An actor dressed as an orderly steps out from the shadows. "Go ahead, test the water. Anybody want to go in?" A young man from my group is pushed forward by a young woman. Laughing, he sticks his hand in the water and instantly pulls it out. "Ow! It's freezing!"

The orderly disappears through a doorway and returns, leading a man in a straitjacket. He takes the man to another tub and tells him to strip.

The patient slowly looks around at us, staring into our eyes. It's unnerving. "In front of everyone?" he asks.

"Doctor's orders," the orderly says, then unbuckles the straitjacket. For a moment, I'm afraid the man will actually undress, but as soon as his arms are free, he swings at the orderly, knocking him down, and starts pushing through the audience to escape.

The orderly gets to his feet and grabs the patient, struggling to buckle the straps, then hauls him over to the box. The man shouts, then begs, "No, please. Don't! I'll be good. Please!" But the orderly opens the door, shoves the man inside, then shuts and locks the door.

We all know it's a play. Yet, everyone is frozen in place. My heart starts to pound. I remember how terrifying it felt inside that box, even with the door open a crack. What is the actor going through right now?

The silence is absolute and seems to last forever. A sudden loud bang comes from inside the box, and we all jump.

Then there's a heart-rending scream, and the lights go down.

When they come back up, the actor in the straitjacket is standing beside the open door in a spotlight. "Patients were put into isolation anywhere from a few hours to several days. There has been no evidence that this isolation has any benefit. Yet this treatment continues to this day."

The spotlight dims and the actor leaves the room. The main lights come up, and everyone starts to mill around, murmuring softly before I remember it's my cue.

"That is all for the main building. If you would please follow me outside…"

I lead the way out a side door. There's still a little light in the sky. I see two other groups waiting, and when I turn back to the building, I see Dad leading his group out to join us. I know what comes next, and I steel myself.

Six people emerge from a side door carrying a simple pine coffin. As it passes the group, Mom calls for us to follow, handing out electric lanterns to the audience, and we follow in near silence.

Once we enter those tall pines, the lanterns barely break the darkness. Some people are talking low, and I hear some stifled nervous laughter.

I haven't been to the cemetery since that last time with Mary. Everything looks bigger in the dark, or maybe it's my eyes searching for an end to the shadows and not finding them. I hear the words *graves* and *cemetery* passing among the guests as they quiet down.

The place where Mom stops has tall posts planted in a circle, and she motions for the lantern bearers to hang their lanterns there. In the surprisingly bright light, I can see we're in our circle, Mary's and mine. A chill runs through me. Why did Mom pick this spot?

The pallbearers set the coffin outside the circle and cover it with black fabric. Mom talks about a woman who lived and died in Thornwood. She is standing beside her headstone and grave. I can see it isn't Mary's, but tears fill my eyes.

Mom's talking about a sister and descendants, but I only see

Mary's angry face. She hates me. And I deserve it. With all my heart, I wish Mary could be here. Maybe if she saw this, she'd understand what we're trying to do. I'm crying harder now, sucking in air so I don't sob.

And that's when someone's hand slips into mine.

Chapter 51 - Mary

I hear footsteps coming toward me, the sound of the lock rattling. When they open the box to let me out, the light blinds me, and I shut my eyes against it.

They've come for me sooner than I thought. Blackwell didn't want to break me, not this time. He just wanted to give me a taste, to remind me of how things work here.

I've been folded up like a paper doll in that stinking box for so long my legs won't work at first. One of the guards reaches out to take my arm and steady me, but I push his hand away.

"Here, I'll take her."

I turn and see Kathleen step out of nowhere, fixing the guards with a steely look. She's taller than both of them. And her voice doesn't sound like she's asking for permission. The guards look at each other, then walk away, leaving me with her.

"So," Kathleen says, "D'you need a hand, then?"

"No," I say. "I'm fine."

"Sure you are."

I shuffle forward and she goes along, walking slowly to keep next to me.

"What did you do to piss him off this time?"

I don't answer. To answer, I'd have to tell her about the Quakers. I haven't done that yet. I didn't want her to know I was going to leave without her.

"So," Kathleen says, "I guess the Quakers aren't coming for you now."

I stop and stare at her.

Kathleen turns and looks at me. "When were you going to tell me about that?"

All the words I want to say rise up in my throat but won't come out. She must see it.

"I know," she says. "You didn't want to tell me. I get it. Hell, I would've done the same thing."

"No. You wouldn't."

"Yes I would. If I could get out of here and I couldn't take anyone else with me, you think I wouldn't do it? I'd do it in a fucking heartbeat."

We walk along in silence for a minute. Hunger makes me feel faint, and I start to weave a bit. Kathleen catches me by the arm.

"Hungry?"

I manage to nod. She guides me to the kitchen, sits me down at a table, and brings me a loaf of bread and a hunk of cheese. The bread is dry, and the cheese tastes foul as ever, but I chew and swallow it down as best I can. Kathleen sits with both arms folded in front of her, watching me carefully.

"So," she says, "How many more times are you going to let that happen to yourself?"

"You think I *asked* to be thrown into that stinking box?"

"Yes. You're always asking for it, Mary. That's what you do. You can't keep crossing Blackwell like that. It's like poking a mad dog."

"I can handle him," I say. Kathleen leans closer to me.

"He's going to *kill* you, Mary, don't you know that? Sooner or later, he's going to kill you. And I'm not going to sit here and watch it."

The fury in her eyes stops my heart.

"So," she finally says, lowering her voice, "You still want to get out of here?"

"Jesus, what do *you* think?" I say, wondering why the hell she's asking such a stupid question—then I look up and see how her green eyes are drilling into mine.

"My cousin," she says, "He knows the new laundry man. The one who comes here every week. The next time he comes, we get in the cart, hide in the laundry, and ride out of here…"

My head is spinning. I want to believe this, but I'm afraid to. The matron walks near us. Kathleen stops talking and waits for the woman to pass.

"My cousin," she whispers. "He'll be waiting a half-mile off with some fast horses. He'll take us to your Quaker friends."

"Wait…" I say. "Won't the Quakers tell Blackwell?"

"They fucking hate Blackwell!" she says. "*Everyone* does. Besides, they won't turn you away, a couple of poor souls in need. It's not their way."

"Jamie too," I say. "I'm not leaving without him."

"Jesus, Mary," she whispers, "Don't you think I know that? *Of course,* Jamie, too!" She pauses again. "Do you think he can do it?"

"What do you mean?"

"Jamie. Do you think he can keep quiet?"

"He'll be fine," I say.

"We'll be riding out of here right under the guards' noses. He'll have to be quiet the whole time."

"He'll be with me, won't he?" I say. "He'll be fine."

She gives me a hard look, then sighs, "Alright, then."

"When?"

"Tomorrow night. Seven o'clock. Can you be ready then?"

Tomorrow. My heart leaps in my chest.

Then I remember. The manuscript. The proof Anne needs. The final nail in Blackwell's coffin.

"There's something I've got to do first," I say.

"What?" She glares at me suspiciously. When I don't answer, she rolls her eyes and sighs. "I know. You can't tell me?"

"I'm sorry."

"Well, whatever it is, you've got to do it by seven o'clock tomorrow. Can you do that?"

"I can."

"Seriously, Mary. I don't want to be standing around that fucking laundry cart, waiting for you. I'm not going to do that. I won't wait for you, do you understand? You've got to promise."

"I know," I say.

"You've got to promise. Promise me."

"Alright," I say. "I promise."

So many promises. I've tried to keep them all. I promised to take care of Jamie, and I've done that, though I'm not finished yet. And that girl, Anne. I promised to help her too. For saving Jamie's life. How can I ever repay her for that?

I think of the last time I saw her, the angry words I said, the devastated look on her face. It burns me to think I'm the one who put it there.

I can try to make it up to her. Give her the proof she's been looking for.

I know where it is. It's been there all along, in that locked drawer in Blackwell's desk. I knew there was something special about those pages and the writing on them, even before I understood what it was.

I remember what Anne told me this would do to Blackwell one day. Maybe I can't destroy him in my world. But I can plant the seed that will destroy him in hers.

Then I remember—Anne doesn't know about those pages in Blackwell's desk. She thinks it's all over. She's given up.

I've got to tell her. Find her and tell her what I've found.

The sun has already set when I slip out through the kitchen door and start walking quickly across the field toward the woods. It's even darker inside the trees, and I have to feel my way with my hands in front of me. What if she's not here?

Suddenly, I see a light. I move closer and see it's not one light but many, all hovering in the air in a circle like a great ring of fire.

And people, so many people; some dressed in strange-looking clothes. Others are dressed like me, women in long dresses and high collars. I even see a few holding those magic picture-lights in their hands, like pilgrims holding candles.

Why are they all here? It's like the hole between our two worlds—the one that was only big enough to let Anne and me slip through—has torn open wide.

I see a woman in a long grey dress holding a piece of paper, reading some words I can't quite make out. A chill goes through me. All these strange people gathered here in the dark, standing in a circle under their ring of light. Are they witches? The ones who come to the woods at night to do terrible and unholy things?

I look to my left and see a face I know. *It's Anne.* She's wearing one of those long grey dresses like mine. Someone has pulled all that wild, curly hair behind her head, and her face looks naked in the strange light. She's crying, and it makes my heart hurt to see it.

Without thinking, I steal behind the ring of people as quietly as possible, step close to Anne, and take her hand.

She turns and sees me. Her eyes go wide and startled, then she lifts my hand to her face and presses it against her cheek. Her cheek is soft and warm on my hand. I feel something start to move inside of me, and I pull my hand away.

"What are you doing here?" she whispers.

"I was looking for you," I say.

"You were?" she smiles. The happiness on her face is so evident I have to look away.

"What's all this?" I whisper. "Who are all these people?"

"It's…it's a play."

"You mean…they're like actors and such?"

"Some of them are…" I can see her figuring out how to explain it to me. "It's a show my mom is putting on. To tell people about Thornwood."

"Why?"

"To tell people how important it is. To get them to help save it."

It's suddenly quiet, and I realize the woman has stopped reading from her paper. Another woman in a long grey dress and white apron steps out of the line and into the circle of light. She speaks in a firm, clear voice.

"My name is Anne Compton. Orphaned at five years old. Brought to Thornwood when I was six. Died at eighteen. Buried here with no name. Remember me."

The woman steps back into the line, and a man standing near us steps into the light.

"My name is Joseph Callahan. Born with cerebral palsy. Brought to Thornwood when I was seven. Died at sixteen. Buried here with no name. Remember me."

The man steps back in the line, and another woman steps into the light.

"My name is Annabelle Colwin. Had dementia when I was sixty-seven. Brought to Thornwood by my own children when I was sixty-nine. Died here at seventy-three. Buried with no name. Remember me."

One by one, they keep coming. *Remember me,* they all say. *Remember me. Remember...* The lantern light blurs and swims in my eyes, and I reach up to wipe the tears away with the back of my hand before anyone can see them.

Finally, no one else steps forward. No one speaks. The silence now is so deep, like the silence of a church.

Then, the people around us start applauding. A tall, slender woman steps forward and speaks, thanking people for coming.

"That's my mom," Anne says proudly.

"Really?" I look for a trace of Anne's face in the grown woman's, and it's not hard to find—the bright eyes, that round chin, and masses of curly hair.

"She's a fine-looking woman," I say.

A man steps out of the crowd and takes his place beside Anne's mother. This time, the resemblance is even more apparent.

"Your da…that's him, right?" I ask. Anne nods and smiles proudly.

The two of them exchange a few words, then Anne's mother steps aside, and he speaks to the crowd.

"My name is Jackson. Jackson Blake…" I hear a few whoops and scattered applause. It seems to startle him. Then he grins and continues. "I just want to thank everyone for being here tonight. I want to thank my wife, Carolyn, for all this. For everything. I'm so proud of you." He looks down for a moment, and I can see him gathering his words.

"I just want to say…I came here to help save a building. A beautiful old building. With a history that…well, wasn't always so beautiful. I've helped save a lot of buildings. And I've lost some too…" He stops, swallows, then keeps going.

"But this one…this one is different. This time, it's not just about a beautiful building or about history. It's about people. Real people. Living right here today in this community. You probably know some of them. The thing is…these people are going to have something very important taken away from them. Unless we can stop that from happening. The services and the care that this place provides…these people need them. I guess I never knew how important that was…until I was one of them, too."

It's so quiet I could swear everyone has stopped breathing. Anne's father stands there like he's unsure what else to say. A few people start whooping and clapping, then more and more. Anne's mother wraps her arms around him, and the two of them stand there, rocking back and forth while the people keep clapping and cheering. I look over at Anne. It's dark, but I'm sure I can see tears rolling down her cheeks.

Then the people around us start to move and talk, men and women in strange clothes walking up to people in clothes like mine, smiling and hugging each other.

"Wait," I say, "Can they see me?"

"I don't know…" Anne says.

"I need to talk with you," I say.

"Alright. I just need to talk to my mom first."

I see Anne's mother look our way and start walking toward us, and my heart leaps into my throat.

"What should I do?" I whisper.

"Wait here," Anne says, then runs to greet her mother.

I watch them meet, wrap their arms around each other, and stay that way for a while, gently rocking back and forth. They break apart and talk for a moment, still holding onto each other. *You're lucky*, I want to tell her. *D'you know that?*

Finally, Anne's mother bends down and kisses her cheek, then smiles and waves at Anne as she walks away. A moment later, she's back by my side, holding one of the lanterns.

"I told her I wanted to stay here a while," she says. "You want to go over here?" I follow her deeper into the trees, away from all the people. Anne sets the lantern down on a tree stump, and the light shines upon her face. She's looking at me anxiously like she's afraid I might disappear again.

"Are you alright?" she asks.

"I'm fine."

"I didn't…I didn't know if I was going to see you again," she begins. Her eyes fill with tears. "Mary, I'm so sorry…"

"That's enough of that," I say quickly. "I've got something I need to tell you. That writing you've been looking for. The book that other woman wrote. I know where it is."

"WHAT?" It's almost a shout, and she covers her mouth with both hands. Then she drops them and says softly, "You…you *found* it? Where?"

"It's in Blackwell's desk. I've seen it. I saw it a while ago but I didn't know what it was."

"Oh my God…it's true," she says, and I see her tremble. "She *was* here! You found it! Where is it now? Is it in the painting?!"

"Not yet. Tomorrow."

I think of how I'm going to do that, how I'll have to break into Blackwell's office, the danger of that. And for a moment, I almost feel afraid.

"Tell me again…" I say, "Tell me what this will do to him. To Blackwell."

She looks confused at first. Then I see understanding fill her eyes. She speaks slowly and clearly, as if she knows how much I need to hear every word.

"Everyone will know what a terrible person he really was. They'll know that everything he wrote was stolen from someone else. From a young woman, he used and tried to get rid of. And that the only reason people remember him is a lie. He won't be an important person anymore. He'll be a joke."

I close my eyes and let out a long breath. When I open them again, the fear is gone.

"When will I see you again?" she asks.

"I don't know… I'm leaving here. Tomorrow night."

"What?" I've startled her.

"A friend of mine here, she knows some people. They're getting us out of here tomorrow night. They'll be taking us to the Quakers."

A sad look comes over her face, and she can't look me in the eye. I realize what she's thinking, and a bit of the old anger rises up.

"I don't care what your history books or your magic lantern says. They're not going to bury me here. I'm leaving. Tomorrow. Jamie and me."

When she looks back up at me, the hope in her eyes nearly kills me.

"Okay," she says, "But…how will you know it worked? That I have it? Can't you come back one more time?"

I shake my head, "Do you think I'd want to risk my life coming back here?"

"No! Of course not…"

"Anne," I wait for her to look at me, "I'll know it worked because I see you now. You follow?"

She shakes her head.

"Why are we here, you and me? For this. All for this. Right? It'll work. Check the painting tomorrow."

Then she smiles, a small one, but a smile nonetheless. "Thank you, Mary. Good luck."

You're my luck, I think. "Good luck yourself."

As soon as the words leave my mouth, she's gone. This time, there's no misty light, no shimmering colors.

She's just gone.

Chapter 52 - Annie

I take my lantern and walk out of the circle, even as Mary's dissolving. Even as, in her eyes, I am too. I thank her silently as I head back to the party, to the great lawn, and to the band whose music I can just now hear.

Mom sees me and comes over with a bag in her hands. "Everything okay?" she asks, and when I nod, "Here, go inside and change, then come back and have some food."

All the lights are on, but no one's here, and my footsteps echo. I picture Mary walking these same halls, entering Blackwell's office, as I'm doing now. Instead of a living man, I see his portrait hanging as it's hung for all these years.

Is it a little crooked?

I hold my breath, then rush over to take it down. I lay it on the ground and look at the nails. I can't tell if they're different from how I left them. I find a letter opener, pry them loose, and lift the backing…

There's nothing there.

I close it up carefully and hang the painting. There's a trace of a smile beneath Blackwell's beard, and I want to hit him.

You haven't won yet, I think. Mary promised it would work. And I believe her.

I change and return to the party. Daphne and Carson are closest to me and appear to be arguing. They both look up as I approach.

"Tell him he can't leave yet," Daphne says, holding onto Carson's arm. "Party's just starting."

"I have to go. You don't get it. This is triggering."

Alarmed, I study his face. He looks mildly annoyed, not upset.

"Which is?" I ask. "The play or the party?"

Carson looks at me gratefully. "The party. I loved the play. Your mom did a great job!"

"Yeah, that was amazing!" Daphne adds. "How did she come up with all that?"

I shake my head. "A lot of research. And practice. She does events all the time. Pretty moving, right?"

They nod and Carson gently disengages his arm from Daphne's grip. "Let's grab coffee tomorrow, okay? I gotta go." She nods.

We watch as Carson goes to Mom and Dad to say goodbye. They each smile and hug him, and he looks so happy it makes me want to cry.

"Did his folks come?"

Daphne looks around, "I don't see them. I don't think so. He told me they didn't want him to get involved in the first place."

"What?!" I remember how Carson's mom spoke to him in the hospital, her voice full of uncertainty and overcompensation. Then I look at Mom and Dad, happy and relaxed, and realize how lucky I am to have them.

"Don't tell him I told you," Daphne says. "He doesn't want your dad to know. They're super protective." Then, looking around, she asks, "Is your friend still here?"

I look at her. "What?"

"Your friend. The one you were talking to. Is she from back home?" And then, "Hey, are you okay?"

"You… saw her?"

Daphne squints at me, then says, "Yeah, the one in costume. I don't remember her from the show. What was her part?"

For a moment, my throat closes up and I can't speak. Finally, I say, "Can you describe her?"

"Uh… okay," Daphne frowns. "Thin, shorter than you, long black hair, big eyes. She had a plain grey dress, long. I guess she was playing a patient."

She saw Mary. I can't take it in. "Oh, yeah," I say. "Her. She had to leave."

"Where's she from? I didn't recognize her…"

"Yeah, yeah. From back home."

I want to tell her the truth so badly it hurts. I look at her face, open, confused, friendly, and make a decision.

"Are you doing anything tomorrow?"

"Other than pushing ice cream with you? Nope."

Shit. We have work tomorrow. "After work, maybe?"

"Sure. What's up?"

"Just … I want to hang. Okay?"

"Sure." She studies me for another moment, then smiles. "C'mon. Let's sneak a drink. I know the bartender."

The next morning at breakfast, Mom says to me and Dad, "I've gotta help strike the set. Wanna come?"

Dad glances at his office but nods.

I think about the painting, what's waiting for me there. "Sure. Love to."

Once there, we're joined by a few other people, and Mom divvies out tasks. We work hard, emptying the tubs and disassembling set pieces and lights. I'm happy to do the work, but my mind and heart are in Blackwell's office. Will I find it this time? I can see myself taking down the painting, pulling out the manuscript.

I check the clock. It's been long enough to justify a bathroom break. I tell Mom, then head straight to the office. I open the door slowly and peer inside. It's dark and empty, so I go in, and close the door behind me.

This is it, I think, my breath coming fast.

I take the painting down and see two nails are missing. I'm sure I put them back. One of the remaining nails is bent at an odd angle as if hammered in too quickly. I can pull it out with my fingernail, giving me just enough space to lift the paper and see inside.

There's nothing there.

I put my fingers inside and feel around the cavity, but it's empty. Mary's been here. I know she has.

I pick up the painting and shake it, peering into the hole in case the documents are stuck further up inside. But there's nothing.

There are footsteps in the hall, so I quickly hang the portrait back on the wall and try to plan an excuse if someone enters. The footsteps pass, and everything is quiet again.

It's not here. What do I do now? My stomach cramps as I imagine what happened to Mary. Was she interrupted? Caught?

I rejoin my folks; they're helping pack lights. Mom looks up. "It's nearly twelve. Do you work today?"

I nod, and Dad jumps in with, "I can take you." He kisses Mom. "I want to check some things at home. I'll come back by 1 or 1:30, okay?"

She hesitates, clearly wanting him to stay, but smiles and waves us off.

Dad moves slowly through the rooms to the front door, looking all around as we go. He shakes his head. "I'd hate to lose this." He points to the ceiling in the hallway. "Look at that molding. It's plaster. Isn't it gorgeous?" I stare at the design in the center, outlined by a simple square with concave corners. The trim around the ceiling looks like oak leaves, and at the center of each wall, a face.

"Yeah," I say. "Beautiful."

"How can they tear it down?"

I look at his face; it's so sad I can't bear it. "We'll find something, Dad. I know we will."

He pulls me to him for a brief hug. "That's my girl."

It doesn't seem fair that I know the truth, and he doesn't.

"Dad?"

"Yeah?"

I hold my breath, then let it out. I can't tell him about seeing Mary. I just can't.

"Nothing."

On the drive to work, I wonder what Mary is doing. What interrupted her? Will she try again?

I think about Daphne. She *saw* Mary! Will she believe me if I tell her everything? The thought of someone else knowing makes me yearn for it so badly. Daphne's so cool. She didn't hesitate when I asked her to take me to the farm. She's got to believe me.

Customers are waiting when I get to the shack, so I jump out quickly and wave goodbye to Dad.

Daphne gives me a wink and a shrug. There's no pause in the stream of customers from opening until our shift ends, leaving no opportunity to talk.

"This is our best day yet!" Daphne says as she finishes counting the cash and credit card charges.

A long-haired, skinny boy steps inside the shack and stands behind Daphne. "Can I get in there, please?" Daphne stands and gives a mocking bow as she puts a stack of bills inside an envelope and sticks it in the lockbox.

She turns to me. "Where do you wanna go?"

I shrug, then say, "The cemetery." Maybe Mary will come while we're there.

"Whoa. Okay. I'm gonna need a drink for this." She grabs a cup and makes herself an ice cream soda. "Want one?"

The boy says, "Easy on the inventory," and Daphne makes a face at him. She makes my drink, then we exit the shack and walk towards the cemetery, slurping as we go.

"So, how'd you make out?" she asks. "With the fundraiser?"

"Really well, I think. Mom seems happy. Says donations are still coming in."

"How about your dad?"

I know she means well, but the question hurts. "He's okay. Still doesn't have what he needs for the Historic Preservation application."

"Yeah. Too bad about that guy, what's his name? Jamie? And those papers."

We turn onto the trail that leads to the cemetery.

"Why here?" she asks. It isn't just because I'm hoping Mary will appear. It's something rising from the ground. Some kind of peace.

"You're gonna think I'm crazy," I begin.

"I *know* you're crazy. So don't worry about it." Again, the Daphne grin. I can't help but grin back.

I look around the woods, listening for that whoosh of sound that often accompanies Mary's arrival. But all I hear are birds and the occasional car going past. I take a deep breath, then I start.

"You know that girl you saw me with last night?"

She nods.

"I only see her here."

Her eyes grow wide, and then she smiles. "Ah. Good one. She's a ghost, right? Former patient of Thornwood?"

I just look at her and nod.

"You're serious?"

"She's...not a ghost exactly. It's more like in a parallel timeline or something. Her name is Mary Donovan."

Now, Daphne shakes her head. "No...what? *That* Mary Donovan? The one your dad's looking for?"

"No. I thought she was…"

"So, this Jamie…"

"He's her brother. *My* Mary's."

"Whoa."

Daphne is silent for a long time. Finally, she speaks.

"How do you do it? Do you call her or something? Can you make her come now?"

I look at her in surprise. Her face is open and curious, maybe a little scared. She's not making fun of me.

"No. It just happens…when it happens." I look around the circle and say, "I don't know why, but I don't think we'll see her today."

I look back to find Daphne peering through the trees, scanning the area. "Too bad. I'd like to meet her."

So would I, I think, longing with every part of me to see her, to find out if she's okay. Maybe I should have told her to forget it. Is she in danger? My guts clench as I remember those words etched inside the box: *Help me, Anne.*

Daphne shoves me with her shoulder. "Hey. Where'd you go?"

I blink away the tears that started to gather in my eyes. "You believe me?"

"Sure. I mean… I saw a girl with you. You say she only comes to you here." She shrugs, "Who knows? The world is a funny place."

Now my chest feels light, and I realize how hard it was to keep this secret, how much I needed to tell someone. I don't even care if she thinks I'm nuts. I'm not alone anymore.

So I tell her everything. All about Blackwell and the presentation. Jamie and TB, the Quakers, their offer, and Blackwell's refusal to let Mary go.

"She found the papers!" I almost shout it, and Daphne stares at me. "The document Blackwell copied. The one written by the Mary Donovan Dad's looking for."

"She found them?" Daphne looks around the circle and back to me. "So she can bring them to you? Here? You've won!" She pumps her arms in the air. "Woohoo! Your dad's gonna be so happy…"

"Wait. You don't understand."

She puts her arms down and looks at me. Before I can say anything, she says, "Of course. How are you gonna explain finding them? 'Here, Dad, a ghost from Mary's time gave these to me in the cemetery.'"

I shake my head. "No, that's not it. I mean, yeah, that's a problem." Then I tell her about the disappearing food, about the painting, and our test run.

Now her eyes are enormous. "So she has the document, she'll put it in the painting… when? Is it there now?" She stands up.

I shake my head, and she sits back down. "She was supposed to do it by today. I checked this morning…"

"And it wasn't there." She finishes for me, then stares closer at my face, "What? You found something…"

"It's nothing. Maybe. The backing on the painting is nailed in. A couple of the nails were missing, and one was bent."

"How do you know that didn't happen sometime between her time and ours? Someone else fixing the painting or something."

"I checked it last night. The nails were all there."

I watch her face as she processes this, thinking again how great it is that she believes me.

"This dude, Blackwood. Would he hurt her?"

"Blackwell," I correct her. "Yeah. I think he would. I should have told her to forget it. She was getting out, escaping with Jamie…" Tears come again, and I rub my eyes hard. "What if she got caught?"

Daphne drapes an arm around my shoulder. "It's okay. We'll figure it out." She squeezes me, then says, "We know they got out, right? Because of Jamie."

I hang my head. I didn't tell her about the grave. "We know Jamie got out."

"Okay, if she was interrupted or something, if she couldn't get the manuscript into the painting, what would she have done with it?"

Hope slowly rises inside. *She could have hidden it somewhere else.* "But what if Blackwell caught her? Took it from her?" I don't realize I'm clenching my fists till Daphne grabs them.

"Easy, cowboy. Let's see what we know." She looks off in the distance, eyes slightly squinted. "We know Jamie got out, right? And last night, the painting was intact, all the nails were there. You're sure of that?"

I nod.

"This morning, it's different, right? Like someone's been at it."

I nod again.

"So Mary was interrupted. She didn't have time to hide the

manuscript there, but she *did* have time to put back one nail. Why? She heard someone coming and left. It's gotta be what happened, or the backing would be wide open, right?"

Again, hope surges inside me. "I guess. I mean, she's smart. And she'll do anything for Jamie. So she gets out before they find her…then what?"

"She hides it somewhere else! What was her escape plan?"

"I'm not sure. She just said they were getting out." I look around the circle, see the grave and look away quickly.

"She takes it with her!" Daphne slaps her forehead and stands up. "Of course she does. She takes it. And, if we're lucky, Old Farmer Joe still has it in those papers we didn't see!"

I jump up, unable to keep still. "You think so?" Of course she's right. Of course Mary did. "Can you drive me there now?"

"Wait." Daphne puts a hand on my arm.

"What?"

"You have to tell your dad."

"What?"

"We need him. Remember, that guy didn't believe us last time. But they'll believe your dad. Besides, he's part of all this. You gotta tell him."

"He'll never believe me. I can't make him think I'm crazy. *You* can convince that guy to let us see the papers. I'm sure you can. We can leave Dad out of this…"

"No. He needs to be there! It authenticates the find. How will it look if we show up with papers we say came from some guy's farm?"

I hate how logical she is. Everything she says is true. We need Dad. I have to tell him.

"If you don't think he can handle it," Daphne says, "just tell him it's a dream. The dream-Mary led you to Jamie, and now you're sure that the papers are there. *Please, please Daddy!*" She's holding her hands clasped in front of her to show me how.

I realize it's getting late and check my phone. "I gotta get back for dinner."

Daphne stands. "So. What are you going to do?"

"Tell him…something… I guess."

I start walking toward the parking lot, and Daphne walks beside me. Having her close by is so comforting I want to take her hand, and even as I think about this, I feel hers slip into mine. It's different from Mary's hand; a little bigger, less bony, but for a moment, I can feel both Daphne's and Mary's hands in mine, and I know I will tell Dad tonight.

"You believe me?" I ask.

Daphne snorts. "Nah, I just go with the flow." When I stop to stare at her, she shakes my hand a little. "'Course I do. It's too crazy for you to make it up."

I grin, and that grin stays with me after we separate, the whole way home.

Chapter 53 - Mary

Today is the day.

I'm already awake when the first dim light of morning starts to glow in the high windows. I've been lying here wide awake in the dark, waiting for it. Just a little light, that's all I need.

As soon as I can see my hand in front of my face, I get out of bed and start down the hallway. I keep one eye out for any guard or matron who might try to stop me, but there's no one. Just the dim light and the sound of my bare feet echoing off the walls.

Tonight. We're leaving tonight.

How am I going to get Jamie ready for this? Jamie's drawings. There are so many of them. Jamie makes drawings the way a tree makes leaves. He'll not want to leave them behind, that's for certain.

I walk quickly down the hall to the stairs, climb to the top, open the door, and step out into the cool morning air.

Jamie is standing a short distance away, leaning against the wall, looking out across the fields where the rose-colored light is gathering on the horizon.

"Jamie." He doesn't answer or turn around, so I walk over next to him. "So, what are you looking at?"

"Shhhh," he hushes me, raising one finger to his lips, then he points to a place on the horizon that's starting to glow brighter and brighter. I watch with him, and a moment later, the first white-hot glare of the sun peeks over the edge of the earth, and the clouds are all aflame with red and gold. It's a sign, I think.

We stand there for a while, watching the sun rise higher and all the fiery colors fading to blue. Then I look at Jamie, the last of that rosy light still on his face. I have to get him ready for what's going to happen.

"Jamie, do you remember the nice lady who came here a while ago? The one who liked your drawings?"

"You mean…" he says, "The lady…" He uses his fingers and traces a line in the air, circling around his face, and I understand. He's drawing her bonnet.

"That's right," I say. "You remember her?"

"I showed her my drawings."

"Yes. Would you like to see her again?"

He studies me closely, his eyes narrowing. "She's gone," he says. "She's not here."

"That's right, but we can go see her. Tonight. Would you like that?"

He looks at me for a long time while I wait for his answer.

"How?" he says.

"In a wagon. Tonight. I'll come get you. Then you and me and my friend Kathleen, we're all going to get in a wagon and ride out of here."

I watch him thinking about this. Jamie doesn't always take well to change. I'm hoping this isn't one of those times.

"I can take my drawings…." he says.

"Yes, yes, you can take them," I say. "But Jamie, you have to promise me something. Can you promise?"

"What," he says.

"You have to promise to be quiet. No talking, no yelling. Nothing. It's a game, alright? And those are the rules. No talking until I say so."

"It's not a game," he says, and it startles me. "It's so we don't get caught. I know that. You talk to me like I'm a little child. I'm not a little child."

I look at those clear grey eyes of his looking right back at mine, and I notice how slim his face has become, not from hunger or illness but from time itself. I know Jamie better than anyone, but there's part of him that I don't really know. I can see that now.

"Alright," I say. "You're not a child. I know that." We both stand there in silence for a moment. "So…I'll come for you tonight, then."

"I can bring my drawings," he says.

"Yes. You can bring your drawings."

It seems like the sun will never set. While I'm waiting, I go over the plan in my mind. Six o'clock, Blackwell leaves his office for the day, I get Jamie and bring him to Kathleen who'll be waiting by the wagon. Six-thirty, I go to Blackwell's office, get the manuscript from his desk, hide it in the painting for Anne to find. Six forty-five, I run down to meet Kathleen and Jamie at the laundry wagon and we all ride out of here forever.

It sounds so simple, but I'm already wondering: What if Blackwell doesn't leave when he's supposed to? What if he leaves and then decides to come back before I'm done? What if Jamie can't keep still like I asked him to, and he gives us all away? And the manuscript. What if it's not there?

I know you're not a child. Now it's my da's voice coming back to me again from wherever it's been hiding itself.

I know you're not a child, Mary, so you'll understand.

He was standing in the rain outside the kitchen door to Aunt Bridget's house, the water running down his face, his shirt soaked to the skin. The things he said to me broke apart like pieces of a broken plate, all scattered bits and sharp edges. They're still like that in my mind, so when I try to piece them together, I never know if I'm doing it the right way. All I have are the pieces—the one where he tells me of the danger he's in and the evil men coming for him. The one where he tells me of the beauty of the world and the special place I hold in it. The one where he makes me promise to take care of Jamie. Time and again, I gather all the pieces and try to make something of them, and time and again, I fail and watch them fall from my hands.

I know you're not a child, Mary, so you'll understand…

Understand what? What is it that he wants me to understand? He's asked me to understand so much already. Why Mother was taken from us. Why I had to take care of my brother. Why he couldn't do the things that other fathers do, and had to disappear from us without even leaving a gravestone to mark his passing. I said that I understood because I knew it was what he wanted me to say, but I never did. Not any of it.

All I understood was that I had to keep going. Because if I just kept going, there'd be something on the other side of all this pain and sorrow and humiliation. Maybe not something better, but something *else*. That's all I've ever hoped for.

Maybe now I'll get to see it.

Finally, the sun starts moving from where it's been frozen all day, and the light begins to dim. I wait until the clock says it's six-thirty. I go down the hallway and climb the stairs to the roof.

Jamie is there waiting for me. His shoes are on and tied, and a big stack of drawings is by his side.

"Are you ready, then?" I say. He nods. "Alright, let's go."

I open the door to the stairwell and listen to hear if anyone else is coming up the stairs—only silence, so we start walking down together.

When we reach the bottom, I poke my head out the door and look up and down the hall. There's a matron coming, and I duck my head back in before she sees me and wait for her to pass by. I don't have to tell Jamie to be quiet—he stands very still, right next to me, silent as the grave.

The matron's footsteps fade away, and I signal Jamie to follow me. I know some girls will be in the kitchen at this hour, so I lead him through the deserted laundry room, past the smell of lye and dampness. I push the little door open, then we're outside where it's almost full dark now.

We steal along behind the big building where no one goes but the rats. I see a big one scamper out of our way behind some rubbish. *Goodbye and good riddance,* I think. *You won't be seeing me again.*

Just around the corner, I see the wagon at the gate and Kathleen waiting near it.

"So this is Jamie then, is it?" she says, looking him up and down.

"Jamie," I say, "This is Kathleen. You're going to wait here with her, and I'll be back in a minute."

"There's no time for that!" Kathleen says. "You should've been here before now."

"I told you," I say. "I have to do something."

"Damn it, Mary, we're trying to get out of here together. What's more important than that?"

"I *said* I'll be right back! Did you hear me that time?"

Kathleen shakes her head. "Fuck, Mary, you're gonna get yourself killed, sure as hell."

I notice Jamie starting to rock back and forth a little the way he does when he's getting anxious, so I turn to him and smile.

"Jamie…why don't you show Kathleen your drawings? She'd like to see them…" I turn to Kathleen, "…wouldn't you?"

Kathleen looks at me, then at Jamie. I see something soften in her face.

"I'd love to," she says. Before I go, she whispers to me. "Twenty minutes, Mary. That's all. We can't wait, I'm telling you."

"I know," I say. Then I'm off and running as fast as I can.

When I reach the main building, I steal along the side of it, keeping in the shadows. I count the windows until I reach the one I know is Blackwell's office. It's no good trying to get in through the door inside. I don't know how to pick a lock, and if I tried to break in, the noise would bring the guards and matrons running.

I reach into my pocket and take out the stone and rag I've brought. I wrap the rag around the stone to muffle the noise and aim at the pane of glass closest to the lock. I have to do this with just one blow—any more might attract attention.

I hit the glass and it breaks. I wrap my hand in the rag to protect it, then reach through the jagged hole. My fingers find the lock and unfasten it. The window slides open easily, and I climb through.

The office is dark, but just enough light is coming through the window for me to see. I go right to Blackwell's desk and try to pull open the drawer, but it's locked.

I look around quickly and grab a heavy brass letter opener. I force it under the lip of the drawer, pull hard, and the drawer comes open with an ugly, splintering sound. Then I drop the blade and start digging through the big stack of papers, praying it's still here.

Just when I think I might never find it, there it is. That same beautiful, careful handwriting. And right there on the top page, I see my name.

Her name. Our name.

Mary Donovan.

And below that name, these carefully written lines:

To whoever finds these words, my thanks. Take courage, and never let yourself be silenced.

My heart stops for a moment. When it starts again, it feels so full that I think it might burst.

I pull those pages out and stuff them into a big envelope I've found. I go to Blackwell's hateful face, glowering down from the wall, lift the painting off the nail, and lay it face-down on the floor. Then I grab the letter opener and start prying away at the nails on the back.

I've almost got the third nail out when I hear footsteps outside in the hallway, getting closer. I hold my breath to listen better, praying they'll keep going and pass me by, but they don't. They come right up to the door and stop. The latch rattles, then I hear a key sliding into the lock.

Quickly, I grab the envelope with the papers inside. I crawl out the window, drop to the ground, and start running. How long will it take for them to raise the alarm when they see what I've done? I don't look back. I keep running harder than I've ever run before.

I round the corner, and there they are, Kathleen and Jamie, waiting for me at the gate. I can see the glow of a lantern in front, a driver holding onto the reins and looking nervous. Kathleen sees me and starts waving me on to hurry up.

Running harder than ever, I finally reach the wagon and jump in, my breath coming in big, ragged gasps. I can't believe it—I made it. Jamie is grinning at me.

"It's about fecking time!" Kathleen says, then a look of alarm crosses her face.

That's when I hear them—angry voices shouting in the distance, growing closer. Blackwell's men. Right now they're only after me, but in another moment, they'll be close enough to see the wagon. And that will be the end of everything for all of us.

I can't let that happen.

I shove the envelope I'm holding into Kathleen's hands and climb out of the wagon.

"Mary, no!" Kathleen says, "What the hell are you doing?"

"Go on, I'll catch up with you!" I tell her, "Get out of here, now!"

"No, Mary!" Kathleen says, "Get in!"

I run to the front of the wagon, grab the lantern, and shout at the driver, "Go on! *Go!*" I slap the horse with the flat of my hand as hard as I can.

The horse bolts, and the wagon lurches away. The last thing I see before the wagon disappears into the dark is Jamie reaching out for me as they speed away, and Kathleen with both arms wrapped tight around him, holding him back.

I take a deep breath and swallow back the pain.

Then I turn to face what's coming.

Chapter 54 - Annie

"Dad?" I poke my head in the door of his office. He's sitting at his desk, laptop closed. He turns to look at me.

"Hey." He glances back at his desk, then at me again. "I'd say I'm busy, but I'd be lyin'." His grin is sweet and sad. "What have you got there?"

I'm holding the papers we got from the farm. I've been over and over what to tell him so he'll help us, but I'm still not sure.

"Remember the artist Jamie Donovan? We found these," I hold up the papers for him to see. "His great-great grandson lives in Boxford, and they saved them."

"Jamie?" Hope passes across Dad's face like a beam of light and then goes out. "The one you thought was related to Mary Donovan? When did you get these?" He reaches for the papers, and I hand them to him.

"Dad?"

He's rifling through the pages as I did, even though he knows there's nothing there. He looks up and says, "You never told me why. Why you thought this man, Jamie, was related."

"Yeah, well, that's what I—"

"Look at this!" He holds up a drawing of Thornwood that I missed. "Wow." He squints at the inscription and reads the date. "He was there after Mary. But I might be able to use this in the application."

"Dad. We need your help."

"We?"

"Daphne and me. Listen…" I pull up a chair and sit across from him, knees almost touching. I lean in and try to speak…but I can't.

He looks at me with curiosity morphing into alarm. "What is it? Are you okay?"

I want to tell him the truth so badly it makes my stomach cramp, but I'm afraid of how he'd take it.

"I had a dream…" It just pops out, and once it's there, I'm committed.

He leans back, a smile starting on his mouth. "What kind of dream?"

I take a deep breath. "There's this girl. In the cemetery. She's from the 1800s, dressed like the women in that picture in the laundry room."

"Thornwood cemetery? Okay. Then what?"

"She says her name is Mary Donovan, and—"

"You had a dream about Mary Donovan?"

"She wasn't *that* Mary Donovan. She just had the same name. Anyway, in the dream, she says that Dr. Blackwell is grooming her for a presentation in front of bigwigs to raise money…"

"Blackwell? This is some dream."

I sigh, "Yeah, well, she also tells me she has a brother with TB."

Dad is looking at me differently now. He leans in. "Jamie."

I nod. "I tell her about you and the project to save Thornwood. How we're looking for her writing… but then the dates didn't match."

"This dream Mary told you what year it was?"

I nod. "And when she was born. She's ten years younger than our Mary."

He's studying me exactly the way I was afraid of. Like he's worried about me. I have to make this work.

"So…that was a few weeks ago. Last night she came to me… I mean, I dreamed about her again."

Dad's face relaxes a little.

"This time, she told me she found it. Mary's writing. She said she could hide it, make sure it was saved, so I…so we could find it now."

Dad makes a sound in his throat, then starts to speak, "Dream Mary told you she would save Mary Donovan's papers?"

I think of movies and books where the ghost or dream person always says where to look. "She told me to look in Jamie's papers." I let out a breath and wait.

Dad studies my face for a long moment, then looks back at the papers I handed him. "*Did* you find something? Something that's not here?"

"There are more papers. We didn't look through all of them. Can we go back, please? Can you take us? The farm guy didn't believe Daphne and me. I'm sure you can convince him…"

"That a dream Mary Donovan told you to look in her brother's papers for a document written by someone else named Mary Donovan?"

"Dad, it's possible. Jamie and Mary were in Thornwood not long after our Mary was there. What if she did find something? What if she did save it? It's worth a try."

He looks at me closely, frowning. "You talk about her like she's real."

"She *is* real!" I pull out the cemetery drawing and gravestone picture from the papers he's holding. "This is real. I've seen it." The tears come and I don't stop them. Dad studies the papers, looks at my face, then stands and pulls me into his arms.

"Shhh, okay. She's real. And you want to help. I know you do."

"I know it sounds stupid, but I think she came to me. I think she really did. So she could help us. Please, Dad, please? Can you take us to the farm?"

He holds me for a long time. It's good to be hugged this way, and even though I never want to worry him, it feels good to have him concerned for me. He sighs, pulling away from me to look into my face.

"If I agree, will you accept whatever happens?"

I'm so relieved I almost miss the question. "What do you mean?"

"This man, what's his name?"

"James Marsh."

"He might refuse us."

"But he can't…"

"Of course he can. It's his property." I start to speak, but he holds up a hand. "I'll do my best, but if he says no, you have to agree to drop it."

I clench my teeth, remembering how Marsh turned us away last time. But I nod.

"Okay. I promise. I'll drop it." Then I look at him and start to smile. "You'll do it? You'll take us?"

He nods, smiling back, and I throw my arms around his neck. "Thank you. Thank you so much!"

Time slows down and it makes me want to scream. First, Dad insists on calling Marsh. Of course he doesn't get him. Then I have to wait and wait as the hours drag by until the next day when I'm at work. I get a text from Dad saying, *'We're in!'* Daphne and I do a little victory dance, making the waiting customers laugh.

'When?' I text.

He takes way too long to answer. Again, minutes stretch into hours, but finally, he texts, *'First thing tomorrow.'*

"Tomorrow?!" I moan, and Daphne pats my arm.

"It's okay. Just one more day."

Then she leans in and whispers, "Have you seen her?"

I shake my head—I did go back to the cemetery this morning before work. I didn't stay long. It's a little like Mary's expecting me to work it out on my own.

At dinner, Dad seems better. He's excited to talk to Marsh about Jamie's drawing. I'm not sure how much hope he has in anything else, and a sudden guilt descends. How will he react if there's nothing there?

I picture Mary's face the last time I saw her, how thin and tired she looked. Then that headstone in the cemetery…But I know how strong and smart she is. She had to find a way to keep her promise. I know she did.

When I go to bed, I shut down my phone and turn off the light, hoping sleep will take me. I think about the first time I saw Mary, how miserable I was, how she suddenly appeared. How she brought me food when she thought I was starving. Her expression of bliss eating ice cream, the chocolate around her mouth. The way she looked when I told her things that could help Jamie. That little shine of hope on a hard face.

I must have fallen asleep because the next thing I know, I'm standing in the cemetery and Mary is holding my hand. I'm so glad to see her I start to cry and she laughs at me. She squeezes my hand, and I can feel her bony fingers. Then there's another hand on my arm, and my Dad's voice comes through.

"Time to get up, kitten."

Shortly after breakfast, I hear Daphne's car pull up.

"Ready?" Dad asks, and I nod.

It's easier to navigate this time, and we're soon at the long driveway to the farmhouse. "Turn here!"

As the barn comes into view, my heart begins to race. "Remember what I said," Dad tells me. I nod, but everything inside me is sparking like a cut power line in the wind.

Please, Mary. These words go through my head over and over like a mantra.

The farmer steps from the barn before we get out of the car and offers a hand to Dad. "G'morning. James Marsh," he says, and Dad smiles.

"'Morning. Jackson Blake. And this is Annie and Daphne. Thanks for letting us come."

Mr. Marsh nods at Daphne and me, then says, "C'mon inside."

I hesitate, but Dad's already following him through the door, and

Daphne gives me a shove.

It's cool inside the house. Mr. Marsh offers us seats around a kitchen table. There's a coffee pot and a bottle of orange juice.

My heart's still beating hard. We're wasting valuable time, but I have to follow Dad's lead. I pour some juice, then sit on my hands, glancing at Daphne. She seems perfectly at ease.

Mr. Marsh clears his throat. "I'm glad you called. Few years' back, we had some interest in my great-great grandfather's art, but then it dried up. Never knew he was at that institution." He's staring at the drawing of Thornwood that Dad left on top of the papers we brought back to him. "Then I got this." He holds up one of the invitations to Mom's event.

"Turns out we got several folks on both sides of the family that spent time in that place. Probably a few buried there." He pushes an envelope across the table to Dad.

"What's this?" He picks it up.

"A little help."

Dad opens the envelope and pulls out a check, then whistles. "Wow. This is … very generous."

"My mom told me not to talk about it. Kids at school liked to tease, you know? But I've seen what the drugs do, booze, depression," he looks up at the ceiling for a moment. "That hospital now, it's doing good work. Should keep on."

He looks down at his hands and we all remain silent. Then Dad breaks it. "Thank you. This just might put us over the top."

"Really?" I stare at him.

"Mm-hmm," he smiles. "But, as I mentioned on the phone, we're trying to save the old buildings, and that land isn't covered by these donations. We need the status of National Historic Preservation."

Mr. Marsh nods, "So, what can I do? You wanna look through that trunk?" He gives me and Daphne a long look. "Again?"

"If you don't mind," Dad says, and I push my chair out to stand. "Would you let me use this drawing? It's signed and dated, clearly

Thornwood. It could help.”

Mr. Marsh nods, then stands up. “I think you two know the way.” He looks at us first, then turns back to Dad. “I’ve got things to do. Let me know what you find.”

Dad stands, shakes his hand, then tells me, “Lead the way.”

We head back to the barn, the inside dark and cool, ripe with the scent of manure and full of soft animal sounds. I lead the way up into the loft, pointing out the hole in the floor to Dad before skirting around it.

The trunk is just as we left it, closed with a couple of handprints in the dust. I look at Dad, then we both look at Daphne, but nobody moves. Dad finally takes a deep breath, says, “Okay then,” and opens the trunk.

“How should we do this?” Daphne says.

“Methodically.” Dad looks at the envelopes and stacks of documents for a moment, then pulls out one stack and hands it to me and another to Daphne.

“What are we looking for?” Daphne asks.

“Anything with the name Mary Donovan,” Dad says. “Anything that looks like a description of the inside of an asylum. Anything mentioning care or treatment of mental patients.”

Dad reaches into the trunk and pulls out his own stack, then the three of us stand by the table, side by side, looking through the papers.

I scan each page, looking for words like the ones Mary read to me. I look for Mary’s name, not Dad’s Mary, but mine. I want to see it somewhere, but it’s not in this stack.

Dad’s reading something slowly. I can see his lips moving. “Hmmm,” he says, “That’s funny…”

“What?” I ask.

“*For A. 2022,*” Dad reads aloud. My heart jerks and everything becomes still.

I’m aware of rustling paper as Dad lifts the sheet and starts to read what's underneath, but all I can see are the letter *'A'* and the year *2022.* Again, I feel her thin fingers in my hand.

"On Treatment in Hospitals for the Insane," Dad's voice starts to shake, "I think…this might be…" He turns that page and reads silently for several moments. He flips through several more pages, then stops. He puts the papers on the table and turns to me, his eyes stunned. "Mary Donovan. Dated. Signed."

"Can I?" I reach for the pages. Dad hands them over to me, and I see elegant handwriting covering page after page. I see the words Mary read to me: *Imagine the worst moment you have ever had.* I'm shaking as I turn to the signature page and see not only the name and date but the place: *Thornwood Lunatic Asylum and Almshouse.*

"Will this do it?" I ask Dad.

He nods, still stunned, and I turn back to the first page, written in a different hand, a hand I know. I remember how she called me *Miss Twenty-twenty-two.* I want to kiss the page. *You did it, Mary! You did it!*

Daphne says, "I don't know about you, but shouldn't we be celebrating?" And with that, she lets out a loud *Whoop!* and slaps us both on the back. Dad smiles and mocks throwing a punch at her, then hugs me and spins me around. "We did it! You did it! You and your dream ghost! Woohoo!"

I pull Daphne in and we bounce up and down in a group hug.

"Let's tell Mr. Marsh and get out of here," Dad says, putting away the other papers and shutting the trunk.

Dad and Daphne leave the barn before me and miss the soft voice saying, "Excuse me?"

I turn to find Marsh's daughter standing in the shadows.

"Looks like you found what you wanted," she says.

I nod. "I know you're not interested in Jamie Donovan," she says. "but I was wondering if you might know…" She steps into the light.

"There were several of these." She holds up papers, which I can see have pencil drawings of someone. "I always loved her face, but he didn't write a name. Maybe you know?"

My fingers tremble as I take the drawings from her hands.

The top one is a pencil sketch on thin paper, a child's drawing, yet there is no question who this is.

Mary looks up at me, chin high, eyes boring into mine as if to say, *Took you long enough.*

I blink away sudden tears, then turn to the next drawing.

"You know who it is?"

I nod, staring at another drawing. This time, the hand is more sure, the drawing more detailed. And it has the year on it, 1866. Before I turn the page, I wonder if I'm about to see what she'll look like as an adult. The paper trembles as I turn to the next one and find Mary, same pose, more detailed, dated 1870. The following three drawings are even better; the dates later. But Mary never ages. The last one is dated 1880, the image so perfect from years of practice, she nearly leaps from the page.

"Her name is Mary. She's Jamie's sister."

"His sister! I wonder what happened to her." She takes the pictures back from me. "She must have died young."

It's true, I think. It's true. Even though I wanted so much for it not to be.

I glance up and see the woman looking at me carefully. She holds the drawings out to me and says in a gentle voice, "Would you like to have one?"

I can't answer. I'm picturing Mary and what happened to her. Rescuing the manuscript. Staying behind.

Then I realize Marsh's daughter is waiting for me, so I nod and take the one from 1870. "Yes. Thank you." And holding Mary's face in my hand, I walk to Daphne's car and wait for her and Dad to emerge from the farmhouse so we can all go home.

Chapter 55 - Mary

I watch the wagon rolling away into the darkness. Jamie's voice cries out for me, getting fainter and fainter until I can no longer hear it. There's a pain in my heart like nothing I've ever felt, like something stretching and tearing loose inside of me.

The angry voices are getting louder. I turn and see the light from lanterns bobbing and swaying in the darkness, coming closer. In another moment they'll see the gate standing open and guess what happened. They don't know about Kathleen and Jamie—not yet. When they find out, they'll go after them for sure.

I remember what Kathleen said—in thirty minutes, they'll reach where her cousin is waiting with fast horses to take them to the Quakers. They'll have a chance if I can hold off Blackwell's men till then.

I see the men now, charging down the hill toward me. I may not be able to stop them. But I can sure as hell slow them down.

I quickly open the lantern, pour the oil all over the road, and then throw the burning lamp down. The fire leaps up, throwing a hellish light on all the angry faces approaching me. One of them tries to cross the flames to get to me, but then I hear him curse and he draws back.

The flames are already dying, so I look around, pick up a stone from the road and throw it at them as hard as I can. I hear a loud curse and know I've drawn blood, so I pick up all the stones I can and keep throwing them until the fire dies and the men come charging through at me. I'm still throwing stones when they reach me and drag me down, beating me with their fists and their boots and their clubs. I try to cover my head and take the blows with my arms, but one club gets through and cracks my skull so hard that everything goes black.

When I can see again, the lighted windows of Thornwood are

hovering in front of me, growing closer. My feet aren't touching the ground, and for a moment, I wonder if I'm flying until I feel rough hands clutching my arms, dragging me forward.

They bring me into Blackwell's office, where he's standing at his desk, digging through the drawers. He looks up at me, his eyes red and angry.

"Where is it?"

I say nothing.

"Where is it?" I can see beads of sweat forming on his brow.

I still say nothing.

He turns to the guards and shouts at them. "Get out!" They hesitate. *"Get out!"* he shouts again. The men leave, and Blackwell slams the door, locks it, and turns to face me.

"Alright," he says, "Tell me where it is."

I take a quick look at the clock. Ten more minutes for Kathleen and Jamie to find her cousin and take those fast horses out of Blackwell's reach.

"So," he says, "You refuse to talk. Do you think that means you've won? You're going to tell me, sooner or later. You might as well tell me now."

I say nothing. Eight more minutes. All I have to do is wait.

Blackwell takes a step closer, the blood starting to gather in his face, reddening it. "Tell me where it is, or I swear I'll make you sorry you were ever born."

Again, I say nothing. I'm not giving him a thing, not a goddamned thing.

"I could throw you back in the box," he says, "But I suppose that's starting to lose its charm for you." He pauses and a terrible gleam comes into his eye. "What about your brother?"

"Fucking bastard," I say, "He's just a child!"

"Exactly. That would be a whole new experience for him, wouldn't it? How long do you think he'll last in there?"

"Jesus, man," I say. "If you could fucking hear yourself, you'd cut your own throat."

Blackwell opens the door and calls to one of the matrons. "Find Jamie Donovan in the men's ward," he says. "Bring him here."

I take another quick look at the clock. Five more minutes. It'll take the matron that long to find Jamie's gone and report back here. Relief rushes through me like a river. They're safe. Jamie and Kathleen. They're both safe.

There's a sudden pounding on the door. The matron's back already. "The boy's gone," she says in a quavering voice.

"Where is he?" Blackwell sputters at me, then turns back to the matron. "Search the building and grounds…"

"You won't find him," I say.

The blood drains from Blackwell's face so fast I think he's going to faint. Without Jamie, he's got nothing; no way to threaten or control me.

Blackwell shoves the woman out of the room, slams the door, and again turns to face me. His mouth moves, but no sound comes out. He bends down suddenly—when he stands up, he's clutching the letter opener in his hand like a dagger.

"Do you know what the punishment for thieves used to be?" he says. "They had their hands cut off."

"You're the fucking thief. Are you going to cut your own hand off? I'd like to see that."

He stands staring at me. I try to imagine what's going through his head, but I can't.

Blackwell drops the letter opener to the floor. It lands with a harsh, clattering sound. When he speaks, his voice is hoarse and weak, like he's running out of air.

"Give it back…please."

Please? Jesus Christ. I can't believe what I'm hearing.

"I believe that must have cost you something to say that," I say. "Am I right?"

"What do you want?" he asks.

"Nothing," I say. "I don't want a goddamned thing from you. Not anymore."

"Give it back." He sounds like a begging child as if saying it enough times can make it happen.

"I can't," I say. "I don't have it."

I see him realize what's happened, and a desperate light enters his eyes.

"We'll stop him," he says. "We'll stop him and bring it back."

"No," I say. "You won't."

"What do you mean?"

"You won't stop him."

"How can you say that?"

"Because," I say. "I know what happens."

He tries to laugh—it's a pitiful, half-choked sound. "Oh, so you can tell the future now, can you?"

"No," I say. "But I know someone who can. Would you like me to tell you *your* future?"

He looks afraid now. Good. He should be.

"Here's what's going to happen. First, you're going to wonder if you should publish that book, the one you stole from that girl who was here before me because you're afraid someone's going to find out. But you won't be able to stand it because you want people to pay attention to you and tell you how brilliant you are. And for a while, you'll be getting what you want, people talking about you, about how smart and important you are. But the whole time, you'll know it's a lie, and it'll be eating you up inside, not because you know it's wrong, but because you're afraid to get caught. So you'll never have a moment's peace because you'll always be waiting for it to happen. And when it does, when it finally does, everyone will know what you really are..."

I watch Blackwell's face grow more and more red as he listens to me, and his lips start to tremble.

"You want people to talk about you and remember you? They'll remember you, alright. How the only thing you ever did was steal from a girl who was ten times smarter and ten times better than you ever were."

He walks toward me. I think he's going to hit me, but he moves past me to the door, flings it open, and calls to the guards. Then he returns with two grim-looking men following close behind him like hunting dogs.

"You think *you'll* be remembered?" he says. "Who's going to remember *you*? You'll have plenty of time to think about that where you're going."

Two rough hands grab my arms, someone pulls a burlap sack over my head, and everything goes dark. Now they're hurrying me along through long, twisting hallways and down drafty stairs, more and more of them, deeper than I've ever gone before until the air on my skin grows colder and colder. There's a wet, rank smell in my nostrils, like the smell of old cellars or caves.

The men stop. I hear the rattle of keys and the groaning of old hinges. Then someone shoves me from behind, and I stumble down a few stairs and fall face-down onto cold, damp stone.

I pull the bag away from my head, but it's too dark to see anything. I hear the creak of rusty hinges, a heavy door slamming shut, the rattle of keys, and footsteps fading further and further away.

I don't leap up and pound at the door. I don't scream and curse the men who've left me here. Something inside is telling me it's no use.

I sit and wait for my eyes to grow used to the dark. Finally, I stand up, my head still pounding from the blow it took. I shuffle forward, reach out and put my hands on a stone wall, damp and rough with moss.

There's something else here, too. Cold, hard metal fixed to the wall rattles when I touch it. I run my fingers down long lengths of heavy chain, then stop. I know what I'm touching. Manacles. Prison chains.

I let go of what I'm holding—if there's something at the other end of these chains, I don't want my fingers to find it.

The rattle of the chains echoes and dies. Now there's only the slow dripping of water and the sound of something small scurrying off in a corner. I know where I am. This is the place Kathleen told me about. The place where Blackwell hid her. The first Mary Donovan, who wrote all those beautiful words.

If that's true, then maybe I'm not alone. Maybe she's still here.

I listen hard for any sound, any sound at all, but there's only the echo of water dripping.

I have to know.

"Mary?" I whisper. No answer.

I call out again, louder this time, "Mary?"

The sound of my name echoes back to me. It's the loneliest thing I've ever heard.

She's not here. Of course she's not. She's gone off to do what she's meant to do. And I'm glad for her.

It's plain to me now. If I hadn't stayed behind like I did, Jamie would be here next to me in this awful place. Instead, he's far from here, on his way to a new life.

I think of all the things that Anne told me. *Jamie lives.* He grows up and grows old. One day he'll die, like the rest of us, but not before he does all the things he's meant to do in this world.

Like me. I've done what I was meant to do. I've kept my promises. Maybe now I can rest.

The old familiar fire rises inside me again. *No.* This can't be it. This can't be all of it. Not while I'm still breathing.

The words come back to me, the ones I saw today in that plain, beautiful handwriting.

Take courage.

Mary's talking to me now, clear as anyone ever has.

Take courage

She speaks. And I listen.

Chapter 56 - Annie

The cemetery is different now. Smaller and no longer mine. I go directly to the circle, sit on the bench, and close my eyes. I've been coming here every day for the past two weeks and still haven't seen her.

"Mary," I say, "You did it! I got the manuscript. Dad's so happy." I listen for a sound, any sound at all, but there's nothing. Even the wind in the branches of the pine trees is silent. "Jamie kept it all his life. And his grandson, great-grandson, they kept it, too. Isn't that amazing?" I look into the trees all around me, but there's no one here but me.

"Mary, please come. I need to see you. Please. Please come!"

I can't stand how hollow and lonely my voice sounds. Tears fill my eyes, but she doesn't come. Still, I stay there in this place, in our place, as long as I can until it's time to go to work.

Daphne's busy with a customer, and there's a line by the time I arrive. So I hurry inside and grab an apron. It's my last day here. I realize with a pang that, next to Mary, I'll miss Daphne most.

"You could move here," she says when we finally have a lull. "We make a good team."

I smile. "Don't tempt me. Mom gets work in New York City and needs to be near the train."

"Guess you'll be glad to get back with your friends."

I picture Bess and my body clenches. Only this time, there's no longing, no wish that we were reconciled. Her last words to me still sting, but I'm starting to think they were more about Bess than me. Even though the memory of the kiss and her rejection still make me cringe, it hurts less.

Daphne interrupts my thoughts. "Still leaving tomorrow?"

I nod. "Mom's anxious to get back, settle Dad with a new doctor. He's already done most of the drawings for the renovations. And school starts soon…"

Daphne makes a face. "School, bleh. I got one more year. After I graduate, I'm free."

"Where will you go?"

"Where *won't* I go," she grins, then studies me for a moment. "You look sad. What's up?"

The concerned look on her face makes me want to tell her—she's let me tell her so much already.

"The other day," I begin, "At the farm, after you and Dad went to the car, that guy's daughter showed me a bunch of drawings. Ones Jamie did of Mary."

"Cool."

"No. I mean…all those drawings. He drew them over, like, twenty, thirty years. But she never gets any older."

I can't say the rest. I look into Daphne's face to see if she understands, and I see her get it.

"Oh…" she whispers. "Oh, man…"

"If it wasn't for me, she might have made it out."

"So you think it's your fault?" Daphne scoots a little closer to me puts one hand on my arm. "Listen, I didn't know her like you did. But from what you told me, she didn't seem like the type of person who'd do anything she didn't want to do."

"I don't know," I say. "Maybe…maybe it would have been better if we'd never met."

Daphne looks at her arms and traces a line of one of her tattoos. "What about Jamie? Wasn't he sick? And you helped them, right?"

I nod.

"She helped you help your dad, didn't she? I bet she'd want you to remember that."

Car doors slam, and a stream of kids and parents run up to the window and form a line so we get to work.

At the end of the shift, I wash the scoops and hang up my apron––for the last time, I realize. I turn to Daphne and she pulls me in for a quick hug. "Don't forget me."

"Not possible," I smile at her.

She waggles her phone at me. "Keep in touch."

I go straight home, knowing Mom and Dad are waiting for me. I walk into the house and Mom hands me an empty box. "Finish packing your room, please."

I go to my room and start filling the box. Gremlin watches from the bed. Mary watches from her frame on my wall. I take it down and put it on top of my things. *Why won't you come to me,* I think. *I want to say goodbye.*

There's a soft knock at my door. Dad peeks in and says, "Can I come in?"

"Sure," I stop packing and look at him. "What's up?"

"I found something," he says, holding an envelope and tapping it against his free hand. He's frowning and staring at me. Something about his look frightens me.

"What?"

"An envelope. With your name on it."

I reach for it, then frown. Who would send me a letter? "Can I see it?" I hold out my hand, but he doesn't give it to me. "Who's it from?"

He holds it up for me to see. The envelope is old, yellowed and looks fragile. Instantly, I recognize the handwriting.

"It was next to the printer. It must have fallen out of Mary Donovan's manuscript when I was scanning." My heart starts to pound. I stare at Mary's words *For Anne.* I want to rip it from his hands.

"The handwriting's different from the manuscript. But it's signed *Mary.*"

He read it?

"What does it say? Is she okay?" I reach for it again, but the look on Dad's face stops me.

"You know who wrote this?" His voice sounds strangled. The envelope in his hand shakes a little. "I sent the manuscript to the Historic Preservation Society. For their specialist to authenticate. What are they going to find?"

He's scaring me now. "What do you mean?"

"Is it a fake? Did you fake it? Fake this?" He shakes the envelope at me.

"No!" I don't mean to shout, but it comes out loud. "No, of course not. It's real. I promise."

"You told me Mary Donovan had a brother, but you couldn't tell me how you knew. Then you told me a dream that Mary told you where to find the manuscript… I don't know what to believe anymore."

How can I explain?

"Please, Dad. Please believe me. Look at the paper. How could I fake that?"

"I know you thought you were helping me…"

"DAD! Trust me, please." My eyes go to the envelope—I can't help it. "I can explain everything. I promise. Just let me read it. Please?"

I look at his face and see that he's wavering. He sighs and hands me the letter.

"Okay. Your mom and I will be waiting out here." And then he's gone.

My legs are shaking, so I sit on the bed, open the envelope and pull out a thin sheet. The paper rattles and almost rips, I'm shaking so hard. As I unfold it, I see an unfinished sketch of a sunrise; Jamie, of course. On the other side is a page filled with crooked handwriting. I have to force myself to breathe.

Dear Anne -

I am leaving tomorrow with Jamie. We are going to live with the Quakers.

I am glad to leave this awful place. But I think it means that we will not see each other again, so there are some things I want to say to you now.

When we met, I wanted to save my brother, and you wanted to save your father. We made a bargain so we could both get what we wanted.

I think we both got more than that.

I am not easy to get along with. I know that. But no matter how angry I got, no matter what I said, you came back. You always did. And whenever we failed, or thought we did, you always wanted to try again. I couldn't believe it. You always came back.

I think you are more like me than you know.

Whatever happens tomorrow, I want you to know I'm not sorry about any of it, about the things we did, you and I, whether they worked or not. Because there was more to it than that.

It's not easy for me to speak of such things, but I want you to know that I'm glad you are my friend.

I hope you get all the things you want. I'll not forget you.

Please remember me.
Your friend,

Mary

I don't know how long I sit on that bed, crying. All this waiting and she finally speaks. I cry and cry it all out until there's nothing left. I put the letter next to me on the bed and reach into the box for

Mary's picture. She stares at me, that pointy chin jutting out, as if to say, *Enough of that.*

She wrote, *Whatever happens tomorrow…* For a moment I can picture Blackwell catching her, finding out what she took and punishing her. My heart aches.

I'm not sorry, she wrote. Whatever happens.

"You did it, Mary," I tell her. "You saved everything. You're a hero."

And that's when it hits me; no one knows but me. I have to tell someone. She deserves that.

Mom and Dad are waiting for me.

Holding Mary's picture, I stand up and open my door.

I'm ready now. Ready to tell them. I hope they believe me, but it doesn't matter. I just want them to know.

I'm going to tell them. About everything.

About my friend Mary.

David Surface lives by the Hudson River in a 160-year-old brick house with his wife and writing partner, Julia Rust. He is the author of two collections; the Shirley Jackson Award nominated, *These Things That Walk Behind Me* from Lethe Press, and *Terrible Things* from Black Shuck Books. David enjoys writing, teaching, old movies, bookstores, and good coffee.

Julia Rust is a practicing Buddhist, cat lover and sometime actor who lives and writes in the Hudson Highlands with husband, David Surface. With David, she wrote *Angel Falls,* winner of the 2023 Whippoorwill Book Award, published by YAP Books. She loves illuminated manuscripts, wild swimming and everything her daughter bakes.

To learn more about the books David and Julia write together visit rustandsurface.com.

www.ingramcontent.com/pod-product-compliance
Lightning Source LLC
Chambersburg PA
CBHW060853210726
48293CB00006B/1776